TEMPLARS IN AMERICA

TEMPLARS IN AMERICA

From the Crusades to the New World

TIM WALLACE-MURPHY

and

MARILYN HOPKINS

WEISERBOOKS
Boston, MA/York Beach, ME

First published in 2004 by
Red Wheel/Weiser, LLC
York Beach, ME
With offices at:
368 Congress Street
Boston, MA 02210
www.redwheelweiser.com

Library of Congress Cataloging-in-Publication Data
Wallace-Murphy, Tim.
    Templars in America : from the Crusades to the New World /
    Tim Wallace-Murphy and Marilyn Hopkins.
            p. cm.
    Includes bibliographical references.
    ISBN 1-57863-317-6
    1. America--Discovery and exploration--Pre-Columbian.
    2. Templars--History, 3. Sinclair, Henry, Sir, 1345-ca. 1400.
    4. America--Antiquities. I. Hopkins, Marilyn, 1950- II. Title.
E103.W35 2004
970.01'1--dc22   2004012867

Typeset in Sabon by Sky Peck Design
Printed in Canada
TCP
11 10 09 08 07 06 05 04
8 7 6 5 4 3 2 1

Photo credits—pp. 98, 101, 104, 111, 134, 174, 220, 222, 223, 230 © Tim
Wallace-Murphy; pp. 78, 126, 132, 138, 139, 163, 164, 165 © James P. Whittal;
p. 100 © Malcolm Pearson; p. 154 © 1955 John T. Hopf.

CONTENTS

ACKNOWLEDGMENTS

THIS WORK IS THE FRUIT OF TEN YEARS of research into trans-Atlantic exploration spanning over 1400 years, from Roman times to the fifteenth century. Like all such undertakings, it has been aided by the insight and knowledge of many willing helpers on two continents. We gratefully acknowledge the generosity of spirit that led so many people to contribute to our understanding.

In Italy: the Morosini Naval Academy of Venice, the Municipality of Venice, and our good friends Nicolo and Eleanor Zeno of Venice.

In France: Guy Jourdan of Bargemon, Provence; and Dr. Biorn Ivemark of Belvezes-du-Razes.

In England: Captain Jack Lammaman; Vic Rosati of Totnes; Lord Malcolm Sinclair, Earl of Caithness and the hereditary Chieftain of the Clan Sinclair; and Tony and Anna Sinclair of London.

In Scotland: Stuart Beattie of the Rosslyn Chapel Trust; James Mackay Munro of Penicuick; the staff of the National Library of Scotland in Edinburgh; Andrew Pattison of Edinburgh; Ian and Joan Sinclair of the Niven Sinclair Study Center, Wick, Caithness; Josh and Cath Gourlay of Orkney; the Islands Council of Orkney; the organizers of the Orkney Science Festival, and all the contributors to the Sinclair Symposium in Kirkwall.

In the United States: D'Elayne and Richard Coleman of New York, founders of the Prince Henry Sinclair Society of America; the Clan Sinclair Association of America; the staff of the J. V. Fletcher Memorial Library of Westford, Massachusetts; Elizabeth Lane, also of Westford, the members of the Westford Historical Society; Connie Whittal of Rowley, Massachusetts; Michael Kerber, Mike Conlon, and all at Red Wheel/Weiser of Boston, Massachusetts.

In Canada: the Clan Sinclair Association of Nova Scotia; the Clan Sinclair Association of Canada; Rob Cohn of Halifax, Nova Scotia; Warden Hines and his colleagues from the Municipality of

Guysborough, Nova Scotia; the Italian Consul to Nova Scotia; Leo F. McKay of Stellarton, Nova Scotia; Councillor Miles McPherson of Guysborough; Bill Sinclair of Halifax; Jack Sinclair; and Rory Sinclair, the Clan Piper.

From the Mi'qmaq Nation: Grand Chief and Mrs. Benjamin Sylliboy; Donald Julian, Executive Director of the Confederation of Mainland Mi'qmaqs; Dr. Peter Christmas; Mr. and Mrs. Daniel N. Paul of Halifax, who gave so generously of their time, understanding, and hospitality; and Mr. and Mrs. Kerry Prosper.

Last, and undoubtedly first among equals, three remarkable people whose lives have been a constant inspiration: Dame Rita Joe, poet laureate of the Mi'qmaq people; Laura Zolo, the courageous and beautiful yachtswoman of Elba who recreated the Zeno/St. Clair voyage from Venice to Nova Scotia; and Niven Sinclair of London, without whose unstinting help, insight, and encouragement, this work would never have been written.

INTRODUCTION

OSCAR WILDE FAMOUSLY DECLARED: "Many people discovered America before Columbus, my dear boy, but most of them had the good sense to keep quiet about it." In making this comment, he was aware of the mountain of controversy that exists concerning pre-Columbian trans-Atlantic travel. On one hand, some subscribe to the theory "that there was no European contact with the Americas before Columbus"—a belief that resulted in the flawed archaeological axiom: "The ground rules for archaeology state specifically (although they are unwritten) that any site uncovered in the United States must be Indian, or colonial, and cannot have been occupied by humans other than Indians prior to 1492."[1] At the other extreme are those who believe that people from many countries repeatedly visited the Americas throughout recorded history. Opinions are not merely divided on reasonable grounds on this vexatious question; sometimes they trespass into the realm of fantasy. The author Eric von Danniken even claims that aliens from outer space used the Nasca lines in South America as a landing ground. Somewhere between these extremes there lies a demonstrable truth that backs up Oscar Wilde's view. Many people did cross the Atlantic to America, and mostly they did keep quiet about it—usually to protect their commercial trading interests.

We explore several of these journeys in this book. The complex and fascinating story of European exploration of the Americas in the time of ancient Egypt and classical Rome is based on hard archaeological evidence, archival records, and, surprisingly, modern scientific, forensic evidence. The ship-building and navigational skills that enabled the Viking people to cross the Atlantic as often as they did are well documented, as are many of their voyages. The age-old traditions that link both the Irish and the Welsh to medieval exploration of the New World, while still classed as myth and legend as no verifiable evidence has yet been found to substantiate them, are fascinating nonetheless.

Equally legendary is the tradition that the medieval warrior monks of the Knights Templar had trading links with the Americas. Unlike some legends, however, this one does have a solid factual basis. One hundred years after the suppression of the heretical Order of the Knights Templar, and nearly a century before Columbus, two leading European Templar families combined forces in an attempt to create a new commonwealth in America far beyond the repressive reach of Holy Mother the Church and the long arm of the Inquisition. This book tells their story.

In 1396, Henry St. Clair, Earl of Orkney and Lord of Roslin, placed his fleet under the command of two of the sons of the renowned Zeno family of Venice and sailed with them to explore the North Atlantic and visit America—not once, but at least twice. Steeped in Templar tradition and spirituality, they sailed across the North Atlantic in the manner of Earl Henry's Viking ancestors. They left proof, carved in stone, on both sides of the Atlantic, as well as documentary evidence that is accepted by the majority of academics and borne out by a strong oral tradition that has withstood the test of time. Perhaps the most enduring legacy is not the round Templar church built on the North American continent, but the enduring friendship and amity that has lasted for over 600 years between the worldwide Clan Sinclair and the Mi'qmaq people of northeastern Canada. This friendship was based from the beginning on shared spiritual values and the principles of truth and justice, values that ensured that these voyages would be of enduring peace, respect, and tolerance, completely free from the lasting legacy of distrust, hatred, and genocide that marred almost every other contact between the white invader and the Native American peoples.

Although the voyages had little immediate political or commercial impact, they acted as beacons to a centuries-long process of spiritually inspired actions that affect us all today. Earl Henry's grandson, Earl William St. Clair, was instrumental in transforming the craft guilds of Scotland, of which he was hereditary Grand Master, into the fraternity of Freemasonry, whose beliefs and traditions molded the thinking of the founding fathers of the United States of America. Thus this spiritually inspired brotherhood gave the world an enduring and vitally important political legacy—the American Constitution.

The voyages to America by Earl Henry St. Clair and Antonio Zeno nearly 100 years before Columbus have generated a considerable degree of controversy and a wealth of accounts over the last fifty years.[2] In various books, claims have been made for the date, itinerary, and duration of the voyages for which we can find no justification whatsoever. We have been careful to use the relevant passages from the Zeno Narrative where they are in accord with the geography, in conjunction with Henry's undoubted knowledge of previous Viking voyages to Vinland. We can also follow the trail of this considerable exploration through archaeological artifacts, which those interested can still view and assess for themselves. While we have made every attempt to keep speculation to a minimum, we consider the hypotheses we do put forward reasonable in the light of the evidence and dispassionate logic. We accept *a priori* that there is no way that even this rational methodology will convince those who hold the entrenched position that there was no European contact with America prior to 1492. We also accept that previous accounts suggesting a more wide-ranging span of activities by Earl Henry and his men on the eastern seaboard of America will still retain their adherents. Our account, evidentially based and incorporating only justifiable speculation, will, to some readers familiar with the subject, seem sparing and cautious. We submit, however, that it is the fundamental and definitive account of the voyages, firmly based upon the known evidence and is, therefore, one that can be defended with confidence. It can and will, we believe, provide a basis capable of development and extension, if and when further valid and relevant evidence comes to light.

PART I

SETTING THE STAGE
FOR EXPLORATION

Chapter 1

THE LORDLY LINE
OF THE HIGH ST. CLAIRS AND
THE KNIGHTS TEMPLAR

IN EUROPEAN HISTORY, IT IS A MATTER OF RECORD that royal dynasties come and go; they arise, rule for varying periods of time, and are then replaced by others as a result of *coups d'état*, acts of war, or as a consequence of simple biological sterility. The fate of certain aristocrats who attain "royal favor" is even more transient and ephemeral, for, the more rapid the rise of such individuals, the faster and harder they fall and, as often as not, end their brief careers in spectacular fashion on the scaffold or at the end of a rope. There is one aristocratic family, however, that proves the exception to the rule—a dynasty who never sought a throne, yet were always close to the seats of power as advisors to kings, and who have wielded virtually unbroken power and influence of a subtle and all-pervasive kind from the last years of the ninth century until the final decade of the second millennium. Their history is one that is of as much interest to students of British or Scottish history as it is to those fascinated by the medieval Knights Templar or to historians of pre-Columbian exploration of America. This distinguished family is known as "the Lordly Line of the High Sinclairs," whose present hereditary Clan Chief, the Earl of Caithness, was a cabinet minister in the United Kingdom under Prime Minister Margaret Thatcher in the early 1990s.

The St. Clairs of Roslin are of true Viking stock, descended from Rognvald, the Earl of Möre, in Norway.[1] In the latter part of the ninth century, Earl Rognvald fought alongside the Norwegian King, Harald Fine-Hair, who made him *Jarl*, or Earl, of North Möre, South Möre, and Romsdale, all of which lay in the vicinity of the modern town of Trondheim, Norway.[2] Rognvald had three legitimate sons: Ivar, Thorir the Silent, and Hrolf. He also had three illegitimate sons: Hallad, Hrollaug, and Einar, who was the youngest of them all.[3] Ivar accompanied Harald Fine-Hair on his campaign to subdue Shetland, Orkney, and the Hebrides, and on the massive raid on the Isle of Man that left it in ruins. Ivar was killed during this campaign, and, as compensation, the king gave Rognvald the Earldom of Shetland and Orkney.[4] Rognvald passed the rule of the islands to his brother, Sigurd, who, with Thorstein the Red and Aud the Deep-Minded, conquered all of Caithness, Moray, Ross, and a large part of Argyll in Scotland.[5] After Sigurd's death, his son ruled for one year and then died childless. Rognvald's son, Hallad, became the next earl, but he proved to be an ineffectual ruler and Rognvald had to think again.[6]

Turf Einar, Earl of Orkney

Rognvald's problem lay in deciding which of his surviving sons would now become Earl of Orkney and Shetland. Hrollaug simplified the problem by announcing that he had decided to emigrate to Iceland, possibly to evade the somewhat oppressive rule of Harald Fine-Hair, who was more autocratic than was traditional for Norwegian kings.[7] Hrolf, possibly for similar reasons, declared his wish to carry on the family tradition of raiding and pillaging and announced that he was going to raid the western coast of Europe.[8] This left Einar to inherit the earldom of Orkney. The *Orkneyinga Saga* puts a rather more diplomatic gloss on the whole episode and describes it in the following terms:

> "Do you want me to go, then?" asked Hrollaug.
>
> "You're not destined for the earldom," replied Rognvald, "Your fate will take you to Iceland. You'll have plenty of descendants there, and they'll be brought up as the noblest of men."

After that the Earl's youngest son, Einar, came forward.

> "Do you want me to go to the islands?" he asked. "I can promise you the greatest favour you could wish for, and that's never to have to see me again. There's little enough here to hold

me, and I don't see myself as being any more of a failure elsewhere."

"Considering the kind of mother you have," said the Earl, "slave-born on each side of her family, you're not likely to make much more of a ruler. But I agree; the sooner you leave and the later you return, the happier I'll be."[9]

Einar ruled Orkney well for many years and was responsible for introducing the custom of digging turf, or peat, for fuel at Tarbat Ness in Scotland, as firewood was in short supply on the islands. As a result, he was henceforth known as Turf Einar.[10] Strangely, for a Viking, he died in his bed leaving three sons: Arnkel, Erlend, and Thorfinn Skull-Splitter.[11]

The Duchy of Normandy

Hrolf, known as the Ganger[12] because of his great size, sailed southward to the northern coast of France and into history. He led his raiding party up the River Seine and determined he would settle in this lush and fertile land. After Hrolf's unsuccessful siege of the city of Chartres, King Charles the Simple decided to use him as a buffer against further Viking incursions and made peace with him in 912. The treaty awarding Hrolf the dukedom of the territories that became known as Normandy (the Land of the Northmen) was signed at the castle of St. Clair-sur-Epte.[13] This treaty refers to Hrolf by the Latin version of his name, Rollo, which was used thereafter. Rollo was given the province of Normandy as a vassal of the King of France, conditional on his marriage to the king's daughter, Gisele, and the conversion of him and all his party to Christianity.[14] Part of the ritual of signing this solemn and binding treaty was an act of homage to the king; Rollo was supposed to kiss the king's foot as a sign of allegiance. Feeling that this task was beneath him, he delegated one of his senior lieutenants, a tall strapping man of more than six feet in height, to take his place. The Viking gravely bent double and took the king's foot in his hand. He raised the king's foot to his lips as he stood up to his full height; the king was tipped over backward from his stool and lay floundering like an upturned crab.[15]

According to one tradition, Rollo and his senior officers were solemnly baptized in the miraculous waters of a fountain fed by a spring named in honor of Saint Clair, who was martyred there in 884.[16] Many villages in Normandy were named after this saint, whose cult lasted for over 1000 years. The saint's day was particularly celebrated in the areas associated with him: the present-day towns of Gourney, Carentan, Saint-Roche, Saint-Sylvain, and Saint-Lo.[17] Despite a long-held belief among the St. Clair family, St. Clair-sur-Epte, as important as it was to Norman history, never actually belonged to Rollo or any of his successors. The Chaumont family owned the castle and the land for several centuries, and the lands themselves were part of the Ile de France under the aegis of the king and not part of Normandy.[18] According to L-A de St. Clair, writing in 1905:

> It is therefore highly unlikely the any family used the name of St. Clair-sur-Epte as its family name. It is the town of St. Clair near Saint-Lo, near the western limit of the Bessin, that is the true origin of the name of the noble house of St. Clair.[19]

The use of the family name of St. Clair can be traced to the reign of the fourth Duke of Normandy, Richard II, when the names of the territories that they occupied began to be applied to the individuals who ruled them.[20]

The first Dukes of Normandy resided in the town of Caen, and the lands near their seat of government were given to their relatives and trusted companions-in-arms. As Rollo and Gisele had no children, Rollo remarried, choosing Popée, the daughter of the Count of Bayeaux, who gave him a son known as William Long-Sword. William, in turn, was succeeded by Richard I, whose daughter, Emma, married King Ethelred the Unready of England. Another of his daughters married Geoffrey, Count of Brittany, while a third, Mathild, became the wife of Eudes, Count of Chartres.[21] Not content with joining with the royal house of Saxon England and the family of the Count of Brittany, Rollo's family married into the aristocratic families of Chaumont, Gisors, d'Evereaux, and Blois, the family of the Counts of Champagne. They were also linked to the ducal House of Burgundy, the Royal House of France (the Capetians), and later, through the House of Flanders, to Godfroi de Bouillon, the first Christian ruler of the Kingdom of Jerusalem and an ancestor of the Habsburgs.[22]

Aristocratic Allies of the Vikings

When one considers the reputation of the Vikings as fearsome raiders and uncouth barbarians, the readiness of the leading aristocratic families of France and elsewhere to marry into this bunch of piratical warriors is a little difficult to understand. The lands of Normandy, important though they may have been, do not of themselves explain this headlong charge by some of the oldest families in Europe into matrimonial alliances with the Vikings. When you study the genealogies of these families, you find that they made repeated dynastic alliances with one another, and furthermore, you find the same patterns recurring over time. Is there an explanation for this, or were they simply bereft of ideas? When you study the history of the noble houses of emergent Europe in conjunction with a map of the territories they occupy, you find that strategic considerations were only a minor factor. Something else is at work here—something that is difficult, if not impossible, to explain by the accepted standards of history.

The breeding, or should we say interbreeding, of these families resembles the creation of bloodstock in the farming sense more than normal human behavior. Even within the exclusive ranks of the nobility, one particular group of families stands out. All of their marriages are conducted from within a select group, and the same family names repeatedly appear in the genealogies of all of them every third or fourth generation. There is an esoteric legend that has persisted for centuries that, bizarre though it may seem, may give us an insight into the belief structure that spawned such strange behavior—the tale of Rex Deus.[23]

Rex Deus

There is a group of families in Europe, known among themselves as Rex Deus, who have a long-held oral tradition that they are all descended from the twenty-four high priests of the Temple of Jerusalem of the time of Jesus.[24] To keep their bloodlines pure, they restricted their matrimonial alliances, wherever possible, to other families claiming the same descent. In this, they are replicating the traditional behavior of the high-priestly families of biblical Israel. Most people are aware that the priestly class at that time was hereditary and drawn from the tribe of Levi. Less commonly known is the existence within the Levites of the Cohens, an even more exclusive group from whom were chosen the high priests. The general Levitical priesthood were allowed by Jewish law and tradition to marry outside the tribe. A Cohen, on the other hand, was not merely forbidden to do so, but was strictly enjoined to marry only within the wider Cohen family, thus preserving, or so it is believed, an unbroken and direct genealogical link to the priesthood instituted by Moses.[25]

The families of Rex Deus claim to preserve the true teachings of Jesus for future generations and are dedicated to bringing about "the Kingdom of Heaven upon Earth." They knew that Jesus came to reveal and not to redeem, and as their version of the "true teaching of Jesus" was considerably at variance with the dogma of Holy Mother the Church, they had to keep their traditions secret in order to avoid persecution.[26] The Church, as the self-appointed guardian of divinely revealed truth, instituted a regime of intolerance and repression against all who had the temerity to disagree with its teaching; those who did not swallow Church dogma hook, line, and sinker were deemed heretical.[27]

The Council of Nicea in 325 promulgated the doctrine of the Holy Trinity, which declared that Jesus was divine and coequal with God the Father and the Holy Spirit. Books written by heretics were burned immediately afterward,[28] and it was not long before the burning of heretical books was followed by the incineration of their authors. Therefore, in order to survive, the Rex Deus families outwardly followed the prevailing religion of the district within which they lived, but kept their hidden teaching alive by passing it down orally through the generations to selected children as they became mature enough to be initiated.

Richard II, the fourth Duke of Normandy, had three sons: Richard III, who became the fifth duke, Robert the Devil, and Mauger the Young. He also had two daughters who made important dynastic marriages: Alix became the wife of the Count of Burgundy and Eleanore, the wife of Baudouin, the Count of Flanders. As neither Richard III nor Robert the Devil left any legitimate children, most of the Norman barons would have preferred the succession to pass to the son of the duke's younger brother, Mauger.[29] However, a party led by Raoul, the Constable of Normandy, was formed that supported the claims of William, the bastard son of Robert the Devil; this man became known to history as William the Conqueror.

Mauger had three sons: Hamon, Walderne, and Hubert. Hamon and Walderne were both killed at the battle of Val-des-Dunes, where the succession of William the Bastard was ensured. Two of Walderne's children, Richard and Britel, became reconciled with William the Conqueror and played a part in the conquest of England, where they were later given estates. This left two other children, William and Agnes. They were both quite young when their father was killed at the battle of Val-des-Dunes, for which William never forgave William the Conqueror.[30] His sister, Agnes, married Philip Bruce, who was also of Norman origin and an ancestor of Robert the Bruce who became King of Scotland after the Battle of Bannockburn in the early fourteenth century.[31]

The First St. Clair Lord of Roslin

William attached himself to a branch of the royal family of the Saxons and accompanied the Atheling and his daughter, Margaret, from Normandy to Hungary. Known as William the Seemly because of his courage and courtesy, he was chosen, along with Bartholomew Ladislaus Leslyn, to escort Princess Margaret to Scotland, where she was to marry Malcolm Canmore, King of the Scots.[32] As a reward for his services, he was granted the barony of Roslin in "life rent." He later commanded the Scots army when they fought against William the Conqueror, who was by now the King of England. William the Seemly was killed in a skirmish with the English in Northumberland.[33]

The first St. Clair born in Scotland, Henri de St. Clair, was confirmed by King Malcolm as Baron of Roslin and also Baron of Pentland. He too carried on the family enmity with the Royal House of England and took the side of the deposed brother of King Henry I of England, Robert Courte-Heuze, whom he accompanied on the First Crusade to the Holy Land in 1095.[34] They traveled across Europe with a crusading army led by one of William's relatives, Godfroi de Bouillon, the head of the Royal House of Flanders. After the capture of Jerusalem in 1099, Godfroi de Bouillon, whose family were Rex Deus, was offered the crown of the Holy Land, but refused the honor and chose to rule as Protector of the Holy Sepulchre.[35] Godfroi died childless and was succeeded by his brother, Baudouin (Baldwin), who showed no reluctance in accepting the crown and reigning as King Baudouin I of Jerusalem.[36] He was succeeded by Baudouin II, who was king at the time of the foundation of one of the most controversial and maligned orders in the history of Christianity—the Order of the Knights Templar.

The Knights Templar

The cofounder of the Knights Templar and its first grandmaster, Hughes de Payen, reputedly traveled to the Holy Land with yet another Henri de St. Clair from Normandy.[37] Another cofounder of the order, André de Montbard, was a relative of the Duke of Burgundy and the uncle of one of the most influential people in medieval history, Bernard of Clairvaux. Both cofounders were vassals of the Count of Champagne, who played a strange and mysterious role in both Templar tradition and the generation of the stories of the Holy Grail.[38]

The Counts of Champagne owed allegiance to the King of France, the Holy Roman Emperor, and the Duke of Burgundy. Despite this, they were virtually independent princes who occupied lands somewhat larger than the country of Wales, which lay to the east and southeast of Paris.[39] The Counts of Champagne were linked by blood and marriage to the St. Clairs, the Capetian Kings of France, the Duke of Burgundy, and the Norman and Plantagenet Kings of England.[40] In 1104, the Count of Champagne, Hughes I, met in secret conclave with members of the noble families of Brienne, de Joinville, Chaumont, and Anjou, all of whom were Rex Deus.[41] Almost immediately afterward, he departed for the Holy Land and did not return to his family estates until 1108; he journeyed to Jerusalem again in 1114. On his return to Europe a year later, he made a substantial donation of land to the Cistercian Order, on which was built the Abbey of Clairvaux.[42] Bernard of Clairvaux became its first abbot, and he too played a pivotal, if somewhat shadowy, role in the foundation of the Knights Templar.

The Order of the Poor Knights of Christ of the Temple of Solomon, more commonly called the Knights Templar, was founded in Jerusalem in 1118 by Hughes de Payen, André de Montbard, and seven other knights.[43] This new order of nine knights, also known as "le Milice du Christ" (the Militia of Christ), announced that their vocation was to protect the pilgrimage routes within the Holy Land. Acting on information provided by the secret traditions of Rex Deus,

the nine knights began a mammoth excavation immediately underneath the quarters they had been granted, which were known as the
Stables of Solomon.[44] Opinions vary as to what they found, but a consensus has emerged that they found documents and artifacts containing the fruits of thousands of years of sacred knowledge,[45] as well as
an inordinate amount of treasure. The excavations took nine years,
and when they were completed, the knights returned to Europe with
their discoveries, visiting first Provence, then Normandy, England, and
Scotland.[46] In Scotland, they went straight to the St. Clair lands at
Roslin. In fact, several authors have claimed that Hughes de Payen was
related to the St. Clairs by marriage.[47]

The new order was granted their rule at the Council of Troyes,[48]
which was dominated by the thinking of Bernard of Clairvaux, who
wrote what we would now call an advertising blurb for the order entitled *In Praise of the New Knighthood*.[49] Following the return of the
nine knights to Europe, the order received numerous donations of
property throughout Provence, the Languedoc, the Ile de France,
Normandy, Christian Spain, Portugal, England, and Scotland, where
King David I gave them a tract of land at Ballantradoch adjoining the
estates of Roslin.[50] Their rise to wealth, power, and influence was
rapid and sustained. Over the next fifty years, they acquired further
lands in the Low Countries, Denmark, Norway, Poland, Germany,
Italy, and Hungary.[51]

Owning estates in every climatic zone in Europe, the Templars
became skilled in every variety of farming. Protection of the pilgrimage
routes and the transport of their own men and materials to the Holy
Land, as well as the transport of pilgrims, led to the creation of a large
and well-disciplined fleet,[52] much of which was built in the shipyards
of Venice. The order became long-term allies of the Most Serene
Republic of Venice, and their combined naval might helped to sustain
the Christian kingdom of Jerusalem against the growing power of its
Muslim enemies.[53] The commercial profits of the European activities
were principally used to maintain the numerous castles and establish-
ments that they owned in the Holy Land, where they were, in effect,
Europe's first professional full-time army since the decline of the
Roman Empire.[54]

The commercial interests of the Templars were many and varied
and included viniculture, agriculture, the raising of livestock, ship-

building, quarrying, mining, and building.[55] Learning from their Muslim adversaries, they adopted the Sufi instrument known as the "note of hand" and used it in financial transactions that spanned the length and breadth of Europe; they became bankers to kings, popes, barons, and bishops.[56] Protecting the trade routes made long-distance trade both feasible and safe, and as a result, the balance of political power began slowly to shift from the squabbling barons to the newly emerging merchant classes in the growing towns and cities. The transformative effect of the Order's activities on European culture was almost total. Peace, safe travel, and the establishment of an efficient banking system were all factors that, in combination, created ideal conditions for the long-term accumulation of capital and the ultimate rise of capitalism.

The most visible reminder of the activities of the Knights Templar is architectural. The entire development of the Gothic style, which, according to architectural historians, did not evolve from its Romanesque predecessor is often attributed to the discoveries made by the Knights in their excavations in Jerusalem.[57] They were certainly involved in financing the building of many of Europe's great cathedrals, such as Chartres and Amiens, whose towering spires are a permanent memorial to the Order.[58] So closely entwined were the Knights Templar with the craftmasons known as the Children of Solomon who physically built the cathedrals, that their precise relationship is still a matter of dispute.[59] Were they both branches of the same Order, or were the Knights simply the patrons and teachers of the craftmasons?

One thing that is certain, however, is that the founders of the Knights Templar ensured that it would always be governed by a grandmaster drawn from the ranks of Rex Deus. While any trained knight of noble birth could join the order, the list of those who served on its inner councils always reflects the names of the families claiming descent from the high priests of the Temple of Jerusalem.[60] One family name remains intimately entwined with the Order from the time of the crusade that led to its creation, throughout its history, and in the long battle to preserve its traditions after its dissolution—that of the St. Clairs of Roslin.

The Fall of the Templars

The persecution of the Knights Templar began on Friday, 13 October, 1307 with the arrest of the majority of Templars in France. After many years of torture, they were tried on charges of heresy and the grandmaster, Jacques de Molay, and his companion, Geoffroi de Charny, were roasted to death over a slow fire on an island in the Seine in central Paris.[61] The reason for the sudden arrest and torture of the Templars was the greed and envy of King Philippe le Bel of France. Despite his carefully laid plans and the instantaneous arrest of the Templars, however, the news must somehow have been leaked, for when the king's men arrived at the temple in Paris to seize the convoy of bullion that the king himself had seen unloaded there only a few days before, the treasure had vanished.[62] The fleet of eighteen ships that had brought de Molay and his entourage from Cyprus to La Rochelle had also disappeared. Painstaking detective work by a variety of modern authors, including John Robinson, Michael Baigent, and Richard Leigh, all tends to confirm with hard historical fact the traditions passed down in French Freemasonry, that the treasure of the Templars was sent for safekeeping to Scotland.[63] We know that the St. Clairs of Roslin were members of the secret group that had founded and directed the Order throughout its history. Therefore, it is hardly a surprise that their wealth, which was already considerable, became far greater after the suppression of the Templar Order. It was recorded by one leading St. Clair genealogist that, from this time forth, when the Lords of Roslin traveled, they were accompanied by 100 mounted gentlemen; the ladies of Roslin were attended by eighty ladies-in-waiting, and the family dined off gold plate.[64]

Sanctuary in Scotland

After the suppression of the Templars, a substantial number of knights also sought refuge in Scotland. The reason was simple: in the course of the civil war for the Scottish crown, the main claimant, Robert the Bruce, was excommunicated for the ritual murder of his rival, John Comyn, on church premises. As this papal action did not produce the desired result of Bruce's deposition, his nobles were also excommunicated, and the entire country was put under papal interdict. This meant that the pope's writ did not run in the kingdom of the Scots, making it a safe refuge for Templar Knights in flight from the clutches of the Inquisition.[65] Their military skills and the armaments they brought with them were warmly welcomed by Robert the Bruce, who had by now effectively secured the succession and was fighting a war of survival against the English king. Matters finally came to a head at the Battle of Bannockburn in 1314. According to most accounts, the Scots, who were heavily outnumbered, created a strong defensive position and managed to repulse repeated attacks by the invading army. As the day drew to its close, the English mounted an overwhelming assault. A band of Scottish reserves came over the brow of a hill, and at the first sight of these new arrivals, the English army took to their heels and fled without striking another blow. The official story is, quite frankly, incredible. The reserves that supposedly put the battle-hardened English to flight by their mere appearance are described as "the small people," a collection of stable boys, horse handlers, and local peasantry. To any rational historian, this is a most unlikely scenario; the truth is far more credible. The Scottish reserves were a division of disciplined cavalry in full armor, fighting under the readily recognizable banner of the Beausseant, the distinctive black-and-white battle flag of Europe's finest fighting force—the Knights Templar.[66]

Robert the Bruce, in 1320, laid the foundations for future relations between the King of the Scots and his people by the Declaration of Arbroath, which defined Scottish independence for all time. One of the many signatories was Sir Henry St. Clair of Roslin. The new king was, above all, a realist, and while Scottish tradition tells us that he became the sovereign grandmaster of the Templar Order, it also recounts that he advised them to go underground and operate in secret. The reason why is not hard to find, for Bruce knew that he would have to reestablish relations with the Pope and with countries who acknowledged papal power, and he did not wish to reward the allies who had saved his throne by allowing them to become visible targets of the Inquisition. The fate of Templar estates in Scotland was also somewhat different from the pattern established elsewhere in Europe. Some reverted to the families who had originally donated them and who had maintained close ties with the Order throughout its existence. The remainder passed into the hands of the Knights Hospitaller—but in Scotland, they were always accounted for separately, as though they were being held in trust for their original owners.[67]

Bruce began to establish international alliances as part of his strategy to restrict English encroachment on his kingdom. One of these, above all others, dates from this period and lasted for so many centuries that it became known as "the auld alliance." Thus the relationship between the Scottish and French branches of Rex Deus was formalized in a way that was to influence the political and economic development of Europe until well into the eighteenth century and beyond.

Chapter 2

TRADE AND POWER
IN POST-TEMPLAR EUROPE

ROBERT THE BRUCE ESTABLISHED VIABLE TRADING links with France, the Low Countries, Denmark, Scandinavia, and the Baltic seaports. The trading patterns that emerged in Northern Europe over the coming century were dominated by a consortium of German seaports that became known as the Hanseatic League, which used the neo-Templar Order of the Teutonic Knights as their mercenary army.[1] The first known meeting of representatives of the merchant cities of Lübeck, Hamburg, Lüneburg, Wismar, Rostock, and Stralsund took place in 1256. From that time forward, their concerted power was used with growing efficiency to gain a monopoly on trade within Northern Europe and the Baltic.[2] The rise of the Hanseatic League, or the Hansa as it became known, occurred at a time when the greatest trading nation in the European world was passing through a period of decline due to developments much further to the east.

Venice had dominated trade in the eastern Mediterranean for centuries.[3] She controlled the trade routes to the Holy Land, dominated trade with Byzantium, and exerted a virtual monopoly over the spice and silk trades. The Aegean was, in effect, a Venetian lake, and Venice sustained her dominance over Mediterranean trade in the face of stiff opposition from her major rivals, Pisa and Genoa. The Venetians were always on the lookout for ways and means to extend their trading empire and, by the time of Bannockburn in 1314, had established trading links with Western Europe as far north as Flanders and England. They were only restricted from further northern activity by the growing power of the Hansa.

The Founding of Venice

The paradox is that Venice, which exerted so much power for so many centuries, was founded by a frightened people. The city was created in the improbable setting of the Venetian lagoon for protection from successive waves of invaders.[4] This strange mixture of marshland and 200 square miles of salt water is, in part, shallow enough for men to wade through, and yet is crisscrossed with channels deep enough to carry the merchant shipping that has sustained its economy throughout its existence. Therefore, it is Alaric, the leader of the Goths, and Attila the Hun whom we should really thank for the foundation of "la Serenissima," Venice, which is still one of the most beautiful cities in the world.

Protected by its lagoon, Venice achieved a degree of self-government even during the latter years of the Roman Empire. By the middle of the sixth century, she possessed the most powerful fleet in the Adriatic. In 726, when the Byzantine Empire in Italy was in crisis, the Byzantine provinces in the peninsula were encouraged by the Pope to turn against their political masters in Constantinople. It was at this time that the lagoon communities that developed into the city of Venice chose one of their number, Ursus of Heraclea, as their leader and gave him the title of *dux*, or duke.[5] Similar developments took place elsewhere, but Venice was, and remained, different in that the position of their dux, or in Venetian dialect, *doge*, was elected and not hereditary. At first, the doge was elected by the mass of the people, but this soon changed into election by the Grand Council. This elective leadership lasted through 117 successors, until Napoleon dissolved the Venetian Republic at the tail end of the eighteenth century.[6]

Venice and the Crusades

At the time of the First Crusade in 1095, while Pisa and Genoa, both burgeoning maritime powers, sensed new opportunities in the East and began to prepare their fleets, Venice hung back. Her merchant class was far too practical and hardheaded to get involved in religious hysteria about the salvation of Christendom, and furthermore, they knew only too well that war was bad for trade. From the perspective of Venice, the goodwill of the Arabs and the Seljuk Turks was essential if the caravan routes to Asia were to be kept open.[7] Much of her trade was with

Egypt, which had become the major clearinghouse for the spice trade in India and the East, and which was a ready market for European timber and metal. Thus it was after 1099, when Jerusalem had already fallen to the Crusaders, that a Venetian fleet of 200 sail made its way to the Holy Land.[8]

This expedition resulted in a battle with the Pisan fleet off the coast of Rhodes in which twenty Pisan ships were captured and over 4000 prisoners taken. As usual, Venice had put her own interests first, for her fleet had still not struck one single blow for Christendom. The Venetian fleet docked in Jaffa in the middle of June 1100. Godfroi de Bouillon went to Jaffa to negotiate with the Venetians, but was forced to return to Jerusalem in a state of collapse. As a result, his cousin, Count Warner of Gray, represented the Protector of the Holy Sepulchre.[9]

The Venetians' terms reflected their true status as merchants rather than pious Crusaders. In return for their help to the emergent state, they demanded free trading rights throughout the land, a church and a market in every Christian town, a third of any town or city that they might help to capture in the future, and, finally, the entire city of Tripoli, for which they were prepared to pay an annual tribute.[10] The speed with which the crusading state accepted these terms demonstrates how badly they needed naval support.

The first city assaulted by the fleet was Haifa, which surrendered on 25 July, one week after the death of Godfroi de Bouillon. The citizens of Haifa enjoyed the same merciful Christian treatment as those of Jerusalem had before them. Christian, Jew, and Muslim alike were slaughtered without mercy. It is highly unlikely that the Venetians played any part in this massacre, but the pious Crusaders were behaving in their normal manner, for they had indulged in similar acts of butchery in Jerusalem and Galilee.

As the Crusaders gradually consolidated their hold on Outremer, the Christian population increased, and opportunities for trade expanded with the population. In order to exert a dominant role in this new market and limit the influence of Pisa and Genoa, another Venetian fleet of 100 sail arrived in the Holy Land in October 1110. The fleet rendered assistance at the siege of Sidon, and Venice was rewarded by a substantial grant in the city of Acre. In view of increasing trade in the Levant, an ambitious new shipbuilding program was called for in Venice. The doge, Ordelafo, nationalized the shipbuilding industry and founded a huge complex of dockyards, foundries, and workshops that eventually became known as the Arsenale.[11] Over the next few decades, the port of Venice became one of the many centers of activity of their allies, the Knights Templar, who had strong connections with many of the leading families among the Venetian nobility. Furthermore, the renowned Templar war galleys were built in the shipyards of their Venetian allies.

When the city of Jerusalem fell to the Saracens on 2 October 1187,[12] Pope Urban III died of shock.[13] His successor, Gregory VIII, promptly called another crusade, and for once, Venice responded enthusiastically. With the effective collapse of the crusader state, this trading nation suffered a series of financial blows, for the markets of the Holy Land were gone. Acre and its Venetian quarter had surrendered, as had Sidon, Beirut, and most of the cities of the coast and hinterland. Venice dispatched a war fleet at Easter 1189 carrying an army of Italians, with later additions from England, France, Denmark, Germany, the Low Countries, and Sicily.[14] Among them were Richard, Coeur de Lion, King of England, and King Philippe Augustus of France.[15] After a two-year siege, Acre was recaptured.[16] Venice's contribution seems to have been limited to providing the transport and grabbing the spoils.

The Sack of Constantinople

The real blot on Venice's reputation came with another Crusade. In 1195, with Saladin dead, the Holy Land looked ripe for plucking. In 1201, the Venetian Republic agreed to transport 4500 knights and their horses, 9000 squires, and 20,000 foot soldiers, and supply them with provisions for nine months.[17] The cost would be 84,000 silver marks, and out of a sense of Christian duty, Venice agreed, from her own resources, to provide fifty fully equipped war galleys in return for 50 percent of all the territories conquered.

It is interesting to note that none of the records of the negotiations make any mention of which country was the immediate objective of the Crusade. The rank and file Crusaders believed they were going to the Holy Land, but their leaders had Egypt in mind, while the Venetians had other ideas, for they had just concluded an extremely profitable trade agreement with the Sultan of Egypt.[18] There must have been a leak, for public knowledge of the intention to invade Egypt became widespread in a remarkably short time. Many intending Crusaders made their own way directly to the Holy Land; others who had no intention of invading Egypt returned to their homes. As a result, less than one third of the expected army arrived in Venice.[19]

The Venetians had kept their side of the bargain and demanded payment in full, refusing point blank to allow any ship to sail until the money was forthcoming.[20] The ultimate result was shameful in the extreme. Far from sailing to liberate the Holy Land from the infidels, the fleet sailed to the Christian city of Constantinople and indulged in an orgy of plunder.[21] This struck a mortal blow at the already weakened Byzantine Empire, one from which it never recovered. The greatest treasure house of art and knowledge in the Christian East was virtually destroyed forever, while Venice, the Machiavellian prime mover in this tragedy, simply filled her coffers once more.

In 1256, Venetian and Genoese rivalry led to outright civil war within the remnants of the Kingdom of Jerusalem. In a quarrel over which state had proprietorial rights over the hilltop monastery of San Sabas at Acre, Genoese forces occupied the disputed building and fighting soon broke out.[22] The dispute rumbled on for several years and became the principal cause of a series of battles on both land and sea between the Venetians and their allies on the one hand, and the Genoese and their supporters on the other. The resident crusaders and other civilian merchants took sides in this war, which lasted until 1261. The principal allies of the Venetians were the Knights Templar who, according to the Templar historian John Robinson, lost no time in siding with their "ancient allies," the Venetians.[23] The Knights Hospitaller, the traditional rivals of the Templars, supported the cause of the Genoese. The matter was finally brought to a head in a land battle, won by the Templars, and a series of naval battles in which the Venetian fleet prevailed, although heavily outnumbered.[24]

Venetian shipbuilding skills were probably the best in the world, and their shipyards and armament manufactures were a hive of constant activity. The marine compass appeared in about 1275, aiding navigation and assisting mapmaking, which led to far more accurate charts. Another innovation at this time was the development of the ship's rudder, which led in its turn to larger ships, thus enabling maritime trade to continue on a year-round basis for the very first time.

According to historian John Julius Norwich, it was the opening up of trade between Venice, England, and Flanders that:

> . . . more than any other single factor, led to the introduction in about 1320 of a revolutionary new ship design. Until this time oars had never been used for commercial vessels; they had been kept for warships, where high speeds and manoeuvrability was essential. . . . Now merchant men too needed to move quickly—and, with more precious cargoes to carry, they demanded increased protection. The answer was found in the merchant galley. [25]

These early merchant galleys were of 150 tons burden. As well as being equipped with sails, they were propelled by 200 oarsmen, all of whom were free men. The expense of maintaining such a crew was high, but this was outweighed by more rapid voyages, larger profits, and near immunity from piracy. These galleys' maneuverability and speed reduced the risk of shipwreck, and the oarsmen could easily be armed in the event of attack.

The Venetian Trading Empire

The necessities of trade had, to a certain extent, made Venice into an almost colonial power. She had colonies in Greece and satellites, towns, and cities dotted throughout the Mediterranean. Some, such as those on the Dalmatian coast, were acquired in her campaigns against the pirates who infested the area. Others were glorified trading posts such as Modone, Acre, and Negropont. On 24 January 1339, as a result of a peace treaty, Venice acquired territories on the mainland of Italy, including Padua,[26] the immediate advantage of which was assurance of the continued provision of corn and meat. In Padua, the House of Carrara was restored to power under the suzerainty of the Venetian doge. In the other towns and cities, she used a watered-down version of the system that had worked so well in the Republic itself. Cities were administered by a *podesta* and smaller towns by a *capitano* or *provveditore*. These positions were broadly similar to that of the doge. Their manner of election was equally Byzantine, and their power of independent maneuver was strictly limited. In Venice, the doge, for all his pomp and splendor, was in fact the servant of the Council of Ten,[27] who were the effective cabinet to the Grand Council's parliament. In the dependent cities and towns, the podesta was the servant of a shadowy official known as "the Rector," who was always a true Venetian and owed direct responsibility to the Senate of Venice and the Council of Ten.

By 1340, the presence of a Turkish armada of 230 ships threatened the eastern Mediterranean and exerted a real menace, not only to Venetian possessions, but to the southeast of Europe itself. Most of Asia Minor was under Turkish domination, and the Turkish lines were established less than sixty miles from the walls of Constantinople.[28] The once-powerful Byzantine Empire was riven by theological dispute and political rivalry, and on the verge of bankruptcy. The only powers with any chance of halting the Turks were Venice and Genoa.[29] Sadly, the continuing bitter rivalry between these two maritime states went on unabated, precluding an alliance.

Despite the Turkish menace, Venice was at peace and riding on the crest of a wave of commercial prosperity that has never been exceeded in her entire history. The Venetians began to adorn their capital with new buildings, artworks, and the outward trappings of prosperity. In January 1341, the reconstruction of the doge's palace began. This, among other things, gave the building the façade that we know today.[30] This administrative center provides a startling contrast to the appearance of the corresponding seats of power in the cities of mainland Italy, for the outward façades of all of these buildings tend to reflect the relationships between the rulers and the ruled in each case. Machiavelli declared that the Palazzo della Signoria in Florence was built to protect the civil authorities from the wrath of the people. Centuries later, John Addington Symonds wrote of Ferrara as

> . . . where the Este's stronghold, moated, draw bridged, and portcullised, casting dense shadow over the water that protects the dungeons, still seems to threaten the public square and overawe the homes of men.[31]

The Doge of Venice, however, had no need for protection from his people. His palace was not built to intimidate, but to celebrate; it is a hymn of praise and gratitude to Almighty God for the political stability, prosperity, and serenity that Venice, alone among all other Italian cities, seemed to enjoy. The architecture of the palace is described by John Julius Norwich as imbued with "a dazzling fusion of grace, lightness and colour."[32] The prosperity and rebuilding that went with it did not, however, blind Venetian authorities to the political and commercial realities that would ensue from the advance of the Turks.

The Plague

One cargo carried by Venetian and Genoese ships from the Crimea in the early weeks of 1348 was the most devastating in history. Whatever else these merchant vessels carried in the way of trading goods, they had some unpleasant and extremely prolific stowaways—rats infested with fleas that carried the plague bacillus.[33] The Black Death had arrived in Europe, and by the end of March, Venice was in its grip, with deaths running at more than 600 a day.[34] By the time the epidemic had run its course, over fifty noble families had been completely wiped out, and Venice had lost in excess of 60 percent of its population. A similar situation prevailed in Genoa.[35]

It would be nice to record that such traumatic and shared experiences united the trading rivals, but sadly, that was not the case. A series of vigorous naval wars took place, with the advantage first accruing to one side and then to the other. The casualties in men and shipping were horrendous. One peace treaty between the two, signed in 1355,[36] was followed on the Venetian side by war with Hungary, which ended with the Treaty of Zara on 13 February 1358.[37] This adventure cost Venice her Dalmatian colonies. A further war with Genoa, which continued intermittently for some years, broke out in 1373. In 1377, the Genoese, in alliance with remnants of the Byzantine Empire, launched a concerted attack on Tenedos,[38] which lay at the gateway to the Hellespont and controlled the entrance to the straits and the Sea of Marmara beyond. If Tenedos were captured by the Genoese, all Venetian trade with Constantinople, the remaining Byzantine Empire, and the area around the Black Sea would be completely terminated. Fortunately, this attempt by the Genoese-Byzantine alliance failed.[39]

The truly significant battles that put an end to this war between Venice and Genoa were fought much closer to home, off the coast of Anzio in Italy,[40] and then, finally, in the Venetian lagoon itself. A Venetian fleet under the command of Pisani defeated a Genoese force at Anzio, only to lose another even more fearsome battle almost a year later at Pola, when only six battered Venetian galleys survived and made their slow and painful way to the port of Parenzo. Pisani was deprived of his command, imprisoned for six months, and debarred from holding any office in the Republic for a period of five years,[41] thus depriving the Venetians of one of their leading admirals at a time when the other, a certain Carlo Zeno, was away in the eastern Mediterranean. With Zeno's fleet somewhere off the Turkish coast, the only ships available for the defense of Venice were the battle-scarred ships lying at Parenzo. Luckily, the Genoese had lost their admiral at the Battle of Pola, and their fleet was inoperative until a replacement could be sent from Genoa.

The Battle of Chioggia

During this brief period of grace, the Venetians strengthened the defenses of the city, with the whole population playing its part. Some rich families put their entire fortunes at the disposal of the state; many nobles fitted out ships or subsidized the cost of defensive works. Meanwhile, Venice's territory on mainland Italy was under attack by Genoese allies, including an army of 5000 Hungarians.[42] Soon, an advance squadron of the Genoese navy was in sight of the city, waiting just beyond the Lido, which had been fortified with stout walls and a triple defensive ditch. Three heavy hulks were chained together as a boom across the entrance to the lagoon, and the rows of piles and stakes normally used to mark the shoals in the channels were stripped from the seabed in order to confuse the invading navy. An army of 4000 horsemen, 2000 infantry, and a large body of crossbowmen garrisoned the Lidi, a chain of small islands, and armed boats constantly patrolled the lagoon to block any attempt at communication between the Genoese fleet and their land-based allies. The defenses were completed in the nick of time, for on 6 August, a Genoese fleet of forty-seven galleys, commanded by the newly appointed admiral Pietro Doria, appeared off Chioggia on the malodorous marshes at the southern end of the Venetian lagoon.[43]

The Genoese fleet had sailed down from the north, burning Grando, Caorle, and Pellestrina on its way. After capturing Malamocco, Doria sailed to Chioggia, where the line of Lidi met the mainland, hoping to unite with the land-based invading forces. Chioggia was defended by a garrison of 3000 men, but fell on 16

August 1379 after a brave defense that imposed an immense cost on both the Venetian and Genoese forces. For the first time in Venetian history, a fortified town within the lagoon, commanding a deep-water channel that led directly to the city itself, was in the hands of the enemy.[44] Things were so desperate in the city that, in deference to the demands of the populace, the disgraced admiral, Pisani, was released from prison and placed in supreme command of the city's defenses. Morale in Venice began to rise dramatically, and workers in the shipyards labored round the clock until forty galleys had come off the slipways. A new defensive wall along the Lido was completed within fourteen days; a boom was stretched across the western end of the Grand Canal, and this, in turn, was protected by ships armed with rockets. Luckily for Venice, the Genoese admiral decided against a frontal attack and opted to blockade the city and starve it into submission, which gave Pisani the time to create the formidable defensive structure that made it virtually impregnable.[45]

The first sign that the Venetians were beginning to take the initiative occurred when a small squadron under the command of Giovanni Barbarigo fell upon three Genoese ships guarding one of the mainland forts and destroyed them all. At the same time, Giacomo de'Cavalli made a slow and sustained advance southward along the Lidi and recaptured Malamocco. When winter approached, the Genoese commander withdrew his forces into Chioggia itself. This gave Pisani the opportunity he had been waiting for. Chioggia was almost landlocked, apart from three narrow channels. Pisani's plan was simple—to sink a large stone-filled hulk in each of the channels.[46] The remaining possible points of escape for the Genoese could then be effectively controlled by Venetian patrols.

The Venetian blockading expedition set out on 21 December 1379, with Pisani on the leading vessel accompanied by the doge. The expedition was successful; the hulks were sunk, effectively blocking the channels, and within a few hours the Genoese fleet were bottled up within Chioggia.[47] Tight control was difficult during the winter storms, and the Venetians had to patrol the northern entrance to the lagoon as well as the approaches to Chioggia. There is some doubt as to whether they could have sustained their position for very long. On 1 January 1380, however, the welcome sight of sails on the horizon heralded the arrival of Carlo Zeno with the main Venetian fleet. The siege of

Chioggia continued into the spring, when a new Genoese fleet arrived under Marco Maruffo. Despite his best efforts, he could not relieve the siege of Chioggia, and, on 24 June, the 4000 starving Genoese sailors surrendered unconditionally.[48] Venice went wild with joy. Virtually the entire population took to the water in boats of every shape, sort, and size to accompany the doge's state barge as it sailed out to meet him, for he had remained with the fleet throughout the siege. The victory of Chioggia was, in reality, the victory of an entire people. It brought credit to Pisani and to the doge himself, but above all, to the timely savior, Carlo Zeno.

Carlo Zeno

Carlo, known as *il Leone*, the Lion, came from one of the oldest and most respected families in the ranks of the Venetian nobility. The Zenos were a family that, for their nobility, service to the state, and quality of their actions, was as celebrated in Venice as the St. Clairs were in Scotland. From time immemorial, the name of Zeno can be found in the records of the highest offices and dignities in the state. In 1203, Marin Zeno took part in the conquest of Constantinople and became podesta, or governor, of the Venetian enclave in the city in 1205. His son, Pietro, was the father of Rineri, who was elected doge of Venice in 1282 and who governed well for seventeen years. Rineri carried on a war against the Genoese with considerable success and was the grandfather of Pietro who, in 1362, was the supreme naval commander in the league of Christians against the Turks. Pietro was nicknamed *Draconi*, from the dragon he had emblazoned on his shield. This warrior had three sons: Carlo il Leone, whom we have already mentioned, Nicolo il Cavaliere, and Antonio.[49] It was during a voyage to the northern capitals of Europe by Carlo Zeno in 1364 that the destiny of the three Zenos and that of Henry St. Clair of Roslin became intimately entwined.

Chapter 3

THE FIRST ST. CLAIR
EARL OF ORKNEY

EVEN THE MOST CURSORY EXAMINATION OF THE history of the St. Clairs of Roslin clearly demonstrates the courage of successive generations of that family. The first St. Clair Baron of Roslin, William the Seemly de St. Clair, was killed as he and his forces protected Scotland from English invasion.[1] His son, Henri de St. Clair, in company with knights from other leading families in Scotland, played a significant role in the First Crusade[2] in the army led by Godfroi de Boullion and was present at the capture of Jerusalem.[3] For the next 150 years, the St. Clairs defended the border against constant English incursions and also contributed to the inner councils of the Order of the Knights Templar.

Yet another Sir William St. Clair, the newly wed Baron of Roslin, destroyed three British armies on his wedding day in 1303, before returning to Roslin Castle to consummate his marriage. This triple victory is known as the Battle of Roslin Moor and is commemorated by a memorial erected in Roslin village a few years ago.[4] Sir William and his son, Sir Henry St. Clair, are believed to have led the charge of the Templar cavalry at the Battle of Bannockburn in 1314.[5] The grave marker of Sir William St. Clair, decorated with Templar symbolism, has been preserved and now rests in the sanctity of Rosslyn Chapel.[6] Henry's son, the knight Sir William St. Clair, passed into legend when, in company with his brother John and Sir James Douglas, he set out to carry the heart of Robert the Bruce in a silver casket to the Holy Land with the intention of burying it in Jerusalem. En route, when they stopped at a Spanish port, they learned that the Christian King of Spain was at war with the Moors, who had occupied southern Spain for many centuries. The three Scottish knights volunteered their services, and on 25 August 1330, during the Battle of Theba in Andalucia, their outstanding bravery ensured that they would be remembered in the annals of warfare for all time. The St. Clair brothers were cut off by the Saracens, and Sir James Douglas charged to their rescue. The knight carrying the heart of Bruce threw the silver casket containing the royal relic forward into the throng of Saracens; all three knights charged after it and were killed. The Saracens were so impressed at the bravery of the Scotsmen that they returned their bodies and the silver casket to their Spanish opponents.[7] In the manner of the Templars of old, the skulls and thighbones of the three knights were returned to Scotland for burial, along with the casket containing the heart of the late king.

This signal act of bravery was well recorded and forms a strange, almost mystical, replication of a much earlier Spanish legend. A fascinating piece of mythology arose after the battle of Clajivo in the Ebro valley in 844 when Santiago Matamoros (St. James the Moor Slayer) is said to have descended from heaven mounted on a fearsome white charger to ride at the side of King Ramiro I. Brandishing his sword, St. James galloped straight at the assembled ranks of the enemy, rallying the Christian forces behind him in a massive charge that defeated the Moors. Estimates vary widely as to the number of infidels decapitated by this apostle of the Prince of Peace.

The Early Life of Henry St. Clair

The St. Clair hero who died so bravely at Theba did not live long enough to inherit the Barony of Roslin, which passed from his father directly to his son, yet another William St. Clair.[8] This new Lord of Roslin married Isabel, the daughter of Malise Spera, the Earl of Stratherne, Caithness, and Orkney.[9] She gave birth to a son, Henry St. Clair, in the Robin Hood tower of Roslin Castle in 1345.[10] Danger of a dramatically different sort soon threatened the infant heir to the Barony of Roslin. The outbreak of bubonic plague brought back from the East by Venetian and Genoese merchantmen in 1348 had reached Scotland and, by 1350, was in full sway. The plague culled the Scots far more viciously than any English invader had ever done. It has been estimated that one third of the population were laid low by the Black Death. The survival of the St. Clairs of Roslin and young Henry in particular is recorded in the family histories almost as an act of divine intervention. The records disclose that they prayed for the abatement of the plague on a daily basis at the church of St. Matthew in the castle grounds. Later, family historians attribute their apparently miraculous survival to their use of the healing waters of the Balm Well, which lies some four miles from Roslin Castle and was named after the patron saint of the family, St. Katherine. Its black, oily waters were believed to be "a precious oyle . . . from her [St. Katherine's] bones."[11] The family smeared their bodies with the exudates from this miraculous well and claimed thereby to have survived the plague. It is a claim that, in scientific terms, may well have considerable merit, as the oily substance is believed by many to be a form of insecticide and, in any case, would have made it difficult if not impossible for any flea to have breathed long enough once entrapped in its embrace to give its bacillus-laden bite to the body beneath.

When Henry was only thirteen years of age, his father, William, was killed in battle in Lithuania.[12] Sir William, accompanied by Sir William Keith, Sir Alexander Lindsay, Sir Robert Clifford, and Sir Alexander Montgomery, was fighting with the Teutonic Knights. Each of the Scottish nobles brought with him sixty horsemen and a strong body of footmen from his estate. The Teutonic Knights had sought help in their war against the Lithuanians under the usual conditions for crusade—the chance of plunder and the opportunity of pleasing God by killing heathens. The financial reasons that lay behind this expedition were pressing, for King David II of Scotland was being held for ransom in England for the huge sum of 100,000 marks, and every nobleman in the land had to assume his share of the financial burden.

Following his father's death, Henry became, according to the St. Clair historian Father Hay writing in the seventeenth century, "Baron of Roslin, Baron of Pentland Moor, in free forestry, Baron of Cousland, Baron of Cardain Saintclair and great protector, Keen defender of the Prince of Scotland . . ."[13]—heavy responsibilities for a thirteen-year-old. Another early historian and descendant, Henry Lord Sincleer, writing in 1590, claims that Henry was also a knight of the Order of St. Michael in France.[14] In 1363, five years after succeeding to the barony, Henry was appointed ambassador to Denmark and took up residence in Copenhagen for the next two years.[15] One of his first official duties was to attend the marriage of the ten-year-old Princess Margrette of Denmark to King Haakon VI of Norway. Attendance at this ceremony began a close friendship between Margrette and Henry that was to last until his death.

The Knutson Expedition

Henry's presence at the Scandinavian court brought him up to date on events in the Viking settlements of Greenland and the New World. The colony in Greenland had, despite the harsh climate, survived for 350 years and maintained regular trading links with Norway, Bristol, Flanders, and Cologne.[16] Early in the 1340s, relationships between the settlers and the Eskimos broke down and erupted into hostility. A priest by the name of Ivar Baardson was called upon to accompany a fleet of volunteers who were dispatched from the Eastern to the Western Settlement to help combat the Eskimos.[17] He reported that, on their arrival at the settlement, the Eskimos were in full control and apparently the settlers had sailed away as a group. Another report from Bishop Oddson in Iceland claimed that the settlers had given up the true faith and fled to settle among the Viking people of Vinland.[18]

The desertion of the Western Settlement is apparently confirmed by the record of *Peter's Pence*, dispatched to Rome from the island, which declined dramatically after 1342.[19] These reports reached Iceland in 1347 and Norway one year later.[20] It took some time before the Norwegian King, Magnus, was in a position to act. There is a letter from him dated in 1354 in which he authorizes a special expedition to Greenland under the command of Sir Paul Knutson, the former Lawspeaker, or Judge, of Gulathing:

> . . . We desire to make known to you [Paul Knutson] that you are to select men who shall go in the Knorr [the royal trading vessel] . . . from among my bodyguard and also from the retainers of other men whom you may wish to take on the voyage, and that Paul Knutson the commandant shall have full authority to select such men who he thinks are best qualified to accompany him, whether officers or men. . . .[21]

The objective of the expedition was to bring the apostates back to Christianity.[22] Paul Knutson was not merely the Lawspeaker of the largest of the four judicial districts in Norway, but also a trusted member of the royal council and a man of considerable wealth. Knutson was given a free hand in choosing which men were best suited to accompany him, but it was suggested that some of them be drawn from the king's bodyguard. Membership in this body, restricted to young men of noble birth, was regarded as the first step toward knighthood. The role demanded bodily fitness, considerable skill in arms, tact, courtesy, and good sense.

It is believed that Knutson first went to Greenland to seek whatever information he could find about the colonial apostates.[23] He would have known from the sagas and the Viking history about the earlier voyages to Helluland, Markland, and Vinland, and it would have been easy for him to gain a pilot from the settlers of the Eastern Settlement to chart his course to these lands. From the sagas, it was apparent that Helluland, or Flat Rock Land, which was good for nothing, was an unlikely place of refuge for the fleeing colonists. While Markland was a good source of timber and would have to be investigated, Vinland, which was renowned for its climate and fertility, was the most likely area in which to find the one-time colonists.[24] The search of Vinland would have necessitated a safe harbor and a defensible settlement inland that was sufficiently fertile to support the members of the expedition.[25] According to historian Hjalmar Holand, Knutson appears to have split his expedition into three parties.[26] One small group and at least one ship were based either in the St. Lawrence estuary or Hudson Bay, another penetrated deep inland, and the third was based at Norembega, the supposed site of the earlier settlement of Leif Ericson.

Written proof of the fate of the overland exploration is inscribed on a Norse artifact known as the Kensington Runestone, discovered in Minnesota in 1898.[27] The inscription is dated 1362 and was translated by Hjalmar Holand as:

> (We are) 8 Goths (Swedes) and 22 Norwegians on (an) exploration journey from Vinland round about the west. We had camp by (a lake with) 2 Skerries one day's journey north from this stone. We were (out) and fished one day. After we came home (we) found ten of our men red with blood and dead. AVM (Ave Virgo Maria) save (us) from evil.
>
> (We) have ten men by the sea to look after our ships 14 days-journeys from this island. (In the) year (of our Lord) 1362.[28]

Holand's translation of the runestone and his claims for its authenticity were about as welcome in American academic circles as a cobra at a cocktail party. The dispute over the provenance of the Kensington Stone was prolonged and bitter. Blinkered by their long-standing rejection of any suggestion of pre-Columbian contact with Europeans, the academic community first responded by accusing the farmer who found the Kensington Stone of forging it, despite the embarrassing fact that the stone was originally discovered when the farmer, removing a tree from his land, found it embedded in its roots. How a forgery could have been planted so that the entire root system of a tree would have had time to grow around it has never been satisfactorily explained. However, over the last decade, the authenticity of the stone has been grudgingly accepted by the historical establishment in North America,[29] but then quietly ignored in the pious hope that, in the public memory at least, the long-lasting bitter dispute over the stone's provenance would prove to be far more memorable than the eventual and grudging verification of its authenticity.

The great majority of European historians who have investigated Knutson's expedition unite around the consensus that places their main base, Norumbega,[30] at or near the present site of Newport, Rhode Island, in the superb natural harbor of Narragansett Bay.[31] This consensus arises from the precision with which this area agrees with the descriptions in the *Flateyabok* (see chapter 6), from the nature of the natural harbor, which would have had a strong appeal to a seafaring people such as the Vikings, and, finally, from the stone artifacts that have been discovered there, which we will discuss in later chapters.[32] Regrettably, this cannot be confirmed by the records of the Knutson Expedition, for very few of its members returned to Europe, and Knutson himself does not appear to have been among them.[33] However, the information brought back by the survivors regarding the death of the Bishop of Greenland[34] tends to confirm the judgment of Professors Storm and Nansen, who claim that there is conclusive evidence that the remnants of Knutson's expedition finally reached Norway on or about the New Year of 1364, while Henry St. Clair was still an ambassador at court.[35]

In 1360, while the Knutson Expedition was still in progress, an English monk by the name of Nicholas Lynne completed a voyage of exploration northward along the west coast of Greenland and to

Hudson Bay.[36] Lynne was known as the "man with the astrolabe" and was a renowned traveler.[37] He was able to plot latitude with the aid of this new instrument, and it is recorded that he gave an astrolabe to Ivar Baardson.[38] Lynne's activities were recorded in the work *Inventio Fortunatae*, copies of which were given to the Norwegian king and to Pope Urban V.[39] The American historian Gunnar Thompson breaks ranks with other academics in his translation of the title of this work. He states that the most accurate translation is *Discovery of the Fortunates* and then defines the Fortunates as the legendary isles that the Romans are said to have found in the far west beyond the Atlantic Ocean.[40] Jacob Cnoyen, a Belgian who was at the Swedish court at the time of King Magnus, gave an account of Lynne's activities that was noted over a century later by the great geographer Gerard Mercator.[41] Cnoyen also confirmed that eight survivors of Knutson's expedition returned to Norway in 1364.[42]

The Meeting of Henry St. Clair and Carlo Zeno

Word of the Knutson Expedition was only one event among many to affect Henry St. Clair. It was at about this time that he either became betrothed to or married Princess Florentina of Denmark.[43] Several manuscripts in the Scottish archives state categorically that this was a marriage,[44] while other, seemingly equally authoritative, sources claim this as only a betrothal. It was also in 1364 that Henry made his first contact with the man who was later to become the savior of Chioggia, Carlo Zeno of Venice. Zeno was touring the capitals of Northern Europe with the chancellor of King Peter of Cyprus, Philip de Mezieres, in order to promote a new crusade.[45] Their objective was twofold. First, they sought to raise funds to pay for this expensive expedition. Second, they wanted to recruit forces to fight the infidels. According to the London scholar Niven Sinclair, Henry was recruited by King Peter of Cyprus himself in 1365,[46] and agreed to take part in the Crusade. He accompanied the substantial body of Scottish knights who joined the main crusading army in Venice in 1366, where he renewed his friendship with Carlo Zeno.[47] A large fleet of over 300 ships set sail for Cyprus and then for Egypt, where they indulged in another orgy of looting and slaughter in the ancient city of Alexandria.[48] Henry, as a result of his participation in this sacred butchery, acquired a bizarre nickname; one of his brothers, somewhat sardonically, called him Henry the Holy St. Clair from that time on.[49]

The Struggle for the Earldom

On his return from the crusade, Henry was left free to marry his childhood sweetheart, Janet Halyburton, the daughter of Lord Dirleton, Princess Florentina having died before reaching puberty.[50] There were only two other women who ever exerted any influence over Henry St. Clair—Queen Margrette, whom we have already mentioned, and his mother, who never allowed him to forget that, through her, he was the rightful heir to the Earldom of Orkney, Caithness, and Stratherne.[51] The succession to the earldom of the islands had been a matter of dispute since the previous earl, Erngisle, was deposed for his part in a plot against King Magnus II of Sweden.[52] This left three legitimate contenders for the earldom, Henry St. Clair, Malise Spera, and Alexander de Arde, who were all grandsons of Earl Malise Spera.[53] According to the generally accepted laws of inheritance of the time, the historian J. Storer Clouston claims that the true heir was probably Alexander de Arde.[54] Henry's claim was based on Earl Malise's will, which left the title to Henry's mother and her heirs.[55] To further bolster his claim, Henry could point to direct lineal descent from Turf Einar, Earl of Orkney and natural son of Rognvald the Mighty.[56]

To Henry St. Clair's intense dismay, Alexander de Arde was appointed governor of Orkney and commissioner for the king on 30 June 1375, but at least he was not installed as the earl. This commission was only for one year, after which de Arde resigned his position, having used his time on the islands to strengthen his relationship with many of the leading inhabitants.[57] Orkney was in desperate need of a strong hand as governor for, since Earl Erngisle's deposition, the islands had descended into near anarchy, a situation that was exacerbated by the activities of the local bishop, who was constantly at loggerheads with the king's representatives. The bishop's behavior was such that two commissioners were sent by the archbishop to investigate his actions. They reported that:

> He had appointed "aliens, vagabonds and apostates" for short periods of time for a commission which he put into his own

pocket. As to his method of spending these ill-gotten gains, he occupied himself "so frequently with hawking and clamorous hunting and that kind of levity—to say nothing of other things —that he attended little or not at all to the government of the Church."[58]

As a result of the misappropriation of all available funds by the corrupt bishop, the king's bailiff, Haakon Jonsson, found it virtually impossible to collect taxes and rents for the king.[59] These problems were part of a wider scenario of financial pressure being endured by the kingdom of Norway at that time. Her ability to trade was severely circumscribed by the Hansa, whose monopoly over Baltic trade placed a complete stranglehold on all of Norway's efforts in the East and whose imports of fur from Russia were in direct and powerful competition with the export of furs from the Norwegian colonies in Greenland, Markland, and Vinland.[60] This perilous situation was exacerbated by bands of pirates who infested the North Sea and exerted a devastating effect on Norwegian shipping elsewhere. It has been suggested that one of the contributory factors that led to the appointment of Henry St. Clair as the first St. Clair Earl of Orkney was his ability to pay 1000 English nobles for the title and the rights that went with it. Under the circumstances we have described, the need of a strong man as earl who could restore peace and order to the islands themselves, boost their revenues, limit the depredations of the bishop, and put a stop to piracy was all too apparent, and with the benefit of hindsight, Henry seemed the ideal candidate on these grounds alone.

Henry St. Clair, Earl of Orkney

In light of the Orcadian historian J. Storer Clouston's comments regarding the greater degree of legitimacy of Alexander de Arde's right to the succession, it is perhaps a little difficult to discern precisely why Henry St. Clair was granted the earldom. He undoubtedly possessed sufficient strength of character, but so did Alexander de Arde, who had already established good relations with many of the islanders during his year as governor. Was Henry's appointment merely a matter of money? Was the preferential treatment of Henry simply a reflection of the close relationships he had established with the crown while he was ambassador? Or, on the other hand, was his preferment yet another subtle symptom of the influence of Rex Deus? Or had a secret agreement been reached between Henry and the Zeno family of Venice, one that might solve Norway's economic problems at one fell swoop?

Henry St. Clair was formally invested with the earldom of Orkney on 2 August 1379.[61] In the document of installation, Malise Spera was instructed to cease his claim and demit his rights, so that the King of Norway would suffer no further vexation from him or his heirs. Another clause gave the same instructions in respect of Alexander de Arde. J. Storer Clouston, lists the remaining terms of the document as follows:

1 - on three month's warning the earl shall serve the king, outwith the Orkneys, with 100 good men or more fully armed.

2 - if Orkney, or the land of Shetland, is invaded the earl shall defend it, not only with the aid of the islemen, but with the whole strength of our kin, friends, and servants.

3 - to the same effect as one.

4 - the earl shall not build castles or other fortifications in the islands without the king's consent.

5 - he shall cherish and protect the lands and inhabitants of Orkney, cleric and lay, rich and poor.

6 - he shall not sell or wadset any lands of the earldom.

7 - he undertakes to assist and provide for the king or his men if they come to the isles.

8 - he promises not to raise war, litigation or dissension that may cause damage to Norway.

9 - if he commits notable injustice to anybody he shall answer to the king.

10 - he shall attend the king whenever summoned.

11 - he shall not violate any truce or peace made with other countries by the king.

12 - he shall make no league with the Bishop of Orkney, nor to

enter into or establish any friendship with him unless with the good pleasure and consent of our said lord the king, but that we assist him against the said bishop until he shall do what of eight or deservedly he ought to do in those things which our said lord king desires or may reasonably demand of the said bishop

13 - the earl's heirs are to seek infeftment in the earldom from the king (i.e. his heirs would not inherit the earldom unless the king granted them the title).

14 - the earl to pay 1000 nobles sterling to the king.

15 & 16 deal with Spera and Arde's disavowal of the title.

17 - the earl promises "that we shall assume in no manner of way to ourselves the lands of our said lord the king. Or any rights and others which his progenitors and our said lord the king have reserved to themselves, nor shall we intromit with those lands or rights in any way whatsoever, which lands and rights within the earldom of Orkney they have reserved as aforesaid, but such lands and rights shall remain in all respects reserved for them."[62]

The importance of the earldom of Orkney in Norwegian terms can hardly be overestimated. The islands of Orkney and Shetland not only produced badly needed revenues for the king, but their geographical position gave them enormous strategic importance. As a base of naval power, they could be used in the campaign to eliminate piracy in the North Sea and to create a new trading link with Venice routed by the west coast of Ireland, which would bypass the stranglehold that the Hanseatic League held over trade between the Mediterranean and Northern Europe. If, on the other hand, the islands fell under the control of the Hansa or their allies, the consequences for the kingdom of Norway would be disastrous.

Dual Allegiance

The earldom of Orkney was the last surviving earldom in the kingdom of Norway, and the earl took precedence over the entire aristocracy.[63]

Consequently, the earl's signature on national documents is always to be found immediately after that of the Archbishop of Nidros and before that of the bishops and the other nobles. The earl was viewed as akin to royalty and entitled to use the honorific "Prince."[64] Within Orkney itself, his power was virtually absolute and carried the right to issue coinage, make laws, and remit crimes. When he issued new laws, he wore a crown on his head, as he was esteemed to be second only to the king.[65] Following Rex Deus tradition and to strengthen his position, Henry arranged dynastic marriages for his children when they were of age. His son and heir, yet another Henry, married Egida Douglas, the granddaughter of King Robert II of Scotland. Ingeborg, a daughter of Waldemar, King of Denmark, married Henry's second son, John.[66]

Earl Henry St. Clair was installed by King Haakon VI of Norway, who died one year later. The royal widow, Queen Margrette, became Queen Regent,[67] as their son, Olaf, was still too young to rule in his own right. It is probable that this made it easier for the new earl to gain permission from the crown to build the castle at Kirkwall, which had been forbidden by his installation document. Power only exists when it is exercised. Theoretical powers granted to Henry at his installation would have been illusory indeed in the chaotic circumstances that obtained in Orkney at the time of installation if he did not have the strength to impose the king's law on all his new subjects. Obeying the basic principle of the German strategist Clauswitz to "first secure your base," Henry carved out a stronghold for himself and his troops. Like many Sinclair castles, it was on the coast and had a sea gate so that it could be supplied from the water. Henry's castle, which no longer exists, was described in the following terms:

> I protest to God that the house has never been biggit without
> the consent of the Devil, for it is one of the strongest holds in
> Britain—without fellow.[68]

Two factors that probably made it easier for Henry to obtain permission from the Crown to build his castle are matters of public record and date from the year of his installation. The first was a solemn pledge from Henry himself, in which he stated that:

> . . . I do promise to the most excellent prince and my lord, the
> Lord Haakon, King of Norway and Sweden, the illustrious,

that I shall in no way alienate or pledge or deliver as security the land or islands of the country of Orkney away from my lord the aforesaid king, his heirs and successors, or surrender them without the consent of my lord the above-mentioned king, his heirs or his successors.[69]

Henry swore this document in front of impressive witnesses, including Lords William and Walter, the Bishops of St. Andrews and Glasgow, Earl William of Douglas, Earl George of March, and a host of barons and knights. The second document was perhaps even more important. It was a contract on the part of King Robert of Scotland, who formerly had denied that the kingdom of Scotland had any claim to the earldom of Orkney, to recognize King Haakon's right to give the earldom "to our beloved relative Henry, Earl of Orkney." By means such as this, Henry clarified his somewhat ambiguous position, which might otherwise have been a reasonable cause for concern by King Haakon. As Baron of Roslin, Henry was a member of the feudal aristocracy owing strict allegiance to his lord and sovereign, the King of the Scots. As Earl of Orkney, however, he was the premier nobleman of Norway and owed his allegiance in this position to King Haakon and his heirs. As a result of King Robert's declaration that he laid no claim to Orkney, we can reasonably assume that any reservations on the part of King Haakon were firmly put to rest. Permission to build the castle at Kirkwall must have been officially granted, as there is no record of any complaint emanating from the Norwegian crown on what, in any other circumstance, would have been a serious breach of the terms of installation. Royal approval of Henry's actions in general, and his castle building in particular, is demonstrated by the fact that Henry and his heirs held the earldom for three generations, under the aegis of the Norwegian crown. Using Kirkwall Castle as his base, Henry progressed to the complex and difficult task of bringing law and order to the islands of Orkney and Shetland.

Chapter 4

HENRY CONSOLIDATES
HIS POWER

IN CONSOLIDATING HIS POWER OVER HIS NEW island dominion, Henry St. Clair had a considerable advantage by virtue of his family descent, for the Norse bailiff in Orkney in 1364 was his uncle, Thomas St. Clair. The native families of both Orkney and Shetland were descendants of the Viking colonists and numbered among their ancestors the land-owning nobility who had served in either the Orcadian or Shetland ruling assemblies, or Lawthings.[1] They included the families of Berstane, Clouston, Cragy (Craigie), Cromarty, Peterson, Petrie, Heddle, Halcro, Ireland, Kirkness, Linflater, Ness (later Peterson, Petrie, Tulloch), Paplay, Rendall, Scarth (formerly Harraldson/Bolt), Scalter, and Yenstay. According to the genealogist Nicholas Cran-Sinclair, all of these families would now be entitled to wear the St. Clair tartan and be officially recognized as regional septs and dependants of the Clan Sinclair.[2]

One author of note, Eric Linklater, records that "Unlike his immediate predecessors Henry I did identify himself with Orkney and apparently lived there in considerable style."[3] Henry had come to the islands to stay. His grant of the earldom was, however, merely a royal license to try to gain power over the islands by dint of his character and force of arms; it offered the opportunity, rather than the right, to rule. His opponents were many and varied and included all those who broke the law: illegal tax collectors, the corrupt bishop, and the varied collection of pirates and smugglers who infested the islands. Henry was under no illusions and knew that he would have to fight to establish his authority. He had one advantage granted to him at the time of his installation:

Malise Spera and Alexander de Arde were forbidden to leave Norway,[4] which kept his two most serious adversaries firmly out of the way for a while at least. Henry's new castle, surrounded in its entirety by the waters of Kirkwall harbor, gave him a fortified base that counterbalanced the bishop's palace, which housed a large garrison used by the prelate to enforce his illegal seizures of land, taxes, and rents.[5] In his opposition to the bishop, Henry was not merely fulfilling the king's wishes, but also gaining popularity with his new people, who understandably resented the venal priest who had been exploiting them for many years. Hatred of the bishop was intense, and every move that Henry made to curb his power increased his popularity and raised the hopes of the islanders.[6] In 1382, the people rose in violent rebellion against the aberrant churchman; the records disclose that "then was heard the mournful tidings that Bishop William was slain in the Orkney's . . . killed or burnt by his flock."[7] The bishop was a Scot; his flock were Norse. In consequence, the chapter of the Cathedral of St. Magnus in Kirkwall asked Pope Urban in Rome to nominate John, the parish priest of Fetlar, to be their new bishop. Due to a papal schism, there were two popes at this time—one in Rome and one in Avignon. The Avignon pope appointed Robert Sinclair as Bishop of Orkney, but he never gained possession of his see.[8] Earl Henry used the time of the disputed succession to consolidate his power, recover lands stolen by the previous bishop, and restore them to the king, the people who had been dispossessed, or the earldom itself.

Mastery of the Sea

At the time of Henry's accession, Orkney and the Shetlands were prosperous, each supporting a population of approximately 25,000. The islands exported large quantities of fish, pork, sheep, and hides to Scotland and the Hanseatic merchants. They imported timber, flax, pitch, wax, salt, and pewter wares.[9] The prosperity of the islanders ensured that tax revenues were high, if only they could be collected. However, as Henry increased his hold on the islands, he became ever more aware of the stranglehold exerted on their trade by the merchants of the Hanseatic League.

Henry was a man of remarkable character and courage, and under his rule the islands began to enjoy what was probably the most successful and prosperous period in their history. Over time, he gained political and military control over the main island of Orkney, but there was no way he could extend his power over the lesser islands or over Shetland unless he first gained mastery of the sea. When the castle in Kirkwall was completed, he began to exert his power over the island and made plans to build a fleet. As Orkney is virtually treeless, Henry had to look to his estates in Scotland for the raw material for his ships.[10] Pentland forest, near Roslin, had good oak and pine trees in abundance, which were used to build a battle fleet of thirteen seaworthy vessels: two galleys, un-decked ships rowed with oars, one long-decked battleship, and ten decked barks.[11]

The historian Frederick Pohl, who has made a series of in-depth studies of North Atlantic exploration, claims that Henry armed his new fleet with cannon,[12] claiming that the earl had learnt of the use of this form of sea-borne firepower when he received news of the Venetian victory at Chioggia. While this is a theoretical possibility, it is highly doubtful, as there is no contemporary evidence confirming that cannon were used at Chioggia. Furthermore we have grave doubts that detailed news of this victory would have reached Henry in time to influence this particular shipbuilding program.

The prime importance of sea power to the earldom was recorded heraldically. The new coat of arms was a shield divided into four quarters. In the second and third quarters was the familiar engrailed cross of the St. Clairs in argent on a sable background, replicating the Templar colors of the Beausseante, black and white. The first and fourth quarters had an armed galley in gold figured against an azure background, within a double tressure counter-flowered, also in gold.[13] Thus the new heraldic crest combined the old with the new. The engrailed cross of the Lordly Line of the High St. Clairs spoke of an old and courageous family, while the galleys denoted naval strength, and the double tressure border indicated a rank akin to royalty.

Henry was not just the Earl of Orkney; he was still Baron of Roslin, Pentland, and Cousland, and he had to make occasional trips to Scotland to look after his estates and discharge his obligations to the Scottish crown. He visited Roslin in June 1384 to invest his cousin, James St. Clair, Baron of Longformacus, with a donation of land, the deed of donation being witnessed by Thomas Erskine of Dun, George Abernethy of Soulston, Walter Halyburton of that Ilk, and John

Halyburton of Dirleton.[14] The earl was also away from the islands for a prolonged period during 1385, when a large English army under King Richard II marched on Scotland. Henry spent several weeks in this campaign. Troops under his command harried the invading English forces and then carried the battle into the northern provinces of England, laying siege to Carlisle.

This defense of Scotland prevented Henry from returning to Orkney for several months.[15] When he did return, he continued with his preparations for the subjugation of the Shetlands, while still making occasional visits to his estates in the south. On one such visit to Edinburgh in 1387, both he and his earlier rival, Malise Spera, signed a treaty of amity that, by its very nature, implies that there were still a number of problems to be resolved between them. His preparations were further interrupted in the latter part of 1387 by pressing duties in Scandinavia.

Queen Margrette

Queen Margrette was Queen Regent of the three kingdoms of Norway, Denmark, and Sweden, reigning in that position while the infant King Olaf was a minor. King Olaf died in 1389. As one of the senior electors for the throne of the three kingdoms, Henry's first duty was to the court. On 2 February 1388, the thirty-five-year-old beauty, Queen Margrette, was elected for life as Queen of Norway and Sweden and as the rightful heir and regent of Denmark.[16] This shrewd and intelligent woman had wisdom beyond her years and has been described as "the Semiramis of the north."[17] The Queen Regent, in her wisdom, recognized that her subjects would, in the normal course of things, prefer to be ruled by a king. To secure her position, and also to provide continuity in the future for her kingdom, she adopted a five-year-old boy, Eric of Pomerania, as her heir. Margrette then persuaded the Council of Electors to recognize Eric as the rightful heir to the three kingdoms, which, in effect, left the reins of power in her hands until he came of age.[18] The charter proclaiming Eric as heir to the throne of Norway was signed by Vinold, Archbishop of Drontheim; Henry St. Clair, Earl of Orkney; various bishops; and the nobles of the council.[19] Henry was at Helsingborg in Sweden on 9 July 1389, when Eric was acclaimed as king of that country, and was also present in September 1389 when Eric

was crowned King of Norway.[20] On the same day that Eric was proclaimed King of Sweden, Earl Henry signed a solemnly binding undertaking to Haakon Jonsson, the royal bailiff of Norway:

> Let it be known by these present that we, Henry St. Clair, Earl
> of Orkney and Baron of Roslin, with our heirs, are held and
> bound to a man of the nobility, Haquin the son of John, or his
> successors, in £140 sterling of Scottish gold, to be paid to him
> or his heirs or sure deputies at the Church of St. Magnus the
> Martyr in Tingwall in Shetland, at terms of the year, without
> fraud or trick; that is at the first term, being St. Lawrence's
> Day, 1390, £40, at the second term the same day of 1391, £40,
> at the third term the same day of 1392, £40, and at the fourth
> term the same day, £20, all at the same place. If we or our heirs
> fail to pay Haquin Johnson or his successors, they may seize all
> our rents for their loss and the delay, with escheats from the
> islands of Sanday and Ronaldsay in Orkney, not lessening in
> any way the said sum of £140, and they will enjoy the rents
> and escheats till fully paid. Our seal is appended at
> Helsingborg Palace.[21]

At first glance, this agreement seems to contain an extremely unusual
promise, made by the senior Earl of Norway to the king's bailiff. Henry
is, in effect, binding himself to pay four substantial sums of money to
the bailiff in an area where he has not, as yet, set foot, and under a
penalty clause that would deprive him of the substantial revenues of
some of the islands he had subdued. Yet there is no indication as to
what these payments are for. The explanation is simple. The document
clearly demonstrates that, as Henry's rule was now effectively established in Orkney, where he had discharged a similar obligation not long
after his appointment as earl, he was now being commanded to extend
the rule of law to the Shetlands and subdue them in their turn. Unless
the Shetland Islands were pacified and returned to a law-abiding state,
Henry would be incapable of making the payments that he had
pledged. This solemn undertaking reinforces the second clause of the
installation document and proves beyond all doubt that the Earldom of
Orkney granted to Henry St. Clair was the traditional Viking one that
included the Shetland Isles. Furthermore, it is a clear recognition of the
difficulties that Henry faced on his installation: he was first expected to

subdue Orkney under a similar undertaking to pay dues at Kirkwall[22] to the king's bailiff, and he was now deemed powerful enough to bring the rule of law to Shetland as earl of those islands. It is clear, from the time difference between the date of signature of this document and the date of the first-due payment, that Queen Margrette was aware that Henry was now in command of sufficient troops and a fleet to transport them and, therefore, could move promptly to wrest control of the Shetland Islands.

Henry Gains the Shetlands

The earl's campaign against the Shetlands, despite the size of his fleet, was fraught with difficulty. To add to the troubles inherent in any naval venture in those troubled waters at that time, it must be remembered that the Shetland islanders numbered over 25,000 and were descended from the same combative Viking stock as the people of Orkney. Furthermore, there could be no element of surprise, as his intentions must have been obvious for months. In the spring of 1390, Henry had been at Scone in Scotland to pay homage to King Robert III, who had just acceded to the Scottish throne.[23] It was only after that obligation had been discharged that he could begin his naval operations against the Shetlands.

His first point of attack was the island of Fer (Fair Isle), which lay a little more than halfway between Orkney and the Shetlands.[24] The rocky coast of Fer Island was lashed on one side by the full fury of the Atlantic and on the other by the North Sea, which is, from time to time, equally violent. The whole island measures about 3½ miles (6 km) long by ½ mile (0.75 km) wide. It has an inhospitable rocky coast, is surrounded by a multitude of reefs and shoals, and is scoured by strong tidal currents.[25] From Henry's perspective, although the island was small and relatively sparsely populated, it provided a stern challenge, as there were only three possible landing places for his fleet. We have no details of his actual landing, but we do know that, once ashore, he began negotiations with some of the islanders. As negotiations proceeded, he was surprised when, without warning, the islanders snatched up their weapons and began to run toward the coast, where a large vessel had been driven hard on the jagged rocks.[26] The inhabitants of Fer Island were, like the Cornish and other races inhabiting dangerous coasts, not averse to making profit from the misfortune of those unlucky enough to be shipwrecked on their shores. The cargo of any ship cast up on the shoreline was considered fair game, and any survivors from a shipwreck were given short shrift by the hardy islanders.

As Henry watched, he noticed that the ship's masts had snapped, presumably on impact, and the crew were clinging desperately to the rails and tangled rigging to keep from being washed from the wreck and drowned. None made an attempt to swim to shore, as that was lined with islanders brandishing weapons and signaling their murderous intent.[27] Henry dispersed the bloodthirsty crowd with his troops and somehow cast lines aboard the wreck, enabling the crew to scramble to safety. To establish communication with the shipwrecked sailors, Earl Henry used the one language in Christendom that any educated man understood—Latin—to enquire whence they came. They replied that they were from Venice. The captain's name, it transpired, was Nicolo Zeno.[28]

The Zeno/St. Clair Alliance

Nicolo Zeno was a younger brother of the hero of Chioggia, Carlo Zeno, whom Henry had met on the Crusades and who had earlier visited the Norwegian court in 1364. We know that the Venetians made an annual voyage to visit Flanders and England and were restricted from sailing further north because of the monopoly exerted by the merchants of the Hanseatic League. We are also aware that Venetian trading patterns were in a state of flux as the increasing power of the Turks was severely curtailing their activities in the eastern Mediterranean and their trading empire was under pressure from their Genoese rivals. During his voyages to the north, Carlo Zeno, scion of one of Venice's leading mercantile families, became acutely aware of the potential for profit in the trade of fur and fish that was pouring into the Scandinavian countries from the new-found lands in the West. He was at court in Norway and Sweden when news of the Knutson Expedition reached home and information about the voyages of Nicholas Lynne was being dispatched from Norway to Rome, so he could not fail to have noted the possibilities for trade that lay in the New World. As agreements with the Hanseatic League insisted that Venetian merchandise could only be carried to Northern Europe and the Baltic in Hansa ships, the presence of a Venetian ship in waters this far north would have been regarded as an act of extreme provocation by the northern monopoly. Is there an explanation for why Venice risked the wrath of the Hansa in this provocative manner? We submit that there is.

Venice needed to expand her trade routes and circumvent the Hanseatic monopoly over northern trade. While in Norway, Carlo Zeno had learned of new lands to the west and was shrewd enough to appraise their true potential for profit. He had met Henry St. Clair and was well aware that he, too, would be under pressure to initiate effective change in the trading patterns of the earldom of Orkney. Both Carlo and Henry were Rex Deus and steeped in the Templar tradition, which gave them a secure basis for a partnership based upon secrecy and trust. They were also acutely aware that persecution and repression was an inherent part of European Christendom. Holy Mother the Church was constantly engaged in a hunt for heresy, and after the genocide against the Cathars[29] and the arrest and torture of the Knights Templar,[30] no one was truly safe. From the Rex Deus perspective, there was a clear need for a northern trading commonwealth far beyond the reach of the Hansa and the Church, where men of talent could prosper and practice their true beliefs openly and without fear. Each step in Henry's early career was made with one supreme objective always in view—to gain the earldom of Orkney. What is now becoming apparent is that this was simply intended as the first step of many. Henry, supported by the brothers Zeno, would utilize his power, his fleet, and their naval expertise to achieve a common objective—to use the islands of his earldom as stepping stones across the northern Atlantic and create a settlement in the New World based upon the principles of toleration and freedom.[31]

Nicolo Zeno

Nicolo Zeno was almost as skilled and experienced as his brother Carlo, having been a captain of a galley in the war against the Genoese.[32] He had served at one time as the Venetian ambassador to Ferrara in northern Italy, and his personal wealth, which he used to build and equip a ship for his voyage to northern waters, was such that he was one of the richest men in Venice.[33] At all times, he kept his family informed of his progress by a series of letters, continued by his brother Antonio, which a later descendant edited and published as the beginning of what later became known as the Zeno Narrative.[34] Nicolo describes passing the Straits of Gibraltar and sailing northward on the route established by the annual Venetian voyage to England and Flanders, and continues with an account of a terrible storm that resulted in the shipwreck we have already described. Nicolo's account names this island as *Frislanda*, a corruption of the Latin term *Fer Island*. Earl Henry is described as warlike, valiant, especially famous in naval exploits, and "a great lord who ruled certain islands called Portlanda which lay to the south of Frislanda."[35] Portlanda has now been accepted as an Italianate version of the ancient name for Orkney, Pentland.[36] Besides being named as the lord of these islands, Henry was also described as the duke of certain estates in Scotland. Nicolo and his men were invited to serve aboard Henry's fleet,[37] and their navigational skills were used to good effect. Indeed, if it had not been for the skill and experience of the Venetian sailors, there is a strong possibility that, owing to the nature of these hazardous waters, Henry's combined naval and land operations against the Shetlands could well have come to grief. Within a relatively short time, his courage and skill, backed up by the might of his army and the presence of this fleet, resulted in the subjugation of the Shetlands. With the islands secure, Henry complimented Captain Nicolo for "the preservation of his fleet and the winning of so many places without any trouble to himself."[38]

Nicolo Zeno was rewarded for his services in the campaign with the honor of knighthood conferred on him by Earl Henry.[39] The contribution of his men was marked by the gift of very handsome presents. The triumphant expedition then progressed toward the chief's city, which lay to the southwest of the island on a bay whose waters abounded with fish, the principal item of trade of the islands. Shetland had grown very wealthy indeed from trading in herring, ling, cusk, and cod, which was in great demand in Flanders, Brittany, England, Scotland, Norway, and Denmark.[40]

The fishermen of Shetland were accustomed to making prolonged voyages in the North Atlantic. On one occasion, it is reported that the island was host to 2000 fishing vessels from Flanders and other countries. Surprisingly, the people had little use for money and worked on a barter system, paying their taxes in butter, fish oil, and homespun cloth. In the Zeno Narrative itself, the account of these matters is said to have been taken from a letter by Sir Nicolo to Sir Antonio, his brother, requesting him to commission another ship to come out to the islands to join the expedition. The narrative continues:

> Since Antonio had as great a desire as his brother to see the world and its various nations, and to make himself a great name, he bought a ship and directed his course that way. After a long voyage full of many dangers, he joined Sir Nicolo in safety and was received by him with great gladness, as his brother not only by blood, but also in courage.[41]

Henry's Control over All the Islands

Henry used the main port of Shetland as his chief naval base in the islands and instituted a system of beacons, for in clear weather, a smoke signal from the southern tip of Shetland was visible from Fer Island, and a similar signal from there could easily be seen from Ronaldsay in the Orkneys.[42] Under Henry's rule, the king's bailiff could now land without hindrance, and as clear proof that the islands were now under the rule of law, Henry's representative made payment to the bailiff under the terms of the bond. Leaving Sir Nicolo in charge of his navy, Henry returned to Kirkwall en route to Scotland for the coronation of King Robert III.

Henry's possession of the Shetlands is confirmed by a charter he signed on 23 April 1391 that authorized the donation of certain lands in Aberdeenshire to his half-brother in return for a renunciation of the half-brother's rights to the Orkney and Shetland earldom. It reads:

> To all who shall see or hear these present, Henry St. Clair, Earl of Orkney and Lord of Roslin, safety in the Lord! I concede to my brother, David St. Clair, for life, because of his claim through our mother Isabella Sperra in Orkney and Shetland, all the lands of Newburgh and Auchdale in Aberdeenshire, to return to me if his heirs fail.[43]

Within three months of this signing, the seething resentment and rivalry between Malise Spera and Earl Henry came to its final, bloody conclusion. Matters came to a head at the annual legislative and judicial assembly, or Lawthing, at Tingwall in Shetland. This was held on an island in a small lake to which access was gained by a stone causeway. The Lawthing was not only legislative in nature, but was also empowered to hear complaints and petitions and to witness pledges and charters. It was a democratic institution in Viking tradition at which the king, or the earl or his representative, presided but did not dictate. In 1391, a case involving Malise Spera was brought to judgment.[44] Despite being bound by Henry's act of installation and having signed a treaty of amity with him, Malise unlawfully retained certain lands he had seized earlier. The lawful heirs to these lands, John and Sigurd Hafthorsson, claimed their rights before the Lawthing. Contrary to public custom, Spera arrived accompanied by a body of armed men, and when he forcibly resisted the judgment against him, Earl Henry took prompt and appropriate action. A contemporary account states that "it seems the Earl was about to hold a court to settle the legal rights of the parties concerned. A conflict taking place, the dispute was terminated by a strong hand . . . Malise Sparre, with seven others, was slain in Hjaltland by the Earl of Orkney."[45] Henry's subjugation of the Shetlands, which was soon followed by a significant victory against pirates, made a lasting impression in Scandinavia. In the eyes of his sovereign and friend, Queen Margrette, Earl Henry St. Clair, with the aid of the Zeno brothers, had acquired a well-deserved reputation for his maritime skills.

By 1392, the Kingdom of Norway had, due to the depredations of pirates and battles with the Hansa, almost completely lost its power at sea.[46] As a stopgap to remedy these matters while shipbuilding could proceed, Queen Margrette entered into correspondence with King Richard II of England to obtain safe-conduct for Henry St. Clair, Earl of Orkney and Lord of Roslin, to travel to London to lease three warships to make good the deficiency in the Norwegian fleet. On 10 March, safe-conduct was granted to "Henry Seint Cler, Comes Orchadie et Dominus de Roslyne" to enter England with a party of no more than twenty-four people. Anyone who was a fugitive from English law was excluded from the safe-conduct, which was good until 29 September of the same year.[47] It is highly likely that Henry brought some of his Italian advisors with him on this visit, and in view of what was to follow, it is reasonable to assume that he used this occasion to purchase rigging, tools, and naval armaments for his own purposes, as well as to discharge his duties to his queen. And so the stage was set for exploration to the west.

PART 2

FOLLOWING IN THE WAKE OF HISTORY

Chapter 5

PRE-COLUMBIAN MYSTERIES

THE FIRST SUGGESTION THAT THERE MAY have been contact between the Eastern and Western Hemispheres in pre-Columbian times comes from the writers of ancient Greece and Rome. Lands situated far to the west of the ocean beyond the Pillars of Hercules are mentioned by Aristotle (or one of his pupils),[1] Plato,[2] Didorus Siculus,[3] Theopompus of Chios,[4] Plutarch,[5] Strabo,[6] and Erastosthenes of Cryrene.[7] While many of these references may well have a legendary foundation, certain of the reports have the ring of truth and speak with the voice of experience:

> The impassable farther bounds of Ocean not only has no one attempted to describe, but no man has been allowed to reach: for the reason of obstructing sea-weed and the failing of winds it is plainly inaccessible. . . . This same ocean has in its western region certain islands known to almost everyone by reason of the great number of those who journey to and fro.[8]

As a description of the perils to navigation posed by the Sargasso Sea, this can hardly be excelled and is obviously based upon direct experience. More intriguing, it is allied to the bald statement that the West Indies was visited regularly. Even stranger still, what are probably the most important references to pre-Columbian trans-Atlantic travel come from the most unlikely source of all—Columbus himself.

What Did Columbus Know?

In 1959, the Russian Professor Isypernick discovered a letter written by Columbus to Queen Isabella of Spain that shows that Columbus was well aware of the existence of the West Indies before he set sail on his momentous voyage and that he carried a map of the islands made by earlier explorers. This assertion is given further credence by G. R. Crone of the Royal Geographical Society, who claims that there are charts in the Library of Congress that prove the point.[9] Professor Ivan Van Sertima of Rutgers University recounts that Columbus confirmed the existence of a secret trade route between Africa and the New World that was mentioned in conversation by Don Juan, King of Portugal. The Genoese navigator claimed that, on his second voyage to the Americas, natives told him of traders whose spears were tipped with gold and who, furthermore, were black.[10]

Black contact with pre-Columbian America was apparently confirmed in 1970 by Alexander von Wuthenau, Professor of Art at the University of the Americas in Mexico City.[11] After extensive examination of a large number of private collections and museums in the Americas, and as a result of his own excavations in Mexico, he discovered a substantial number of Negroid heads in clay, copper, copal, and gold. The heads, found in a variety of strata whose dates ranged from the earliest American civilizations right up to the period of Columbus, are of undoubted African influence. The Negroid facial features, fullness of lip, noses, tattoo markings, and typical curly hair are unmistakable— all recorded skillfully by American sculptors and artists of the pre-Columbian period.[12] According to the American writer, Frances Gibson:

> Black colonies were found in Panama when the Spaniards arrived. The white man, the black man, the red man in the costume of the Indian of North America, and the yellow man are all distinctly depicted on the murals of Chichen Itza.[13]

Cultural Diffusion?

Another early Spanish explorer who hinted at pre-Columbian contact by European and Mediterranean peoples, Father Gregorio Garcia, described the immense racial diversity of the Native Americans in his book *The Origin of the Indians of the New World*, which was published in 1607:

> The Indios come from many nations of the Old World. Some are probably descended from the Carthaginians; some are

descendants of the ten lost tribes of Israel; others come from Atlantis, Greece, Phoenicia and China.[14]

Naturally enough, Father Garcia attributed the racial diversity he saw to origins that arose from his own frame of reference—European knowledge and legend, moderated by the biblical studies that were the foundation of his faith. He was not alone in suggesting that Native Americans were descended from the ten lost tribes of Israel, but such suggestions are not proof. Much has also been made of the similarities between pyramid building in Central America and Egypt, but these ideas have long since been dismissed. Other Spaniards remarked on the wide range of species of plant life that was quite unknown to them, but also gave detailed descriptions of other flora that was common in Europe.[15] The English author and one-time M.P. Nigel Davies, who has spent many years residing in Mexico, posed the question: "How did Old World plants reach the New World and was Man responsible for their arrival in pre-Hispanic times?" In light of the vast expanse of ocean separating the two continents, we suggest that man is the only credible vector in this case.

The cultural historian Professor Joseph Campbell, who has a well-deserved international reputation for his insight and understanding, has studied the myths of the people of the Americas in a worldwide context. In this, he has broken ranks with the majority of his fellow American academics, for he wrote:

> We can reasonably suggest that the mythologies underlying and represented in the art forms of the high cultures of Middle America were finally not merely similar to those of ancient Greece and the Orient, but were actually of one piece with them—a remote provincial extension of the one historic heritage and universal history of mankind.[16]

The idea that the early megalith builders of Western Europe may also have crossed the Atlantic could attest to this type of cultural diffusion. This strange suggestion has a distinguished pedigree and was proposed by Professors Sean O'Riordain and Glyn Daniel of University College Dublin, leading experts on megaliths and passage graves in Europe who wrote in the 1950s.[17] Their ideas may yet explain the cultural links between the megalithic structures of Western Europe and those of New England on the east coast of the United States.

Despite the widespread belief that the culture of the Native Americans was a true Stone Age one, evidence does exist of metal working at a time of remote antiquity. The oldest metal artifacts in North America have been found in Minnesota and Wisconsin. Manufactured from copper, they include axes, knives, and chisels dated to between 3000 and 4000 B.C.E. The naturally occurring copper is found as ingots in a relatively pure state and did not have to be smelted.[18] One modern American researcher and author, Dr. Gunnar Thompson, claims that the abandoned mine shafts near Lake Superior, some of which are several hundred feet beneath the surface, are a visible legacy of ancient seafarers. He states that the local tribes, who often made blades and ornaments from nuggets lying on the surface, claim that the mines were not the work of their ancestors. American archaeologists have estimated that over half a million tons of copper were removed from these mine shafts and yet only a tiny proportion of it has so far been located in burial mounds and other archaeological sites in continental America. Thompson speculates that the bulk of the copper was exported overseas.[19] One bizarre anomaly has yet to be explained. Assays made and reported in 1991 show that some of the copper artifacts found in North American burial mounds were not made from pure copper, but from zinc-copper alloys of Mediterranean origin.[20]

The fact that trans-Atlantic voyages were possible even in the distant past is made abundantly clear by a discovery on the island of Corvo, the most westerly island of the Azores, which lies only 1000 miles from the American mainland. A pot full of Phoenician coins dating from 330 to 320 B.C.E. was discovered there in 1749.[21] Furthermore, in the Mayan book, *Popol Vuh*, Aztec religious belief and Mexican tradition all tell the same story of a fleet of ships crewed by white-skinned, bearded people that arrived on their shores many centuries before. This was noted in the sixteenth century by Father Bernardino de Sahagun,[22] who left the most complete record of the habits, traditions, and beliefs of the Central American people. This twelve volume masterwork, *Historia General de las cosas de Neuva España,* which was described by the historian Paul Johnson as the greatest work of the Renaissance, was deemed dangerously heretical at the time; it was suppressed and did not see the light of day for several centuries.[23]

Egyptian Petroglyphs in North America?

Two sets of petroglyphs that indicate possible Egyptian contact with the Americas were first fully described in 1993 and are subject to ongoing investigation. One is situated in the state of Oklahoma and the other at Rochester Creek in central Utah. If they do eventually prove to be of Egyptian origin, they will indicate a far deeper penetration of America than has previously been imagined.

In 1978, Gloria Farley was the first to suggest a possible Egyptian connection for the Oklahoma site when she identified a dog-like figure in one of the caves as that of Anubis.[24] Certain inscriptions indicate that the site is equinoctial (relating to an equinox), while others give details of additional "interactions with the sun at that time of year." These translations have been validated, as the "interactions with the sun" have since been observed and recorded by Rollin Gillespie, Phil Leonard, Bill McGlone, and Jon Polansky. This discovery was reported in the TV documentary *History on the Rocks* that was produced by Scott Monahan of Denver, Colorado.[25]

Near the Anubis figure in cave 2 of the Farley site is a carving of a woman displaying her birth canal, which was identified as a *sheila-na-gig* by Gloria Farley. Sheila-na-gigs are "rude" medieval carvings of female genitalia found commonly in many medieval churches and cathedrals in Europe. The possibility of an Egyptian/Phoenician source for this figure has been clearly demonstrated[26] by two similar depictions discovered on the Phoenician coast, dating to the first millennium B.C.E. These were illustrated by Stern in 1989.[27]

Similarities between certain North American petroglyphs and ancient Egyptian hieroglyphs have also been reported by archaeologist Phil Leonard during investigations conducted at Rochester Creek. Leonard and his colleagues attempted to interpret one of the Rochester Creek panels by using the meanings assigned to the figures in Egyptian iconography. The majority of the similarities depict the journey of the soul after death, with all its attendant perils, before it reaches its final destination. The right side of the main panel is framed by a large rainbowlike arch. Beneath the arch is a female figure exposing her birth canal, which frames a light-colored circle. Immediately under this carving is a reclining ithyphallic male figure (a symbol carried in ancient festivals). According to Egyptian beliefs, the goddess Nut gives birth to the

Sun each morning. She is frequently shown giving birth to the Sun with her consort, Geb, reclining beneath her.

There are also two beetles shown within the area framed by the arch; in Egyptian iconography, the dung beetle or scarab was intimately associated with the rising Sun. A serpentine figure under the left end of the arch clearly portrays an Egyptian cobra; also depicted are hippopotamus-like creatures, crocodiles, and a dog baring its teeth and tongue. In Egyptian tradition, the soul, on its final journey, is subject to attack by a strange creature known as "the Devourer of the Unjust." This creature was part crocodile and part hippopotamus. There are numerous other figures of possible Egyptian origin, and David Kelley, after a personal examination of the site, claims that "the mere presence of a possible hippo is highly suggestive of a tradition originating outside this continent."[28] Drawings of the inscriptions, along with the team's Egyptian suggestions, were forwarded to a senior Egyptologist, Professor J. Gwyn Griffiths of the University College of Swansea in Wales. He made the following comment:

> Several of the individual units and groups are in my view attractively explained by these suggestions. The central arch seems to be a vault of heaven (rather than a celestial river), but this supports the idea that the daily birth and course of the sun are depicted.[29]

We are in total agreement with William McGlone, Phil Leonard, James Guthrie, Rollin Gillespie, and James Whittall that the remarkable similarities to ancient Egyptian iconography displayed at this site are not properly accounted for by the term "Amerindian rock art."[30] Appreciable Egyptian impact of some type seems to be present in the glyphs. Open-minded and meticulous investigation of sites such as these is essential. They cannot simply be dismissed without further analysis, especially as the former president of the New World Foundation, Thomas Stuart Ferguson, has reported that seals marked with Egyptian hieroglyphs have been discovered in southern Mexico at Chiapa de Corso.[31]

Egyptian Trade with America?

Further intriguing evidence that gives proof of sustained Egyptian contact with the Americas has been discovered in Europe, which indicates the motive for these voyages—namely trade. In 1976, Dr. Michelle Lescot of the National History Museum in Paris, examining the wrappings of the mummy of the Egyptian Pharaoh Rameses II (c. 1290–1224 B.C.E.) to determine the reason for the degeneration in its condition, was looking for bacterial or viral causes. To her consternation, she found that she was looking at shreds of tobacco.[32] Her discovery caused considerable controversy. When she continued her examination deep inside the mummy itself, her findings were confirmed. Later tests proved beyond all doubt that the internal organs, which had been placed in canopic jars during the mummification process, had been preserved using a mixture of vegetable products including plantain, wheat, nettles, black pepper seeds, chamomile, and chopped tobacco leaves.[33] As the mummification process based upon these procedures was of long standing, sustained trade must have taken place with the American continent, for at that time, this particular variety of tobacco was indigenous to America and did not occur elsewhere. The trading implications of these findings were simply ignored, as they were too uncomfortable for the academic community to contemplate.

In 1992, several incredible discoveries were made by the German toxicologist Svetlana Balabanova in the course of forensic examination of portions of nine Egyptian mummies belonging to the Munich Museum. Taking samples from bone, skin tissue, head and abdominal muscles, she found a high level of drugs. All nine samples showed traces of hashish—not surprising, as this was common in Egypt. Her other findings were so startling that she immediately took steps to have them independently verified by three other laboratories. Eight of the mummies displayed clear evidence of nicotine usage and—the most bizarre result of all—each of the nine clearly demonstrated traces of the active alkaloid of the coca plant—cocaine.[34] The most probable source of the nicotine contamination was explained by the ethnobotanist Dr. Michael Carmichael during The Alternative Egypt Conference 2000 in London, as arising from the Egyptians' use of mood-altering drugs derived from mandrake or the nightshades that were in common use in that era. The use of the coca plant as a drug, however, has been proven in ancient Peru from circa 2500 B.C.E., but was unknown on the other side of the Atlantic until the mid-nineteenth century. Dr. Balabanova is an expert witness whose evidence, in her capacity as a toxicologist, is accepted without question in the courts of Germany, so her methodology is beyond question. Since 1992, further tests have been conducted on over 3000 preserved bodies, and a high number of these have proved positive for the presence of both nicotine and cocaine.[35] These results were considered so perverse that, of course, they had to be independently verified.

Professor Rosalie David of Manchester University in England was asked by a leading TV company in 1996 to conduct similar tests on mummies kept in her own department of Egyptology. The skeptical David found, to her surprise, that three of the mummies she examined tested positive for nicotine, but all her samples were negative for cocaine.[36] Since then, albeit grudgingly, scientists have been forced to consider seriously what, to them, was the least likely, but is now the only possible conclusion: trade had taken place between Egypt and the Americas. While it is possible that tobacco could, theoretically at least, have been cultivated in Africa after its importation from America, no such case can be made for cocaine. Therefore, the only reasonable explanation for this high level of usage must be sustained trade between Egypt and the American continent. Egyptian reed boats could, theoretically at least, have crossed the Atlantic, as Thor Heyerdahl showed in the mid-twentieth century when he sailed a reed boat named *Ra* from North Africa to Barbados.

Trans-Atlantic Voyages?

Roman shipping, which was of a far more sophisticated type than the Egyptian, would have had no trouble at all making this voyage. Roman ships considerably larger than Columbus's flagship, the *Santa Maria*, were common by the time of Jesus. Lionel Casson, an historian who specialized in ancient shipping, has stated that the Romans had cargo carriers of about 340 tons burden and grain ships of 1200 tons. The cargo ships were constructed of pine, fir, or cedar, and their hulls were often clad with sheets of lead below the waterline, with a layer of tarred fabric sandwiched between the lead and the wooden hull. The sails were made of linen and the cordage of flax, hemp, twisted papyrus, or, sometimes, leather.[37]

Several Roman shipwrecks have been located off the coast of the United States, Honduras, and Brazil. Clearly identifiable artifacts have been recovered from many of them, mainly *amphorae,* or ceramic wine casks. As early as 1971, two amphorae were found in Casting Bay, Maine, by a scuba diver at a depth of twelve meters. Colleagues at the Early Sites Research Society in Massachusetts identified them as being of Iberic/Roman manufacture of the first century C.E. Another was discovered near the shoreline of Jonesboro, Maine.[38] In 1972, large quantities of amphorae were discovered at the bottom of the Caribbean Sea off the coast of Honduras. Scholars who examined them identified them as originating in North African ports and applied for a permit to do a proper excavation of the wreck. Honduran government officials denied this responsible and legitimate request because "they feared further investigation might compromise the glory of Columbus."[39]

North African amphorae seem to abound in the Americas. In 1976, a Brazilian diver, Roberto Teixeria, found several on the seabed near Rio de Janeiro. Following his discovery, more were recovered. As a result, the shipwreck was inspected by archaeologist Robert Marx. He passed some of the amphorae on to Professor Elizabeth Will of the Department of Classical Greek History at the University of Massachusetts, who identified them as Moroccan. She was able to narrow their point of manufacture down to the Mediterranean port of Zillis and dated them to the third century C.E. Marx recovered several thousand pottery fragments from the wreck before (surprise, surprise) he was denied a permit for further excavation.[40] This time, it is not "pro-Columbian" bias we have to thank; the Brazilian authorities were concerned that any further evidence of ancient Roman voyages would diminish the fame of the "official discoverer of Brazil," Pedro Alveres Cabral.[41]

Artifacts of Roman origin in North America are not restricted to shipwrecks. In 1943, James Howe bought a farm on the banks of the Roanoke River near Jeffress, Virginia. His first find was bog iron followed by slag, and he concluded that he had found the site of an old colonial forge. He could find no records, however, of iron being worked anywhere near his property. Intrigued, he continued his search and found 400 pounds of iron and a natural draft furnace that had been used by these unidentified ironworkers. He began to excavate carefully and found various quantities of iron down to a depth of 80 cm. Then he discovered a superb bronze cup in relatively good condition, two fragments of bronze, and a bronze spindle. The finding of bronze amid the debris of an ancient ironworks indicates that the bronze artifacts had been imported from abroad and not made on the spot, for no trace of either copper or tin, the constituent metals of bronze, were found anywhere near the sites.[42] The bronze cup is fascinating; six cups of a similar type and metallurgy were found in the ruins of Pompeii and are indisputably dated as being over 2000 years old. A nearly identical cup in the Smithsonian Museum in the United States carries no date, merely a question mark. Similar bias is easy to find. A nail head found at a Roman site at Saalfeld Fort in Germany is dated at 200 C.E.; it was found in Europe. A virtually identical nail head exhibited in the Smithsonian carries no date, merely a question mark; not surprisingly it, too, was found in America.[43]

One sixteenth-century commentator, Marinaeus Siculus, recounts in his *Chronicle of Spaine* that a certain quantity of Roman gold coins were discovered in a gold mine in America: "certaine pieces of money engraved with the image of Augustus Caesar: which pieces were sent to the Pope for a testomonie of the matter, by John Rufus, Archbishop of Consentium."[44] Presumably, they still languish somewhere in the Vatican. One indisputably Roman artifact, a terracotta head found by a reputable archaeologist during a properly supervised and recorded dig in Mexico is dated to the second century C.E. The archaeologist, Jose Garcia Payon of Mexico's National Museum, made the discovery in 1933. It was found beneath a cement floor that dates to the eleventh century C.E. and, therefore, cannot be attributed to colonial importation.[45] Because of the circumstances of the find, which occurred in the course of a museum-sponsored excavation, there can be no argument whatsoever about its authenticity. Yet this proof of Roman contact with Central America has been greeted with deafening silence by the academic establishment in the United States.

The Celtic Voyages—Myth or Reality?

Just as Thor Heyerdahl's epic voyage in the *Ra* proved that Egyptian visits to America were feasible with even the most primitive forms of shipping, Tim Severin's re-creation in 1976 of the voyage of St. Brendan indicated the plausibility of many early Celtic myths. Irish legends tell of many voyages of return to a magical land far to the west. The story recounting the Voyage of Bran tells of an Atlantic crossing to a place over ten times the size of Ireland. One Celtic clan, the Formorians, are believed to have sought refuge there after their defeat in battle. Several Irish heroes are said to have sailed west to an idyllic land called Mag Mel, or *Tir na n'og*.[46]

Moreover, the legends of trans-Atlantic Celtic travel are not restricted to the Land of Saints and Scholars. The folk traditions of the Native American people tend to confirm the blarneying stories of the native Irish. One Abanaki researcher, Bernard Assiwini, spoke to a native elder who told the following story:

> Our chiefs speak of strangers who came to us by boat from the sea about two thousand years ago. They established their colonies on our territories trying to take us by force. But after they had destroyed their vessels, our Algonquin fathers convinced them to live with us. They called themselves "Kelts."[47]

Perhaps the most famous Celt reputed to have traveled to the New World is St. Brendan, the Abbot of Clonfert. Three versions of this legend were recorded: Two were from the eighth century, the *Vita Brendani* (*The Life of Brendan*) and the *Navigato Sancti Brendani* (*The Voyage of St. Brendan*). A third is found in the twelfth-century work known as *The Book of Lismore*. St. Brendan reputedly crossed the Atlantic in 565 C.E. and spent seven years in North America before returning to Ireland. The eighth-century versions of his voyage describe his boat as a *curragh*, a wooden-framed skin boat; but the twelfth-century *Book of Lismore* claims that the crossing was made in a large wooden ship manned by sixty monks.[48] No archaeological evidence exists that indicates the truth of this legend, with the possible exception of a stone beehive hut at Upton, Massachusetts. This intriguing structure stands on land that was owned at one time by our colleague Malcolm Pearson and is generally similar to early Celtic monks' cells found on the Blasket Isles off the coast of Kerry, southwest Ireland.[49]

The romantic Irish were not alone in creating poetic folklore claiming contact with the Americas. The Welsh claim that prince Madoc ab Owain Gwynedd was the true discoverer of America.[50] Madoc is reputed to have sent three expeditions across the ocean: "the first to reconnoitre the ocean passage, the second to scout for suitable land and the third comprising a fleet of ten ships carrying settlers, cattle and farm animals." The legend of Madoc's historic voyages was recorded by Caradoc of Llancarfan in *Historia Cambria,* which was edited and translated into English in 1584 in order to substantiate England's claim to settle North America. Another account can be found in *De Originibus Americanus* (Book IV), published in the Hague in 1652. This work claims:

> Madoc, a prince of Cambria, with some of his nation, discovered and inhabited some lands in the west, and that his name and memory are still retained among the people living there scarcely any doubt remains.[51]

Although St. Brendan's and Madoc's expeditions can both still only be classified as legendary, it must be noted that the Spanish reported ancient stone forts in Florida and attribute their origin to ancient Welsh settlers.[52] Native tradition tells of meetings with whites sailing up the rivers, and the chief of the Shawnee, Black Hoof, claimed in 1851 that there was an ancient story that spoke of a white race that lived in Florida long before the Spanish arrived. Numerous unsubstantiated reports of Welsh-speaking Native Americans occur in the early years of colonial settlement. One tribe, the Mandans of North Dakota, was described as "white men in red men's dress who understand Welsh."[53] The Mandans, however, cannot be consulted on this matter as, due to the colonial gift of smallpox, the tribe is now extinct. These legends provoked John Evans of London, to explore the Americas in 1792 to find firm evidence for the Welsh-speaking natives. Sadly, he came too late. His supporters declared "that all the frontier reports were either part of a conspiracy to defraud Columbus of his rightful glory, or they were the consequence of an enduring mass hysteria."

American antiquarian Arlington Mallery claimed that many of the sites he investigated in the eastern United States during the 1940s were iron-smelting furnaces of Celtic origin. In 1986, Joseph Gardner and his team found what they believed to be archaeological support for the Welsh legends near Chattanooga (Old Stone Fort), Tennessee; Desoto Falls, Alabama; and Fort Mountain, Georgia. In Gardner's view, these three ruined forts were not of Native American construction; they apparently dated from the twelfth century. The Tennessee site in particular bore a close resemblance to medieval ruins found in Wales.

Clear and undeniable evidence of Celtic habitation far from Ireland or Wales has been found, however, not in mainland America, but in Greenland, where archaeological excavation has found that Celtic foundations were reused by later settlers for their own dwellings. These later builders came from a race noted for their seafaring skill, who undoubtedly did reach mainland America—the Vikings.

Chapter 6

THE VIKINGS CHART
THE COURSE

BIAS AMONG HISTORIANS IS NOT RESTRICTED TO Americans of the twentieth century; they are simply following the somewhat dubious example set by their medieval European counterparts. The history of the Dark Ages of the eighth to tenth centuries was first recorded in written form by the only literate class in Europe—the clergy. The priests and scribes recorded the oral history, myths, and legends of the people they converted, giving a Christian gloss to pagan legend, adding this, omitting that, in order to create stories that reinforced the superiority of Christian dogma and belief. These devoted "historians," working in the *scriptoria* of monasteries and cathedrals, rich and cloistered oases of peace in semi-barbaric Europe, became prime targets for the wild raiders from the North who became known as the Vikings. Understandably, the Vikings got a very raw deal from the Christian clergy, who described them as fearsome pagan raiders intent on despoiling the churches and Christian communities that surrounded them. It was many centuries before this partially accurate, and somewhat circumscribed, vision of the Norsemen was expanded to create a more realistic picture.

Viking Culture

Fearsome raiders the Vikings undoubtedly were, and their incursions into the Outer Hebrides, the Scottish and English coasts, Ireland, and European coastal towns are the valid basis of the records written by a terrified clergy. In fairness, however, it must be stated that the Vikings were certainly no less cruel than their Christian foes; in fact, the only difference between them was that the Christians did not attack Church property as a rule, while the Vikings made it a prime target. This vio-lence, nonetheless, was only one aspect of a complex multifaceted emerging society that, through its seafaring skills, was able to reach right across the known world and become one of its most transforma-tive elements.

Above all, the Vikings were masters of the sea. This gave their cul-ture an exceedingly long reach, for, not only were they raiders, they were also explorers and traders of considerable acumen. Between the eighth and tenth centuries, their explorations became the foundation of a network of trading links that brought back to their homeland the products and ideas of the entire Mediterranean coast, from Byzantium[1] to the Pillars of Hercules, now known as the Straits of Gibraltar.[2] One Viking tribe known as the "Rus" founded Moscow, and Viking ships traveled the entire length of the rivers spanning what is now greater Russia, reaching both the Caspian and the Black Seas.[3] Due to popula-tion pressures in their homelands, the Vikings also became settlers and colonizers in Orkney, Caithness, York, the east and southern coasts of Ireland, northern France, Sicily, and, ultimately, the islands of the North Atlantic, including Iceland and Greenland.[4]

Far from being simple brutal heathens, the Vikings had a rich, sophisticated, and complex culture imbued with ideals that we would now describe as democratic. The rule of the Viking Kings of Norway was moderated by a parliament of leading nobles.[5] Under this regime, Scandinavia became, in many respects, the cultural crossroads of the world, where ideas from its far-flung trading network were imported, resynthesized, and, in many cases, re-exported to areas of Viking set-tlement. When most of Europe was still building in wood or wattle and daub, the Vikings built in stone. One particular Viking skill that remained unequaled elsewhere for centuries to come was bridge build-ing. Their craftsmen created jewelry with a sophistication and beauty that is still a source of wonder to archaeologists and historians. A vivid example can be seen in the hoard discovered in Ireland in January 2000. But above all else, the Vikings are remembered as shipbuilders *par excellence*.[6]

The Viking Longships

The longship was, in many respects, the supreme achievement of Viking culture, for it provided the means by which raids, trade, and exploration could take place. Thus it was not simply a mode of transport, but a source of power and, in the case of chieftains and nobles of note, the final resting place on the road to Valhalla. It is this practice that has provided the means by which modern historians and archaeologists have gained such intimate and detailed knowledge of Viking shipbuilding techniques.

Three huge man-made mounds once adorned the edge of Oslo fjord—one on the eastern shore at Tune and two on the west, at Gokstad and Oseberg.[7] Each was erected over a ship. All three vessels, excavated in the latter half of the nineteenth century and the early years of the twentieth, are now on view at the ship museum on the Island of Bygdoy, a short boat ride from Oslo city. The first to be excavated was the Tune find in 1867;[8] the second, at Gokstad,[9] which is the largest and is believed to date from about 900 C.E., was excavated in 1880. The third and final excavation occurred at Oseberg in 1904.[10] A further five Viking ships were discovered, almost perfectly preserved, underwater at Skuldelev in Roskilde Fiord in Denmark in 1962.[11] Another discovery made in 1970 is now on display at the Vestfold County Museum in Tunsberg.[12] Thus, in the space of a little over 100 years, artifacts have been discovered that give a superb basis upon which we can assess Viking shipbuilding skills with great accuracy and that enable us to comment on their seamanship with considerable precision.

The most superb example among these finds is the one at Gokstad. This ship was built to be both sailed and rowed. The ship is of clinker construction, consisting of sixteen rows of planks, each plank overlapping the one beneath and caulked with threads of tarred wool.[13] The planking is lashed to the ribs with withies held in cleats, not nailed. Furthermore, the ribs are not fastened to the keel, a method of building that endows the hull with considerably more flexibility than modern shipbuilding techniques. There are sixteen oar-holes in the fourteenth row of planking on each side of the vessel, each furnished with wooden shutters that could be closed when the vessel was under sail. Therefore, there is a two-plank gunnel above the oar-holes, giving the boat greater freeboard under sail.

Figure 1. Replica of a Viking longship.

The keel is 20.10 meters in length and is cut from a single piece of wood in such a manner as to derive the greatest possible strength with the least possible weight.[14] The height from the keel to the top of the gunnel, amidships, is 2.02 meters. The overall dimensions of the ship are 23.30 meters from stem to stern; the maximum beam is 5.20 meters, and the weight of the hull, fully equipped, is estimated at 20.2 metric tons. A specially constructed timber burial chamber lay across the stern, in which was found the skeletal remains of a finely dressed Viking chieftain.[15] Sadly, due to the attentions of grave robbers, his weapons are missing. Grave robbers apparently concentrated their efforts on weapons and valuable artifacts with male burials, and with jewelry from the graves of females. Despite the depredations of the robbers, however, what remains is rather interesting: fine textiles embroidered with gold, the remains of a peacock, and an abundance of kitchenware.

Thor Heyerdahl and Tim Severin were not the first modern adventurers to demonstrate the feasibility of Atlantic crossings in ships of ancient design. In 1893, a replica of the Gokstad ship under the command of Captain Magnus Andersen crossed the Atlantic in time for the Chicago World's Fair.[16] The captain remarked that the ship's performance was remarkable and that her rudder was a work of genius. On

15 May 1893, she out-sailed the steamships of that time by covering 223 nautical miles in twenty-four hours, an hourly average of 9.3 knots. The same year, a replica of Columbus's flagship, the *Santa Maria*, also crossed the Atlantic, but averaged only 6.5 knots.[17] Thus it can be clearly seen that, in design quality, build, and performance, the tenth-century Viking ships were far superior to the fifteenth-century vessels used by Columbus. Of all the Viking ships that have been excavated so far, the Gokstad ship is the closest in design to the Viking longships that sailed to Iceland, Greenland, and on to Vinland, as recounted in the Viking sagas.

The Viking Sagas

Viking culture, for all its sophistication, produced no early written literature. Their history was passed down orally in stories or sagas describing particular events or linked episodes. These sagas, including, among others, the *Islendingabok*,[18] the *Flateyabok*,[19] the *Hauksbok*[20] and the *Orkneyinga Saga*,[21] did not achieve written form until between the twelfth and fourteenth century.

At first regarded by historians as mere myth or folklore, over the course of the last two centuries these sagas have come to be accepted by academics. Although told in narrative form, they are rich in historical material,[22] which has served as a form of literary signpost pointing to irrefutable evidence of Viking occupation in Iceland, Greenland, and, most dramatically of all, Newfoundland. The authenticity of the sagas as historical documents is now accepted, and the only point upon which historians seem to differ to any significant degree is the exact dating of the events described, and even here there is a strong consensus that limits the variation to not more than two years. For our purposes, we will use the average dates among those quoted by reputable authorities.

The earliest saga to take written form was the *Islendingabok*, recorded by the Icelandic priest and historian Are Frodi, also known as Ari the Learned.[23] His account, written down between 1122 and 1132, provides some useful gems of information about the Viking exploration and settlement of the islands and coasts of the great northern ocean. Vinland is mentioned four times. He also records that the Viking settlers in Greenland found the remains of habitations and stone implements left by earlier settlers, and that these were similar to the ruins discovered in Vinland. Naturally enough, Ari came to the conclusion that the tools belonged to *skraelings*, or natives.[24] The historian Ian Wilson suggested in 1991 that the pre-Norse Vinland ruins mentioned in the *Islendingabok* may well have belonged to Celts who once inhabited Greenland.[25] If the ruins were as similar as Ari suggests, this could well be true, for fairly recent excavations in Greenland have shown conclusively that many Viking buildings there were constructed on the foundations of earlier Celtic structures. According to Hjalmar J. Holand, the earliest mention of Vinland is found, not in the Icelandic sagas, but in a runic inscription on a stone unearthed in Norway.[26]

A degree of confusion can easily arise when studying the Vinland stories, as there are two different sources for the history of the Vinland exploration, each seemingly authoritative. One, written in Old Icelandic in the latter part of the fourteenth century, was given to the King of Denmark in 1647 by a Mr. Hakonarson. He lived on Flatey, an island in one of the fjords of Iceland, from whence comes the name by which the saga is commonly known, the *Flateyabok*.[27] The other principal source lies in the Arnamagnean Library in Copenhagen. This is the so-called *Hauksbok* written by Hauk Erlendsson, who died in 1334. Erlendsson was a descendant of Thorfinn Karlsefni, and the *Hauksbok* contains "Karlsefni's saga."[28] Many scholars believe that, although the *Hauksbok* is the earlier of the two, the *Flateyabok* comes from far more direct Greenland sources—it is often referred to as the *Greenland Saga*.[29]

The derivation and nature of the two books is very different. The *Hauksbok* contains a rather flattering account of the deeds of Thorfinn Karlsefni and, in common with medieval practice, is richly embroidered with episodes that are, in all probability, lifted from other sources. The *Flateyabok*, which most authorities believe is the more historically accurate of the two, has a spare and direct narrative form and contains within it far more accurate sailing directions, as might be expected from a seafaring people.[30]

Exploration in the North Atlantic

The seafaring race of the Vikings was ceaselessly driven by the twofold motivation of scarcity of land and a strong sense of adventure and greed to seek new lands to plunder, or better yet, settle. Iceland was discovered by accident by Gardar Svarvasson in 861, when he was blown off course in a gale during a voyage from Norway to the Hebrides.[31] The first Viking settlers arrived nine or ten years later. At that time, the island had already been settled by Celtic monks from Ireland, who had been there for centuries. They were less than enamored of the new settlers and returned whence they came, leaving behind them, according to the *Landnamabok*, "bells, books and croziers."[32]

Iceland was the birthplace of the explorer Eric the Red who, even today, is a household name. In 982, Eric set sail to the west and made his first landfall on Greenland at a place he called Mid Glacier, an ice-covered mountain that was later called Blacksark. He then sailed south along the east coast, constantly on the lookout for pastureland that would be suitable for settlement. In true Viking tradition, he sought such land in the coastal areas near the rocky fjords, where it would be irrigated by the meltwaters of the rocky icecap. He rounded the southern tip of Greenland to the southwest coast, where he made winter camp on a large island, to which he gave the name Ericsey, in the Briedifjord.[33] After the spring melt, he was able to sail in through the fjord, now called Tunugdliarfik. Finding suitable land at the inner end of it, he chose this place for his permanent farmstead.

Eric the Red is often wrongly credited with the discovery of Greenland, but, as we mentioned earlier, we now know the Celts were there before him. According to the saga, he found fragments of boats and stone tools left by people who had previously inhabited the Greenland fjords. During the following summer, he explored the western region, naming every island, fjord, and headland as he went. It is claimed that, in the hope of encouraging settlement, he called this glacier-ridden land by the misleading yet attractive name of Greenland.[34] This assertion is highly questionable, for the modern historian Kare Prytz records that Pope Gregor IV wrote to Ansgar, the papal legate of Scandinavia, as early as 831 instructing that Greenland be administered by the Archbishop of Hamburg.[35]

By the summer of 986, Eric had gained all the support he needed for his new settlement, and over a thousand people crammed into thirty-five ships and set sail with him. Many of the ships were scattered by adverse winds or lost at sea; only fourteen reached their final destination, and the number of settlers who landed is estimated as little more than 400.[36] Less than a year later, a young man called Bjarni

Herjulfsson set sail from Iceland to join his father in the newly settled Greenland. Swept off course by a North Atlantic gale, his ship was carried far to the south, to within sight of an unknown land. This new country was described as being heavily wooded, with low hillocks and no mountains. Keeping to his original intention of joining his father, Bjarni turned northeast. His ship skirted the shores of two other unknown lands and sailed on to the southwestern corner of Greenland. When he finally arrived, he described his adventures in such precise detail that those who wished to could easily find the lands he had seen.[37]

Frederic Pohl, a twentieth-century historian who made a prolonged study of pre-Columbian voyages to America, plotted Bjarni's course back to Greenland. Comparing Bjarni's account of his first sight of the new land with topography of America's east coast, he suggests that Bjarni's first landfall was at Cape Cod, where the coast fits the Viking's description.[38] According to the saga, Bjarni then sailed for two days in a northeasterly direction, out of sight of land, and came to a flat country covered in timber, which both Pohl and Holand suggest, quite logically, is southern Nova Scotia.[39] Following the coast (and the logic of this argument), the third sighting of land was the mountainous island of Newfoundland, whose features again match those of the saga.

Even though the temperature in Greenland 1000 years ago was appreciably warmer than at present, the country was still remarkably bleak and inhospitable. Yet Eric's newfound colony thrived for several hundred years,[40] eventually sustaining sixteen parish churches, a cathedral, a monastery, and a nunnery. Thirteen years after the colony's foundation, Eric sent his son, Leif, to Norway. During the voyage, Leif's ship was driven off course and landed in the Hebrides, thereby setting a record for the longest voyage by a Norseman across open ocean in that era—over 1600 miles. When Leif arrived in Norway in the summer of 999, he converted to Christianity under the direct orders of King Olaf Tryggvason. The king's evangelical methods were somewhat brutal and direct; his subjects were given the option of Christianity or a vat of boiling oil.[41] Leif wintered at Indoors, now called Trondheim, and then, acting under royal command and protection, was sent home on an evangelical mission to Brattahlid in Greenland. As a result of his ministry in his homeland, the people, with one notable exception—his father—converted to Christianity.[42]

Leif Erikson's Vinland Voyage

Leif, imbued with the Viking sense of adventure and curiosity, asked Bjarni for sailing directions to the new lands he had discovered. He set sail with a crew of thirty-five men and made his first landfall at the last mountainous island that Bjarni had seen. They explored the island and found that, inland, were great ice-covered mountains. According to the saga, from the sea to the mountains was like one great flat rock, almost totally devoid of good qualities. Leif called it Helluland—the Land of the Flat Rock.[43] There is one point on the Newfoundland coast that matches this description with uncanny accuracy. If Leif had landed at what is now called Flat Rock Cove near St. John's, it would have provided an ideal harbor for his ship, and the nearby land of Flat Rock Point mirrors the description given.

The saga then recounts that Leif and his men returned to their ship and once more put to sea. They sailed until they found the second of the new lands. Unlike Bjarni, however, they landed there. This was a wooded land fringed with white sand. Where they made landfall, the shore sloped gently toward the sea. Leif named this country Markland—the Land of Forests.[44] Leif and his men left Markland in some haste, as they had detected an unusual wind blowing in just the right direction. After sailing for two days to the southwest, in which time a Viking ship of that era would have covered 300 miles, Leif made landfall once again. This would have placed him in the region of southern New England.[45]

This place seemed almost ideal. The rivers abounded with salmon, and it appeared that cattle would have no problem with winter feed, for there was no frost and the grass did not wither much.[46] The area was also well wooded. The hours of day and night were more equally divided than in Greenland, so the Viking party set to and built houses for the winter. When their shelters were finished, Leif divided his party in two; one group guarded the houses and the other explored the countryside, changing roles from time to time. The saga[47] recounts that, one evening, one of their number, Tyrk the German, went missing. The search party found him in high spirits, for Tyrk had found grapevines and grapes.[48] Leif, therefore, named the land Vinland, the discovery of which was made, according to Hjalmar R. Holand, in 1003.[49] After wintering in Vinland, Leif and his party returned home with a boatload of produce from this new land.

Thorwald's Voyage

On Leif's return to Greenland, his brother, Thorwald, inspired by the tales of the new land, determined to set sail for Vinland to continue its exploration. Thorwald's departure would have been in the year of Leif's return, 1004, or at most one year later.[50] On his arrival at what had been Leif's settlement, he divided his party in two and, with one group, took the shore boat and explored the coast to the west of the settlement[51]—probably the area of the present-day Block Island Sound and Long Island Sound. The following summer, Thorwald sailed eastward with some of his men, passing present-day Nantucket Sound, and then northward, where they encountered a gale near a headland and were blown ashore. This headland was most probably Cape Cod.[52] When the boat was beached, the keel was badly damaged and took some time to replace. When this task was completed, they sailed on in a northerly direction, which kept the coast to the west, and explored for the first time the coastal areas between Vinland and Markland. They reached a headland with deep water, moored their vessel alongside the shore, and put out a gangplank. The countryside was so beautiful that Thorwald decided that it was here that he would build his home.[53]

As they made their way back to their boat, they discovered three upturned canoes on the beach in the shelter of the headland; under each were three sleeping Indians whom they took prisoner. One escaped and the saga records that "they killed the eight."[54] The circumstances surrounding this slaughter are not mentioned, but, as events proved, it was an extremely imprudent act. Later, when the Vikings returned to their boat, they were attacked by Indians in a fleet of canoes and showered with arrows. They responded by putting their shields along the gunwales of the boat in traditional battle array, and after a short time, the attackers withdrew. There was, however, one casualty among the Norsemen—Thorwald himself, who had an arrow in his side. In the certain knowledge that he was facing death, he instructed his men to bury him at the site he had chosen for his new home.[55] This they did, and then returned to Vinland, where they remained throughout the following winter, spending their time cutting timber to take back to Greenland.

Thorfinn Karlsefni's Exploration

Thorfinn Karlsefni, who was of royal descent and a man of considerable substance, arrived in Greenland in 1008 or 1009 accompanied by Snorri Thorbrandson, an old friend of Eric the Red, and a crew of forty men. Shortly afterward, another Viking ship of approximately the same size arrived under the command of Bjarne Grimolfson and Thorhall Gamalson. Leif Erikson invited the leaders of both ships, with their crews, to be his guests for the winter.[56] It was during this time that Thorfinn married Gudrid, a widow who was a ward of Leif Erikson.[57] During the long winter nights, Thorfinn was brought up to date on the explorations in Vinland, and he determined to sail there and see this wondrous land for himself. The expedition set sail in 1009 or 1010, and there is some dispute between the *Hauksbok* and the *Flateyabok* about the number of people who actually took part. The *Hauksbok* claims 160 men and women; the *Flateyabok* claims only sixty men and five women. What is not in dispute, however, is that the party included residents of Greenland and that, as the intention of the expedition was settlement, they took cattle with them.

There is a startling contradiction between the accounts in the *Hauksbok* and the *Flateyabok* as to the route taken by this expedition. The most credible version is found in the *Flateyabok*, which states that, after discussions with Leif Ericsson, Thorfinn and his party arranged to borrow his houses in Vinland and sailed there directly by what had become the traditional route. Then follows a description of a two-year stay in Vinland during which trade was established with the *skraelings*, or natives. Ultimately, however, the Viking party was subjected to a concerted attack by the natives. As a result, Thorfinn resolved to return to Greenland.[58] The saga tells that the birth of Thorfinn's son, Snorri, took place during their stay, which makes him the first person of European extraction recorded as being born in the New World.

In the *Hauksbok*, the voyage is described more as an exploration, with Karlsefni being wrongly credited with both discovering and naming many of the places en route. A description of a prolonged stay at a place called Straumsfjord is given; all attempts to identify its location have only created difficulty and confusion. It is a classical case of the truth of the old Latin tag *quot homines, tot sententiae*—there are as many opinions as there are people. Depending upon which author you read, Straumsfjord has been supposedly located on Cape Breton Island, 600 miles further west on the shores of the St. Lawrence River, Sandwich Bay in Labrador, the Bay of Fundy, west of Nova Scotia, Long Island Sound, or Chaleur Bay to the north of New Brunswick. This entire episode in the *Hauksbok* smacks strongly of the medieval churchman's habit of hagiography—the use of material from very different sources to embellish or enhance the reputation of the principal subject, in this instance, Thorfinn Karlsefni. We have no doubt that the description of the Straumsfjord episode is based on fact—either the records of an earlier, or perhaps even a later, voyage by quite a different expedition—for the descriptions of Straumsfjord have the ring of truth. The saga records that "there were mountains there and the view was beautiful." Working from logic, the accounts of other voyages, and gut instinct, we suggest that the true site of Straumsfjord may well have been L'Anse aux Meadows in Newfoundland.

The *Hauksbok* account states that the long winter was severe and the food supply so bad that, if it had not been for the discovery of a stranded whale, they might well have starved. Snorri's birth, in this version, is recorded as occurring shortly after their arrival at Straumsfjord. With the coming of spring, matters improved and the expedition searched in vain for grapes. Harsh though the winter had been, they spent a year on this site before some of the party left in disgust. It was then that Thorfinn and the others sailed southward for "a long time" in search of Vinland.[59] We find this account incredible for, as Karlsefni had spent a winter in the company of Leif Ericsson, it is impossible to believe that he would not have been given precise sailing directions that replicated the instructions given to Ericsson himself by Bjarni Herjulfsson. However, the *Hauksbok's* account of events in Vinland does mirror, in some respects, the version given in the more authoritative *Flateyabok*.

There have been many investigations over the years to establish the exact location of Vinland and Markland, resulting in a consensus that identifies Markland as Nova Scotia and Vinland as somewhere in New England. The area identified with Leif's original settlement has been variously claimed as near the Gulf of Maine in the vicinity of Boston, but more credibly as Narragansett Bay and the area surrounding present-day Newport, Rhode Island.[60] Modern archaeology and the records of Viking trade tend to confirm this, for the Norwegian archaeologist Helge Ingstad reports that anthracite coal that originated in Rhode Island was found in Viking settlements in Greenland.[61] From the time that Leif Ericsson brought his first cargo of timber and grapes back to Greenland, the Viking lands in the New World were used as a rich source of raw materials, with Markland being a primary source of timber for the Greenlanders. The manifests of cargoes landed at Bergen in Norway tell us that Greenland shipping brought to the home country a variety of furs of great value,[62] including the skins of marmot, otter, beaver, wolverine, lynx, sable, and black bear, yet none of these animals were native to Greenland; all were from the New World.[63]

Ecclesiastical Records of Vinland

Church records also confirm the discoveries in the New World for, prior to 1070, the scholarly Adam of Bremen, who later became rector of the cathedral school in the town, spent several years studying the history of the Archbishopric of Hamburg. This diocese was vast, comprising northern Poland, the Baltic States, Russia, Finland, Prussia, the Scandinavian countries, and all the islands of the North Atlantic other than Britain and Ireland. He talked to King Sven of Denmark, who told him "of yet another island, discovered by many in that ocean, which is called Wineland because grapes grow wild there, producing the best of wine. Moreover that self-sown grain abounds there we have ascertained not from fabulous conjecture, but from the reliable report of the Danes."[64] According to some reports, King Olaf II of Norway is believed to have visited Vinland in 1016.[65] Ingstad mentions that the Icelandic annals for 1121 suggest that the Bishop of Greenland also set out in search of Vinland.[66] This bishop, Eric Gnupsson, was born in Iceland and appointed by King Sigurd in 1112. According to Father Ivar Bardsson in the fourteenth century, Bishop Eric never returned from his Vinland expedition.[67] Trade and contact continued between Norway, Greenland, and Vinland, and a settlement based upon Leif Ericsson's original home in the New World became known as Norumbega.[68] This area may have been the country annexed by King Haakon Haakonson in a treaty dated 1262.[69] The annexed territory included Iceland, Greenland, and a place called "Landa-nu," which was supposedly discovered by an Icelander called Rolf in 1258. Bishop Gissur Einarsson noted that the sailing directions to this land from Iceland were to the southwest, where one would land in Newfoundland or Nova Scotia. Despite the fact that this land had been settled before, the use of the word "new" may well have simply been a stratagem to claim ownership.

Thus documentary evidence attesting to the kingdom of Norway's claims to sovereignty over "new" lands to the west was plentiful by the mid-fourteenth century. In the final decade of that century, Queen Margrette of Norway charged her principal adviser, Henry St. Clair, the first St. Clair Earl of Orkney, with the task of exploring and exploiting these lands in a manner that would free the kingdom from the stranglehold on trade exerted by the Hanseatic League.

Chapter 7

NICOLO ZENO EXPLORES THE NORTH ATLANTIC

WHEN HENRY HAD ESTABLISHED HIS RULE in Shetland, according to the Zeno Narrative, he then built a fort in Bres, which most modern scholars assume to be Bressay. In the opinion of Niven Sinclair, the probable foundations of this castle are still visible on Learaness, which, in Henry's time, would have been the end of a long peninsula jutting into the sound of Bressay (Bressasund).[1] Since then, the sea has eroded the neck of the peninsula, and the tip is now an island to which it is still possible to wade at low tide. This would have been an excellent site for a fortress, as it gives a superb view of the approaches to Bressay Sound, which comprises the north and south harbors of the present-day town of Lerwick. There is, however, some dispute over the site of Henry's fort, which, according to Frederick Pohl, "was in all probability where a later fort was built in the 17th century, at the water's edge in Lerwick."[2] Sir Nicolo Zeno remained at Bres and, the following year, in 1393, equipped three small barks for a voyage of exploration. He sailed northward in July and landed in Egroneland, or Greenland.

> . . . Here he found a monastery of the Order of the Preaching Friars and a church dedicated to St. Thomas by a hill which vomited fire like Vesuvius and Etna. There is a spring of hot water there which is used to heat both the church of the monastery and the chambers of the Friars. The water comes up into the kitchen so boiling hot that they use no other fire to cook their food. The also put their bread into brass pots without any water, and it is baked as if it were in a hot oven.[3]

Later critics, wishing to discredit the Zeno Narrative, tried to use this passage to support their case that the Zeno voyages were a complete fabrication. In this attempt, all they demonstrated was their scant knowledge of the history of Viking settlements in Greenland. Was their criticism based upon the assumption that the only Viking settlements were those on the west coast, which had been deserted more than fifty years prior to the Zeno voyage? Or did they base their case on the mistaken belief that the southerly segment of the east coast was the only part of this barren land to have been inhabited? As they rightly pointed out, in that part of Greenland, there was no monastery or church that accorded with the description in the Narrative. What they missed, or willfully chose to ignore, however, was that there was a site some distance north of the main Eastern Settlement that mirrors precisely the description written in the 1390s by Nicolo Zeno.[4]

The existence of formerly active volcanoes and thermal springs on the east coast of Greenland was demonstrated by the twentieth-century archaeologists Alwin Pedersen, Helge Larsen, and Lauge Koch.[5] Nearby ruins in Gael Hamke Bay have been identified by Dr. William H. Hobbs, a geologist at the University of Michigan,[6] as St. Olaf's Monastery, which had been described centuries earlier by Ivar Bardsson, who claimed that the hot springs "were good for bathing and the cure of many diseases." In respect of Nicolo Zeno's description of the monastery, volcano, hot springs, the nature of the harbor, and a populous settlement of Eskimos, Dr. Hobbs claims "evidence for all these have been found there." The nineteenth-century historian Dr. Luka Jelic confirms this when he mentions an account written by papal emissaries in 1329, who reported to Pope John XXII that there were two monastic centers in Grotlandia (Greenland), one called Gardensi (Gardar)[7] and the other Pharensi, a name that is virtually diagnostic of St. Olaf's proximity to the volcano, for the glow of such a mountain would resemble that of a lighthouse, or pharos.

The Zeno Narrative also describes how the thermal springs at the monastery were used to irrigate herb gardens and heat the quarters of the monks.[8] Nearby, on the coast where the springs drained into the sea, was a harbor that never froze, despite the nine-month-long winter. Because of the warm temperature of the water, fish and seafowl were so abundant that they became the main source of provisions for the monks. Many vessels were detained in this harbor for the winter, for the sea beyond it froze and the sailors had to wait until the ice melted before they could leave.[9] As a result of the severe climate that he endured in Greenland, Sir Nicolo, not being used to such cold, became ill and returned to Fer Island, where he died. His brother, Sir Antonio, succeeded him as admiral of Henry's fleet and inherited all Nicolo's wealth and honors.[10] The account of Nicolo Zeno's survey of Greenland and his death soon after was confirmed by Marco Barbaro in *Discendenze Patrizie,* which was published in 1536, twenty-two years before the eventual publication of the Zeno Narrative itself.

The Fisherman's Tale

At this time, another voyage of exploration was being planned, the origins of which, according to the Zeno Narrative, were very strange indeed. A local Orkney fisherman told that some twenty-six years earlier, four fishing boats had put to sea and been driven westward by a heavy storm. When it subsided, they discovered an island, which they called Estotilanda, over 1000 miles from Iceland. One of the boats was wrecked, and the six crewmen were brought to a "fair and populous city," where the king found an interpreter, another shipwrecked mariner, who spoke Latin and requested that the men remain in his country.[11] The fisherman described this new land as "very rich and abundant in all things." He claimed that the inhabitants were "intelligent and as well-versed in the arts as we are and that they had obviously had dealings at some time with our people for in the king's library were Latin books which they did not now understand."[12] They traded with Greenland, exporting furs, sulphur, and pitch, and grew corn and made beer. According to the fisherman, these people did not have the compass, and for this reason, the fishermen were highly valued and sent on a voyage to the south to a country called Drogio. There they were captured by savages and, except for the fisherman, eaten. He was spared because he showed the savages how to fish with nets and, as a result, was held in such esteem that he was allowed to live there for thirteen years, moving from one group to another teaching them this art.[13]

He described this country as "a new world" peopled by savages who were uncultivated, had no kind of metal, lived by hunting, and carried lances made of wood sharpened at the point. They were very fierce and had deadly fights among themselves, and, while they had chieftains and laws, these differed from tribe to tribe. After many years, he made his way back to Drogio, and hearing that some boats had arrived, he was delighted to discover that they had come from Estotilanda. He arranged passage with them and eventually, after many adventures, returned home to Orkney, where he met Earl Henry St. Clair.[14] According to the Zeno Narrative, this fisherman's tale was the principal cause of Earl Henry's voyage to the New World.

The Dream of a New Commonwealth

No one will ever be certain whether the story of this voyage was the last in a series of events whose cumulative effect was to provoke Earl Henry St. Clair into making his momentous voyage of exploration and settlement to the New World, or whether the inclusion of this tale in the Zeno letters was simply a piece of clever camouflage to hide the long-planned nature of this heretical enterprise. To imply, as the Narrative does, that this was the first news of the New World across the Atlantic to reach the ears of the earl is to fly in the face of reality. From his contacts at the Scandinavian courts, Henry was already aware of the ill-fated Knutson Expedition, the voyages of Nicolas Lynne, and the long-standing trade between Greenland, Markland, and Vinland. He would, like any other child of Viking descent, have been fully conversant with the earlier voyages to these lands from his knowledge of the Viking sagas.

It is also reasonable to assume, although it cannot be proved, that Henry would have apprised Carlo Zeno of many of the details of the lands across the Atlantic, or that Carlo would have learned at least of the Knutson Expedition first hand when he was at the Norwegian court in 1364. The question then arises, would it have been safe for Nicolo or Antonio Zeno to have mentioned in plain speech in any letter susceptible of interception the fact that the true intention of the voyage was to found a settlement that lay beyond the reach of the long arm of the Inquisition and which, furthermore, had as one of its prime objectives to break the stranglehold of the Hanseatic League on Northern European trade?[15] Or did the fisherman's convoluted story simply tip the balance in favor of immediate action to implement a plan that had been maturing for nearly twenty years?

There is also a degree of uncertainty surrounding the details of events immediately prior to Earl Henry St. Clair's momentous expedition. The only clear indication we have about his intent and the number of people involved is that contained in the Zeno Narrative, which includes a letter written by Antonio Zeno that states:

> . . . this nobleman [Earl Henry] is now determined to send me out with a fleet towards these parts. There are so many that want to join on the expedition on account of the novelty and the strangeness of the thing, that I think we shall be very well equipped, without any public expense at all.[16]

The editor of the Narrative, a later Nicolo Zeno, linked the various letters with comments of his own and, after the quotation above, he said of this voyage by his ancestor Antonio, "he set sail with many vessels and men, but he was not the commander, as he had expected to be." He goes on to explain that the earl himself was in charge and that, three days before their scheduled departure, the fisherman, who was to be their guide, died. Despite that, however, the expedition went ahead.[17]

The Size of the Expedition

Previous authors who described the Earl Henry voyage have tended to overestimate the size of the fleet he took with him and been somewhat imaginative in their attempts to assess both the number and the nature of the people involved in the expedition. Apart from the comments that "a fleet" was involved and that many wanted to join the expedition, there is nothing in the early part of the Narrative on which we can base such assumptions. There are, however, one or two passages in the description of the latter part of the voyage that clarify matters slightly, and we will mention these in their proper context.

Some very fanciful claims have been made that Henry sailed with members of the Knights Templar[18] and Cistercian monks,[19] carried massive quantities of treasure with him,[20] and even, incredible though it may sound, took the Holy Grail across the Atlantic.[21] Not one shred of evidence exists to justify these bizarre speculations. The Knights Templar had been suppressed more than seventy-five years before and no longer existed. Henry was a member of a family with long-standing and intimate associations with the suppressed Order and was undoubtedly imbued with Templar philosophy, but short of raising the dead, how could he have been accompanied by Templar Knights? Furthermore, there was no need for vast quantities of treasure for trade, nor would there have been room to carry it even if Henry had taken every ship in his fleet. While it is possible that he may have been accompanied by a priest who acted as chaplain to the fleet, it is highly improbable that he would have taken with him a number of Cistercian monks on what was, after all, an armed reconnaissance in the first instance.

It is not clear from the Zeno Narrative how many ships were used. The implication, intentional or accidental, is that Henry used his entire fleet, although this is an extremely unlikely prospect. Henry's original fleet of two oared ships, one battleship, and ten barks[22] had been augmented by the Venetian galley brought by Antonio Zeno.[23] If Henry intended to be away from his islands long enough to make a return voyage across the Atlantic, he would have been obliged to leave his islands in a defensible position. Due to the numerous pirates and the depredations of the Hansa who blockaded Bergen and burned the Norwegian fleet in 1394, we estimate that the size of the home fleet needed to protect the islands and maintain communication between them would have been at least one galley, one battleship, and six or seven barks. This would have left Earl Henry with one Venetian galley and its 200 oarsmen, who could be armed rapidly if attacked, one of his own Orkney galleys, whose crew would be similarly prepared, and three or four barks for scouting purposes. An expedition of this size would have been more than adequate to make the voyage to Vinland, and would most certainly have been capable of withstanding any attack by pirates while en route. While it is impossible to prove that this was the full extent of his fleet for the voyage, it is, we believe, a reasonable estimate in the light of our knowledge of his total resources in shipping and the demands of the defense of his realm while he was away.

Following in his Ancestors Footsteps

It would have been very strange if Henry St. Clair, with all his knowledge of the previous Viking voyages to the Americas, had chosen to follow a route substantially different from those who had blazed the trail before him. Starting from his base in Orkney and Shetland, he sailed westward on a voyage that, like those of Leif Erikson and

Thorfinn Karlsefni, used Iceland, Greenland, and Newfoundland as stepping-stones to his first continental landfall in the Americas. The Zeno Narrative recounts:

> . . . Then at last we discovered land. As the sea ran high and we did not know what country it was, we were afraid at first to approach it. But by God's blessing, the wind lulled, and then a great calm came on. Some of the crew then pulled ashore and soon returned with the joyful news that they had found an excellent country and a still better harbour. So we brought our barks and our boats in to land, and we entered an excellent harbour, and we saw in the distance a great mountain that poured out smoke.[24]

It continues by stating that an exploration-in-force of 100 armed men was dispatched to the smoking mountain, with strict instructions to bring back an account of any inhabitants they met. Those who remained with the ships took in a store of wood and water and caught a considerable quantity of fish and seafowl, which were found in large quantities.[25]

> While we were at anchor here, the month of June came in, and the air in the island was mild and pleasant beyond description. Yet as we saw nobody, we began to suspect that this pleasant place was uninhabited. We gave the name of Trin to the harbour and the headland which stretched out onto the sea we called Capo di Trin.[26]

The prolific historian of North Atlantic voyages, Frederick Pohl, used this passage to try and establish the date of Henry's landfall.[27] He assumed, not unreasonably in light of voyages by other explorers, that Henry and Antonio named both the harbor and the headland "Trin" because they made landfall on Trinity Sunday.[28] The habit of naming landfalls according to the religious calendar was certainly not unique to Henry St. Clair and Antonio Zeno. However, Pohl made a fundamental error of calculation that places it two years later than it actually happened. He quoted the date of Trinity Sunday, which is a moveable feast, as 6 June 1395, 28 May 1396, 17 June 1397, and 2 June 1398,[29] and then opted for the latter as the most probable. A careful reading of the Zeno Narrative, however, discloses that they had arrived at this harbor before the beginning of June—"While we were at anchor here the month of June came in[30]—indicating that the expedition was comfortably at anchor before the end of May. The choice of Trinity Sunday as a commemoration of their time of landfall would have been in celebration of their first sighting of land or their day of anchorage, and in light of the phrase quoted above, they were already at anchor when June came in. If Pohl's reasoning connecting Trin with Trinity Sunday is correct, then the only date that accords with this and yet allows sufficient time thereafter for Henry's exploits to take place prior to the earliest date suggested for his death is 28 May 1396.

Having established a more credible date for the voyage, can the description in the Narrative be matched to actual geographical and geological features on the ground in any part of the northeastern coast of North America? If this can be done, is there any evidence or plausible reasoning that can tie that site to previous Viking exploration? The knowledge that the area was well-wooded, teeming with fish and seafowl, and had a safe harbor is, taken in isolation, virtually useless as this description could be applied to sites on the northeastern coast far too numerous to count. The key is the smoking mountain and the discoveries made by the force sent to investigate it:

> . . . After eight days the hundred soldiers returned and told us
> that they had been through the island and up to the mountain.
> The smoke naturally came from a great fire in the bottom of
> the hill, and there was a spring giving out a certain matter like
> pitch which ran into the sea, and there were great multitudes
> of people, half-wild and living in caves. These were very small
> of stature and very timid; for as soon as they saw our people,
> they fled into their holes. Our men also reported that there was
> a large river nearby and a very good and safe harbour.[31]

The Narrative describes the landfall and the exploration to the smoking mountain as being on an island. We can use this information to rule out one early suggestion that it was Greenland, because that island is treeless[32] and the settlers there had to trade with Markland for wood. Therefore, it is reasonable to assume that the landfall was in Markland itself. And in light of the information brought back by the expedition to the smoking mountain, the land was surrounded by water on several sides, and so was either an island or a peninsula.

In Search of the Smoking Mountain

The armed expedition crossed well-forested land and spent eight days away from their shore base. They would not have spent that time on the return journey from the coast to the smoking mountain; part of it would have been spent investigating the fire and the river of pitch that ran into the sea. No sailor would have noted a safe harbor without giving it a detailed examination. So, allowing for the time spent at the harbor, tracing the river of pitch, and examining the naturally occurring fire, a maximum of three days' travel either way can be conjectured. The site of the smoking mountain must, therefore, be within a radius of forty-five to sixty miles of the harbor where the ships anchored. As none of the islands on the western side of the North Atlantic, such as Martha's Vineyard, Nantucket, or Long Island, are wide enough to take three days to cross, our search for this site must be restricted to the coast of the mainland itself.[33] Open deposits of pitch do occur on the island of Trinidad, in the higher reaches of the Orinoco River in South America, and in North America in Alabama, California, Kentucky, Missouri, Oklahoma, Texas, and Utah. The nearest of these, however, is more than 1000 miles from the northeast coast where Earl Henry landed. According to the geologist Dr. William H. Hobbs from the University of Michigan, the only plausible site where one is likely to find a great fire at the bottom of a hill in conjunction with a spring from which issues a pitch-like substance that runs into the sea is the present-day town of Stellarton in the Pictou region of Nova Scotia.[34]

On the railway serving Stellarton, there is a flag-stop called Asphalt, which is on a slight elevation just outside the town near an asphalt road formed of pitch whose surface has solidified to the extent that it can be walked on for a distance of about 100 yards. The surface has been described as spongy, flexing beneath a man's weight and then springing back into place. Being relatively soft, the substance was easily dug up and was used by people at the turn of the twentieth century as fuel.[35] From the Asphalt halt, a stream known as Cole Brook flows down to the estuary of the East River that eventually empties into Pictou harbor.[36] Below Stellarton, the East River is tidal, and at low tide, the muddy bottom is black with oily waste. This region is traversed by several coal seams, one of which is known as "the oil coal seam," which again runs close to Asphalt. The indigenous Mi'qmaq

Figure 2. The Miners' Memorial at Stellarton, Nova Scotia.

people informed Frederick Pohl that there was an opening in the ground near the banks of Cole Brook that had burned and smoked repeatedly over the centuries.[37] Local records disclose that three times between 1828 and 1830, a channel had to be cut from the upper reaches of the East River to near the smoking hole so that the river water could extinguish the fires in the coal seams below ground. There was another fire in 1832, and a prolonged one in 1870 that continued to burn for more than twenty-six years.[38]

Leo F. McKay, a retired government official who has a profound knowledge of local history, told us when he showed us around Stellarton in October 1999 that mining in that area had been terminated as all the coal seams were so highly charged with flammable gas that it was too dangerous to continue. While there, we visited the memorial in the town commemorating one particular disaster that occurred prior to the closure of the mines.

He also informed us that the last spontaneous fire that he could remember was as recent as 1947.[39] There can be little doubt that the smoking hole near Cole Brook and the asphalt spring nearby, taken in conjunction with the presence of the oily pitch-like waste in the East River that can still be seen today, fulfill the description: ". . . The smoke naturally came from a great fire in the bottom of the hill, and there was a spring giving out a certain matter like pitch which ran into the sea, ..."[40] We wholeheartedly agree with Frederick Pohl that the present town of Stellarton is the site of the smoking mountain and river of pitch, and that the good anchorage nearby, described by the armed party, is Pictou harbor. Can we use this conclusion and any relevant passage from the Zeno Narrative to pinpoint the first landfall of Henry's expedition?

Establishing Henry's Landfall

The distance between the landfall and the smoking mountain is, at most, sixty miles. If we draw a circle with this radius, centered on Stellarton, on a map of Nova Scotia, Henry's landfall must be within it. The Zeno Narrative tells us that the first landfall was made with the wind aft and from the southwest, and that the bay terminated in a headland that stretched out into the sea. There is a further clue: ". . . Some of the crew then pulled ashore and soon returned with joyful news that they had found an excellent country and a still better harbor."[41] In other words, there was a harbor that was hidden from the view of those on board Henry's ships at the point of their first landfall. With this information, we can pinpoint this as Chedabucto Bay on the northeastern coast of Nova Scotia. This wide and beautiful bay is flanked at its southern extremity by a headland that juts out into the sea exactly as described in the Zeno Narrative. This headland, the present Cape Canso, is called Cape Trin by Henry's expedition. At the eastern extremity of Chedabucto Bay, we again find a replication of the circumstances described in the Narrative for, as one approaches this side of the bay from the sea, the coast seems to be continuous and well-

Figure 3. Viking axe head found at Cole Harbor, Nova Scotia.

wooded with no sign of a hidden harbor. When approached in a small boat, however, the view changes and a small gap in the coastline leads past a wooded sandbar into Guysborough harbor, a long and completely sheltered waterway that stretches inland for more than ten miles.[42] The sandbar masking the entrance provides complete shelter, not only from the wind, but also from any tide and currents affecting the bay, while the trees on it conceal a ship at anchor from any vessels passing to seaward. We can imagine the excitement that Henry and Antonio must have felt when they cautiously rounded the sandbar and

Figure 4. Prince Henry Memorial at Guysborough, erected by the Clan Sinclair Association of Canada.

entered the welcoming waters of this maritime haven. The low range of hills that clothe the southern side of the harbor are in many respects reminiscent of the west of Ireland, in that they seem to change in shape and mood with the ever-changing light. Miles MacPherson, a local councilor from Guysborough, kindly gave us a guided tour of the full extent of the harbor in his boat, during which he informed us that the bottom of the harbor is of cobbled rock, with a depth that varies from 60 to 100 feet throughout most of its length.

The case for Henry's landfall at Chedabucto Bay and anchorage in Guysborough harbor was first made by Frederick Pohl some fifty years ago[43] and has been readily accepted, not only by ourselves, but also by several other authors whose work has touched upon this voyage. Further proof that Henry was following in the footsteps of the Vikings was the discovery of a Viking axe about ten miles south of Guysborough, which now resides in a museum in Connecticut. In celebration of Henry's voyage, the Clan Sinclair Association has erected a memorial in a public park in Guysborough, in the appropriate form of an upturned prow of a Viking ship. A few miles away, on the southern shore of Chedabucto Bay, is a large, rough-hewn granite rock with a suitable plaque, erected as a more permanent commemoration by the Prince Henry Sinclair Association of North America at the most likely site of Henry's first point of anchorage.

The woodlands surrounding Guysborough harbor are still the haunt of bear, moose, and other game, despite the depredations of modern man. In the late fourteenth century, these lands were the perfect hunting ground for the Mi'qmaq, the Native Americans who inhabited this region. The only brief mention of these people in the Narrative is the one we have already quoted, which describes them as small, rather timid, and living in caves. We prefer to use the word "circumspect" rather than timid, for any people of that era faced with a large body of men in strange attire who proceeded as a military party would have been understandably cautious until the true nature of the incursion was revealed. There are one or two caves in the vicinity of Stellarton, and it has been suggested that, because the natives most probably took shelter within them at the sight of the warlike scouting party, they were mistakenly described as "cave dwellers." Who were these people and what can we discern about the impact of Earl Henry's arrival upon them from their traditions, beliefs, and culture?

Chapter 8

THE MI'QMAQ— PEOPLE OF PEACE

THE MI'QMAQ PEOPLE WHO LIVE IN THE REGION of Earl Henry's landfall have occupied what are now described as the Maritime Provinces of Canada for over 10,000 years, since the retreat of the glaciers at the end of the Ice Age.[1] This area includes Nova Scotia, Prince Edward Island, Cape Breton Island, and a good part of Maine. The Mi'qmaq were part of the Algonquin or Wabanaki Confederation, which included the Malisett, Passamaquoddy, and Abanaki peoples, among others, and which extended geographically as far south as Cape Hatteras on the coast of North Carolina.[2] This confederation of tribes was primarily defensive, providing protection against the war-like Iroquois. It lasted until the early 1700s, when a combination of disease and wars with the British rendered it ineffectual.

According to Daniel N. Paul, a leading Mi'qmaq historian, the tribe lived within seven distinct districts, each of which had its own territory and was governed by a district chief and a council of elders. Each council of elders, in its turn, was made up of a band of village chiefs and other distinguished members of the community. In many respects, each of these districts had much in common with self-governing countries of today, in that the district government possessed conditional powers to settle disputes, apportion hunting and fishing areas to designated families, and, more important, make war or peace. The seven districts comprised Kespukwitk, Sipekne'katik, Eskikewa'kikx, Unama'kik, Epekwitk Aqq Pitktuk, Siknikt, and Kespek.[3] The people of these districts lived in villages of from fifty to 500 inhabitants, and although the number of villages at the time of

Figure 5. Mi'qmaq historian Daniel N. Paul.

Henry's arrival is a matter of conjecture, the total population of the Mi'qmaq in that era is estimated to have exceeded 100,000.[4] The two districts that concern us most are the Eskikewa'kikx, which occupied most of the northeastern coast of Nova Scotia including Chedabucto Bay and Guysborough harbor, and the Epekwitk Aqq Pitktuk, whose lands included the present-day town of Stellarton, the smoking mountain, and Pictou harbor. The English translation of these two names is interesting. Henry's landfall fell within "the skin dressers," the Eskikewa'kikx territory, and his armed scouting party investigated the smoking mountain and the river of pitch in Aqq Pitktuk, otherwise known as "the explosive place."

The overall government of the entire tribe was a responsibility that devolved upon the Grand Council, which was composed of the seven district chiefs, who chose one of their number to be the Grand Chief. It may be more accurate to describe this Grand Council as the trusted senior servants of the tribe, for its only real powers were those assigned to it by the districts and it exerted its influence by persuasion and example rather than by force in the European manner. The district councils were open to all who wished to contribute, and thus the claim that the Mi'qmaq had developed one of the "most democratic political systems that has ever existed" is a simple statement of truth.[5] It is generally believed that the name "Mi'qmaq" derives from their habit of greeting fellow tribesmen, friends, allies, and even newcomers from Europe as *Nikmaq*,[6] which translates as "my kin-friends." Among themselves, they simply referred to the tribes as *Lnu'k*, or "the People."[7]

Social Customs of the Mi'qmaq

The entire community considered themselves members of one large extended family and, until fairly recently, used greetings that would easily lead an outsider to believe they were all blood relatives. Daniel Paul relates that, when he was younger, children addressed all the elders of the community as aunt or uncle,[8] a good custom that he hopes will be revived as his people rebuild and strengthen their traditions. One Mi'qmaq practice that we could well adopt is that children within the tribe are never abandoned. If a child cannot be cared for by its natural parent, for any reason whatsoever (e.g., it has been orphaned), either a childless couple or another with children simply take the child and treat it as their own.[9] Children born out of wedlock are also accepted without stigma.

A Mi'qmaq aspiring to leadership had to achieve certain demanding standards in intelligence, courage, and wisdom. Leadership was by selection and not by birth, and the term of office was always indeterminate. If the leaders did not perform well, they were rapidly replaced. If their governance was satisfactory, it was only terminated by death.[10] Competition among the native people of the Americas was, contrary to beliefs held about them by the Europeans, quite intense. In a complete reversal of the standards found among European societies, however, this competition focused not accumulating personal wealth, power, or prestige, but on providing the highest standards of service or the most benefit to the society as a whole.[11]

Mi'kamagi—Land of the Mi'qmaq

The nature of the countryside of Nova Scotia in the late 1300s was distinctly different from that seen today. Nowadays, there are large areas of open countryside used for pasture and the growing of crops, punctuated by towns and cities, and criss-crossed with roads. At the time of Earl Henry's arrival, the land was almost completely forested with birch, maple, beech, oak, pine, spruce, and fir.[12] The natives used their bark in their housing, canoes, and as containers for food. The roots were used for binding, and the wood was used, not only for fuel, but also to make tools, lances, and weapons. The only clearings were natural meadows, sections seared over by forest fire, or open areas of marshland and bog. Here, the people found useful food plants such as cranberry, blueberry, raspberry, and strawberry, as well as those used for medicines or for making baskets and mats. These large areas of forest were home to bear, moose, porcupine, hare, grouse, and passenger pigeon—all animals essential to the survival of the Mi'qmaq.[13]

The lakes and rivers swarmed with fish, especially salmon, and on their banks were beaver, muskrat, raccoon, and otter.[14] The bays, coves, and rivers provided them with the greatest supply of food and other materials for their needs. These waters were a seemingly inexhaustible source of clams, mussels, whelks, squid, crab, and lobster. The fish were as varied as they were prolific, and included flounder, smelt, shad, skate, salmon, and eel.[15] The Mi'qmaq were as skilled on the water as the Orcadians or the Vikings, and in their deep-water fisheries, they caught porpoise, sturgeon, swordfish, and small whales.[16] The riverbanks, lakesides, and coasts were ideal nesting places for geese and ducks, while the beaches and rocks provided an ideal location for huge herds of seal and walrus to sun themselves. In such a rich environment, where most daily needs could be acquired locally, it is not surprising that the Mi'qmaq developed an almost encyclopaedic knowledge of the habits of the animals they hunted, the relationship between plants and animals, and the details of the seasonal fluctuations in their food supply. This intimate knowledge of the living world engendered a deep respect for life that was incorporated into their system of spiritual beliefs and traditions. Like all hunter-gatherers, they learned to live in harmony with the land without despoiling it.[17]

Spiritual Beliefs of the Mi'qmaq

The religious beliefs of the indigenous people of North America differed very markedly indeed from those current in Europe in the late fourteenth century. The Europeans, as Christians, were required to believe in a fixed body of dogma from which no deviation was permitted without risk of imprisonment, torture or burning at the stake for heresy.[18] While lip service was paid to the precept of "love thy neighbour as thyself," how could the European love himself when he was assailed on the one hand by the guilt-inducing doctrine of original sin and on the other by constant reminders that he was sinful, tempted by the Devil, and liable to spend eternity in hell.[19] The prime purpose of his religious exercises was the rather selfish one of attaining personal salvation. Inherited wealth, the pursuit of personal greed, and a social structure based on force and exploitation formed the acceptable outward face of European Christianity.

Native American religion and spirituality could not have been more different. The dependence of the Mi'qmaq on the fruits of nature and their relationship with the living world of plants and animals with whom they shared their land led them to develop a religion based upon respect for nature or Mother Earth. Mother Earth provided all the essentials of life, and the people knew that they were bound to revere and respect her, for without her bounty, they could not exist.[20] In one major respect, the stark difference between the Mi'qmaq and European attitude to the land was crucial. The Mi'qmaq venerated the land, lived on it, and thanked it for its bounty, but they did not, by their beliefs, ever own it; they shared it with the trees, the flowering plants, and the animals that were part of it.[21] The concept of land ownership was so foreign to their experience that it was totally beyond their understanding.[22] They knew that reigning over the Earth was a supreme being and creator, the Great Spirit, who had created all things and was personified in them—in the air they breathed, the rivers, the forests, their families and friends, and in love, kindness, compassion, knowledge, and wisdom.

When the Native Americans offered tobacco and other tokens of respect to the Great Spirit, the Europeans described them as heathen savages. Yet when they offered bread, wine, and incense to their own God, this was perceived as a sign of Christian civilization.[23] The spiritually aware natives of North America knew that the Great Spirit was goodness incarnate, and they loved and respected him and had no need to fear him. European Christians, on the other hand, feared hellfire and damnation from their God in the afterlife and persecution from his priesthood in the present.

These startling differences in religious belief between the Mi'qmaq and the Europeans underscored the differences in attitudes toward sex and nudity in the two civilizations. As a spin-off of the doctrine of original sin, Europeans viewed sex as a source of depravity or, at best, a necessary evil when limited to the confines of marriage.[24] Sex among the Mi'qmaq was accepted as a perfectly natural and pleasurable act when performed by consenting individuals in private. Like all other cultures, they took great exception to inappropriate sexual advances being made to their wives and daughters, but they had no concept of any form of racial barrier to sexual relationships between them and other peoples, as long as that liaison was conducted according to Mi'qmaq custom.[25]

It is a matter of record that a great number of marriages took place between later French settlers and the Mi'qmaq. This tolerant attitude extended into all areas of life, for the Mi'qmaq, used to their own respected democratic forms, treated all people as equal among equals. This left them remarkably free from the intolerance, class distinction, and racial prejudice that so distorted the worldview of their European counterparts. This principle, when applied in the light of their religious belief, reinforced the idea that hospitality toward one's fellows was a test of civility. They welcomed visitors and settlers alike without opposition because, as one is recorded as saying, "how could one refuse to share the bounties of Mother Earth?"[26]

In the light of later European settlers' claims to have brought civilization to the indigenous peoples of North America, an unbiased examination of the differences in lifestyle, beliefs, and actions between the "civilized" Europeans and the so-called "savage" North American natives is very revealing indeed. While the Native Americans undoubtedly lagged far behind their European counterparts in matters of engineering and technology, they far exceeded them in the things that really matter. Flowing from their spiritual beliefs was a respect for nature and all life—human, animal, or vegetable—and a strong sense of community that pervaded every section of society. The sheer effectiveness and inclusivity of their democratic form of governance, which incorporated respect for the elders and gave a courteous and considered hearing to every voice in the tribe, has not yet been attained by modern European democratic states, much less exceeded. The only competition among the Mi'qmaq people was to discover who could make the best contribution to society as a whole[27]—a startling contrast to the greedy scramble for personal riches that characterized the culture of the "civilized" Europeans. A Mi'qmaq's word was his bond, and any treaty he entered into on behalf of his people was scrupulously honored, which placed him at a gross disadvantage with the British colonial administration[28] that ruthlessly used and abused treaty-making with the Mi'qmaq as a means of exploitation, expropriation, and slow genocide.[29]

The Mi'qmaq way of life, with its gentle disciplines enforced by diplomacy and persuasion and not by force, developed into one that was not merely harmonious with nature, but that promoted a system of real fraternity among the people. It was an inclusive society that valued all its members, young or old, with reliable social systems, mutual respect, and a true sense of belonging. The gentle rhythm of seasonal movement and activity was dictated by nature, and the minutiae of daily living were laid down by custom for which there was total acceptance and respect. This stress-free nonexploitative way of living was not restricted to the Mi'qmaq, nor simply to the Algonquin Federation, but was largely shared by the vast majority of the native peoples of the Americas, even among the more hierarchically structured nations of Central America prior to the Spanish invasion:

> . . . a Spanish boat with sixteen men and two women on board was wrecked on the coast of Yucatan six years before Cortes arrived; the crew were all sacrificed and ritually eaten, with the exception of Gonzalo Guerrero and Jeronimo de Aguilar[30] who were instead enslaved by two local chieftains. Of these survivors, Guerrero had gone so far native that he adorned himself with the accoutrements of his adopted tribe, including elaborate use of nose plug and earrings, and refused on any account to abandon his new life to join Cortes; even Aguila, when first found by the Spaniards, had become indistinguishable from an Indian.[31]

If Europeans could be assimilated into American Indian cultures that had much in common with their European counterparts (such as brutality and hierarchically rule),[32] how much more attractive would such assimilation be with tribes whose fraternal, democratic, and harmonious values were like those of the Mi'qmaq?

Strange Hieroglyphs

Even in the twenty-first century, the white man's view of Amerindian culture at the time of their first contact with Europeans is grossly distorted and tinged with a patronizing form of elitism that classes most of the tribes as primitive, and therefore illiterate. While the vast majority of the Indian nations did not employ writing as Europeans knew it, they did have a means of communication using symbols that, while it had produced no literature, had nonetheless achieved a high degree of sophistication. The Mi'qmaq had developed this much further than most and had a well-developed hieroglyphic form of written language whose origin poses questions about earlier contact with Europe and North Africa that no one can as yet satisfactorily answer. According to Nigel Davies, languages are rather like plants, in that several variants springing from a common trunk are often described as a family of related tongues. Davies states:

> . . . a single language cannot be born twice; a linguistic group must have one place of origin and one only, regardless of its subsequent spread. Thus if two languages, current in two widely separated regions, can be shown to belong to the same family, then a close connection existed between the ancestors of their respective speakers.[33]

We contend that this is just as true of the language of symbolism as it is for the spoken word. When hieroglyphs so close in form and interpretation are used by two cultures widely separated by geography and time, we contend that they may have had a common root. However, this concept poses difficulties if the possibility of contact between ancient Egypt and the Native American people is ignored.

We were given a graphic example of how close this strange linguistic relationship between Egypt and North America really is at a seminar in Orkney in 1997. At the Sinclair Symposium held in Kirkwall to celebrate the 600th anniversary of Earl Henry's voyage, we had our first contact with representatives of the Mi'qmaq people—Chief Kerry Prosper; Donald Julian, the Cultural Curator; and Dr. Peter Christmas, a Mi'qmaq historian. A party brought to the symposium by Niven Sinclair was invited to a reception at the Masonic Lodge in Kirkwall, where we were shown their most treasured possession, an eighteenth-century artifact known as the Kirkwall Scroll.[34] This scroll, which in part denotes in symbolic form a spiritual pathway of enlightenment, is liberally adorned with Egyptian hieroglyphs and religious symbolism. Our hosts informed us that, sadly, the meaning of many of these had been lost and that, therefore, they were unable to interpret them for our benefit. To their intense

Figure 6. Dr. Peter Christmas of the Mi'qmaq and the Kirkwall Scroll.

surprise, this matter was immediately remedied by the eldest of the Mi'qmaq, Dr. Peter Christmas, who took some delight in explaining the meaning of many of these symbols, which he had learned as a child and which he instinctively knew would be remarkably close to the meaning of the Egyptian symbols. The question that naturally arises from this is: Where did the Mi'qmaq learn to use a highly complex pictographic system of writing whose manner is identical in many respects to that used in the Pyramid Texts at Saqqara? As far as we are aware, only one rather specious theory has been advanced in explanation—that is, that the Mi'qmaq were taught hieroglyphic Egyptian by the French missionaries who originally converted them to Catholicism.

Grand Chief Membertou and his family were converted to Roman Catholicism by the French in 1610[35] as part of an extensive missionary movement initiated under the direct orders of the King of France. Britain assumed total control of Nova Scotia in 1713, thus removing any political link between the French priests there and the French Crown.[36] It is fatuous to suggest that the French missionaries could have taught the Mi'qmaq how to use hieroglyphs accurately at this time or for some considerable period later, as no one in Europe had the faintest idea how to translate them until Champollion first deciphered the Rosetta Stone in 1821(2).[37] Therefore, in answer to our own question, we have to say quite simply that we do not know. Bluntly, no one will ever know the answer to this and many other questions of a similar nature until academia further explores the apparent contact between Europe and North Africa on the one hand, and the Americas on the other, prior to the voyage of Christopher Columbus in 1492.

The Controversy over the Mi'qmaq Flag

The Mi'qmaq party presented their hosts at the Islands Council in Kirkwall with some interesting mementos in gratitude for the hospitality they received. The largest of these gifts was a beautifully drawn map of the Mi'qmaqi, the Land of the Mi'qmaq; the other was a flag of the Grand Council of the Mi'qmaq nation suitable for wall display. The flag is a simple design of a red Christian cross lying on its side, with a red five-pointed star in the upper quadrant near the flagpole. In the lower quadrant of the same end, separated by the central bar of the cross, is a crescent Moon, also in red. The symbolism of this flag gave rise to considerable comment and a degree of misunderstanding among some of the Europeans present. The confusion arose because the Mi'qmaq Grand Council flag is a vertical inversion of another shown on a well-known, beautifully illuminated, medieval illustration of King Louis IX of France (St. Louis) departing from the port of Aigues Mortes at the mouth of the River Rhone in a fleet of ships en route to the Crusades.[38] Certain members of our party mistakenly thought that this was a Templar flag and, as Earl Henry sprang from a family steeped in Templar tradition, assumed that it must have been brought by him to the Mi'qmaq, who erroneously used it upside-down.[39] Sadly for the romantics among us, the truth is far more prosaic: this particular flag was never a Templar emblem. St. Louis did not, as it was mistakenly believed, travel to Cyprus in Templar ships, but in vessels of the Genoese fleet.[40] The flag was that of St. Louis and his entourage, and it was used as a royal symbol in his bid to extend the boundaries of Christendom. His successors spent considerable effort in the same evangelical endeavor, sending missions acting under royal patronage to convert the Native Americans in Acadia, the French colony that later became the province of Nova Scotia. Thus it is the French missionary priests who first converted the Mi'qmaq who deserve the credit for the tribe's use of a European flag.

Earlier, we established the site of Henry's first landfall in the Maritime Provinces by using the account in the Zeno Narrative and matching that with considerable precision to the geography and unique geology of the northeast portion of Nova Scotia. It is not just the silent witness of the landscape that confirms his presence here, however; it is also recounted in the vibrant oral traditions of the Mi'qmaq who, in common with other civilizations that used written forms of communication very sparingly, had a complex body of creation myths, allegorical legends with a deep spiritual impact, married to a strong oral tradition encompassing their history. Like the oral histories of other nations such as the Jews of biblical Israel, the Celts of Western Europe, and the tribal cultures of West Africa, these traditions were sung or chanted rather than merely spoken.[41]

According to Professor Leland of Harvard, the chants were characterized by primitive rhythms that were "quite irregular, following only a general cadence rather than observing any fixed number of beats in each line . . . Amerindian metres are not all like that of Hiawatha."[42] Frederick Pohl recounts that "Several passages in the Micmac chants are of a higher order of poetry than we have generally credited to American Indians, as we judge from the songs translated into English poetry by C. G. Leland of Harvard, and revised for strict literalness by J. D. Prince, Amerindian linguistic scholar at Columbia University."[43] Leland and Prince recount the most important aspects of the mythology of the Mi'qmaq in their work *Kuloskap the Master and Other Algonquin Poems*, which includes selections from the traditions of the Passamaquoddy, Penobscot, Abanaki, Mi'qmaq, and Delaware—all tribes from the Wabanaki branch of the Algonquin Federation. The central character in all of these legends, which were first translated from the native language by Father Silas Tertius Rand in the latter part of the nineteenth century, is Kuloscap, also known as Glus-kabe, or the Mi'qmaq variation, Glooscap.

Glooscap

Glooscap is the pivotal figure to such an extent that his actions and those of the animals that surround him are used to explain the creation of the landscape, its exploration, and how the ideal man should behave within creation and in his dealings with his fellows. Writing in the

1950s, Frederick Pohl claims to have discovered seventeen "identical" correspondences between certain aspects of the Glooscap legend and the life of Earl Henry St. Clair, Prince of Orkney, and he states:

> The numerical chances are so astronomical that the equating of the Prince of Orkney with the prince of the Micmac legend [Glooscap] is incontrovertible. Prince Henry Sinclair and the hero of the Micmac tales surely are one and the same person.[44]

When we consider that this all-encompassing statement is made about the creation legends of so many Amerindian nations in which the central character is held up to be the spiritual archetype of idealized behavior, we are tempted to simply dismiss it out of hand. While Pohl's overzealous enthusiasm may well have led him to exaggerate, however, we must examine his assertions in some detail lest we throw the baby out with the bathwater. As the whole body of the Glooscap legend is part of a living and growing tradition, we must recognize the probability that, just like the biblical tales of Israelites of old, it acquired accretions and additions reflecting the actions of various exemplary figures through the ages.

Those figures in the biblical context were the prophets, kings, and judges of Israel; in the context of the Mi'qmaq, they are outstanding characters from their nation and others whose actions made significant contributions to their way of life.[45] Therefore, the possibility that some part of the Glooscap story reflects the arrival of a real historical personage from another strange and exotic culture cannot be ruled out. This possibility is transformed into a high degree of probability when we consider a statement made by Vaughan Doucette, a Mi'qmaq from Eskasoni on Cape Breton Island, who stated that "there could have been several Glooscap figures spread out over a period of time, each one possessing unusual and praiseworthy abilities."[46] This does reinforce the ideas first mooted by Pohl, that a visit by the Prince of Orkney may well have been commemorated in some fashion in the oral traditions of the Mi'qmaq. The problem, therefore, is to discern if and where the Glooscap legend comments directly or allegorically on the arrival of Henry St. Clair, and where the account merges back almost imperceptibly into the main body of legends of far greater antiquity.

Pohl claims that there are seventeen significant and identical correspondences between the characters of the Prince of Orkney and the

Glooscap of legend.[47] He prioritizes twelve of these[48] as being of the utmost importance:

> The visiting hero was a "prince": He was a "king"[49] who had often sailed the seas: His home was in a "town" on an "island,"[50] and he came with many men and soldiers: He came across the ocean via Newfoundland and first met the Micmacs at Pictou.[51] His principal weapon was "a sword of sharpness":[52] He had "three daughters":[53] He explored Nova Scotia extensively: He slept for six months in the wigwam of a giant named Winter:[54] He remained in the country only from the sailing season of the year of his arrival to the next sailing season: The prince had "made long trips across the ocean with his feet on the backs of whales."[55] He was entertained by the playing of "flutes."[56] He possessed "money, iron and a store."[57]

While we accept that the arrival of the St. Clair/Zeno expedition in Nova Scotia would undoubtedly make some mark on the oral history of the Mi'qmaq people, the claims that Pohl makes for Henry's wide-ranging activities quite frankly stretch the bounds of credulity much too far. First, Pohl claims that the European party spent an entire year in Nova Scotia and recounts as substantiated fact a list of activities that would probably have taken twice that time to accomplish. We can find no evidence that Henry and his party lingered that long in Nova Scotia, nor is there any corroborating evidence whatsoever to substantiate the claim made in the Zeno Narrative that he implemented his "idea of staying there and founding a city." The editor of the Zeno Narrative made his own comment, over 150 years later:

> What happened afterwards I do not know beyond what I gather from a piece of another letter which maintains that [Henry] settled down in the harbour of his newly discovered island and explored the whole of the country thoroughly as well as the coasts on both sides of Greenland.[58]

We do not believe that this brief comment is sufficient justification for the highjacking of the creation mythology of a people of great antiquity for the greater glory of Earl Henry St. Clair, who was rightly described by Antonio Zeno as "a man worthy of immortal memory,"[59] and who has no need for such overzealous false claims to honor. We restrict our comments on Henry's activities in Nova Scotia to those in the region of Guysborough and Stellarton, and such explorations in that area as it is reasonable to assume he made.

To the reasoning advanced earlier in respect of this landfall, we can now add the following extracts from the Glooscap legend that tend to corroborate the known facts recounted in the Zeno Narrative.

> *Kuloskap was first,*
> *First and greatest,*
> *To come into our land -*
> *Into Nova Scotia . . .*
> *When the Master left Ukakumkuk,*
> *Called by the English Newfoundland,*
> *He went to Piktook or Pictou,*
> *Which means "the rising of bubbles,"*
> *Because at that place the water*
> *Is ever strangely moving.*
> *There he found an Indian village,*
> *A town of a hundred wigwams.*
> *Kuloskap being a handsome*
> *And very stately warrior*
> *With the air of a great chief,*
> *Was greatly admired by all,*
> *Especially the women;*
> *So that everyone felt honoured*
> *Whose wigwam he deigned to enter.*[60]

The probable relevance of the last three lines of this quotation give an ironic confirmation of a comment made by Donald Julian at the Sinclair Symposium, who made the cryptic remark that, if his uncle came into the room dressed in the clothes of Niven Sinclair, no one would be able to tell them apart. While we were in Canada, we came across the photograph of an elder of the Mi'qmaq tribe called Joseph M. Augustine,[61] who quite simply looked like a tanned identical twin of our good friend, Niven. Sensing further proof of the veracity of Earl Henry's voyage when these matters were first brought to his attention, Niven suggested using DNA tests to establish the direct ancestral connection between the Sinclairs and certain members of the modern

Mi'qmaq nation. The persistence of the Sinclair features should be enough, however, for on the European side of the Atlantic, they are readily recognizable from generation to generation. Later in the Glooscap legend, it is stated that "Before he came they knew not how to make nets."[62] And according to the historian Andrew Sinclair, sinkers and floats for nets of a European design that was current at the end of the fourteenth century have been found in the sites of Mi'qmaq coastal camps in the northeast of Nova Scotia.[63]

Validation by Oral Tradition

Leaving the matter of the Glooscap legends to one side, there are certain important oral traditions concerning the visit of Earl Henry St. Clair that are handed down to this day to the Grand Chiefs of the Mi'qmaq nation on their election. In light of one such tradition, there is now no doubt that Earl Henry St. Clair, Prince of Orkney, crossed the Atlantic and landed in Nova Scotia during the final years of the fourteenth century and returned to Scotland at the conclusion of his voyage. Furthermore, he then returned to the North American continent a second time. This claim, which to the best of our knowledge has not been mentioned by any of the more recent historians, rests upon the secret tradition handed down from one Grand Chief to another over the centuries, which states that, when Henry returned to Europe, he took one of the Mi'qmaq with him as his guest. This exotic visitor did not stay in Scotland for long, for tradition tells us that he returned to his people in about a year. This gives us vivid confirmation and proof of the fact that Earl Henry St. Clair crossed the Atlantic not once, but at least twice,[64] and helps us to expand and clarify the timescale of his exploratory voyages to the Americas in a manner that makes his achievements there far more credible.

The accuracy of oral tradition, which used to be taken as myth and legend, has now been proven almost beyond doubt, particularly when it is encapsulated in poetic form, as it is among the Mi'qmaq. The Supreme Court of Canada now accepts the oral traditions of the Mi'qmaq regarding land use and hunting rights as having the force of legal documents. Other examples of the acceptance of the validity of oral tradition are not hard to find: the history and genealogies provided by the African tribal *goriots* are familiar to many millions worldwide, thanks to the work of Arthur Hailey, the author of *Roots*; the Viking sagas, which are simply the written form of earlier poetic oral legends, are now accepted as historical records, with their sailing directions to the Americas that can be replicated today; the oral history of the Celtic peoples, which did not take written form for many centuries; and finally, the first five books of the Old Testament. As in other predominantly oral cultures, one of the major contributing factors to the survival of the Mi'qmaq was their sense of history, which lay at the core of their identity as a people. Without this, they would have vanished without trace, for few other people have survived as a distinct race when subjected to the long catalogue of misdeeds that has been their history since the advent of the European colonial settlers.[65]

The Horrors of British Colonial Misrule

The relationship of the Mi'qmaq with the early French settlers was, as evidenced by their intermarriage, quite benevolent on the whole.[66] But even the French can be justly criticized for replacing the Mi'qmaq's innate spirituality with the guilt-inducing doctrines of original sin and a system of belief based on fear of eternal hellfire and damnation. The British colonial administration broke nearly every treaty they made with the native inhabitants of Nova Scotia and subjected these trusting people to a regime of systematic brutality that included, at one point, paying a bounty on their scalps.[67] It is scant consolation to the Mi'qmaq to learn that the British government was just as brutal, repressive, and unjust to subject populations in India, Africa, and Ireland. Nor is it any comfort that this repressive attitude was at least consistent, in that the British ruling classes treated the lower orders in Britain just as badly as they did the indigenous peoples of their colonial empire. Yet ironically, the British settlers had the gall to call the Mi'qmaq savages.

The work of historian and civil rights activist Daniel N. Paul, entitled *We Were Not the Savages*, is a moving indictment of this shameful and prolonged historical episode, one that is all the more powerful because of its detached, objective, and unemotional approach. In light of the dreadful history of race relations that lasted so long between the Mi'qmaq and people of British origin, it is enlightening to see the lengths to which senior representatives of the Mi'qmaq today are prepared to go to celebrate the arrival in Nova Scotia of Earl Henry St. Clair. Not only did they send representatives to the Sinclair Symposium in Orkney, they have participated in every official celebration of the Zeno/St. Clair voyage that has taken place in Canada and have generously offered their help to all those investigating this historical event. This is a further illustration of the fact that Henry not only arrived in Nova Scotia and stayed there for some time, but was spiritually akin to the Mi'qmaq, for, like the Templars from which he sprang, he worked for the benefit of the community as a whole rather than the acquisition of power and riches for his own selfish ends.

Chapter 9

HENRY SAILS FOR VINLAND

THE SUPERB SURROUNDINGS OF GUYSBOROUGH harbor were the perfect base for Henry's stay in Nova Scotia. We can estimate the length of this with a reasonable degree of accuracy as three to four months, and we are told that he spent this time profitably, exploring the local area with its potential for support of life and trade, and deepening his relationship with the hospitable Mi'qmaq.[1] Archaeological evidence for his exploration was found at Lilly Lake in Waverley near Halifax, Nova Scotia, in the form of a petroglyph. A medieval-type shield has been carved on the top face of a boulder on a rocky outcrop in a clearing. The shield is surmounted by the Roman numeral IV and is quartered in the medieval fashion. The top left-hand quarter contains a badly eroded and slightly flattened circular design; the top right-hand quarter shows a sun in splendor with eight radiating beams; the lower left quadrant contains a crescent moon; the lower right carries what could be a stylized version of the *croix pattée* of the Knights Templar. Various archaeologists who have studied this carving note the similarities in symbolism between it and the rock carving known as the Westford Knight in Massachusetts.

The Zeno Narrative recounts that Henry "noticed that the place had a wholesome and pure atmosphere, a fertile soil and good rivers and so many other attractions, he conceived the idea of staying there and founding a city."[2] There is no evidence that this idea came to fruition, and from the information contained in the Narrative, Henry certainly did not have time to accomplish this on his first voyage, which is the subject of the document. The expedition arrived during the last week in May, and we learn that he ordered the bulk of his fleet to return to Orkney at the beginning of autumn so that they would reach home before winter set in. Antonio's letter recounts that "He therefore kept only the oared boats and those people who were willing to stay with him, and he sent all the rest away in the ships. He appointed me against my will to be their captain"[3] This return voyage took about twenty-eight days.

Frederick Pohl, being a landsman unfamiliar with medieval custom and maritime usage, took the passage in the Narrative about "oared boats" to imply that Henry sent his entire fleet back to Orkney and only kept a limited number of men in small rowing boats with him for the rest of his exploration.[4] This, combined with the attribution of an unduly large proportion of the Glooscap creation mythology to the exploits of Henry St. Clair, led to the creation of a fable of almost unbelievable dimensions bereft of any archival or archaeological supporting evidence whatsoever.[5] Pohl's account states categorically that Henry explored the length and breadth of Nova Scotia in rowing boats, passed the winter at Cap d'Or, near the Minas Basin,[6] which projects into a tidal rip averaging twelve to fourteen knots, and then, unbelievably in light of his reduced manpower, built a ship from scratch.[7] This shipbuilding exercise was supposedly conducted by a skeleton crew working in the depths of a Canadian winter, which is quite ludicrous.

We are not alone in this view; one critic, Colin Clarke, a professional surveyor from Waverley, Nova Scotia, shares our belief that Henry would not have been so foolish as to send all his ships back home and rely on building one in North America to facilitate his return. Clarke, who once worked as a shipwright, declares that he finds Pohl's scenario preposterous: "He was here to explore not to build ships, and, even if he did have the tools with him, where did he plan to find dry wood for the construction?" Clarke shares our view that this aspect of Pohl's story completely lacks credibility. With the maritime technology of the late fourteenth century, sailing from Cap d'Or into the teeth of the prevailing wind, even taking advantage of the riptide, is hardly feasible. Sailing ships of that era could not sail particularly close to the wind and would, in all probability, risk foundering on the coast on the east side of the Bay of Fundy had this been attempted. Even if it had been practicable, the distances involved are so huge that the tide would have changed, leaving the ship to battle against an incoming tidal rip long before it reached the open sea. To merely stand still in the water, much less make headway, would indicate a capacity for sailing at twelve to fourteen knots, whereas a sailing ship of that era would have been lucky to average three to four. Would any experienced mariner have built a ship at a site whose prevailing conditions would have dictated against its being used as a port of embarkation? We submit they most certainly would not.

The Orkney Galley

Any realistic assessment of the options open to Henry after the departure of the bulk of his fleet on their homeward voyage depends entirely upon the interpretation given to the term "oared boats." Earlier, having made due allowance for the defensive and communication needs of the earldom, we estimated that the fleet at Henry's command for his exploration consisted of one Venetian galley, one of his own Orkney galleys, and three or four barks for scouting purposes. It is highly probable that the Venetian galley and the barks returned to Orkney, leaving Henry with the other galley as his means of transport. No responsible leader would have stranded himself or his followers in unknown waters so many thousands of miles from home with only small rowing boats as their sole means of transport. Equally, it would be unreasonable to suggest that Henry retained the Venetian galley, which, although in his service, was the personal property of Antonio Zeno, who had purchased it for his journey from Venice to Orkney.[8] The Orkney galley, being smaller than its Venetian counterpart and powered by both sail and oars, would have given Henry all the flexibility and security he needed. Furthermore, there is hard archaeological evidence on the mainland of North America that tends to support this.[9] The voyage from Guysborough to Vinland in search of the earlier settlement of Norumbega using an Orkney galley is, despite the prevailing southwesterly winds, perfectly feasible. It had been done many times before by Viking vessels, which also used oars and sail.

Henry's route to Vinland would, like all his other steps along the way, have replicated that laid down by his Viking predecessors so many centuries before. Thus, after rounding Cape Trin and gaining some searoom, his true course would have been almost due southwest, in the direction of Cape Cod. The sailing ships of the fourteenth century could not sail very close to the wind, and as the prevailing wind was from the southwest, a direct route would not have been feasible for a vessel dependent upon sail alone. Such a ship would have to have made one tack in a more or less southerly direction, overreaching the latitude of their destination, and then tack and sail crosswind in order to make landfall, thereby more than doubling the nautical distance sailed. Henry's choice of an oared galley as his preferred mode of transport clearly demonstrates his wisdom and maritime experience, for with a vessel of that nature, he could row directly into the teeth of a gentle southwest wind and take advantage of the occasional northeaster, which can sometimes blow for from forty-eight to seventy-two hours at that time of year, and which would impel him directly to the fabled Vinland. While Henry knew how to find Vinland with some precision, it is highly likely that directions to find Norumbega, the settlement founded by Knutson, were extremely vague, as few of Knutson's men had survived to make the return journey to Norway. As this settlement was most likely located in territory controlled by the Algonquin Federation, Henry would need help to find it. And indeed, Mi'qmaq tradition tells us that the earl took several men from the tribe with him to act as guides, emissaries, and interpreters.[10]

The Search for Norumbega

There is no extant documentary evidence to chart Henry's movements from the time he left Guysborough on his first voyage until his return to Orkney. Our reconstruction of his exploration is based on our knowledge of his objective, fleshed out with Mi'qmaq tradition and hard archaeological evidence that has been subjected to prolonged investigation and controversy for many years. We contend, based on this evidence, that Henry St. Clair and his expedition were the sole creators of the first archaeological site we describe and either built or, at the very least, made very significant contributions to the second.

Sailing directions to Vinland were precise and easy to follow; finding Norumbega, the stone-built settlement constructed or used by Knutson, was a different matter entirely. There were no precise directions for locating this Norwegian settlement, and in his efforts to locate it, Henry was therefore very largely dependent on information supplied by the Mi'qmaq and their allies. The geography of the New England coastal plain helped, however, as the area is remarkably flat and the few hills found there were good vantage points for surveying the surrounding countryside. The present town of Westford, which lies approximately two days march inland from both Boston Bay and the mouth of the Merrimac River,[11] is dominated by Prospect Hill, which gives a panoramic view of over thirty miles and, on a clear day, views of the mountains to the north and west. Henry's reason for climbing Prospect Hill was to try and catch sight of a possible site of Norumbega, which had been reported to him by his Amerindian allies. Strange stone structures stand on a hilltop near Salem, which used to be known as Pattee's Caves and are now the tourist site known as America's Stonehenge. This highly complex Neolithic site could easily have been mistaken for the stone-built structures of Norumbega by Native Americans, to whom any form of stone building was unfamiliar. Whatever Henry's reason for climbing Prospect Hill, it is near there that we find an archaeological site that is indubitably a relic of the first exploratory voyage of the Prince of Orkney.

The Westford Carving

As with all other evidence of pre-Columbian European contact with North America, this site went unrecognized for many years and has been the subject of considerable debate for the last five decades. This is hardly surprising, for no one who has been brought up to believe that Columbus was the first European to set foot in the Americas can be expected to welcome the discovery of a petroglyph that shows a medieval knight in full armor with sword and shield. Yet this is precisely what is found on a rock ledge near a busy road on the outskirts of the town of Westford, Massachusetts.

The earliest documentary evidence for this carving that we have found is in a book by the Reverend Edwin R. Hodgeman, who describes it in the following words:

> A broad ledge which crops near the house of William Kittredge, had upon its surface grooves made by glaciers in some far off geological age. Rude outlines of the human face have been traced upon it and the work is said to be that of Indians.[12]

As it is considerably older than the history of European settlement in these parts, it was, not surprisingly, attributed to the Native Americans.

Figure 7. The Westford Knight outlined in chalk.

This carving was examined and photographed by Malcolm Pearson and William B. Goodwin in the early 1940s. In 1946, Goodwin, who was a Director of the Wadsworth Atheneum in Hartford, Connecticut, wrote a book entitled *The Ruins of Great Ireland in New England*, which was illustrated by photographs including one of the Westford carving taken by our colleague Malcolm Pearson. The accompanying text stated that part of the carving was a representation of a broken sword, a Viking symbol for the death of a warrior. The groundbreaking work in the investigation of this petroglyph came much later and was done by the president of the Connecticut Archaeological Society, Frank Glynn, a graduate of Wesleyan University.

Glynn was a regular contributor of numerous research articles to a variety of archaeological journals, but it is for his work on the Westford Knight that he is remembered worldwide. He made several unsuccessful attempts to locate the carving until the winter of 1951, when he was provoked into making an all-out search for it by his colleague and correspondent, T. C. Lethbridge. Lethbridge, who is the author of extensive works on archaeology and a variety of other subjects,[13] was at that time the director of excavations for the Cambridge Antiquarian Society in England and also a director of the Cambridge University Museum of Archaeology and Ethnology, having served in these posts for over thirty years. He was a member of three arctic expeditions and several archaeological explorations of the Hebrides, and made two voyages in the Baltic on square-rigged ships.

Positive Identification

On Lethbridge's insistence, Glynn visited Malcolm Pearson, who stated that he believed the carving had been destroyed during a road-widening operation. This misconception was not corrected until 1954, when, traveling with his daughter, Cindy, Glynn was shown the turn-off to Westford and was told that the carving was located some two miles beyond the town. On 30 May 1954, Glynn was delighted to rediscover the carving that was known locally as the Old Indian. Soon after, with Malcolm Pearson's assistance, a series of black-and-white and color photographs were taken. First, the carving was photographed untouched from every angle and then, with chalk applied to the bulb of percussion of the peck marks in the stone that delineated the design, it was photographed again. The white chalk marks set against the dark rock outlined the figure of a tall knight in medieval armor, wearing a long surcoat reaching to his ankles with, more centrally, the outline of a long pommel-hilted sword that extends from his lower chest to the level of his feet. Behind the hilt of the sword, you can be see the shape of a helmet surmounted by some form of bird. On the knight's left arm, the distinct outlines of a shield can clearly be seen. Glynn sent copies of the photographs to Lethbridge, along with his own verbal description of the carving. Lethbridge was overjoyed and wrote to Glynn:

> Well done! I don't know of course, but isn't there something more on this stone than a sword? Can't it be a medieval knight holding a sword? Right hand below the pommel, . . . Left hand holding the scabbard where you have dotted a triangle below the hilt. Right armpit shown by curve of dots outside pommel. Right shoulder higher up. . . . Throat indicated by line of dots just above the pommel. If it is, there ought to be some trace of a pointed helm. The whole thing never, more than outlined and, perhaps, not completed, because something happened . . .
> I expect that you will be burnt at the stake for finding something pre-Columbian, but it is worth it. I don't see how it can be anything but European Medieval.[14]

Glynn's enthusiasm now knew no bounds, and during the summer, he persuaded A. J. Gagne and E. R. Beauchop, curators at the John Higgins Armory, to visit Westford and examine the carving. At first, they concentrated on the helmet, which they believed was the final part to be completed. It convinced them of the authenticity of the Westford Knight. They described the style of the helmet at first as being typical of a range of dates between 1350 and 1400, and then narrowed even that down to 1376–1400. They further suggested that a pi-nosed visor was represented, and they simultaneously spotted what Glynn described as "the saucy little rampart lion on the round pommel, his tail curving up around the corner of his shield." Glynn's own observations included the outline of a hat with something like a coronet engraved upon it, but he did not know if that was heraldically possible.[15]

At the suggestion of Gagne and Beauchop, Glynn submitted the question of the arms depicted on the shield to the Lord Lyon King of Arms in Edinburgh. The Lord Lyon's reply stated that similar shields

were known from the Elgin-Inverness region during the fourteenth century and suggested that the knight might be a de l'Ard or Sperre. He
also asked for large photographs to aid further study.[16] In a further letter to Glynn, Lethbridge made the following comment: "He looks as if
he is within fifty years either way of 1350 and to be made more in the
nature of a brass than an effigy."[17] This comment is in accord with our
own viewpoint, for we also have described it as being carved in the
design of a memorial brass rather than a Templar-style grave marker, as
suggested by other authors.[18] In a subsequent letter, Lethbridge put his
finger right on the crucial issue with the following comment:

> Either I am quite gaga or we have got this thing solved. No one
> will believe it of course . . . Your knight should be some rela-
> tion of the Sinclairs on the female side. I gather that Sinclair of
> Zeno was put into the earldom by the King of Norway. This
> would explain his rather primitive armour.[19]

Proof of Henry's Voyage

While Glynn continued his investigations in New England, Lethbridge
pursued the matter of the coat of arms in Europe and submitted them
to the "Unicorn Herald," Sir Iain Moncreiffe of that Ilk. Sir Iain was
most enthusiastic over the Westford carving and responded in the following terms:

> . . . The 14th century Knight in Massachusetts is absolutely
> fascinating, and his heraldry certainly seems to point to the
> Scottish noble families of Norse origin, though it looks pretty
> crude, and I wonder if Mr Glynn has traced it quite right on
> his surcoat. A galley would never be on a knight's shield to sig-
> nify 'journey's end'! His shield would only bear his ancestral
> coat of arms. In Scotland, galleys fall into two main groups: (1)
> the galley, usually black, born by descendants in the male or
> female line of the Norse Kings of the Isles (the family of
> Godred Crovan) such as the Macdonalds, Campbells,
> MacDougalls, Macleods, Macleans, Stewarts of Appin etc and
> (2) the galley, usually gold, born by the descendants in the male
> or female line of the Norse Jarls of Orkney, (the family of
> Roganvald the Wise) such as the Sinclairs or St Clairs. . . . The

figure's costume and sword, together with the galley on his shield, all fit so happily into the context of Jarl Henry's expedition, that I'd be very surprised if it wasn't from one of his companions, and indeed from the galley, one of the godings of Northmen of his kindred.[20]

Further study of the armorial bearings on the carving led Sir Iain Moncreiffe to clarify matters still further and state that they were "the armorial bearings for a Clan Gunn chief from Thurso," the heraldic description of which is "Gules a lymph ad, sails furled, oars in saltire, and in chief a mullet Gold between two buckles Silver."[21] The Unicorn Herald's next comments preempted further controversy and put an end to any suggestion of possible forgery of the carving. He stated that only three people in the world, other than himself, would have had the knowledge to depict these fourteenth century armorial bearings with such precision or know enough about late medieval armor to fake a carving such as that in Massachusetts.[22] In other words, it is highly likely that the image is a true medieval memorial carved in North America by the St. Clair expedition commemorating the death of Earl Henry's closest companion, Sir James Gunn, who, it is believed, died during the ascent of Prospect Hill.

Sir Iain Moncreiffe made the connection between the carving and the St. Clair voyage and stated that:

> . . . the effigy of a fourteenth century knight in basinet, camail and surcoat, with a heater-shaped shield bearing devices of a Norse-Scottish character such as might have been expected of a knight in Jarl Sinclair's entourage, and a pommel sword of that period, is hardly likely to be a coincidence. I rather think that the mighty jarl stayed a while—possibly wintered—in Massachusetts.[23]

This funeral effigy had been punched into the natural shelf of rock, as the materials were not available for the memorial brass demanded by European knightly tradition. The effigy had been punched into the rock by the armorer, who would have been among the most skilled craftsmen traveling with the expedition. Detailed examination of the peck marks by Jim Whittal, an archaeologist of the Early Sites Research Society, have clearly shown that the metal punch used became progressively blunted as the carving progressed.[24] Further examination by archaeologists Austin Hildreth and H. J. O'Mara compared the deterioration of the punch marks outlining the Westford Knight with that of punch marks on early gneiss gravestones. This led them to conclude that the punch marks on the Westford Effigy were in the region of 500 to 800 years old.[25] One article about the effigy made the following comment: ". . . done so accurately to detail that every expert consulted has said that it would have had to be done by an armourer of the period."[26]

The fourteenth-century knight's pommel sword is shown as broken, indicating that he died nearby. Also shown is a pointed bassinet helmet carried by the knight, who is wearing a quilted surcoat. The coat of arms showing a ship without sails, but with oars, indicates the Viking ancestry of the Gunns.[27] The mullet, or star, which can mean the third son, appears on every Gunn coat of arms and refers to their alliance with the Sutherlands.[28] The buckles in silver are a heraldic reference to the silver brooch given to the Gunn chief by the King of Scotland when he created the clan chief the royal Crowner, a hereditary office they held for over 200 years.[29] Some of the heraldic symbolism on the Westford Knight replicates that of the shield carved on a rock discovered at Waverley near Halifax, Nova Scotia, which we mentioned above.

Extending the Search

After identifying the carving as a memorial to Sir James Gunn, Lethbridge wrote to Glynn suggesting that further exploration of the area might be worthwhile to locate the winter camp of the St. Clair expedition. Glynn was joined by Frederick Pohl, and they were shown a stone that had been unearthed by a local farmer near Westford bearing a rather strange carving.[30] This stone, which now rests in the J. V. Fletcher Library in Westford, shows a ship with a single mast bearing two sails and, on the upper part of the hull, eight ports for oars. An incised arrow with four feathers on either side of the shaft and the number "184" is also evident. Lethbridge suggests that the numerals may signify paces, and Glynn found that, within 184 paces of the original location of the stone, there were three stone enclosures. These were similar to Viking stone buildings in Greenland known as "storhouses."[31] The details of the carving on the Westford boatstone

Figure 8. The boatstone at Westford, Massachusetts.

confirms our theory that it was an Orkney galley that Earl Henry St. Clair used for his further exploration of the North American coast. The theory that the three rough stone enclosures might be a St. Clair winter encampment, while plausible, demands far greater examination before it can be held to be fact.

The effigy known as the Westford Knight lies within feet of a major road that has sustained ever-increasing loads of traffic over the last few decades, making this medieval carving subject to erosion from traffic fumes and salt contamination thrown up from the road surface during the winter snows. As a result, the carving has been deteriorating rapidly. This situation is made worse by the runoff of water from a nearby lawn that constantly affects the surface of the rock. The deterioration over the last few years has become so marked that we are getting close to the point when the remnants of the carving will have to be interpreted rather than viewed. Earlier photographs by Malcolm Pearson, Frank Glynn, and Jim Whittal, however, have left us a permanent record of the carving before modern pollution began to destroy it.

Official Recognition and Preservation

In 1991, Niven Sinclair commissioned a rubbing to be taken of the Westford Knight by Marianna Lines, who took an impression from the carving using brass-rubbing techniques of her own invention. Instead of simply using a heelball of wax, she used a mixture of vegetable and floral juices with beeswax. She revealed the complex nature of the carving in a far more credible way than any photograph. According to Andrew Sinclair, who was present at the time:

> . . . The shield with the Gunn arms of previous reconstructions had always looked askew and toylike, a primitive effort by an armourer, who did not know of the conventions of medieval military burial. But the cloth impression showed a large shield of arms set squarely below the left shoulder of the figure, with two quarterings at the top, and a ship at the base of the shield similar to the Sinclair ship on the coat of arms of Prince Henry's daughter, Jean St. Clair, whose effigy lies at Corstorphine Church near Edinburgh.[32]

Since that rubbing was taken, the effigy has been fenced off by a suspended chain-link fence mounted on stone pillars. An explanatory plaque that contains a detailed description of the effigy and its origin has been erected with a suitable inscription describing Henry's voyage and the relationship between him and Sir James Gunn.[33] Sadly, this has not prevented an act of almost criminal vandalism by a misguided and somewhat overzealous supporter of the Clan Gunn, who painted over the shield.

To ensure the Westford Knight's preservation and to protect it from further acts of vandalism, our close friend and colleague Niven Sinclair made a presentation to the Archaeological Commissioners of the Commonwealth of Massachusetts in the autumn of 1999. We were privileged to assist him in this, along with such stalwart local historians as Norman Biggart and Malcolm Pearson. Pearson brought with him a letter from Joseph A. Sinnott, a consultant geologist who was once the Massachusetts State Geologist, who had this to say about the Westford carving:

> After lengthy and detailed study of the rock outcropping in the field it is my opinion that a pecked and etched image of an

historical event has been emplaced on the bedrock . . . Natural or glacial markings such as striations, grooves, polishing and weathering are all apparent on the rock, but do not diminish the stature of the image placed there at a much later date. I have been the State Geologist for Massachusetts for twenty two years . . . and also the Director of The Massachusetts Underwater Archaeology Board for five years and understand the commission's desire for authenticity . . . the etching is solidly and authentically placed on the bedrock and deserves historical preservation.[34]

We are happy to record that, thanks not only to the cooperation of the commissioners, but also to the support of the president and the com-

Figure 9. Memorial stone at the Westford Knight.

mittee of the Westford Historical Association, steps are now under way to preserve this important medieval artifact.

Despite the recognition granted to the effigy by this decision to preserve it, the professional opinions of A. J. Gagne and E. R. Beauchop of the John Higgins Armory, the views of the director of excavations for the Cambridge Antiquarian Society, T. C. Lethbridge, the untiring work of Frank Glynn and the president of the Connecticut Archaeological Society, the detached opinions of the Lord Lyon King of Arms in Edinburgh, the definitive comments of the Unicorn Herald, Sir Iain Moncrieffe of that Ilk, and the dating of the creation of the effigy by the archaeologists Austin Hildreth and H. J. O'Mara, we have no doubt that there will still be those who will refuse to believe that this is evidence of pre-Columbian European exploration of North America. Our illustrations clearly show that the effigy known as the Westford Knight fits quite properly into the British and European tradition of memorial brasses of the twelfth to fourteenth centuries. To any open-minded and serious student of our common heritage, the evidence is overwhelming and specific. The Westford carving demonstrates beyond all reasonable doubt that the St. Clair/Zeno expedition described in the Zeno Narrative continued its explorations after its landfall in Nova Scotia, and, following in the footsteps of its Viking precursors, reached New England and explored a considerable distance inland.

Chapter 10

THE NEWPORT TOWER— A PIECE OF THE PUZZLE

THE CONTROVERSY SURROUNDING EVIDENCE OF pre-Columbian European contact with the Americas has often degenerated into bitter and vituperative debate. Perhaps the most prolonged dispute has been over a distinctive structure which, had it been located in Europe, would have been dated to the twelfth to fourteenth centuries without causing the slightest ripple of concern among academics.[1] This building lies in Newport, Rhode Island, and is known locally by the misleading title of the Old Stone Mill. This circular rubble-built stone tower, which stands on eight supporting pillars in Touro Park, is more accurately described as the Newport Tower.

The building is almost circular, its outer diameter measuring just over seven meters. It stands about eight meters above present ground level and is supported by eight round pillars that are linked by Romanesque arches. The arches rest on cylindrical stone-built pillar bases that were originally visible and would have added nearly half a meter to the height of each pillar.[2] The inside surface of the pillars is flush with the inner surface of the walls they support, while their outside surfaces project about twenty-five centimeters from the outer side of the walls.[3] The top of each pillar is marked by a thin sloping stone or slate slab that projects at an angle.[4] The inside of the circular wall is marked by post-holes that once housed substantial beams, and there are also three window openings and several smaller peepholes. There is a built-in fireplace with two flues, faint traces of steps, and several niches of varying size.[5]

Figure 10. *Model of the Newport Tower as it stands today in front of the original in Touro Park, Newport, Rhode Island.*

Figure 11. *Interior view of the Newport Tower model.*

Figure 12. The Newport Tower in Touro Park in Newport, Rhode Island.

This bizarre stone-built structure, ringed by a wrought iron fence in a public park that is surrounded by mostly wooden-built houses, is truly an architectural anachronism. The controversy over its true age and origin has been prolonged and strident, to the extent that it makes the *odium theologicum* of the doctrinal disputes of the early Christian Church seem like squabbles in a kindergarten.

> The most controversial building in America is one of the least impressive structures you ever saw [The Newport Tower] . . . For more than a century now, an occasionally scholarly, often fantastic, usually bitter dispute has ranged about this old round tower. Over 100 books, articles and pamphlets have attempted to throw light on its origin and purpose. The Irish, the Portuguese, the Dutch and even the ancient Druids have been suggested as the builders; but there have been only two theories that hold water—the Norse and the Colonial.[6]

It seems impossible that two such opposite viewpoints could coexist, and the fact that they do, each championed by men of such unswerving conviction that nothing the other side produces can convince them, indicates how little is actually known about the tower.[7]

Pre-Colonial References to the Tower

When the explorer Verrazano landed in Narragansett Bay in 1524, he reported that he found a European-style structure located on the east side of the bay near its mouth, which he called the Norman Villa.[8] He described the people near the tower as the most beautiful and civilized he had met on his expedition; they excelled his own people in size and he called them "white European-Amer-Norse."[9] When the first English settlers arrived in this district in the 1600s, they described a group of fair-haired and blue-eyed natives as "the banished Indians" that were, presumably, the descendants of people described by Verrazano.[10]

A building or settlement of some description is marked on the site of Newport on several early maps. In Mercator's World Map, published in 1569, the tower was clearly recorded and placed in present-day New England, which the geographer called, intriguingly, Norumbega.[11] Another, made by the Dutchman Cornelis Hendriexson before 1614, was later included in his Atlas published in 1635. The original map, found in the Dutch archives of The Hague in 1841,[12] shows the islands and coast of Narragansett Bay, with one small area on the east side of the bay marked "New England," the only part of the map with an English name. On this map, a "Toret" is shown as a small circle on the western end of Newport Island.[13] The Englishman John Smith left a description of this area and a chart of its coast, dated 1614, that accurately charts Narragansett Bay, Mount Hope Bay, and Mount Hope and its Indian village. When passing the future site of Newport, Smith spied some structure there, which he believed was an English settlement, and marked the site on his map.[14] Later, in 1621, he received a letter from "New Plymouth" describing the new colony. Apparently, when he marked its position on his chart, he renamed the original site he had indicated as "an English settlement" as "Old Plymouth."[15]

The structure was described as a "rownd stone towr" by English seafarers in 1629–30,[16] and William Wood mentioned it on a map he derived from coastal observation in 1629. According to Arlington H. Mallery, writing in 1958, Wood's belief that there was an English settlement on the site of Newport in 1629 was not inspired by Smith's map, but by his own sighting of the Newport Tower.[17] In London, records exist of a petition in 1632 by Sir Edmund Plowden[18] to establish a colony in Rhode Island that was to be called New Albion and later became known as Old Plymouth. In this, he describes an existing round tower as an asset for the colony.[19] Neither Sir Edmond nor his heirs ever exploited their successful petition, but a colony was eventually founded in 1636, and the city of Newport in 1639.[20] The tower is mentioned in a property deed dated 1642, which states that the boundary line of the property is "so many lots from the Old Stone Tower."[21] According to Lossing, it was there when the English settlers came, and he believed the natives had no knowledge of its origin,[22] although we have since learned that the elders of the Narragansett Indians have a tradition that states that the tower was constructed by "Green-eyed, fire-haired giants who came in peace, had a battle and then left."[23] So, apart from the oral tradition of the local Native American people, there are eight cartographical or archival references to the tower that all predate colonial settlement.

The architectural style and the nature of the building's construction prove, beyond all dispute, that the Newport Tower was not built by the Native American people of the area or by any of those who built in stone in Central or Southern America. According to Professor Eben Norton Horsford of Harvard, the Newport Tower has the shape and form of a baptistery, and he believes that it indicates a Viking presence in Newport that predates the colonial era by several centuries.[24] In this, he is only echoing comments made in 1879 by R. G. Hatfield, the president of the New York Chapter of the American Institute of Architects, who also claimed that the tower was built by the Viking founders of the Vinland colony.[25] The Professor of Medieval Architecture at Harvard in 1954 was Kenneth J. Conant, who said of this controversial structure: "The actual fabric is medieval while the statistics of the building are Norse. It so happens that the only arch left from medieval Norse construction in Greenland is like that."[26] He is later reported to have said, in reference to the window and doorway of the first floor of the tower: "The semi-circular discharging arch and tympanum are a regular medieval construction, carried down from classical times, and lost sight of by colonial times."[27] The structural engineer Edward Adams Richardson of Bethlehem, Pennsylvania, believed that the tower itself could be questioned to provide information on when it was built. Writing in 1960, he claimed that "The design proves adequate, by modern standards, for a particular structure, while the windows and fireplace form a sophisticated signalling and ship guidance system characteristic of the 14th century."[28] According to Hjalmar R. Holand: "As even a small cannon would be sufficient to shatter the tower, this implies that it was built before 1400, when cannon came into general use."[29]

The Medieval Round Churches

The idea that the Newport Tower may well have been a baptistery or church gains credence when it is compared to Great Hedinge Church in Denmark, St. Olaf's Church at Tonsberg in Norway, the Church of St. Mikael in Schleswig in Denmark, Osterlars Church and Oles-Kirke on Bornholm, Vardsberg Church in Ostergotland in Sweden, the plans of the round church that once stood at Nidros in Norway, and the Church of the Holy Sepulchre in Cambridge, England.[30]

A very similar structure also exists at Lanleff in Brittany, where there stands a round church surrounded by the ruin of a roofed ambulatory. The only difference is that this round church stands on ten columns rather than eight. Originally thought to be Celtic in origin, this church has now been firmly classified as either being built or substantially modified by the Order of the Knights Templar in the twelfth century.[31] Circular churches of similar type were constructed throughout Europe by the Templars,[32] some of which, as we have previously mentioned, can be found on the Danish island of Bjornholm in the Baltic. Every architect who has commented on the Newport Tower describes its design and structure as medieval, and, whether it was built as a church, a lighthouse, or a mill, it is unquestionably pre-Columbian in date. According to Sue Carlson, an architect working for New England Historical Restorations, writing in 1997:

> To all trained architects and architectural historians, the style of the Tower is unquestionably medieval, as indicated by the quality of the rough stone masonry with its round stone columns supporting stone arches awkwardly making a transition to the superstructure above.[33]

European architects and historians who are not bound by the premise that there was no European contact with the Americas before Columbus are virtually unanimous in their conclusion that the tower is of medieval European design. In 1844, Charles Rafn, Professor of

Northern Antiquities in Denmark, "suggested that the tower was a Norse Christian baptistery."[34] Professors Boisseree, Klenze, Tiersch, and Kallenbach, who, in the 1840s, were renowned as authorities in art and what we would now call archaeology, wrote as follows: "Judging from drawings of the Old Stone Mill sent from America, having all declared in favour of the ruin being the remains of a baptismal chapel in the early style of the Middle Ages."[35] In 1951, further reinforcement of the medieval origin of the tower was given by the Danish historian Johannes Brondsted, who stated that "The medievalisms are so conspicuous that, if the tower were in Europe, dating it to the Middle Ages would probably meet with no protest."[36] In 1911, the Swedish architectural historian Hugo Frölen suggested that the tower was Anglo-Norman in design and very similar to Templar churches in Cambridge and Northampton.[37] A similar conclusion was reached by Dr. F. J. Allen, the English architectural historian writing in 1921, who said that the Newport Tower was "Of the shape of the central portion of a 12th century round church, from which the surrounding isle or ambulatory has been removed."[38]

Some academics in North America echo the views of their European colleagues. The Board of Regents of the Smithsonian Institution said, "everything taken into consideration, I am most inclined to regard the Newport Tower as an English watchtower or beacon . . ."[39] A recent comment by author and historian Gunnar Thomson makes a valid comparison between the style of construction used in the Newport Tower and similar buildings in Europe, pointing out that "we do find a similar technique in medieval buildings in the Scottish Isles."[40] Dr. Haraldur Siggurdson, of the University of Rhode Island, stated, after examining the tower, that it was unlikely to be Viking in origin or built before 1200 because of the presence of ancient mortar. However, he went on to say that, nonetheless, the tower had apparently been constructed to Scandinavian design.[41]

In light of the evidence and expert opinion quoted above, it is bizarre that there has been such a sustained effort to date this building as early colonial, when every architectural feature within it clearly proclaims its medieval European design and construction. As we have mentioned, unlike other disputed artifacts, there are eight archival and map references to the Tower that clearly predate the era of colonial settlement on Rhode Island. Just as telling is the fact that there is no evidence whatsoever that stone buildings were constructed in this part of New England in the seventeenth century.[42] It is, therefore, extremely puzzling that academic historians still make a case for the Newport Tower being built by the first colonial settlers—yet that is precisely what many do state with considerable conviction.

The Colonial Theory

There are at least three different schools of thought among those who attempt to explain the origins of this strange building. The first believe that the tower was erected by Governor Benedict Arnold in the seventeenth century; the second are most insistent that it was erected far earlier by Vikings; the third, and smallest, of these groups put forward the theory that it was built by the Portuguese explorer Cortereal. The oft-quoted "first" colonial document to mention the tower was the will of Governor Arnold, dated 24 December 1677. This completely ignores the earlier document of 1642, in which the tower is used as a baseline on a property deed and therefore passes over the embarrassing fact that Benedict Arnold did not come to Newport until eleven years after the tower's first mention in the records. Arnold's will makes two mentions of the tower. In the first, it states "my body I desire and appoint to be buried . . . in or near ye line or path from my dwelling house leading to my stone built windmiln." In a later part of the will, he bequeaths various properties to his wife, Damaris, and specifically includes within them "'my stone built wind miln."[43]

On the foundations of these bare comments, an argument that the Tower is colonial in origin has been constructed. In our view, however, that argument cannot withstand independent and rational examination. Writing in 1811, the American historian George G. Channing stated:

> The problem concerning the origin and purpose of this ancient structure is no nearer solution than it was two hundred years, and more, ago. Speculation of all sorts with regard to it, both here and abroad, have nearly died out; and notwithstanding the allusion in an ancient deed to the ownership of the land, "my stone mill standing thereon," it has never been imagined, that the aforesaid proprietor had anything to do with the construction of this unique pile of stone and mortar. The very style

and grace of the structure preclude the idea that it could have been erected upon almost barren waste, merely to grind Indian corn to powder. Not a vestige of any similar edifice has ever been seen on the continent. The notion that Indian sagacity might, without a precedent, have wrought such a massive and artistic work, is taxing credulity unwarrantably.[44]

Channing is not alone in his scepticism, for a more recent publication makes a claim that is far closer to a dispassionate analysis of the truth: "There is a strong probability, amounting almost to a certainty, that the English colonists found the tower here when they landed and that Governor Arnold modified it to serve the purposes of a windmill."[45]

No one would argue against the pressing need for a windmill in order to grind corn in the early colonies, and indeed colonial records testify to this fact. One of the earliest colonists, Mr. Peter Easton, had the diarist's habit of noting all remarkable events in his pocket book. One specific entry reads: "1663. This year we erected the first windmill."[46] The historian Benson J. Lossing states that this mill was constructed of wood and described its exact location.[47] So important was it to the colony that the general court rewarded Mr. Easton for his contribution to the community and made him a grant of land. The erection of this mill was so noteworthy that it can be checked in the court record, in Lossing's work, and in Easton's diary. It is referred to quite clearly as the first windmill and was built fifteen years before the date of Benedict Arnold's will.

If Easton's mill was the first in the colony, then logic suggests that Arnold's mill must have been built after Easton's and before Arnold made his will—namely, in the fifteen years between 1663 and 1678. Yet, apart from the property deed of 1642, colonial records contain no other mention of the structure whatsoever, much less a note of its erection or even its use prior to Benedict Arnold's will-making.[48] If so much notice was taken of the erection of a wooden mill, why is there no record of the erection of one of such singular form and built of stone in an era when all other buildings in the area were of wood? Is it not odd that there is no record of the building of such a singular and useful facility?

Despite the fact that local people have described the Newport Tower as a windmill for more than 300 years, little realistic analysis has been made to assess whether or not it could be used for any prolonged period as a windmill. The tower is fixed and immobile, yet all known varieties of windmill have one feature in common—the ability to rotate all or part of the building around a vertical axis to bring the vanes into position in varying wind conditions. The Newport Tower does not conform to either condition, as the body of the building is fixed in solid foundations and the upper part (now supposedly vanished) would not be able to rotate because the top of the tower walls do not form a true circle.[49] Furthermore, even if the engineering difficulties of a rotating roof were overcome, the wooden structure required to accomplish this would be far too close to the exit of the two flues from the fireplace within the mill, creating a fire hazard of unacceptable proportions. Benson J. Lossing dismissed the windmill theory in the following terms:

> Its form, its great solidity, and its construction upon columns, forbid the idea that it was originally erected for a mill; and certainly, if a common windmill made of timber was so highly esteemed by the people, as we have seen, the construction of such an edifice, so superior to any dwelling or church in the colony, would have received special attention from the magistrates and historians of the day.[50]

The Chesterton Mill Defense

The arguments put forth by the protagonists of the windmill theory become more and more desperate and strained as they progress. They mounted what they hoped would be their clinching argument in a comparison with the so-called Chesterton Mill in Warwickshire, England. The theory states that the Chesterton Mill, which is also built on columns, was a fully working mill that was known to Benedict Arnold prior to his emigration to the Americas and used by him as a model to construct the mill at Newport. This view, however, ignores certain embarrassing and indisputable facts that completely undermine the argument. First, it assumes that Benedict Arnold was familiar with the Chesterton Mill in England, a theory that flies in the face of the facts, for he was born in the southern part of Somerset well over 100 miles (160 kilometers) from Chesterton.[51] The distance between Chesterton and Ilchester, his hometown, was such that it is extremely unlikely that, under the conditions obtaining at the time, he ever visited Chesterton, and no one has advanced any proof that he did so.

Arnold emigrated to Massachusetts in 1635,[52] came to Newport in 1651, became a freeman in 1653, president of the colony in 1660, and governor in 1663, a position he held until his death. The likelihood that he ever laid eyes on the Chesterton windmill is absolutely nil.[53] The building that later became the Chesterton Mill is extremely well documented, as it was designed by one of England's leading architects of that era, Inigo Jones. It was constructed, not as a windmill, but, according to the family who commissioned it, as a folly or an observatory.[54] It was not completed until 1633, less than two years before Arnold emigrated. The folly was converted to a windmill in 1647, twelve years *after* Arnold left southern England for the Americas, never to return.

Any rational examination of the two buildings known as the Chesterton Mill and the Newport Tower soon discredits the argument that one was the model for the other. The Chesterton Mill is a classically designed and crafted building, as befits the reputation of its architect. It is built in finely dressed ashlar stone, superbly proportioned, with a quality of build that reflects the taste of its aristocratic patron. It is 29 feet in height from its foundations to the top of the masonry, of circular construction, 23 feet in diameter at the outside face of the stonework of the pillars, and has two floors.[55] There are six pillars supporting the structure, with an arched outer and inner face and absolutely straight edges to the stonework on the pillars' sides. Being completely circular and built of solid well-crafted masonry, it easily takes the stresses of the revolving mill head that surmounts it in a way that would be impossible for the Newport Tower. The architectural detail of the Chesterton Mill blatantly suggests its seventeenth-century construction, while the Newport Tower—with its rubble-built, Romanesque arches, eight round pillars, and uneven construction—quite obviously predates the Chesterton building by several centuries. The solidity of the Chesterton Mill is such that it would easily withstand the stresses, strains, and vibrations inherent in its function as a mill. The structure of the Newport Tower, on the other hand, quite obviously would not—which may go a long way to explaining why, although it is called the Old Stone Mill, its suggested use for this function was so brief or nonexistent that it was never noted by diarists or chroniclers of Arnold's day and is, therefore, purely a matter of conjecture.

More Pre-Columbian Evidence

According to Governor Gibbs, who was governor of Rhode Island in 1819, the exterior of the Newport Tower was covered with white hard stucco and, according to Lossing,

> It was originally covered within and without with plaster, and the now rough columns with mere indications of capitals and bases of the Doric form were handsomely wrought, the whole structure exhibiting taste and beauty. . . . Of its existence prior to the English emigration to America there is now but little doubt . . . and if the structure is really ante-colonial and perhaps ante-Columbian, its history is surely worthy of investigation.[56]

While we concur with these sentiments without reservation, we are duty-bound to point out that every attempt to publish the results of examinations of the tower has resulted in more controversy, not less, and that no suggested origin for it has been accepted by a majority of those who have expressed an interest in its history. Professor Rafn, who was the secretary of the Royal Society of Northern Antiquities in Copenhagen, claims that the old mill was built by Scandinavians or Northmen in the eleventh century.[57] While Professor Rafn's other conclusions that the Vikings discovered Massachusetts and Rhode Island in the tenth century and established a colony there in the eleventh are widely accepted, his views on the Newport Tower have simply generated as much controversy as those of anyone else.

The author Hjalmar Holand, writing in 1953, quotes Dr. Frölen, who claimed "the Newport Tower has undoubtedly been the inner rotunda of a carefully built round church."[58] The authors Hjalmar Holand and Andrew Sinclair[59] have come to the same conclusion and go on to claim that one important factor in both the choice of site and the erection of the tower was its alternative use as a watchtower or beacon. In light of these comments, it is interesting to note that the door faces southwest over the inner harbor, while its entrance and two windows, one facing south and the other east, look out upon the ocean. The north wall, which faces inland, the direction from which Native Americans might come, is unbroken, which Holand takes to indicate that the occupants of the tower had no fear of attack from the landward side, but were concerned about "the safety of friends out at sea." The windows aligned with the fireplace indicate its use as a beacon, which again has been used as an explanation for the entire tower being covered in white stucco. The annual report of the Board of Regents of the Smithsonian Institution for 1953, quoted earlier, states that the fact "that the tower is known to have been used as a mill tells us nothing of its original purpose."

A Portuguese Origin for the Tower

The third theory of origin for the Newport Tower was proposed by Dr. Manuel Luciano da Silva, a physician on the staff of the Bristol County Medical Center in Rhode Island. Writing in a medical journal in March 1967,[60] da Silva claimed that the Newport Tower closely resembled the Rotunda of the Monastery of Tomar in central Portugal.[61] Da Silva is indeed correct when he mentions that round churches were built throughout Europe by returning crusaders, especially the Knights Templar, in the style of the Church of the Holy Sepulchre of Jerusalem. The monastery of Tomar was built as the headquarters for the Templars in Portugal and later became the training center for all navigators and missionaries working under the direction of the Knights of Christ, who succeeded the Knights Templar after the suppression of that order. The rotunda, or *charola*, of the monastery has, like the Newport Tower, eight columns and eight arches, giving evidence of an octagonal geometry.[62]

After the Templars in Portugal became the Knights of Christ, Prince Henry the Navigator became the newly formed Order's third grandmaster. Under his direction, the eight-pointed *croix pattée* of the Templars was carried to many continents throughout the era of Portuguese exploration and discovery. According to da Silva, two Portuguese explorers from the Order, Gaspar and Miguel Cortereal, spent approximately nine years in the area of Narragansett Bay evangelizing the natives. He also states that this gave sufficient time to build the Newport Tower and claims that they were most probably motivated to do this by their devotion to their *alma mater*, the Monastery of Tomar.[63]

Da Silva was scathing about the colonial theories of origin for the tower, particularly as he believed that "The feeble locking columns of the Newport Tower could never sustain the tremors and stresses of use as a windmill."[64] He was equally dismissive of the Viking theories of origin, claiming, quite correctly, that Leif Erikson could not have been inspired by the Holy Sepulchre in Jerusalem, as the First Crusade did not take place for a another 100 years. He ruled out Bishop Gnupsson as the architect on the reasonable grounds that he, too, would have been unaware of the architecture of Jerusalem.[65]

Having reviewed the various theories and some of the attitudes of their various protagonists, now let's examine the results of the more prolonged examinations of this puzzling and disputatious building.

Chapter 11

SCHOLARS PUZZLE
OVER THE TOWER

IN LIGHT OF THE MANY CONFLICTING THEORIES regarding the origin of the Newport Tower and the scholarly disputes that have accompanied them, it would be nice to record that a dispassionate and official archaeological or scientific evaluation of the building settled the matter once and for all. Our opinion, however, is that the first official archaeological excavation was marred by bias, flawed methodology, and unwarrantable assumptions. The archaeologist William S. Godfrey, Jr. published his report on his investigation (conducted between 1948 and 1950) in 1951, partially in fulfillment of the requirements for a Ph.D.[1] He entitled this strange document (clearly an example of prejudice prior to investigation) *Digging a Tower and Laying a Ghost*. His bias in the dispute is vividly demonstrated by quotations from the first chapter of his report: ". . . he [Benedict Arnold] purchased some of his Newport property, specifically the section on which he later built his house and the stone mill, the year before he moved[2] . . . At some period before 1677 Arnold built the Old Stone Mill."[3] Godfrey made these statements despite the fact that, three lines later, he also wrote "Indeed, the only contemporary reference that connects Arnold to the mill is his own will."[4]

Godfrey's partiality becomes even more obvious when he writes, "Means reviews the writings on the Tower with great care, but fails to find any Newporter of the period, or of a later period, for that matter, who had lost his head to the Norse."[5] Furthermore, Godfrey suggests that William Gibbs, who was governor of Rhode Island in 1799, supported the Viking theory for political and social expediency: "It would seem that, whatever he [Gibbs] privately thought, it would be expedient for him to espouse the Norse theory."[6] It would seem that our erstwhile twentieth-century archaeologist was also a gifted clairvoyant, endowed with sufficient psychological skills to enable him to analyze the thought processes of a long-dead governor of the state with uncanny accuracy.

While we give Godfrey full marks for dismissing the Chesterton Mill theory,[7] the rest of his report is less credible. Writing of Means, whose work was published in 1941, Godfrey states: "he managed to change from a moderately impartial student to a violent protagonist of the Norse theory. Every sentence in his work must be examined for bias and frequently for malice."[8] The bulk of Godfrey's report is not taken up with an account of the actual archaeology of his digs, but by personal attacks on those who support views other than his own, in which he uses words like "crackpots,"[9] "pygmies,"[10] "zealots,"[11] or "the lunatic fringe"[12] to describe his opponents. By using terminology of this nature, Godfrey merely reinforces the impression that the report itself is the work of a biased and partisan protagonist. He states as a categorical fact that "there is absolutely no proof of the existence of the Mill until 1677,"[13] and ignores all eight previous references that might apply, including those of Verrazano, the Plowden document, and the various early maps. He claims that "the tower is unique, . . . the archaeologists, . . . were never able to find all these features in one building."[14] Yet any reasoned examination of the architecture of round churches in Europe, particularly those in Portugal, Brittany, England, and Scandinavia, many of which have been mentioned earlier, gives the lie to this sweeping statement.

Despite two years of heavily publicized excavation, and the acquisition of both a reputation and a Ph.D., we actually learn little as result of Godfrey's two-year study. According to James P. Whittal, Jr. of the Early Sites Research Society, who worked on the tower for over twenty-five years, no artifacts recovered by Godfrey can lead to a firm conclusion as to the date and origin of the structure.[15] If the date of the tower were judged solely on the evidence of Godfrey's excavated artifacts, a time frame of 1750 to 1800 would be feasible, which contradicts the documentary evidence that the tower was standing in 1677.[16] Even Godfrey himself had the honesty to conclude that "the tantalising fragments of our ancestor's culture . . . do not tell us when, why or by whom the tower was built."[17] Yet, having admitted that, he goes on to make the following statement: "Our excavations set the date of the tower's construction definitely between the dates of the founding of Newport (1639) and 1677 when it is first mentioned historically."[18] He signally fails, however, to produce one shred of evidence, archaeological or archival, in support of this argument. He goes on to claim: "On the other hand, there is very little probability that Benedict built his Tower as a mill . . . the tower mill form, as contrasted to the smock, post and composite forms, was not common in England until the beginning of the 18th century, ..."[19] Indeed, he admits in his final paragraph that, "This study has strayed far from 'pure' archaeology."[20] Truth indeed!

A Dispassionate Examination

Less than four years after Godfrey completed his report, his tower excavations were reexamined by the structural engineer Arlington Mallery, who was assisted by the City of Newport engineers, Gardner Easton and John Howieson.[21] Mallery made no statements in favor of any of the three major schools of thought regarding the origin of the tower; in a spirit of true scientific analysis, he simply reported what he found.

> We also dug plaster from under the bottom stones of the foundation and found that every joint and opening in the foundation was carefully and thoroughly caulked with refill clay containing particles or fragments of plaster to prevent water seepage. Since all that plaster except possibly a few fragments had to come from the superstructure of the tower, it could not have been placed inside the joints and crevices of the present foundation unless the foundation had been installed as underpinning after the tower was built.[22]

> The Tower was probably underpinned in 1675. The quantity of plaster fragments in the excavation indicates that the plaster stucco had so far disintegrated that the Tower must have been more than 300 years old when it was underpinned.[23]

In his opinion, the additional architectural support to the bases of the pillars had been done to strengthen the tower prior to its alleged use as a windmill. This dispassionate and highly professional analysis leads us to believe that it was originally constructed in the latter part of the fourteenth century. No one from any side of the dispute on the

*Figure 13. Arlington Mallery's excavations of the
foundation of the Newport Tower.*

Newport Tower has yet produced any evidence to refute, or even cast reasonable doubt upon, Mallery's assessment.

The Carbon-Dating Controversy

In 1992, a team of researchers from Denmark and Finland led by Heinemeier and Junger took samples of mortar from the Newport Tower for testing. For reasons that are far from clear, while eight core samples were taken, one from each pillar, only those from pillars 6 and 7 were tested. The core sample that was taken from the wall of the fireplace at a level of 420 cm was rejected in analysis for reasons that were not disclosed in the copy of the report that we have seen.[24] Surface samples were taken from the plaster on pillar 8 that gave a range of dates of 1550 to 1770, and a surface sample from plaster in the chimney flue was also taken that gave a range from 1680 to 1810. Two core samples from pillar 6 were tested; sample 1 gave a range of dates from 1750 to 1930, and sample 2, from 1510 to 1640. Therefore, the overall dating of the core sample from pillar 6 ranges from 1510 to 1930. Of the core samples taken from pillar 7, several were rejected arbitrarily, four were tested and gave a range of dates from 1410 to 1855. Even to the untrained eye, carbon-dating results from four samples drawn from two of eight pillars indicating a range from 1410 to the 1930s defy logic. It certainly raises serious questions about the reliability of carbon-dating techniques in mortar in general, and in this investigation in particular.

We are not alone in questioning these results. Several scientists of the highest repute have also made highly critical comments about them. The analytical chemist, James L. Guthrie, condemned the results in the following words:

> The plaster dating results of Heinemeier and Junger are not to be taken seriously because the small number of samples tested, the poor precision of the methods revealed by the only test run in duplicate, and by the unwarranted assumption that all of the mortar and plaster is of the same age. Plaster and mortar applied over hundreds of years during known episodes of repair and reinforcement complicate the analysis, and the reported results suggest to me that the samples were mixtures of carbonates of various ages. The possibility that any of the specimens was a pure sample of the original mortar seems remote. Other things bother me, such as a preference for the more recent dates obtained from the first fraction of the evolved carbon dioxide, the apparent belief that a single ambiguous result from a nearby 17th century house is an adequate control, and the use of a calibration that may not be appropriate for the New England coast. . . . The plaster samples seem to be a mix of older and newer plaster, and there is no evidence that any is from the date of construction. Errors, especially the adsorption of modern carbon dioxide would tend to date samples closer to the present than to the date of mixing.[25]

This matter of slow diffusion of carbon dioxide through the mortar, making some samples appear younger than they really are, is a variable quantity, as it may take several hundred years for carbon dioxide to reach depths of 20 cm.[26] This point was expanded in some detail by Dr. Alan Watchman, a geological dating expert of Data-Roche Watchman, Inc., who wrote:

> The data in table 1 of the article can be used to suggest an age of about 550 radio-carbon years might be obtained from

measuring the more acid resistant carbon in the mortar—taking into consideration possible diffusion, particle size, crystallisation and fractionation effects. If my hypothesis is correct, then the calibrated age for the mortar would be about 1400 A.D. [27]

Professor Andre J. de Bethune, Professor of Chemistry at Boston College, made the most scathing criticisms of the carbon dating of the mortar of the Newport Tower. Professor de Bethune made several criticisms of a highly technical nature that tend to invalidate the thinking and the methodology used in the tests. He echoed the criticisms we have quoted above and stated "there are serious doubts in my mind concerning the mortar testing at the tower. . . . the timing yielded by the tests is close to the time that Governor Arnold . . . referred to the tower in his last will and testament. But does this date truly give us the age of the tower?"[28] Professor de Bethune goes on to explain that this date could only be valid if we could be absolutely certain that, in the intervening period, there had been no exchange of carbon dioxide between the carbonate in the mortar and carbon dioxide gas in the atmosphere. When wood or fiber samples are tested, such exchange ceases when the tree or plant dies. But with a porous ionic solid, such as mortar, an exchange of CO_2 molecules at the gas-solid interface does tend to continue, especially in a damp climate such as New England. While such gas-solid exchanges are extremely slow, we know that, in this instance, we are dealing with a time scale in excess of three centuries, and this continuing exchange would have rejuvenated the mortar, so to speak, with respect to its C^{14} content. With this possibility in mind, Dr. de Bethune states that "an earlier origin for our Newport Tower—Portuguese or Viking—cannot be excluded, even in the face of painstaking C^{14} analyses."[29] Professor de Bethune is emeritus Professor of Chemistry at Boston College and a close colleague of Professor Willard F. Libby, who devised carbon dating in the first place, and therefore his considered professional opinion cannot be easily dismissed.

A Comparative Study across Two Continents

The most prolonged and dispassionate examination of the archaeology of the Newport Tower to date was made by the late James P. Whittal, Jr. of the Early Sites Research Society of Lowell, Massachusetts. Whittal worked as an archaeologist for twenty-five years prior to his untimely death in 1998, and spent the last six and a half years of his life work-ing on the Newport Tower. Unlike Godfrey, Whittal made no *a priori* assumptions that the tower was unique and spent a considerable amount of time and resources examining buildings of similar age and construction throughout Northern Europe. He left an archive devoted to the Newport Tower and related subjects that is far too detailed to be included in a work of this nature, but he also left us with a useful sum-mary and conclusions that we can use as a sound basis for assessing the true origins of the much-disputed structure. Because of its great value and relevance, we include it below in its entirety.

THE ARCHITECTURE OF THE NEWPORT STONE TOWER
by James P. Whittal 1997

The Newport Stone Tower in Touro Park in Newport, Rhode Island was constructed in the style of Norman-Romanesque architecture, inspired by the architecture of the Holy Sepulchre in Jerusalem brought back to Europe by returning Crusaders. In its own unique style, the tower was further influenced by a combination of the architecture of temples of the Templars, the round churches of Scandinavia, and local architectural tradi-tions from whence the builders came. Architectural features found within the construction of the tower would date it in the broad range of 1150 to 1400 A.D. However, some specific fea-tures limit it to a period in the late 1300's. In the course of six years of research I have found the best parallels in the tower's architectural features exist in the Northern Isles of Scotland which were under Norse control during the time frame men-tioned. Other features relating the tower to Scandinavian round churches and Templar buildings have been published by Hjalmar R. Holand, Philip A. Means, and F. J. Allen.

The following are some of my conditions to date.

1 - The architecture of the tower was preplanned. The concept was not conceived on site and built in haste.

2 - The architecture is completely involved with sacred geometry.

3 - The masons were completely familiar with the material on hand with which to construct the tower.

4 - The tower was aligned to east and each pillar (8) was placed on a cardinal point in the manner after the Templars. It was not constructed using a magnetic compass. Today designated pillar 1 is 3 degrees west of the North Pole star.

5 - The tool marks created in the dressing out of the stone work can directly be related to tools manufactured before 1400. These marks are unique and unknown when compared to tool marks noted in colonial stonework.

6 - After extensive comparison with ancient units of measurement, we have found that the unit of measurement for the construction of the tower is best suited to the Scottish Ell or the Norwegian short Men. A photogrammetric survey made in 1991 showed that the unit of measurement for the tower was 23.35cm, which supports the idea that either the Scottish Ell or the Alen was used in constructing the tower. The English foot wasn't used.

7 - The single and double splay windows have prototypes in Medieval Europe and the Northern Isles of Scotland in the 1300's in churches and the Bishop's Palace in Orkney.

8- The arch and lintel design noted in the tower is to be found in Orkney, Shetland, and Scandinavia round church architecture before 1400.

9 - I have found in extensive research, that the triangle keystone feature of the arches in the tower only seemed to have been found in buildings in Orkney, Shetland, Greenland (1 example), and to a very limited degree in other buildings in the Scottish Isles (3), and in Ireland (2).

10 - Built-in niches in the tower have parallel examples in Medieval construction in Orkney and Shetland. Feature basically unknown in New England architecture except in some post 1700 stone chambers.

11 - The plinth, pillar, capital, arch architecture of the tower

has no prototype in New England Colonial architecture, yet is found in Kirkwall Cathedral in Orkney.

12 - The design of the fireplace with its double flues dates to the 1300's and was out of fashion after the 1400's. There are prototypes of this design in Scotland. Research has indicated the probability that the fireplace and its relationship to west facing window was used as a lighthouse and probable signal station. The same can be said for the windows on the third level.

13 - The walls were covered with a plaster stucco finish both interior and exterior. Stucco finishing started in the 1200's and is a feature known in Orkney and Shetland.

14 - The probable layout and design of the floor joists with corbels has parallels in Medieval Scotland.

15 - Probable first floor entry by ladder through the window/entry 3. A trait found in the Round Churches of Scandinavia.

16 - Some architectural features in the tower have been organised to utilise astronomical alignments as a calendar event. Some of the alignments fall on Holy days of the Norse and Knights Templar. There are prototypes in Northern Europe.

17 - Probability of an ambulatory around the tower (planned for but not necessarily built). Examples in Templar construction and round churches.

18 - The tower is located approximately the same latitude as Rome. This would make it an ideal reference point for exploration and mapping.

19 - There is no architectural parallel in Colonial New England for the Newport Tower and its specific architectural features.

20 - I suggest that the tower was built as a church, observatory, lighthouse, a datum zero point for future exploration in the New World.

This prolonged comparative study of the tower, like many of the earlier investigations, also focused on the odd dimensions of the building. Measured in feet and inches, the only linear measure known to the Colonial settlers, the tower displays some rather peculiar anomalies.

1 - the diameter of the pillars = 3 feet 1 inch.

2 - width of wall at arch keystone 1 = 3 feet 1 inch.

3 - interior diameter of tower, pillar to pillar = 18 feet 6 inches.

4 - exterior diameter of tower at pillars = 24 feet 8 inches.

5 - width of wall at arch keystones 2–8 = 2 feet 3¾ inches.

6 - distance from south side of fireplace to niche 1 = 1 foot 6½ inches.

7 - distance across inside of capital = 3 feet 10¼ inches.

8 - distance across outside of capital = 2 feet 3¾ inches.

The Vital Standard of Measure

Investigators have tried to marry Whittal's dimensions to the Norse foot, the megalithic yard, and linear measures of Basque or Portuguese origin.[30] None of these approaches resulted in a satisfactory answer to the problem. The archaeologist, Godfrey, tried to duck the issue by suggesting that the measurements only appear bizarre because they do not include the outer layer of stucco that once covered the building inside and out.[31] This argument, however, regretfully ignores the precision attained by masons and bricklayers from medieval times to the present. Moreover, in 1997, the architect Sue Carlson wrote "It is inconceivable that English builders with English tools and rulers would *not* have used English feet as their unit of measure."[32]

The one measure that is peculiar to the Newport Tower, which was discovered by Whittal and confirmed by the historian Andrew Sinclair, is the Scottish ell.[33] This measure, which equals 37 inches or 93.98 cm, when applied to the measurements of the list above gives the following answers:

1 - the diameter of the pillars = 1 Scottish ell (SE)

2 - width of wall at arch keystone 1 = 1 SE.

3 - interior diameter of tower, pillar to pillar = 6 SE.

4 - exterior diameter of tower at pillars = 8 SE.

5 - width of wall at arch keystones 2–8 = ¾ SE.

6 - distance from south side of fireplace to niche 1 = ½ SE.

7 - distance across inside of capital = 1¼ SE.

8 - distance across outside of capital = ¾ SE.[34]

Whittal's examination of the tower is the most detailed and meticulous examination of the fabric of the structure conducted to date. It even extended to the tool marks on the individual stones of the construction. It is worthwhile to use extracts from Whittal's own words to emphasize the importance of his discoveries:

> The tool marks found scattered about the stonework of the Newport Stone Tower, as far as I know, are unique in New England. Over the last 25 years I have been involved in researching New England stone structures, and I have yet to see any tool marks like the type to be found in the Newport Tower. This is a very important point as it rules out the possibility that the structure was constructed between 1639, when Newport was founded, and 1677 when the Tower is noted in a historical record.
>
> This type of tool mark was made from dressing down the stonework after construction to even off the surface before a stucco mortar coating was applied. The technique does not date the construction of the Tower as its application is lost in the annals of time. The technique was to take a round chisel and place it against the stone where the mason wished to dress out the surface. Hand held, the chisel was struck with a mallet, thus fracturing off a spall, leaving behind a small oval shaped indentation.

It is also possible that a "slate axe" was employed. However, I would rule it out, because one does not have the control over the blow which would be possible with a chisel. . . . the marks are quite consistent, thus we may presume that the same tool, or type of tool, was used throughout the Tower to dress the surface.[35]

Whittal concluded his report with the proviso that, while there were other traits, features, and concepts that still require serious study, for the moment at least, in his opinion, the prime candidate for builder of the Newport Tower is Henry St. Clair, Earl of Orkney and Shetland, and it is more than likely that it was constructed under his guidance in the latter part of the fourteenth century.

Whittal's conclusions must be evaluated in the context of all the opinions quoted in this chapter and the previous one—Verrazano's description of a "Norman Villa" on this site in 1524,[36] Mercator's marking of this area as Norumbega in 1569,[37] the turret shown on the Hiendrixson map of 1614,[38] and the reference in the Smith chart of 1614—which all indicate that the tower has a long recorded history that considerably predates the colonial era. According to Arlington Mallery, writing in 1958, the English settlement marked on the Smith map recorded the Newport Tower,[39] which is also explicitly mentioned in the Plowden petition dated 1632.[40] The tower was again marked, as a "toret," on the Blau map published in Amsterdam in 1635,[41] and, according to the Narragansett Indians, was constructed by "green-eyed, fire-haired giants,"[42] not colonial settlers who did not reach this area until 1636. The first documented mention from colonial times is in a property deed dated 1642.[43]

Professors Boisseree, Klenze, Tiersch, and Kallenbach all stated that the tower was the remains of a baptismal chapel in the early style of the Middle Ages.[44] The medieval theme was again echoed by Brondsted, writing in 1951, who said, "The medievalisms are so conspicuous that were it in Europe dating it to the Middle Ages would meet with no protest."[45] The architectural historians Hugo Frölen and F. J. Allen both described the Newport Tower as in the style of a twelfth-century church,[46] while the Board of Regents of the Smithsonian Institute claimed in 1953 that it had much in common with an English watchtower or beacon.[47] The pro-Arnold school of

Figure 14. Stonework at Eine Hallow, Orkney, closely approximates that of the Newport Tower.

origin was dismissed by the American historian George G. Channing, who stated ". . . it has never been imagined, that the aforesaid proprietor [Benedict Arnold] had anything to do with the construction of this unique pile of stone and mortar. . . . Not a vestige of any similar edifice has ever been seen on the continent."[48] The authorities who

Figure 15. Stonework at the Newport Tower.

have compared the Newport Tower to European round churches of the Templar tradition are too numerous to list here, but many have been mentioned earlier. The New England architect Sue Carlson states that, in her opinion, the tower is unquestionably medieval.[49]

It is obvious, therefore, that the vast majority of the experts who have studied the tower agree it is pre-colonial in origin and of distinctive

Figure 16. Square window at Eine Hallow, Orkney.

Figure 17. Square window at the Newport Tower.

medieval construction. The arguments to the contrary are summarized by the two disputed reports made in the latter part of the twentieth century. The first was the highly biased and prejudicial report of the limited archaeological excavations conducted by Godfrey that, on his own admission, strayed far from pure archaeology. If one attempts to date the tower from Godfrey's report, the only feasible date is 1750, which is more than 100 years after its first appearance in the colonial records and 200 years after being recorded on the Verrazano map. Arlington Mallery's examination of the foundations some years after Godfrey's dig stated quite dispassionately that the tower had been underpinned in 1675 when it was already some 300 years old.

The second dissenting examination was the flawed attempt at carbon dating the mortar. These results were dismissed by Dr. Guthrie, Alan Watchman, and Professor de Bethune, who worked for several years on the Manhattan Project with Professor Libby, the developer of carbon-dating techniques in the first place.

The original controversy over the origins of the Newport Tower was a three-cornered battle between the pro-colonialists, the vociferous supporters of the Norse theory, and a small but vocal minority supporting the Portuguese explorer, Cortereal. In light of the evidence already detailed, we can dismiss the colonial theory. Earlier, we cited expert opinion, which stated that, as the tower used mortar, it was not purely a Viking structure, but could be a post-twelfth-century Norse construction. We have no record in the sagas or in Norse tradition of any settlement in Vinland that was sufficiently prolonged to have constructed the tower, with one exception—that of the expedition of Paul Knutson in the late 1350s. As there are no extant records of the Knutson voyage, we can make no claim that he was the architect or builder of the tower, but the possibility that he may have erected some form of stone-built settlement in the vicinity must be considered. While we have no doubt that the Newport Tower was heavily influenced by Norse tradition, however, the predominant stylistic signature within its architecture is undoubtedly the sacred geometry of the Knights Templar.

This leaves only two possibilities: that it was built by Cortereal following the style of the Monastery of Tomar or by Earl Henry St. Clair in the Templar tradition, his workmen using their native Orcadian rubble-building skills to good effect. We believe that the balance of probability weighs heavily in favor of the tower being constructed during one of the St. Clair expeditions to North America. The question that remains is, which expedition?

The Tower that Henry Built

According to Hjalmar R. Holand:

> It must have been a colossal task to build the Newport Tower without the aid of beasts of burden. Five thousand cubic feet of soil had to be excavated and later refilled. A lime kiln was necessary, and the construction of the building requiring more than a million pounds of stone, sand and lime. The builders must, therefore, have had plenty of time at their disposal.[50]

From this, we can deduce two things. First, that, in all probability, the tower was constructed during Henry's second expedition to the North American continent, as we know that the Mi'qmaq he took to Europe returned home within one year, which probably included Henry's first visit to Rhode Island. Therefore, the timeframe necessary for constructing the tower could only have been available on his subsequent voyage. Second, extensive archaeological excavations in close proximity to the tower should reveal artifacts left by the builders in the course of their construction work. Sadly, no such excavations have as yet taken place. When we remember that Henry came to Rhode Island looking for the earlier settlement of Norumbega, it is highly desirable that the area be excavated to learn the true history of the Newport Tower and of pre-Columbian Viking settlements on the North American continent. One artifact found nearby, an amulet excavated at Touro Park in May 1995, has been compared by Jim Whittal to similar ones from Shetland, which again fits the scenario of the voyage to America made by the St. Clair Earl of Orkney and Shetland.[51] The pressing need for further excavations was emphasized by the results of a ground-penetrating radar survey conducted in Touro Park in 1994.

The Ground Scan

Touro Park has been in existence since 1854; prior to that, the site had been a hayfield. Colonial records indicate that the only known structure located on the site is the controversial Newport Tower. Since

Arlington Mallery's examination of the foundations of the tower in 1956, there had been no subsurface archaeological investigation in the park. A preliminary ground-penetrating radar survey was conducted in 1992 in the immediate vicinity of the tower by Vincent Murphy, President of the Weston Geophysical Company, and Ken Boltz, a geophysicist. This preliminary survey was observed by the Boston City Archaeologist, Steven Pendry, and Jim Whittal.[52] This limited investigation revealed anomalies that warranted further study, and the Early Sites Research Society undertook to carry this out with the further cooperation of the Weston Geophysical Company. Permission was granted by David F. Roderick, Mayor of Newport, and cooperation was obtained from Susan Cooper, the Director of Recreation and Public Service for the City of Newport.[53]

The survey of the site was conducted by the Early Sites Research Society of Rowley, Massachusetts, and the Weston Geophysical Company of Westboro, Massachusetts. The site work was directed by James P. Whittal and the ground scan by Mark Stoughton of Weston Geophysical.[54] The work revealed 181 anomalies, which were duly listed and noted, in the 32,800 square feet (approximately 3,000 square meters) site.[55] The subsurface depth of the anomalies varies from two to ten feet (0.6–3 meters), but not all of them have archaeological potential, as some may be reflections of drains and electrical systems serving the park. According to the report:

> The Newport Tower does not exist in a void. It has a very definitive relationship with the area that surrounds it; Touro Park. The construction of any structure leaves some evidence of the activity in the immediate area, a dropped artifact, or material waste. Locating the area where the binding mortar was mixed would be of major importance. The mortar would not be mixed "clean." Some datable organic substance could be retrieved. Certainly, the groundscan has opened the possibilities of some interesting archaeological evidence relating to the area surrounding the Newport Tower, and perhaps even shedding some further information on the origin and date of the Tower's construction. Out of 181 anomalies there has to be something that has a direct relationship to the construction of the Tower. The high count seems at odds with the site being

only a hayfield. Regardless of various theories put forth today, there is no solid verification as to the origin or date. The best endorsement for an ancient origin is its architectural features which would be "exotic" to a Colonial New England origin.

Thanks to the Early Sites Research Society and the Weston Geophysical Company, the City of Newport, the Newport Historical Society, Redwood Library, the Friends of Touro Park, and the *Senatus Populusque Novae Portiae* of Newport, all of whom cooperated with the ground-radar survey, the 181 anomalies are now plotted with precision. Prior to the death of Jim Whittal, the Early Sites research team recommended a limited number of nondestructive two-inch (5 cm) core probings of some of the more promising anomalies to determine whether a deeper investigation of these was warranted to establish their precise archaeological character. That this investigation should take place is not simply a matter of interest to the citizens of Newport, but to all students of history in Europe and the Americas who are committed to a search for the truth of our history.

PART III

HONORING
THE LEGACY

Chapter 12

REVIVING THE
HISTORICAL RECORD

EARL HENRY ST. CLAIR AND ANTONIO ZENO came from different branches of Rex Deus: Antonio was a member of an aristocratic
Venetian family with a strong maritime tradition, and Henry St. Clair,
a Scots earl of Viking descent. Both families had a long and sustained
relationship with the Order of the Knights Templar throughout its existence. As we indicated earlier, Henry and Carlo had ample time and
opportunity during the latter part of the fourteenth century to plan
their exploratory expedition in search of new lands for settlement and
trade. Their voyages to the New World are indelibly commemorated in
stone on both sides of the Atlantic. These perpetual mementos take
widely differing forms at a variety of sites, but all point to the truth of
the momentous achievements of these remarkable men and their crews.

The Westford Knight and Newport Tower are mirrored on the
European side by stone carvings in Rosslyn Chapel in Scotland and by
a substantial stone plaque on the outside of one of the many Zeno
palaces in Venice. The carvings in Rosslyn Chapel, which was founded
in 1446 and completed in 1482, ten years prior to Columbus's voyage
in 1492, consist of depictions of maize, aloe cactus, sassandras, albidium, trillium grandilorum, and quercus nigra, all native American
plants that were completely unknown in Europe at the time of the
chapel's construction. These carvings, commissioned by Henry's grandson, Earl William St. Clair, were probably based upon drawings of
Native American plants brought back to Europe by Henry and Antonio
at the end of their first voyage.

Figure 18. Detail of aloe cactus at Rosslyn Chapel, Scotland.

Figure 19. Detail of maize at Rosslyn Chapel, Scotland.

A stone plaque on the outside of a Zeno palace erected by the Council of the City of Venice commemorates the North Atlantic explorations of Nicolo and Antonio as a matter of fact in the following terms:

A

NICOLO E ANTONIO ZENO
NEL SECOLO DECIMOQARTO
NAVIGATORI DECIMOQUARTO
DEI MARI NORDICI

PER DECRETO DEL COMMUNE
MDCCCLXXXI[1]

The voyages commemorated in these disparate ways include Nicolo's original exploration of Greenland, Henry and Antonio's first voyage to the North American mainland, and their subsequent return to Europe. Their eventual return to North America can reasonably be deduced from the oral tradition of the Mi'qmaq Grand Chiefs, which clearly states that one of their tribe was taken to Europe by Henry and returned within a year. The fact that the second voyage was prolonged and well-equipped can be inferred from both the time scale and difficulties of construction of its specific memorial, the Newport Tower on Rhode Island.

The St. Clair/Zeno voyages were exploratory in nature, but were most certainly not voyages of "discovery," for they replicated the sailing instructions contained within the Viking sagas and deliberately followed in the footsteps of Henry's Viking ancestors, who, as we have shown, were relative latecomers in the long and complex story of European trans-Atlantic exploration. Indeed, we submit that it was arrogant in the extreme for any European of their era or later to claim to have discovered a continent that had been visited so frequently over the many centuries since the writers of Rome and Greece clearly recorded its existence. This long history of contact with the Americas gives rise to two inevitable questions: Why did Columbus get the credit for the "discovery" of America and why did the exploits of Henry, Antonio, and their predecessors signally fail to attract any recognition whatsoever? These questions are particularly relevant when we consider that the much-vaunted "discoverer" of America, the mysterious figure known as Christopher Columbus, *never* actually set foot on the North American mainland.

The answers to these questions are part of a complex web of inter-related and sometimes disparate events that, in combination, have created a fog of obfuscation that masks the real truth. One significant factor in this complicated equation is academia's choice to ignore the hard evidence of pre-Columbian contact between Europe and the New World. However, in fairness, other circumstances have combined in a powerful manner to hide the truth. These include the mystery sur-rounding the eventual fate of Earl Henry St. Clair, the death of Antonio Zeno in 1405 shortly after his return to Venice, the complex story of the writing and publication of the Zeno manuscript, and the contro-versy that has surrounded it since its publication. All these circum-stances, exacerbated by the adulation accorded to Columbus in the nineteenth century, culminated in the establishment of the American national holiday known as Columbus Day.

Doubtful Accounts of Henry's Death

The actions of Henry St. Clair are recorded many times in the docu-ments of the period in Norway, Scotland, and England, despite the fact that the bulk of the Orcadian archives were lost at sea many years later in the time of King James III. There is, however, considerable mystery surrounding the circumstances of Henry's death. It is not mentioned anywhere in the state papers of Scotland or Norway, and the few ref-erences to it in other documents are decidedly puzzling.

When we were conducting our research in the National Library of Scotland, we came across this obscure reference to Henry's death in the Advocates Library.

> . . . and deit Erile of Orchadie for the defence of the Cuntre was slaine thair cruellie be his Inimies.
>
> . . . of the month of June in the year of our Lord ane hun-dred 4 and 40 sex. [the date of the document].
>
> Translated out of Latin into Scots by me Deine Thomas Gwle Munk of Newbothile at the request of ane honorable man William Santclar Barroun of Roslin, Pentland and Herbershire. An Dom 1554.

Underneath the signature was the following annotation:

> The true date of this paper appears (tho' erroneously) to have been 1406 instead of 1446, the 40 being put with different ink upon the margin, and whereas the spelling here very often varies in the same words, it is so too in the original translation from which this is exactly copied.[2]

The sentences of this extract appear verbatim in two other supposed accounts of Henry's death that are given very different dates—1404 and 1400. Frederick Pohl quotes the date as 1400[3] and cites as his source a man who has proven to be one of the most unreliable chroniclers of Sinclair family history, Father Hay,[4] who, as a Catholic priest, was far more expert at hagiography than history and, in the eyes of most modern historians, is sadly renowned for both inaccuracy and exaggeration. The date of 1404 is quoted in another document that once rested in the family archives of the Earls of Caithness. The fact that the wording of this document is identical to the wording above is a strange coincidence indeed.[5]

Another document, dated 1446, repeats this wording yet again, but in this account, neither the date of Henry's supposed death nor the nature of his "inimies" is recorded.[6] One Danish historian, Van Bassan, reputedly claims that the "inimies" were "southrons." It was generally believed that Henry was killed either by an English raiding party or by an armed expedition against the Orkney Islands mounted by the Hanseatic League. Yet there is only one recorded raid on Orkney in that period, an English incursion in 1401. We cannot fail to be suspicious of the identical wording used in each of the brief accounts of Henry's death that we have located, particularly when it is applied to three very different dates, none of which coincide with the time of the English raiding party. Another strange anomaly arises from the paucity of information concerning Henry's death and obsequies. How could the passing of such an important personage fail to be recorded in the state documents of the period?

There is no record whatsoever of the burial of Earl Henry St. Clair. He was certainly not buried in the family vaults at the original church of St. Matthew's at Roslin,[7] nor was his body later interred in the vaults of Rosslyn Chapel as so many people have erroneously suggested. It is equally certain that he was not buried on Orkney. Therefore, to the confusion over the sparse yet oddly identical accounts of his death on different dates, we have to add not only a breach with family tradition regarding the ritual interment of the Lords of Roslin, but also a complete dearth of any information about his burial at all. To complicate the issue still further, Antonio Zeno, who, according to tradition, is reputed to have asked Henry's permission to return to Venice on several occasions, remained in Orkney until 1404 and then returned home, where he died shortly after.[8] It must be assumed from this that either Henry did not die until 1404 or, as we suspect, did not give Antonio permission to return until that date.

Henry's son, who became known as Henry II St. Clair, Earl of Orkney, was never formally installed by the Norwegian crown as earl. Henry II was captured by the English in 1405 while escorting the heir to the Scottish throne to France.[9] He was imprisoned for many years in the Tower of London,[10] but was released from time to time to attend to family business in Scotland and Orkney, while other members of his family were being held hostage against his safe return. As a result of his prolonged imprisonment, Henry II left virtually no trace whatsoever in the history of the islands.[11] The continuity of the rule of law in Orkney demanded the continuance of the St. Clair earldom as a matter of priority to the Norwegian crown. Therefore it was imperative that Henry II be formally installed within a very short time of his father's death. Henry II did indeed succeed to the title,[12] but for some unexplained reason was never formally installed as the earl of the islands. Why?

Prior to Henry's first voyage to America in 1396, he made certain provisions that would have been regarded as reasonable and proper precautions for a man of property embarking on a hazardous enterprise. Henry transferred his holdings in Pentland to his brother, John. Furthermore, he drew up a deed that was signed at Roslin by his eldest daughter, Elizabeth, and her husband, Sir John Drummond of Cargill, whereby they renounced any claim that they might have to his lands in the Kingdom of Norway so long as Henry had male heirs.[13] The male heirs were not named, and it has been assumed by some scholars that this document indicates that Henry may have intended to take some of his sons with him on his voyage of exploration. If this is so, and he failed to return, then his lands in Norway, which included Orkney and Shetland, would have passed without dispute to his eldest son, Henry II.

Our estimate of the timing of the voyage is, to a certain degree, confirmed by the fact that Henry was not a signatory to the Treaty of Kalmar, which was signed in 1397.[14] He was not present at the negotiations, but was represented by Bishop Jens of Orkney, who was appointed in 1396. The treaty formally united the three Scandinavian countries of Norway, Denmark, and Sweden under the rule of Queen Margrette. The signing of this treaty was a matter of supreme importance to Norway, and there can be only one explanation why the premier earl of Norway did not sign it—because Henry was, with the queen's full blessing and permission, engaged upon a voyage of exploration with the ultimate intention of extending the control of the three kingdoms right across the North Atlantic. Thus we can deduce that, throughout this period, Henry was attempting to discharge his obligations to his Norwegian sovereign and to his family whatever might befall.

To suggest that a man of such meticulous organizational ability would not have left precise instructions as to the succession to the earldom and to the matter of his own burial in the event of his death is inconceivable. Yet no burial appears to have taken place, or at least none is recorded. The passing of such a great and noble lord, whose political position in both Scotland and Norway would have been a matter of considerable note, left no official document recording his demise in either country. The three brief and uninformative accounts of his death and their identical wording are, we believe, simply a matter of camouflage.

Two possible and reasonable explanations can account for the manner of Henry's death and the bizarre silence that followed it. One was suggested to us by Earl Malcolm Caithness, the present Chief of the Clan Sinclair. Earl Malcolm dates the beginnings of the decline in the family fortunes to Earl Henry's mysterious passing and claims, quite plausibly, that the King of Scotland was increasingly alarmed at the growing power of the northern Earl. He suggests that the "southrons" referred to in earlier accounts may disguise the fact that Earl Henry was killed in a naval engagement with the Scottish King somewhere off the west coast of Scotland. Malcolm admits that, so far, he has not been able to substantiate this, but is actively seeking proof.[15]

We have an alternative suggestion to offer that is at least supported by circumstantial evidence. We suggest that Earl Henry St. Clair gave permission to Antonio Zeno to return to Venice and then returned to North America in 1404 with the firm intention of spending the rest of his life among people whose culture and spiritual values were so close to his own. If this is so, we conclude that Henry was neither the first nor the last European to assimilate into the Native American culture. The Templar ideals, which had imbued the St. Clair family over two centuries, stressed the primacy of communal living, service to others, and the elevation of the communities within which they moved. On his repeated voyages to America, Henry had encountered a culture that not only preached these ideals, but lived them. It is not beyond the realm of possibility that the attractions of this way of life easily outweighed the so-called advantages of living in the brutal, dangerous, and intolerant world of late-medieval Europe.

A Strange Tradition

There is one little-known Native American legend that tends to confirm the suggestion that Henry and some of his party may have died in North America. When the Narragansett Indians were asked who built the Newport Tower, they replied by describing the green-eyed, fire-haired strangers that we mentioned earlier. They also have another tradition, which, as it seems to contradict the known facts about their way of life, has been largely ignored. This states that the Newport Tower was built by certain of their ancestors *as a temple*. As Native Americans did not build temples, this statement has been treated as irrelevant. However, if, as we believe, Henry St. Clair did build the Newport Tower as a church and then was assimilated into the Narragansett people, this tradition acquires a startling relevance. In his report of his exploration of the east coast of America, Verrazano commented on the different skin colors of the various American people he met between 1524 and 1545.[16] He identified one tribe on Rhode Island, whom he described as having exceptionally white skin, while a similar report of a distinctly "white tribe" in Nova Scotia was made by Jacques Cartier.

The two people we could expect to exploit and publicize the benefits of the New World were Henry St. Clair and Antonio Zeno. Henry was either killed or returned to settle permanently in the New World in 1404, and thus was rendered incapable of any public exposition of the discoveries he had made. Antonio Zeno returned to Venice and died shortly thereafter, in 1405.[17] The only remaining records of the voyage to be found in Europe are the oral tradition of the St. Clairs on the one hand and a collection of letters from Antonio Zeno gathering dust in Venice on the other. Henry's grandson, Earl William St. Clair, who erected Rosslyn Chapel as a memorial to Templar belief and St. Clair family tradition, left coded reference to the voyage in the carvings of American plants within the chapel long before Columbus set sail.

A Schoolboy Prank

The letters of the Zeno brothers to their homeland lay unnoticed for over 100 years in the Zen Palace in Venice. These were discovered by accident by a mischievous and inquisitive five-year-old boy, yet another Nicolo Zeno, who found them in an unlocked chest along with ancient maps. Some he scribbled on, others he tore up, until an adult stopped him.[18] Later, as a young man who had developed an interest in geography, he reread the portions of those letters that he had not completely destroyed with a deep sense of regret for his childhood misdeed.[19] They described fascinating voyages of discovery made between 1390 and 1404 by his ancestors Sir Nicolo and Antonio Zeno. To make amends for his childish and destructive act and to gain an understanding of the actions of his ancestors, he began the slow and tedious task of reassembling the scraps of old and fragile paper. The faded ink, the tattered fragments of letters, some whose dates had been torn off, did not make his task an easy one. The use of names that were foreign to him, written in an archaic script, complicated the issue still further. Young Nicolo discussed his find and the difficulties of reassembling it correctly with his father, who in turn showed the reassembled letters to a respected relative, Marco Barbaro, who was engaged in composing a history of his distinguished Venetian ancestors.

This book, *Discenza Patrizie*,[20] was published in 1536 and was the first work to bring to public notice the fourteenth-century North Atlantic explorations of Sir Nicolo and Antonio Zeno. The book consists of several volumes, and in one we read:

> Nicolo the Chevalier, of the Holy Apostles Parish, called the Old—in 1379 captain of a galley against the Genoese. Wrote with brother Antonio the voyage to Frislanda, where he died.[21]

> Antonio wrote with his brother Nicolo the Chevalier the voyage to the islands near the Arctic Pole, and of their discoveries of

1390 by order of Zichno, King of Frislanda. He reached the continent of Estotiland in North America. He remained fourteen years in Frislanda; that is four with his brother, and ten alone.[22]

Barbaro's book did not have a wide circulation outside the City of Venice, so the statements within it had little or no impact on European consciousness at that time. It did have an effect within the maritime republic, however, for there are several globes in Venice dating from the mid-sixteenth century that record the Zeno landing in Nova Scotia and date it, erroneously, as 1390.[23]

Some twenty years later, when young Nicolo inherited the torn letters on the death of his father, he prepared an edited account of his ancestors' voyage of exploration using the reassembled surviving portions of these letters. His account ends with a description of the origin of the letters and his childhood act of destruction, and the motivation that impelled him to reassemble them.

> These letters were written by Messire Nicolo (and Antonio) to Messire Carlo his brother; and I am grieved that the book and many other writings on these subjects, I don't know how, came easily to ruin; for, being but a child when they fell into my hands, I, not knowing what they were, tore them in pieces, as children will do, and sent them all to ruin; a circumstance which I cannot now recall without the greatest sorrow. Notwithstanding, in order that such an important memorial should not be lost, I have put the whole in order, as well I could, in the above narrative; so that the present age may, more than its predecessors have done, in some measure derive pleasure from the great discoveries made in those parts where they were least expected; for it is an age that takes a great interest in new narratives and in the discoveries which have been made in countries hitherto unknown, by the high courage and great energy of our ancestors.[24]

The Zeno Narrative

The Zeno Narrative was published in Venice in 1558 with the somewhat clumsy title *The Discovery of the Islands of Frislanda, Eslanda,*

Engronelanda, Estotilanda, and Icaria: made by two brothers of the Zeno family, namely Messire Nicolo, the Chevalier, and Messire Antonio. With a special drawing of the whole region of their discovery in the north.[25] The phrase "a special drawing of the whole region of their discovery in the north" refers to the document that is commonly known as the Zeno Map. This chart was drawn by young Nicolo, who published the Narrative, and not by the original explorers, as many of its detractors would have us to believe. The Zeno Map has been widely criticized because it displays seeming lines of latitude and longitude—concepts that had not even been thought of in the fourteenth century. It also contains certain strange, little-known islands and place names that were copied from other maps. Copying the errors as well as the accuracies from previous documents is not unique to the Zeno map;[26] it had been common practice for many years before and after the map was published. Due to the controversy over this confusing chart, Nicolo did the cause of the Zeno voyage considerable disservice.[27]

Another factor that affected the credibility of the Zeno Narrative was the 140-year delay between the voyage and its publication. According to Norman Biggart, a researcher from Massachusetts, this was a result of state policy on the part of the Venetian authorities. He suggests that the voyages were kept secret until long after trading patterns to the Americas had been established so that Venetian discoveries would not be used to the advantage of her trading rivals in Pisa and Genoa.[28] He goes on to claim that the story of the letters having been torn up by young Nicolo as a child may also be an act of calculated misinformation to create a plausible explanation for some important missing data in the Narrative,[29] and that, furthermore, there is a possibility that the original letters may still exist intact in some long-forgotten archive in Venice.[30]

To answer these points and to gain a realistic understanding of the true causes of the disputes in the Zeno Narrative, we have to address the questions that arise from the complete disinterest of the Venetian authorities in the discoveries made by the Zeno brothers at the time of Antonio's return in 1404, and also at the time of the first publication of the Narrative in 1558.

Reasons for the Delay in Publication

In 1405, at the time of Antonio's death, Venice was beginning a period of unprecedented expansion and prosperity. According to the historian John Julius Norwich:

> . . . the Republic had become a nation. . . . Venice found herself mistress of a considerable area of north-east Italy, including the cities of Padua, Vicenza and Verona and continuing westward as far as the shores of Lake Garda. At last she could treat as an equal with nations like England, France and Austria—in her own right, a European power.[31]

With this enormous growth in power and influence, the Serene Republic's considerable expertise in economic and political matters was deployed in consolidating and exploiting her position and was not to be frittered away on speculative adventures in the North Atlantic. By the time of the publication of the Zeno Narrative in 1558, mainland Italy was a scene of unparalleled strife, as a Spanish army led by the Duke of Alba invaded the papal territories from one side, while the papal allies, a French army of more than 10,000 men led by the Duc de Guise, invaded from the other.[32] Venice, sensibly, refused to be involved and continued to enjoy the longest era of peace in her history, which led one French historian to remark ". . . the history of the Venetians flows on without being marked by any events worthy of the attention of posterity."[33]

Indeed, with the election of Doge Girolamo Priuli in November 1599, the majority of the Republic's foreign policy problems simply melted away.[34] Even the Ottoman Turks were quiescent, as they were preoccupied with civil war at home. Despite these facts, Venice had nonetheless embarked on a long period of decline that precluded her capitalizing on the earlier exploits of the Zeno brothers. Furthermore, following the first voyage of Christopher Columbus, the Pope divided the New World into two strictly enforced zones of influence—one for the Catholics of Spain and the other for his loyal subjects in Portugal.[35] Venice had waited too long. The inactivity of the Venetian authorities, when considered in the light of the endorsement of the Zeno Narrative by both Barbaro and Ramusio, cannot, however, be taken as a statement about the document's accuracy. The contents of the Zeno

Narrative, which was published over sixty years after the exploitation of the New World by Europeans began, posed no political or economic threat to the Spanish, Portuguese, or the later English and French colonists of North America. Why then did it later engender so much controversy and bitter argument?

Chapter 13

THE ZENO NARRATIVE

THE ZENO NARRATIVE WAS COMPILED FROM the tattered remnants of faded handwritten originals in an archaic script. These difficulties were further complicated as Nicolo and Antonio, the original authors, wrote in Italian, using information provided by Norse-, Scots-, or Gaelic-speaking islanders. They themselves would have had difficulty enough in determining how to spell the names of the people, towns, islands, and countries they came across; how much more problematic was it for young Nicolo, over 100 years later, when he tried to reassemble the letters and maps he had destroyed as a child, which spoke of places whose names he could not reasonably be expected to recognize.[1]

The title of the Narrative rather than the text itself, listing the strange names of islands discovered by the Zeno brothers such as Frislanda, Eslanda, Engronelanda, Estotilanda, and Icaria, is baffling enough to anyone with only the most rudimentary knowledge of the geography of the North Atlantic, but this is not the principal source of confusion. The majority of the criticism leveled at the Zeno Narrative arises from the problem of identifying, as an historical personage, the main character described within it, Prince Zichmni. According to Frederick Pohl, Zichmni was ". . . the most troublesome misspelling in history."[2] You can scour the records and archives of Northern Europe and never find a trace of anyone whose name remotely resembles Zichmni. For the two centuries that followed the Narrative's publication, no one appeared capable of even hazarding an educated guess as to the true identity of this elusive prince, who was first identified in 1786 by the historian Johann Reinhold Forster.[3] In a moment of insight, Forster came to the conclusion that Zichmni was simply a muddled misspelling of Sinclair, which derives from St. Clair. While this identification became widely accepted by the majority of historians,[4] it was left to Frederick Pohl, in the middle of the twentieth century, to explain the precise mechanism by which "Earl Henry St. Clair, Prince of Orkney" became corrupted to the enigmatic "Zichmni."

According to the custom of the time, Sir Nicolo Zeno would have referred to Earl Henry as Principe Enrico or, more probably, by the name of the territory he ruled, Principe d'Orkney. Now we shall see how the spelling Zichmni happened:

> In medieval Italian letter forms given by Capelli, "d'O" would most likely be written as

> In the Marciana catalogue in Venice, the capital Z of "Zeno" is written thus:[5]

Dr. Barbara A. Crawford, Lecturer in Medieval Studies at St. Andrews University, states that:

> One has to admit, however, that his [i.e. Pohl's] interpretation of "Principe Zichmni" as a mis-reading of "Principe d'Orkenei" because Z in Italian script can appear to be d'O is ingenious and on the whole satisfactory.[6]

Fred Lucas, the principal critic of the Narrative, who wrote in the latter part of the nineteenth century, held the peculiar belief that Zichmni was actually a Baltic pirate named Wichmann. Lucas made no attempt whatsoever to justify the reasons why two outstanding Venetian noblemen from one of the most powerful and proud families in the Serene Republic were serving under a pirate and taking pride in the fact that such a black-hearted villain could have conferred knighthood upon them.

An English account of the Narrative was published in London in 1582 by Richard Hakluyt, who stated "This discourse was collected by Ramusio, Secretary to the State of Venice or by the printer Tho. Giunti."[7] Hakluyt, whose expertise in voyages of exploration is a matter of international repute, identified six explorers who reached America before Columbus, four of whom were Venetians: Marco Polo in 1270, Nicolo and Antonio Zeno in 1380, and Nicolaus Conti in

1444.[8] According to the historian Jack Beeching, Hakluyt is a reliable source with a well-deserved reputation for sober scholarship:

> He [Hakluyt] was primarily a scholar in the magnificent Renaissance tradition—a man for whom the gratuitous pursuit of knowledge for its own sake, was life's most important end . . . he will go to great lengths to get the facts.[9]

Beeching is not alone in his praise of Hakluyt's accuracy, for the historian Ben Jonson states that Hakluyt's documents were "registered for truth."[10]

Official Approval

Ramusio, whose approval is even more significant, gives an account of the voyage in his publication *Viaggi*, which was published circa 1574. As Secretary to the State of Venice, he was in fact the state censor who had to ensure that anything that was printed was accurate and honest so it could not be used to detract from the honor, prestige, and security of the Republic. Ramusio had to interview and record the exploits of all ships' captains who returned to Venice and was, therefore, perhaps the supreme authority of his time on voyages and discoveries.[11] Thus he was widely known and respected as a geographer and historian.[12]

Venice was internationally renowned for the quality and accuracy of its documentation in records of maritime exploration and trade. According to Professor Taylor of London University, when it came to naval voyages of exploration, Ramusio was "a man who could hardly have been deceived."[13] Ramusio's signature at the bottom of the Zeno Narrative, therefore, signifies two important things: first, the accuracy of the Narrative in so far as it went, and second, state approval of its publication.[14]

The Honorary Secretary of the Royal Geographic Society from 1866 to 1881, R. H. Major, wrote of the authenticity of the Narrative in the following terms:

> The first to do himself honour by vindicating the truth of the Zeno narrative was the distinguished companion of Captain Cook, the circumnavigator, Johann Reinhold Forster, in a work published in 1784 and 1786. Amongst others who uphold the narrative we have the following brilliant array of

savants: Eggers, Cardinal Zurla, Zach, Malte Brun, Walckenaar, de la Roquette, the Polish Geographer Joachim Lelewel and the Danish Antiquary Bredsdorf, also the far-seeing Humboldt.[15]

The position of honorary secretary of the society during the nineteenth century is equivalent to that of the executive director today. Johann Reinhold Forster's comments include the following:

> . . . that the countries visited and described by the two Zeno's, are of the number of those already known, that Greenland was visited by them, and these illustrious adventurers were even not unacquainted with America.[16]

The renowned American historian and author, John Fiske, included a chapter of 108 pages, entitled "Pre-Columbian Voyages," in his major two-volume work, in which he states:

> In a very true sense Henry, as a civilised man, in the modern sense of civilisation, was the one and only discoverer of America; historians of the future are bound to come to this conclusion by all the canons of criticism. . . . The Zeno narrative of which there is an English translation in the Hakluyt Societies Collection of Voyages has had full discussion and complete acceptance.[17]

The majority of modern academics again vouch for the truthfulness of the Narrative, including Professor E. G. R. Taylor of the University of London, who wrote:

> The authenticity of the account has been challenged but on very flimsy grounds. It appears to the present writer to be quite out of the question that any author could invent a story which in every detail reflects facts about which it is impossible that he could be aware.[18]

Professor William Herbert Hobbs of Michigan University penned an article entitled "The Fourteenth Century Discovery of America by Antonio Zeno" in 1951, in which he described the Zeno brothers as ". . . reliable and honest explorers who were far in advance of their age. . . . True they did not reveal a New World to the Old World as

Columbus did but their presence there must be accepted as historical fact."[19] In 1561, Ruscelli referred to Nicolo Zeno as an authority in both history and geography, ". . . universally held to have, at this day, few equals in the whole of Europe."[20]

The authenticity of the Zeno Narrative has been accepted by the prestigious publication *Encyclopaedia Americana* since 1904. In the current edition, the St. Clair/Zeno expedition is described in the following terms:

> Henry Sinclair, the Scottish earl of Orkney, and Antonio Zeno, a Venetian navigator, are reported to have made a westward voyage in 1398 that perhaps took them to Nova Scotia. Zeno wrote an account of the voyage that was not published until 1558, and then in garbled form. The report nonetheless has the ring of truth. Its geographical description of the unknown land fits Nova Scotia. Most significantly, Zeno described pitch flowing out of the ground, a phenomenon that once existed in Nova Scotia. . . . Traditions among the Micmac Indians of Nova Scotia, recalling the arrival of a "prince" with some resemblance to Sinclair, lend further support to the account.[21]

The *Dictionary of National Biography* has also confirmed that it was Henry St. Clair who led the Zeno expedition.

We are in complete agreement with Professor Taylor of the University of London in his belief that there is absolutely no way that any Venetian nobleman writing in 1558 could have had any knowledge of the monastery, the hot springs, or the ice-free harbor in Greenland.[22] Nor is there any mechanism other than the rediscovery of the original letters by which young Nicolo Zeno could have known the details of the topography of the Nova Scotia coast, the harbor at Guysborough, or the smoking mountain at Stellarton. The accuracy of the descriptions of the monastic settlement in Greenland on the one hand and the smoking mountain on the other describe geographical features that, being unique, completely authenticate the descriptions of the Zeno voyages.

The Fate of the "Fly Away Islands"

The matter of these strangely named islands and their apparent disappearance since the time the Narrative was written and the map compiled, is also simple to explain. In compiling the Narrative from the family letters, Nicolo wrote:

> I thought it good to draw a copy of these northern lands from the sailing chart which I find that I have still among our family heirlooms. To those who take pleasure in such things, it will serve to throw light on what would be hard to understand without it.[23]

Sadly, this young nobleman's mapmaking efforts have, for centuries, produced more confusion than clarity. To the "sailing chart" from his family heirlooms he added the islands Frisland, Estland, and Icaria, which were clearly described in the Narrative. Unfortunately, when we consult modern maps of the North Atlantic, there is no sign of them. Many critics denounce both the Narrative and the map as fraudulent because of the inclusion of these apparently fictitious islands.[24]

As most of these were mentioned in earlier historical writings, however, there is no factual basis for asserting that they are figments of the collective imaginations of the Zeno family. Estotiland, Estland, and Drogio are all found in Norse and Viking accounts of Atlantic voyages,[25] and can be seen on the Modena Map of 1350.[26] Frisland was regarded by Columbus as an alternative name for the Icelandic Isles, or Newfoundland. The archaic naming of this mysterious place goes back to the twelfth century, when it was named after the Frisian nobles who supposedly found it in the northern seas. The confusion of identifying Frisland and Fer Island, however, can easily be explained by the difficulties of communication between the Italian letter writers and their northern hosts.

One critic, Samuel Eliot Morison, who focused on the story of the voyage to Icaria and the description of its king, reserves his most scathing comments for what he describes as the "Fly Away Islands." However, Arlington Mallery and other modern mapmakers made a startling discovery that finally proved that the Zeno map was correct. There once was an island group situated between Iceland and Greenland known as "Gunn Biorn's Skerries."[27] They were discovered by the Norse trader Gunn Biorn in 920, and are described in *Description of Greenland*, which was published in 1873. They are now shown on charts issued by the United States Hydrographic Office, but do not appear on normal maps since they are now over 60 fathoms (360 feet) below sea level due to subsidence. They were, however, shown on maps until 1600.

In 1456, the main island, Gombar Skaare, was described as 65 miles long and 25 miles wide. According to Arlington Mallery[28] and Charles Hapgood,[29] this island was considerably larger at the end of the fourteenth century, and it is probable that it was the island of Icaria. The early existence of Icaria is mentioned in medieval accounts of the voyage of St. Brendan. The ongoing subsidence of this island, whose coastal mountaintops gradually disappeared under the waves, could explain the dangerous shoals around its coasts described in the Zeno Narrative.

> The evidence . . . that Iceland had been sinking for thousands of years has been corroborated by the modern explorations of the Norwegian Polar expedition under Fritjohf Nansen. Nansen concluded that the Faroes and Iceland were once connected by a basaltic plateau emerging above sea level at a period when the shoreline stood on an average 500 meters lower than it does now. The Faroe-Icelandic ridge now extends beyond Iceland to Greenland, and the southern end of Greenland is also sinking.[30]

The disproportionate size of Iceland on the Zeno map is explained by Arlington Mallery, who also detailed the submergence of several provinces of the island that subsided beneath the sea after a forty-year period of terrific volcanic explosions. These ended in 1380, but the effect on water levels continued for another century.[31] He states:

> Scholars have been frustrated mainly because they have overlooked the tremendous changes in the natural features of the Greenland-Iceland area due to natural phenomena. Unaware of the consequent sinking of land and the forming of undersea shelves as the surface of the earth shifted under the weight of glacial ice, they have not realised that some landmarks on the Viking trail have even vanished under ice and water.[32]

Paying due regard to the above account of subsidence, Professor Charles Hapgood states that "It would seem highly probable that the Iceland we see on the Zeno map is the greater Iceland that existed prior to the Zeno brothers visit."[33] Months after publishing his first comments on the Zeno Narrative, Mallery read the reports of the three polar expeditions led by Paul-Emile Victor[34] and stated:

In confirming my analysis of the Greenland portion of the Zeno map, Victor accomplished something of magnitude for cartographers, historians, and scholars in general: he restored to the Zeno map its original reputation for authenticity.[35]

Authentication of the Zeno Map

Mallery found that, when compared with the latest United States army maps, all the points of Greenland on the Zeno map were plotted with a remarkable degree of accuracy. Charles Hapgood, who was once a professional cartographer with the United States navy, analyzed the Zeno map in both Portalan and Polar projections. In the Polar projection, he compared thirty-eight locations in Greenland, Iceland, Scandinavia, Germany, Scotland, and the islands of the North Sea in relation to each other. The European points are surprisingly accurate, with Greenland and Iceland's references only fractionally less so.[36] Both John Fiske and Miller Christy agree that, on the Zeno map, Greenland was charted using magnetic coordinates. Fiske wrote:

> The genuineness of the Zeno narrative is thus conclusively proved by its knowledge of Arctic geography, such as could be obtained only by a visit to the far North at a time before the Greenland colony had finally lost touch with its mother country.[37]

The Zeno chart, for all its supposed errors, was deemed authentic by the mapmakers Mercator and Ortelius, in 1569 and 1574, respectively, and by the explorer Martin Frobisher in 1576. Mercator and Ortelius reproduced details from the Zeno map, just as Nicolo Zeno had undoubtedly copied from earlier works, modifying them in line with the discoveries made by his illustrious ancestors who had voyaged to the West with Henry St. Clair. This expedition had undoubtedly used information drawn from the Viking sagas, from Nicolas Lynne, who also drew maps of the North Atlantic,[38] and from maps devised in 1350 by the Dominican monk Ranulf Higden, who lived in Chester, England.[39] Higden's maps, showing "Wineland" and "Svinlandia," were used in a fourteenth-century geographical history called *Polychroricon*[40] and have been reproduced in a modern reference work, *The History of Cartography.*

A Rising Tide of Acceptance

Despite its long and troubled history, the authenticity of the Zeno Narrative is now well established and has been accepted by academics such as Hapgood and Hobbs, the American historian Ridpath, the Albany Herald of Scotland, the late Sir Iain Moncreiffe of that Ilk, Dr. Barbara Crawford, the chief archivist, Gelting, of Denmark, the Swedish archaeologist Rausing, the Danish scholar Aage Russel, Arlington Mallery, Johann Reinhold Forster, the Tudor naval historian Richard Hakluyt, the secretary to the State of Venice, Ramusio, Professor Taylor of London University, the Venetian historian Ruscelli, R. H. Major of the Royal Geographic Society, the American historian John Fiske, the British historian Andrew Sinclair, and, of course, the persistent student of pre-Columbian American exploration, Frederick Pohl.

The Zeno map, despite the fact that it was made 150 years after the event and drawn from information supplied by the Narrative, has now also been authenticated as an accurate chart of the voyage. The importance of the work done by Captain Arlington Mallery and Charles Hapgood in establishing a valid rationale for the seeming disappearance of the "Fly Away Island" of Icaria has defused many earlier criticisms, and the work of Paul-Emile Victor in restoring the Zeno map to its original reputation for authenticity has been vital.

The historical reality of the Zeno/St. Clair expedition to the New World does not simply depend upon the validity of the Zeno map and narrative, however. We also have the evidence of the Westford Knight in Massachusetts, the Newport Tower in Rhode Island, the carvings in Rosslyn Chapel, and the official commemoration of the voyage on a plaque at the Zeno Palazzo in Venice. In addition to these, we have strong indications in the boatstone at Westford, the petroglyph near Halifax, and in a letter from Pietro Pasqualigo, Venetian ambassador to the crown of Portugal, to his brother in 1501. Writing about the expedition of Cortereal, which had returned from Labrador and Newfoundland eleven days previously, Pasqualigo stated:

> . . . There has also been brought here a piece of broken sword, inlaid with gold, which we are convinced was made in Italy, and one of the children had in his ears two pieces of silver which most certainly seem to have been made in Venice.[41]

The ambassador's statement is not in doubt. The question is, which expedition brought the sword and the pieces of silver across the Atlantic in the first place? As no Venetian expedition other than that of Zeno/St. Clair is recorded as reaching Newfoundland prior to Cortereal, were these artifacts a relic of the exploration originating in Orkney?

Despite resistance among academics in the United States, a rising tide of acceptance of the St. Clair/Zeno voyage as fact has been growing in mainland America since the 1850s. While we have no doubt that the entrenched positions adopted by the partisans on various sides regarding the origin of the Newport Tower will continue for some time, the truth about the builders of this architectural anomaly is spreading steadily, thanks to the work of Jim Whittal and others. We had the privilege of assisting Niven Sinclair, Malcolm Goodwin, and Norman Biggart in making a successful presentation to the Archaeological Commissioners of the State of Massachusetts in October 1999 concerning the preservation of the carving of the Westford Knight. Under the aegis of the archaeological commissioners, the preservation of this unique medieval memorial is now being undertaken by the Westford Historical Society, thus preserving for future generations this lasting legacy of the St. Clair/Zeno expedition.

The civic authorities of Guysborough in Nova Scotia have also shown their support by granting permission for the erection of two memorials within their jurisdiction. The first, situated at Henry's original landfall, was erected by the Prince Henry Sinclair Society of North America as a result of the untiring efforts of its president, D'Elayne Coleman. The Clan Sinclair Society of Nova Scotia erected the second memorial in a public park in Guysborough to commemorate the safe-haven used by Henry's ships during his exploration of the province (See Figure 4, page 101). Its opening was attended by a large number of Sinclairs from both sides of the Atlantic, by the Norwegian ambassador, and by representatives of the Canadian government. The memorial was dedicated by the Earl of Caithness, Malcolm Sinclair, hereditary Clan Chief and a direct descendant of Earl Henry.

Chapter 14

THE LORDLY LINE CONTINUES

WITH THE MYSTERIOUS DISAPPEARANCE OF Henry St. Clair, Earl of Orkney, in 1404 or thereabouts, the traditions of the Lordly Line of the High St. Clairs were carried on by his eldest son, Henry II, who was never formally invested with the earldom of the islands, even though this was a prerequisite for holding the office. The only rational explanation for this glaring omission is that neither the whereabouts nor the death of his father could be proved. In the same year, Antonio Zeno, after many years of faithful service as admiral of the St. Clair fleet, returned to Venice and died some months later.[1]

Henry II

Henry II, in his capacity as Lord High Admiral of Scotland, was entrusted with the task of conducting the Crown Prince of Scotland (later James I) to France, but they were captured by the English en route.[2] Some say they were betrayed by Augustinian monks who were English spies; others claim the betrayal was by King Robert III's brother, the Duke of Albany, who was ambitious to gain the throne of Scotland for his own. Regardless of who, if anyone, perpetrated the betrayal, Earl Henry and the prince were imprisoned in the Tower of London.

King Robert died suddenly after hearing the news of his son's capture,[3] and the Duke of Albany acted as regent during the new king's captivity. He certainly did not exert himself unduly to try and engineer the release of his sovereign lord, the king. During the prolonged period of their incarceration, Henry was granted periodic freedom to attend to his Scottish affairs, provided that one of his brothers or a noble from the family of Douglas surrendered themselves to Durham Castle as surety against his return. As a result of his long custody in the hands of the English, the future King James I is said to have become "the best educated king" who ever reigned over the Scots.

Henry St. Clair's prolonged absence from his dominions created an opportunity for anarchy to rear its ugly head once more among the island subjects of the Norwegian crown. To preempt this possibility and to maintain control by the St. Clairs, Henry's brother John was made "fould" of Shetland[4] and his brother Thomas became "mandatory" of Orkney in his absence.[5] Henry was released in 1418 and died in 1420. Due to the mystery surrounding the disappearance of his father from the official record, Henry's early capture and prolonged imprisonment, and the brief period that elapsed between his release and his death, his reign left little mark on the islands and virtually none at all in the official records.

According to the Orkney historian J. Storer Clouston, there is one document that notes Henry's death and the beginning of the reign of the third St. Clair Earl of Orkney, William. It discloses that, after Henry's death, Bishop Thomas Tulloch was appointed to look after the earldom during the minority of William.[6] The bishop was later replaced as governor of the islands by an uncle by marriage of William, David Menzies of Wemyss, who governed so badly that the islanders rose up against him and petitioned the king for a replacement. In 1427, following a petition to the crown, Bishop Tulloch was reappointed as governor.[7]

Earl William St. Clair

Sir William St. Clair was formally invested as the Earl of Orkney at a ceremony in Denmark in 1434, at which Thomas St. Clair and Thomas Tulloch were witnesses.[8] In 1447, he married his cousin, Elizabeth Douglas. It is largely due to the actions and spiritual insight of Earl William that the St. Clairs of Roslin were ultimately, albeit indirectly, able to exert a profound and formative influence on the founding fathers of the United States of America. This spiritually gifted Scot strode like a colossus across the cultural bridge that carried medieval man from an atavistic, superstitious past into the early years of the Renaissance and the era of sustained trans-Atlantic settlement and colonization. He was described variously as "one of the illuminati," as "a nobleman with singular talents," and as "a man of exceptional talents much given to policy, such as the buildings of castles, palaces and churches."

Yet, in so far as it can be established, William founded but one church in Orkney and one at Roslin.[9] The foundations of Rosslyn Chapel were laid in 1446 with the intention of building a collegiate church with "a provost, six prebendaries and two singing boys."[10] It was completed to its present state, which is equivalent only to the choir of the original plans, immediately after the death of Earl William in 1480.

> It is in some respects the most remarkable piece of architecture in Scotland . . . when looked at from a strictly architectural point of view, the design may be considered faulty in many respects, much of the detail being extremely rude and debased, while as to construction, many of the principles wrought out during the development of Gothic architecture are ignored. But, notwithstanding these faults the profusion of design, so abundantly shown everywhere, and the exuberant fancy of the architect strike the visitor who sees Rosslyn for the first time with an astonishment which no familiarity ever effaces.[11]

Rosslyn Chapel

Despite the somewhat mixed architectural influences present in its construction, Rosslyn Chapel is, nonetheless, essentially and undeniably Scottish in character. The variety, candor, and exuberance of its rich profusion of carvings, which have no equal anywhere else in Britain, give Rosslyn Chapel its reputation as a unique shrine.[12] This wealth of stone carving gives the chapel importance, in spiritual terms, to the worldwide brotherhood of Freemasons and to all who seek spiritual enlightenment. There is far more to the innate quality of the carvings than can be attributed to craftsman's competence or even architectural skill; a distinct yet indefinable quality that transcends mere art is discernible here. The deeply mystical symbolic synergy that existed between the founder and his craftsmen seems to radiate from the very stone itself.

The people of the late Middle Ages—craftsmen, patrons, or observers—all knew their artwork should be beautiful, but that mere beauty was not enough. There had to be meaning[13]—not only meaning in the storytelling sense, though this was often an essential ingredient, but meaning at a deeper spiritual level. Carvings, paintings, and even the buildings themselves were deliberately designed for men and women for whom symbolism was the breath of spiritual life[14]—a spiritual life that, in the case of Rosslyn Chapel, was startlingly different from the outworn dogma and ideology of the Church.

The carvings within Rosslyn Chapel represent, with powerful symbolism, nearly every known spiritual pathway that had impinged upon European consciousness prior to the date of its foundation. There is a chaotic mixture of spiritual symbols from the Celtic worlds of Western Europe, Norse and Saxon pagan beliefs, the initiatory practice of Zoroastrianism, the worship of Ishtar and Tammuz from Babylonia, the Mithraic mysteries, Judaic traditions, and, scattered here and there, occasional references to esoteric aspects of Christianity.[15] The all-pervading theme that unites these disparate spiritual streams is that of a hymn to nature in all its bounty so beloved of the medieval Christian mystics.[16] It is within this aspect of the carvings of Rosslyn that we find various references to plants that are native to the New World explored by William's grandfather, Henry St. Clair. As we observed before, these include many carvings of maize, stylized carvings of aloe cactus, sassandras albidium, trillium grandilorum or wake robin, and finally, quercus nigra, or water oak (see Figures 18–19, page 174).

The main heretical theme encoded in the carvings is, however, found in symbolic references to the belief system of the Knights Templar, who were suppressed over 130 years before the chapel's foundation.[17] Three superbly carved pillars separate the main body of the chapel from the retro choir—the Master Mason's pillar, the Journeyman's pillar, and the Apprentice pillar. To the worldwide brotherhood of Freemasons, these have deep symbolic significance. The Master Mason's pillar signifies wisdom, the Journeyman's pillar strength, and the Apprentice's pillar beauty. Each represents not only the named quality, but its significance and function: wisdom constructs and is ordained to discover, strength supports, and beauty adorns. And all must be built upon the foundations of truth and justice.

This concept of the ideal foundation finds echoes in the qualities aspired to by the true initiate.

He who is as wise as a Perfect Master will not be easily injured by his own actions. Hath a person the strength which a Senior Warden represents he will bear and overcome every obstacle in life. He who is adorned like a Junior Warden with humility of spirit approaches nearer to similitude of God than other.[18]

Thus, in the construction and care lavished upon these three magnificent pillars, we have, enshrined in stone, Masonic expression as an integral part of symbolism, of the esoteric, spiritual insight and wisdom with which this chapel is so abundantly blessed.

Standing with your back to the three pillars in the main body of the chapel, your eye is drawn by the architecture up to the stone vaulted roof. This imposing structure is solid stone and over three feet thick. It is divided into five sections powdered with diaper work.[19] The first is decorated with daisies, representing innocence; the second panel contains a profusion of lilies to indicate the pure descending bloodline from the high priests of the Temple of Jerusalem[20]; the flowers opening to the Sun in the third section are in adoration, while the fourth contains roses, a symbol that once decorated the Babylonian temples of Ishtar. The final segment, in the west of the roof, contains a profusion of five-pointed stars, a cornucopia, the dove of the Knights Templar, the Moon, and the glowing orb of the Sun in splendor, which is half-hidden behind a balustrade.[21]

The five-pointed stars also decorated the temples of Ishtar, but in this instance are held to represent the *Via Lactodorum*, the Way of the Stars. This is an allegorical reference to the Milky Way, which forms the Royal Arch joining the Apprentice pillar at Rosslyn Chapel with a similar structure at Cintra and covers the route of the ancient Templar pilgrimage of initiation.[22] The half-hidden Sun in splendor is, to the initiated, the symbol of the Fisher King of Rex Deus tradition.

The Transmission of Templar Principles

The families of the Rex Deus who claimed direct descent from the high priests of the Temple of Jerusalem[23] and, through them, from the ancient initiates of Egypt, nominated one of their number from each generation as the Fisher King, the true heir to the throne of Jerusalem. The much-maligned Order of the Knights Templar, which transformed the face of

European society during its brief 200-year history, is perhaps the most obvious manifestation of the activities of this secretive group.[24] After their brutal suppression, Rex Deus wisely chose other routes by which to pass on their beliefs to the spiritually aware within European society.

Their central belief, that heaven could be created upon Earth if mankind could only learn to change its behavior,[25] was promulgated in many different ways. The stories of the search for the Holy Grail were allegories for the initiatory path to enlightenment promoted by Rex Deus. To them, spirituality did not concern itself with "pie in the sky" after death; it was the mainspring of action here on Earth. Brotherhood, justice, truth, and service to the community were the true foundations of their entire beliefs. No longer content to risk the continuance of this tradition through purely hereditary means, the fifteenth-century Fisher King, Earl William St. Clair, played an instrumental part in spreading these esoteric teachings, which had their origin in ancient Egypt, to carefully chosen men of goodwill of his own time. He had the perfect means at hand, for he was appointed grandmaster of the Craftmasons, the Hard and Soft Guilds in Scotland, in 1441.[26]

> Under the guidance of the St. Clairs, the hidden members of the Templar Order selected suitable candidates from the operative craft guilds for instruction in various branches of knowledge. The subjects covered included science, geometry, history, philosophy and the contents of the manuscripts recovered by the Templars during their excavations in Jerusalem. As a result, Scotland in general and Midlothian in particular became a beacon of enlightenment. The new brotherhood of speculative "free" masons created charitable institutions to support the poorer members of society and their respective guilds also set money aside for the benefit of their less fortunate neighbours. According to Prince Michael of Albany, these were the first charitable institutions to be established in Britain which were outside the direct control or instigation of the Church.[27]

The Foundation of Freemasonry

The absolute secrecy that shrouded the first three centuries of Freemasonry has made it difficult to assess the full range and depth of the wide variety of esoteric influences that formed the fraternity. The history of the St. Clairs of Roslin makes it plain that it was the preservation of Templar tradition that lay behind the transformation of the guilds of operative masons into the speculative and fraternal society of Freemasonry. Under the guidance of the St. Clair grandmasters, the tradition of transmitting secret and sacred knowledge through the rituals leading to higher degrees developed a high level of sophistication and complexity, which led to the development of Scottish Rite Freemasonry and the Royal Arch degrees.

The fact that Scottish Rite Freemasonry draws its teaching from sources of great antiquity is made manifest in the name "Roslin," which, according to Tessa Ranford, translates from the Scottish Gaelic as "ancient knowledge passed down the generations."[28] The St. Clairs and the other families of Rex Deus were descended from the high priests of the Temple of Jerusalem, who were, in turn, descendants of a close-knit priestly group who could trace their lineage and teaching back to the establishment of a hereditary priesthood in ancient Egypt. William St. Clair of Roslin, as the Fisher King of Rex Deus in his time, was thus the chosen route by which the sacred *gnosis* of the Egyptian/Hebraic tradition could reach out and liberate insightful medieval men from the blinkered thinking and despotic dogmatism of Holy Mother the Church. It is therefore no surprise to learn that, in continental Europe, Freemasonry developed an innate anticlerical and anti-Catholic bias and kept particularly close ties with its spiritual parent in Scotland.[29] Like their Scottish counterparts, French lodges took great pains to keep as close as possible to the traditional beliefs that had been handed down over the centuries.

The tradition of hereditary teaching and control of sacred knowledge continued for nearly three centuries after the death of Earl William St. Clair. The founding of speculative Freemasonry always had at its heart the long-term aim of spreading Rex Deus teachings and transformative influence far beyond the narrow confines of the Rex Deus families. Such an important step could not be rushed. It would take considerable time before the teaching was spread to appropriately qualified initiates who, in their turn, would prove their worth by passing on the sacred knowledge for several generations before being granted full control of the fraternity. William St. Clair, as grandmaster of the Hard and Soft Guilds of Scotland, had been the guilds' supreme judge and arbiter at their courts at Kilwinning in the fifteenth century.

The St. Clairs of Roslin retained their hereditary grandmastership of the guilds and of Freemasonry until the beginning of the eighteenth century when, on St. Andrews Day in 1736, yet another Sir William St. Clair of Roslin formally resigned his "hereditary patronage and protectorship of the Masonic craft" to effect the creation of "The Grand Lodge of Ancient, Free and Accepted Masons of Scotland."[30] The minutes of the meeting include the following passages:

1441. William St. Clair, Earl of Orkney and Caithness, Baron of Roslin, &c., &c., got a grant of this office from King James II. He countenanced the Lodges with his presence, propagated the royal art, and built the chapel of Roslin, that master-piece of Gothic architecture. Masonry now began to spread its benign influence through the country, and many noble and stately buildings were reared by the Prince and Nobles during the time of Grand Master Roslin. By another deed of the said King James II, this office was made hereditary to the said William St. Clair, and his heirs and successors in the Barony of Roslin; in which noble family it has continued without any interruption till of late years. . . .

. . . William St. Clair, of Roslin, Esq. (a real Mason, and a gentleman of the greatest candour and benevolence, inheriting his predecessors virtues without their fortune), was obliged to dispone the estate: and, having no children, of his own, was loth that the office of Grand Master, now vested in his person, should become vacant at his death . . .

. . . as hereditary Grand Master over all Scotland, he had called this meeting, in order to condescend on a proper plan for electing of a Grand Master; and that in order to promote so laudable a design, he proposed to resign into the hands of the Brethren, or whomsoever they should be pleased to elect, all right, claim, or title whatever, which he or his successors have to reign as Grand Master over the Masons in Scotland . . .[31]

Sir William's resignation as grandmaster having been reluctantly accepted, the assembled brothers decided that:

. . . they could not confer that high honour upon any Brother better qualified, or more properly entitled, than William St.

Clair, of Roslin, Esq., whose ancestors had so long presided over the Brethren, and had ever acquitted themselves with honour and with dignity. Accordingly, by a unanimous voice, William St. Clair, of Roslin, Esq., was proclaimed Grand Master Mason of all Scotland, and being placed in the chair, was installed, saluted, homaged, and acknowledged as such.[32]

By Their Fruits Shall Ye Know Them

The worldwide fraternity of Freemasonry put their transformative teaching into action and became the mainspring of political and social change in the seventeenth and eighteenth centuries. The concepts of democracy, freedom, and science all benefited from the touch of the spiritually gifted men who derived their insights from the living body of Rex Deus tradition, enshrined within the teaching of Freemasonry.[33] Many such initiates combined in a loose network with tolerant scholars to form the "Third Force," a movement of moderation that campaigned against the excesses of both Catholics and Protestants in the troubled times following the Reformation. The Third Force combined with a Masonically inspired esoteric movement in Holland, known as "The Family of Love," to form a pan-European "Invisible College" of scholars working for change. This movement eventually came into the open in England with the founding of the Royal Society, which was granted its charter by Charles II in 1662.

The Royal Society was formed by scientists who were drawn mainly from the ranks of the Freemasons, including Robert Boyle (1627–1691) and Isaac Newton (1642–1727), and who, like their Templar predecessors, were endowed with knowledge that went far beyond the boundaries of science.[34] A further development of the Invisible College, known as the Correspondence Society, played an important part in shaping the democratic ideals of Liberté, Egalité, and Fraternité that inspired the French Revolution.[35] Freemasonry was, from the very beginning, a political organization that was intimately entwined with the Stuart cause. When the Stuart monarch was exiled in 1691, French Freemasonry received a massive injection of members, which resulted in the spread of Masonic ideals throughout Europe.

The rising tide of Freemasonic liberal influence did not pass without comment from the papacy. In 1738, Pope Clement XII issued a papal bull, *In Eminenti Apostolatus Specula,* the first of a series of denunciations against the craft that provoked the Inquisition into its traditional form of action. Under pain of excommunication, the Pope prohibited any Catholic from joining the fraternity and, in Catholic countries, known Freemasons were harried, imprisoned, tortured, and deported. In the Papal States, membership in a Freemasonic lodge by any citizen was an offense punishable by death.[36] The fraternity of Freemasons played a revolutionary role in Russia and elsewhere in Europe wherever exiled Russian revolutionaries sought refuge. The Italian leaders of the *Rissorgimento,* Garibaldi and Mazzini, were both active Freemasons, and the Marquis de Lafayette attained high rank during his time in America and continued with his membership when he returned to France. Other French revolutionaries who were active in the brotherhood included Danton, Camille Désmoulins, and the Abbé Sieyés.[37]

Not surprisingly, the right-wing and royalist priest, the Abbé Augustin de Barruel, claimed, in his *Memoirs pour Servir l'Histoire de Jacobinism,* published in 1797, that the French Revolution was simply the bloody aftermath of a Freemasonic plot to overthrow royal and ecclesiastical authority.[38] The paradox is that, while Freemasons were undoubtedly active in revolutionary movements, other members of the craft were also heavily engaged in supporting right-wing regimes in Austria, Prussia, and Great Britain.[39] Thus a list of nineteenth-century leading Freemasons is, in political terms, remarkably inconsistent and contradictory. On the revolutionary side, it includes Mazzini and Garibaldi in Italy, Bakunin and Kerensky in Russia, and Daniel O'Connell and Henry Grattan in Ireland. On the other side of the political fence, there were the arch-turncoat Talleyrand in France, three French presidents, the right-wing administrator and poet Goethe, two nineteenth-century kings of Prussia, various kings of England, members of the English nobility, and many Anglican clergy.

Freemasonry in America

It is perhaps fitting that it was in the lands first settled by Earl Henry St. Clair that Freemasonry exerted its most lasting influence. The fraternal brotherhood came to the North American continent during the early eighteenth century as a result of the emigration of Freemasons from the United Kingdom to the colonies and also through the activities of the traveling lodges of the British army. Lodges were formed in Boston and Philadelphia in 1730, and a leading American, Benjamin Franklin, published the first Masonic book in the New World in 1734.[40] By the time of the outbreak of the American Revolution, most of the leading advocates of independence, such as George Washington, Paul Revere, and John Hancock, were members of the craft, as were, of course, many members of the British army of occupation.

After the War of Independence, new Grand Lodges were formed in the United States so that American Freemasons were no longer under the active control of the Grand Lodge in London. Critics of the craft have pointed out that, in America as in Europe, membership appears to be an almost inevitable prerequisite to high office. As we have mentioned earlier, while Freemasonry drew its members from every walk of life, it also tended to recruit a large number of people drawn from the aristocracy, and the professional and the educated classes. Therefore, although its membership is drawn from every nationality, religion, and political persuasion, it is not surprising that, in the historical context, its membership has included a large number of politicians and heads of state. From the time of George Washington to Gerald R. Ford in the late twentieth century, fourteen presidents of the United States are known to have been Freemasons.[41] The Declaration of Independence was signed by nine members of the craft, and Masonic thinking formed the predominant influence on the creation of what many authorities claim to be the embodiment of the highest ideals of democracy, namely the Constitution of the United States.

The American Constitution

The Constitution of the United States was drafted by the Constitutional Convention held in Philadelphia, between 25 May and 17 September 1787. This document is the oldest written constitution of any state that is still in effect today. At its heart is the democratic concept that all forms of government must be confined by the rule of law.

The constitution is in many ways the embodiment of the principles of the eighteenth-century Age of Enlightenment and was heavily influenced, not only by Masonic belief, but also by a variety of European and American philosophers such as John Locke, Voltaire, Montesquieu, and Thomas Paine, all of whom attacked despotic government and suggested that democratic power should arise from below and not be imposed from above. Like the respected thinking enshrined in the Declaration of Arbroath in 1340, when the King of the Scots was held to derive his power from the consent of his people, the American Constitution proclaimed that its government could only derive its powers from the consent of the governed. Furthermore, it was based on the concept that all free men have certain natural and inalienable rights and that these must be respected by any form of governance. Central to this was the concept that men are born equal and should be treated as equal before the law.

The Articles of Confederation, which were framed as a result of the various American colonies hostility to despotic British rule, embodied at their heart the colonists' revulsion against any form of strong national authority in such a way that virtually all effective power was left in local hands. The new constitution was based on the reasonable assumption that it was both wise and possible to distribute and balance powers between different arms of government, giving defined local powers and considerable autonomy to state governments and general powers to the national government. The allotting to the national or federal government of only those powers specifically delegated to it was done in such a manner as to make clear that all residual powers remained with the governments of the states. The extensive powers of the president were prescribed in a number of places by designated responsibilities that were clearly defined. Montesquieu's concept of the separation and balance of power was adopted with enthusiasm and, as a result, John Adams proclaimed that the eight explicit balancing mechanisms within the constitution were prime examples of the document's republican virtue. These checks and balances pertained between:

1. The states and the central government

2. The House of Representatives and the Senate

3. The president and Congress

4. The courts and Congress

5. The Senate and the president (in respect of appointments and treaties)

6. The people and their representatives

7. The state legislatures and the Senate (in the original election of senators)

8. The Electoral College and the people

While the American Constitution contained many human imperfections, it had, nonetheless, been framed with such wisdom that it has been capable of further amendment and development into that superb guarantee of people's rights to be governed under the law that obtains today.

The thinking of the Rex Deus tradition that, through the wisdom of Earl William St. Clair of Roslin, spread through the emerging world of Freemasonry, comes into the open with extremely beneficial effect in the United States. Regrettably however, its application was severely limited in a manner that would have appalled Henry St. Clair and his grandson, William, the hereditary grandmaster of the guilds of Scotland. Despite the concept that "all men are born equal and entitled to equal treatment before the law," there were two groups of people who were rigorously and ruthlessly excluded from its protection: the slave population of the southern states and indigenous Americans. It is perhaps a sad commentary on American history that the slaves, at least, gained some measure of redress long before the native people who had, by and large, welcomed the early colonists and sustained them during their early trials and tribulations. This situation is particularly tragic when we consider the startling similarities in culture, spirituality, actions, and beliefs that sustained and inspired Rex Deus families like the St. Clairs on the one hand and Native Americans such as the Mi'qmaq on the other.

Chapter 15

THE LEGACY OF THE VOYAGES

THE EUROPEAN EXPLORATION AND EXPLOITATION of the Americas that took place with such rapidity after Christopher Columbus's first voyage was marred by repressive and exploitive measures. Within 100 years of the arrival of the Europeans, the total native population fell from an estimated seventy-five to eighty million to between ten and twelve million, a dramatic drop primarily due to genocide. In the context of the total world population at the time, this crime far exceeds in scale, nature, and brutal effect even the Nazi holocaust against the Jews, Gypsies, and Russians in the Second World War. This destruction of native peoples was "justified" theologically, for "The Spanish Conquistadores reached a conclusion that the Native peoples did not have souls and therefore it was perfectly all right to enslave or murder them."[1] The labor problems created by this wave of mass murder were eventually solved by the importation of black slaves from West Africa.

While the birth of Protestant North America was an act of deliberate policy, the behavior of members of the reformed church was little different from that of their Catholic counterparts in the south. The rapacious greed and intellectual and racial arrogance of the colonials might have been enough on their own to prompt the genocide and cultural destruction, but when allied to religious certainty injudiciously mixed with new concepts of science and the Protestant work ethic, it effectively desacralized all of creation in the minds of the colonists. Thus the natural world and all it contained was threatened, along with the native people who so revered it.

The early colonial settlers in New England treated the Native Americans with contempt and derided their cultural values. The Puritans, whose search for religious freedom and a state founded on

Christian principles created the beginnings of the United States, were, in their fanatical religious certainty, singularly ill-equipped to tolerate or live in peace with people of a totally different creed and culture. "To have been genuine reformers, they would have had to accept the New World. But nothing in their history told them how this might be done."[2] The author and civil-rights activist Daniel N. Paul states that "Compassion among the Europeans for Aboriginal Americans was too often non-existent. Yet when recording their relationships with the Tribes for posterity, the Europeans continually harped upon the Tribes benevolent generosity towards them."[3] Who were these people who were so abysmally betrayed and almost completely destroyed?

Native American Spirituality

The Native Americans were, and in their surviving descendants still are, people of intense and deep spirituality—a people who had always instinctively, deliberately, and consciously sought spiritual guidance in all they did; a race who lived in vibrant harmony with the land and all the creatures who inhabited it; a population that perceived through their natural insight that the spirit of God resided within each and every aspect of creation. Their own words describe this intimate spiritual relationship with nature:

> There is no quiet place in the white man's cities. No place to hear the unfurling of the leaves in spring, or the rustle of the insects wings . . . And what is there to life if a man cannot hear the lonely cry of the whippoorwill or the argument of frogs around a pool at night? Whatever befalls the earth befalls the sons of the earth. If men spit on the earth, they spit on themselves. This we know—the earth does not belong to man, man belongs to the earth. All things are connected like the blood which unites one family. Whatever befalls the earth befalls the sons of the earth. Man did not weave the web of life, he is merely a strand in it. Whatever he does to the web, he does to himself.[4]

> Every part of this earth is sacred to my people . . . The sap which courses through the trees carries the memories of the red man. . . . Our dead never forget this beautiful earth, for it is the

mother of the red man. We are part of the earth, and it is part of us. . . . The water's murmur is the voice of my father's father. The rivers are our brothers, they quench our thirst. The air is precious to the red man, for all the things share the same breath. . . . We know that the white man does not understand our ways. . . . The earth is not his brother, but his enemy, and when he has conquered it, he moves on. His appetite will devour the earth and leave behind only a desert. . . . Perhaps it is because I am a savage I do not understand. What is man without the beasts? If all the beasts were gone, man would die from a great loneliness of spirit. For whatever happens to the beasts, soon happens to man.[5]

> Crazy Horse dreamed and went into the world
> where there is nothing but the spirits of
> all things. That is the real world that is
> behind this one, and everything we see here is
> something like a shadow from that world.[6]

All things are the work of the Great Spirit. We should all know that he is within all things: the trees, the grasses, the rivers, the mountains, and all four legged animals, and the winged people: and even more important, we should understand that he is above all these things and peoples.[7]

The Native American people used their spiritual insight as the mainspring of their everyday actions in the world they inhabited. It is from this spiritual source that they derived their sense of honor, which was the foundation for their lifestyle. For them, there was no arbitrary division between the spiritual and the material worlds. Their spirituality pervaded their actions in war, in peace, within families, in relationships between individuals within the tribe, and between the tribes themselves.[8] It was the foundation of their courage, courtesy, and hospitality to the pale-faced strangers from across the ocean.

The white colonizers, all deeply imbued with the Christian precepts of love, truth, and charity, persecuted and betrayed the native people, whom they described as painted, heathen savages. This is in stark contrast to the vision of Earl Henry St. Clair, for his expeditions to North America were part of the overall Rex Deus strategy to found a commonwealth based on tolerance, far from the oppressive hand of Holy Mother the Church. Sadly, due to the circumstances that combined to keep the voyages secret, their objective and their spirituality had no impact whatsoever on the behavior of later European colonizers.

Thanks to the foresight of Earl William St. Clair and the activities of the Freemasons, Rex Deus thinking did exert some degree of formative influence on the development of the American Constitution as described earlier. While the development of the culture and economy in the United States and Canada has been hailed as a beacon for liberty and opportunity for people of European extraction, it has sadly mirrored all other European colonial endeavors in its brutal disregard for the rights of the indigenous peoples.

Impelled by the Protestant work ethic, American economic activity soon overtook that of its European parents and began to dominate, if not control, the world economy as a whole. The philosophy of economic development in the twentieth century flowed from this in a way that has raped, plundered, and pillaged this planet to the extent that mankind itself is now an endangered species. The Western developed countries have sown the wind, but the entire world must now reap the whirlwind of widespread pollution, radioactive contamination, escalating population growth, and the greenhouse effect. Appalling as these consequences most certainly are, they can be mitigated. We can begin to apply the lessons that were put into practice when Henry St. Clair and Antonio Zeno first encountered the Mi'qmaq people of North America.

The Paradigm Shift

Is there any evidence that we, at the beginning of the third millennium, show any readiness to learn from the past? We believe that there is, in both the political arena and among the wider public of the Western developed world. Since the 1960s, the general public has conducted campaigns aimed at redressing the injustice, racism, and environmental destruction that, up until now, has seemed an integral part of society.[9] Perceptions change; paradigms do not merely shift, they are often forcibly displaced; new ideas, until they have proven themselves, are always held by a committed minority who are endowed with the courage to act. Edmund Burke said, "No one has made a greater mistake than he who did nothing because he could only do a little." We must all begin to act responsibly for our own lives and the place in which we live.

The growing awareness of climatic change, increasing levels of pollution, and the escalating world population are compelling reasons for effective action. However, if simple, logical and intellectual argument were enough to change people's perceptions and their actions, the kingdom of heaven of which Jesus spoke would have been well-established for nearly 2000 years. Action is ultimately more compelling than faith or argument, for it is only when our actions are changed and we become the living embodiment of spiritual experience that we can begin to influence others.

William James claimed that "I must act as if what I do makes a difference." This is as vital in our dealings with one another as it is in our overall relationship with nature. As individuals, races, or nations, we must recognize that peace cannot be imposed from above; it is neither the fruit of legislation, nor does it derive from religious strictures and moral codes. Peace grows from within, from the cooperative energies of human beings. As the American psychologist Marilyn Ferguson, remarked ". . . peace is a state of mind, not a state of the nation."[10] Peace and justice are not just political issues; they both have an innate spiritual and religious dimension. The American civil-rights leader, Martin Luther King, Jr., wrote "Any religion which professes to be concerned about the souls of men and is not concerned about the social and economic conditions that can scar the soul, is a spiritually moribund religion only waiting for the day to be buried."[11]

In the United States, massive strides have been taken to combat racial injustice following the civil-rights campaigns of the 1960s. Politicians throughout North America have started to bring a measure of redress to the Native American people who were so cruelly abused by the white invaders. In both the United States and Canada, the law is giving growing protection to the rights of tribal people in reclaiming their cultural heritage.

The constitutional right of American citizens to take an active part in the decision-making process is almost unique in the developed world. It is a tribute to the foresight of the spiritually gifted men who wrote the Constitution that the telling introductory phrase "We, the people . . ." still has relevance today. Individual citizens in the run-up to state elections frame resolutions to initiate changes in the law that, if approved by state referenda, then pass into legislation. We know of no other democracy where this is possible.

In the American democracies, while the political systems enable change and the politicians have initiated some form of redress in favor of the native people, is there a true constituency for further change? There is no doubt that, stimulated by the pressures of the global crisis, people are thinking deeply, reevaluating old conceptions, and looking at the world with new eyes, but are they open to spiritual conceptions?

The answer to both questions is a resounding *yes*. There has been a growing movement to reclaim spiritual values as the foundation for decision making since the early nineteenth century, when a group of American writers known as the Transcendentalists began to build upon earlier European foundations laid down by Blake and Swedenborg. Helena Petrovna Blavatsky strengthened this process, and the Theosophical Society she founded played a catalytic role in opening up Western awareness to the mystical powers inherent in Eastern religious philosophies. The so-called Esoteric Revival in Europe and elsewhere, which extended from the late nineteenth century onward, strengthened the rising tide of perception that mysticism and spirituality had real validity and were of vital relevance to the modern age. Mysticism and spirituality have at their very heart the concept of a change of consciousness, which led the historian William McLoughlin to claim that the 1960s marked the beginning of America's fourth "great awakening," and that it represented a time of cultural dislocation and revitalization that would extend for three or more decades.

> The counterculture that began to emerge during the 1960s was not restricted to the United States however; it spread rapidly through the new and vibrant international popular culture to many nations in Europe. In Scandinavia, Germany, France and England there was already a growing, thinking and questioning group of middle class, youthful people, who were disenchanted and ill at ease with the emotional and spiritual desert that was the apparently inevitable end product of the consumer society. Thus began an informal movement characterised by a spiritual thirst, a time of a growing sense of community and

new cultural synthesis that is in harmony with nature and with the earth itself. The task that confronts us all at the beginning of this millennium is to seek a new ecology of the spirit.[12]

What role can Native American spirituality and the insights of medieval mystics play in bringing about effective transformation in this era of technological change? The foundation of Native American spiritual belief was the certain knowledge that we are a living part of nature, not just observers separate and distinct from it; the human race is one of the subject species of the natural order, not its master. If we utilize that simple truth at the foundation of our belief system and build upon it the principles of tolerance, love, and community service that were the common denominator between the three cultures that reflected those values when the St. Clair/Zeno expedition met the Mi'qmaq people, perhaps we may yet earn our right to survive as a species.

> The earth does not belong to the people; people belong to the earth. . . . This earth is precious to the Creator and to harm the earth is to heap contempt upon the Creator. . . . Our dead never forget this beautiful earth, for it is the mother of the red people. We are part of the earth and it is part of us.[13]

A MODERN VOYAGE
OF DISCOVERY

IN THE AUTUMN OF 1997, AN ADVENTUROUS Italian yachtswoman, Laura Zolo, in her yacht *7 Roses*, was caught in a severe storm off the Orkney coast and took shelter in Kirkwall harbor. During her enforced stay, she was sitting in a local pub leafing through a tourist guide when she came across an article that immediately fired her imagination. Published to celebrate the 600th anniversary of the Henry St. Clair/Zeno voyage to America, the article summarized the evidence for the voyage produced at the Sinclair Symposium held in Kirkwall a few weeks earlier.[1] Laura described her feelings on first reading the article in the following words:

> Why had I never heard of this? And why has such a vital part of maritime history been so completely neglected? I was determined to look into this the minute I got back to Italy. I am an Italian sailor so when I read about Zeno the Venetian navigator, patriotic pride took hold and I thought "Wow! My countryman could have been part of the discovery of America." It is obvious that he did it—and I am going to find the evidence when I do it too.[2]

On her return to Italy, Laura began researching the North Atlantic voyages of the Zeno brothers and resolved to replicate them in her own vessel and to bring the magnificent achievements of the Zeno brothers to wider public and international notice. Seeking sponsorship for her project, Laura received an immediate and generous response from the municipal authorities of Venice,[3] who endorsed not only her efforts,

Figure 20. The beautiful and courageous yachtswoman, Laura Zolo.

*Figure 21. Laura Zolo receiving plaques from the
Venetian Municipality.*

but also the campaign by the Prince Henry Sinclair Society of America to publicize the fourteenth-century St. Clair/Zeno voyages.[4] Laura also gained the backing of the Italian Navy[5] and support from the elected authorities of her island home of Elba.[6]

We first heard of *Projetto Zeno* when we received an invitation to a civic reception to launch the project at the Morosini Naval Academy in Venice on 16 December 1999.[7] When we presented ourselves at the gate of the Academy, the problems and coincidences began. The security guard spoke no English and refused us entry pending authorization from his superiors. While he sought further orders, a young Italian couple arrived who spoke fluent English and offered to act as translators for our party. They introduced themselves as Nicolo and Eleanor Zeno, truly a divinely inspired coincidence. Niven Sinclair, of course, was delighted at this reunion of the St. Clair and Zeno families after a gap of over six centuries. We had time to get to know one another before the official reception began, and our party was joined by Richard and D'Elayne Coleman, the founders and principals of the Prince Henry Sinclair Society of North America. The Colemans had been instrumental in setting up Progetto Zeno. When Laura Zolo arrived, she was the center of attention. She is a delightful lady of considerable charm, whose attributes include courage, practicality, and above all, beauty.

The reception was hosted and chaired by the Cultural Director of the Venetian Municipality. This imposing dignitary outlined the project and gave it the official blessing of the city authorities. Niven Sinclair described the original fourteenth-century voyage in some detail[8]; Nicolo Zeno and D'Elayne Coleman provided further comments. Laura then held center stage, gave a brief history of her involvement, and outlined the aims and objectives of the project. She was presented with a series of commemorative plaques in Venetian glass to pass on to the civic authorities at her various ports of call. Niven later described the project in the following terms:

> It is a wonderful project by a beautiful lady who has already circumnavigated the world. She has the experience, the courage and the determination to complete the voyage. She deserves our unstinted support.[9]

During the next few days, we all enjoyed the company of Eleanor and Nicolo Zeno, Laura, and her partner and crew member Cap'n Jack

Figure 22. Niven Sinclair and Nicolo Zeno in Venice.

Lammiman. We spent many an enjoyable hour drinking coffee and chatting in the comfortable, if somewhat overcrowded cabin of *7 Roses*, which was moored near the old naval dockyard of the Arsenale. Eleanor and Nicolo not only invited our growing tribe to their home in one of the original Zeno *palazzi*, but gave generously of their time to ensure that we had an opportunity to visit many sites in Venice associ-

Figure 23. The yacht 7 Roses *arriving in Guysborough Harbor.*

ated with their illustrious family. They also hosted one of the most delightful dinner parties we have ever attended, at which the humor became completely surreal.

Accompanied by an official escort provided by the Italian Navy and a flotilla of small boats, Laura and Cap'n Jack sailed from the Lagoon in Venice on 6 January 2000. Totally dependent on sail, they were buffeted by adverse winds and endured a variety of weather conditions as they made their slow progress to Elba and on through the Mediterranean to ports in Italy, France, and Spain en route to Gibraltar and the Atlantic. Included in this itinerary were the Templar ports of St. Raphael, Aigues Mortes, and Marseilles in the Mediterranean, Tomar in Portugal, and La Rochelle on the Atlantic coast of France. We will pass over Cap'n Jack's bizarre, if somewhat unfortunate, cycling accident in Hartlepool, where he collided with a gondola (his words not ours), fractured a rib, and ruined a pouch full of pipe tobacco with salt water. After the hiatus in Hartlepool and appropriate medical treatment, the 37-foot yacht set sail in the North Sea bound for Prince Henry St. Clair's old earldom of Orkney; they arrived on Tuesday 20 June.

In company with Niven, and Tony and Anna Sinclair, we flew to Orkney on Thursday 22 June. Immediately after booking into the hotel, we made our way to the harbor, boarded the yacht, and began to hear of Laura and Jack's adventures since leaving Venice. They had been warmly received in every port of call and had already begun to put flesh on the bones of the first Zeno voyage to Orkney. Laura's account made the history of this long-forgotten voyage come alive in a way that appeals to academic historians, the ordinary public, and most important, to children everywhere. The fact that Laura was neither a Zeno nor a Sinclair, was neither Scottish nor Venetian, imparted a degree of impartiality and gave added emphasis to the story she was re-creating.

On Friday morning, we were joined by the Sinclair Clan Chief, Malcolm Sinclair, the Earl of Caithness, a direct descendant of Earl Henry St. Clair of Orkney. Laura was given an official reception by the Island's Council at their offices in Kirkwall, at which she presented them with one of the commemorative plaques entrusted to her by the Municipality of Venice. In return, she was presented with an Orkney plaque. It is most fitting that this ceremony took place beneath the flag of the Mi'qmaq presented to the people of Orkney by Donald Julian, Dr. Peter Christmas, and Chief Kerry Prosper during the Sinclair Symposium in 1997. After the exchange of plaques, Laura received a donation of Orkney delicacies for the voyage and a bottle of whiskey (purely for medicinal purposes of course). She was then entrusted with The Sword of Peace to pass on to the Grand Chief of the Mi'qmaq in Nova Scotia. This ceremonial sword had been specially commissioned from Wilkinson's, the sword makers, and was engraved with the word "peace" in over two hundred languages, including Mi'qmaq. It also carried Mi'qmaq symbolism and the Engrailed Cross of the St. Clairs. It was to be presented to the Mi'qmaq people as a token of respect and gratitude for their hospitable and kindly reception of Earl Henry.

Friday night concluded with a dinner for us all. Tony and Anna Sinclair spent the remaining few hours on Saturday provisioning 7 Roses for the Atlantic crossing, after which our party took leave and flew south once more. Laura and Jack attended a reception in their honor at the Sailing Club and again received presents from the generous people of the island. They sailed from Kirkwall to Shetland on Sunday 25 June, escorted by a small flotilla of boats from the Orkney Sailing Club.

The voyage to Shetland was made with the assistance of a gentle northwesterly breeze, as Laura and Jack reflected upon the warmth of Orkney hospitality and the many presents they had received. Laura remarked that Bressay was a superb natural harbor, and as they sailed through its calm waters, they were passed by an imposing replica of a Viking longship engaged in re-creating voyages recounted in the Viking sagas.[10] History does indeed have a habit of repeating itself, and just as Earl Henry and Antonio Zeno had followed the sailing directions of the Viking explorers, now Laura's re-creation of that voyage once again followed the Viking trail. The yacht stayed in Shetland for six days. Laura and Jack enjoyed a very pleasant meeting with the island's civic dignitaries at the town hall before settling down to tackle the endless tasks necessary to prepare a small yacht for a prolonged voyage in northern waters.[11]

The passage from Shetland to the Faroes was brisk; it took only forty hours to make landfall at Thorshaven for a very short stop—then onward toward Iceland. As an Italian, Laura found the northern waters and conditions a constant source of discovery: the sky was different, the movement and ever-changing cloud pattern a constant source of delight, and the midnight sunset an enthralling sight. Eventually, she spotted the gleaming beauty of a great imposing mountain enveloped in ice on the horizon. The cliffs of Vestmannaeyjar Island off the southwest coast of Iceland stood ready to protect 7 Roses as she anchored in a perfect harbor formed by volcanic action.[12] Laura reflected that this harbor must have given much-needed shelter to many a Viking ship bound for Greenland and Vinland in the New World. After resting there for two days, Laura and Jack sailed on to Reykjavik, the main port of Iceland, where they had to wait for several days for the weather to abate. Luckily, they found that the people of Iceland are kind and generous and ready to help whenever possible. They left Iceland for Greenland on 25 July.

The weather and conditions in Greenland, Labrador, and Newfoundland delayed Laura's estimated time of arrival in Nova Scotia until the end of the first week of September. We flew with Niven from London to Halifax on Thursday 7 September to meet Laura and Jack as they docked in Guysborough on that Friday. D'Elayne and Richard Coleman of the Prince Henry Sinclair Society of North America had done their work well by publicizing Laura's arrival in the local press, and there was a considerable crowd waiting on Jost Wharf in Guysborough that Friday afternoon.

Local people, Mr. and Mrs. Kerry Prosper and other members of the Mi'qmaq, politicians both local and national, the Italian Consul, the press, and our own small party had all gathered in a state of expectation at the small anchorage in downtown Guysborough. Right on time, we saw *7 Roses* complete her long and arduous 7,000 mile voyage by sailing through the narrow passage from Chedabucto Bay escorted by a flotilla of small boats, including the familiar shape of the boat owned by the local Councillor, Miles MacPherson, who had taken us through these waters during our research trip just a year before. As *7 Roses* turned toward the dock, the crowd grew silent, and we both felt quite tearful seeing this voyage reach its culmination. Laura was at the helm, and Cap'n Jack was on the foredeck making ready for the landing. Within a few moments of making fast, it was hugs and kisses all round as we greeted Laura and Jack and welcomed them to Guysborough. There was a special welcome for Laura that she had not expected; her brother Andrea had flown in specially from Elba to meet her at the culmination of her voyage.

D'Elayne and Richard Coleman had organized a reception in the evening on behalf of the Prince Henry Sinclair Society of North America to formally welcome Laura and Jack. This event was attended by many members of the Clan Sinclair Association of Nova Scotia; the Clan Sinclair Association of Canada; several visitors from the United

States; Ms. Elo-Kai Ojama, Consul General of the United States; Mr. Rodolfo Meloni, the Honorable Vice Consul of Italy; Warden Hines of Guysborough Municipal District; Andrea Zolo from Elba; our own party; and, arriving during the proceedings, Rory Sinclair from Toronto, bringing the Sinclair Clan Chief, Malcolm Sinclair from Halifax Airport. Various presentations were made to Laura, including a generous donation from the Prince Henry Sinclair Society; then Laura and Jack each received the gift of a Nova Scotia jacket. Not surprisingly, it was a very emotional occasion that culminated in a speech of thanks from Laura herself. Stimulating as this was, however, the party was only beginning.

Saturday was blessed with bright warm sunshine that showed Guysborough Harbor to wonderful effect. At lunchtime, there was a formal reception at the De Barres Manor Hotel for Laura and Jack, hosted by Warden Hines on behalf of the Municipality of Guysborough. This was attended by all the dignitaries mentioned earlier and Mr. Ron Chisolm, member of the Legislative Assembly for Guysborough and Port Hawkesbury; Mr. Peter MacKay, member of Parliament for Pictou, Antigonish, and Guysborough; Dr. Peter Christmas, Don Julian, and Grand Chief and Mrs. Ben Sylliboy of the Mi'qmaq people; the Earl of Caithness; and our own party from England. Another Venetian glass plaque was presented to Warden Hines, and in return, Laura was given a superb, framed photograph of Guysborough Harbor. After a magnificent lunch, the entire party moved to Boylston Upper Park to the site of the Prince Henry Memorial erected by the Clan Sinclair Association of Canada for the culmination of Celebration 2000, the Sinclair Clan's salute to the Mi'qmaq nations and the Italian mariners.

In this magnificent setting overlooking the grand panorama of Guysborough Harbor, under the direction of Jack Sinclair as Master of Ceremonies, the Clan Sinclair began to celebrate Laura's achievement in re-creating the original St. Clair/ Zeno voyages of the late fourteenth century. The ceremony began when Rory Sinclair piped in a procession headed by Grand Chief Sylliboy and Earl Malcolm Sinclair. Amid the speeches by the various dignitaries, we were treated to a wealth of talent from local people, and by the dancing of the Eskasoni Dancers of the Mi'qmaq in which everyone was invited to join. For the majority of those present, the most moving contribution came from the lady described as Poet Laureate of the Mi'qmaq, Dame Rita Joe, who was awarded the Order of Canada in recognition of her work as a Mi'qmaq writer and spokesperson. This courageous and gifted lady of eighty-two years, who has been battling Parkinson's disease for many years, took center stage, sat before the microphone, and said:

> I am a Mi'qmaq, I speak for my people.
> I welcome
> The Venetian mariners from Italy,
> Laura Zolo and Captain Jack
> Who end their heroic voyage in Guysborough.
> From many lands they have visited
> Then to ours.
> I am a Mi'qmaq representative,
> Like in the days of 1398
> The offered hand is still in place,
> The other on my heart in sign of friendship.
> I am the nation known the world over
> Who helped the broken men, their bodies wasted by scurvy,
> My food, your food,
> My medicine, your medicine.
> My fear the same as yours for the unknown.
> Today there is no fear but a welcome knowledge
> That we are friends as it should be
> And the view that was offered by Antonio Zeno in 1398,
> The friendly reception by the Mi'qmaq Nation,
> I thank him today.
> And from the voyage of Prince Henry Sinclair and
> The Clan thus acknowledging this history,
> By showing the Mi'qmaq as compassionate
> I appreciate and know is true.[13]

This simple and moving speech touched every heart present. Niven Sinclair remarked:

> It was perhaps understandable that Rita Joe established an immediate rapport with that other woman of courage, Laura Zolo. When they embraced, tears drenched each other's shoulders. Two remarkable women, two cultures, one accord.[14]

Niven, himself no mean public speaker, gave the speech of a lifetime. Then came the presentation of The Sword of Peace.

Traditionally, a sword is a symbol of honor, chivalry, and fraternity. It was with this in mind that the Sword of Peace was presented to the Mi'qmaq Nation in recognition of the welcome they extended to Prince Henry St. Clair, Antonio Zeno, and all the generations of Scottish people who made their home in Nova Scotia. The sword was presented by Malcolm Sinclair, Earl of Caithness, in his capacity as the hereditary Clan Chief of the Sinclairs, to Grand Chief Sylliboy of the Mi'qmaq Nation. The Grand Chief is a dignified man who has led his people through many trials and tribulations, but even this experienced man began to show great emotion as he received this gift from his Scottish counterpart. Holding the sword with his arms extended, one hand near the hilt, the other on the blade, his face began to tremble visibly as he spoke his thanks on behalf of his people. Grand Chief Sylliboy welcomed everyone to Mi'qmaq territory and spoke the following words:

> As Grand Chief of the Mi'qmaq Nation, historically and today I have the responsibility of the territorial well-being of our Mi'qmaq people. It is with great pleasure that we greet our friends from the Clan Sinclair and their many followers in the continuation of the saga of Prince Henry St. Clair's voyage to the Mi'qmaq country in the past. We would like to thank the Right Honourable Malcolm Sinclair, the Earl of Caithness and Hereditary Chief of the Clan Sinclair for his presence here today on our Mi'qmaq soil and his great gesture of peace between our two tribes.
>
> We accept this beautiful Sword on behalf of our Mi'qmaq Nation as a symbol of the peace and continued friendship which will re-emphasise the bridging of lasting relationships.[15]

The Grand Chief concluded his speech with a tribute to Laura Zolo and thanked her for recreating the St. Clair/Zeno voyage. He then paid fulsome tribute to the work of Niven Sinclair in researching and publicizing the original voyage to Mi'qmaq territory. He placed the Sword of Peace into the custody of Donald Julian, Executive Director of the Confederacy of Mainland Mi'qmaq, for safekeeping until it can assume its proper place of honor when the Dehert Museum project is completed.[16]

Figure 24. Earl Malcolm Caithness and Grand Chief Benjamin Silliboy with the Sword of Peace.

Niven's words encapsulate the atmosphere engendered by this ceremony:

> It was a moment which will be forever imprinted on the minds of those who were there. It was a moment when history was shared by people from both sides of the Atlantic—indigenous and immigrant. It was a moment when tears were shared and shed in a common bond of understanding and friendship which transcended boundaries of culture and custom.
>
> It was a moment when the spirit of Prince Henry St. Clair manifested itself and allowed those present to realise that the way of progress is the way of peace. He set an example by the exemplary way in which he treated the indigenous people with whom he came into contact—an example which found a generous response in the way in which the Mi'qmaq people received him. It was this lesson which Rita Joe has spelt out in her own inimitable style.[17]

Laura's voyage was not yet finished, however. After leaving Nova Scotia, she continued retracing Prince Henry St. Clair's original voyage and sailed to Vinland. Anchoring in Boston Harbor, she and Jack made their way to Westford to see the carving of the Westford Knight and played their part in the official opening of an exhibition about the history of the carving at the Westford Museum organized by Elizabeth Lane of the J. V. Fletcher Memorial Library.[18] Sailing on to Newport, Rhode Island, she completed the known route of Prince Henry's voyage before traveling to New York. There, ironically, she took part in the Columbus Day Parade.

Christopher Columbus is still believed by many to be the discoverer of America despite the fact that the land had been occupied for over eleven millennia by the Native American people, visited frequently by the Egyptians, Romans, and Vikings, to say nothing of the, as yet unproven, explorations by Phoenicians and Celts. Laura's participation in the Columbus Day Parade reinforced the fact that over 100 years before Columbus set sail on his famous voyage, the Atlantic had been crossed by Prince Henry St. Clair and Antonio Zeno, who came in peace, established good and productive relations with the Mi'qmaq, and created lasting and permanent bonds of friendship with those magnificent and compassionate people that have stood the test of time.

APPENDIX A

GENEALOGY OF
EARL HENRY ST. CLAIR

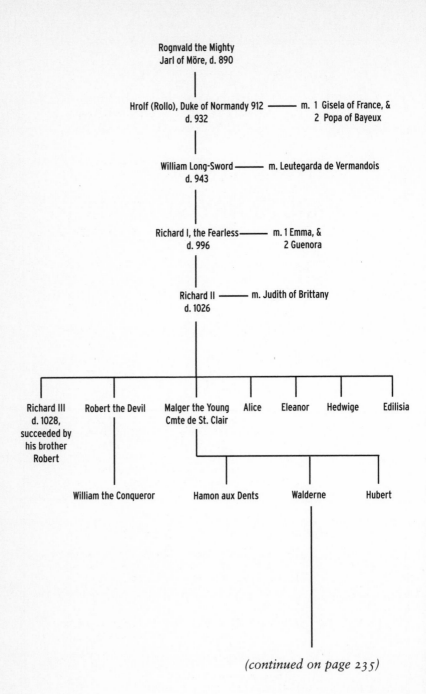

Rognvald the Mighty
Jarl of Möre, d. 890

Hrolf (Rollo), Duke of Normandy 912 ——— m. 1 Gisela of France, &
d. 932   2 Popa of Bayeux

William Long-Sword ——— m. Leutegarda de Vermandois
d. 943

Richard I, the Fearless ——— m. 1 Emma, &
d. 996   2 Guenora

Richard II ——— m. Judith of Brittany
d. 1026

Richard III | Robert the Devil | Malger the Young | Alice | Eleanor | Hedwige | Edilisia
d. 1028,   Cmte de St. Clair
succeeded by
his brother
Robert

William the Conqueror   Hamon aux Dents   Walderne   Hubert

(continued on page 235)

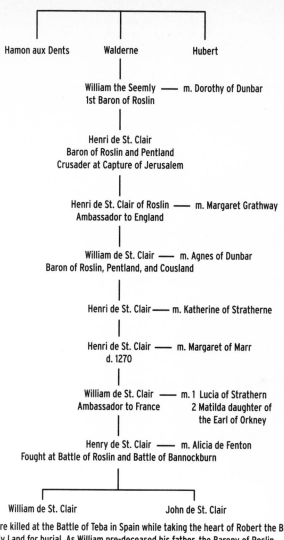

Hamon aux Dents   Walderne   Hubert

William the Seemly —— m. Dorothy of Dunbar
1st Baron of Roslin

Henri de St. Clair
Baron of Roslin and Pentland
Crusader at Capture of Jerusalem

Henri de St. Clair of Roslin —— m. Margaret Grathway
Ambassador to England

William de St. Clair —— m. Agnes of Dunbar
Baron of Roslin, Pentland, and Cousland

Henri de St. Clair —— m. Katherine of Stratherne

Henri de St. Clair —— m. Margaret of Marr
d. 1270

William de St. Clair —— m. 1 Lucia of Strathern
Ambassador to France   2 Matilda daughter of
          the Earl of Orkney

Henry de St. Clair —— m. Alicia de Fenton
Fought at Battle of Roslin and Battle of Bannockburn

William de St. Clair   John de St. Clair

Both brothers were killed at the Battle of Teba in Spain while taking the heart of Robert the Bruce
to the Holy Land for burial. As William pre-deceased his father, the Barony of Roslin
passed to his son, another William de St. Clair.

William de St. Clair ———— m. Isabel daughter of
Killed in battle in Lithuania, 1358   Malise Sperra, Earl of Orkney

Henry de St. Clair, Earl of Orkney,
Baron of Roslin, Pentland, and Cousland.
Voyaged with the Zenos to America in 1396–1400.

APPENDIX B

MAP OF THE
VOYAGE

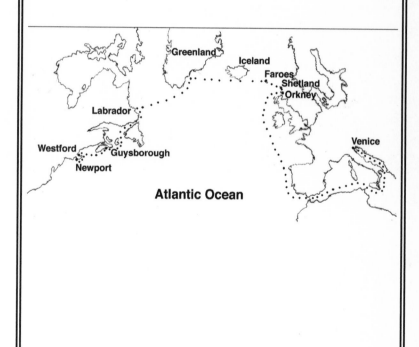

NOTES

Introduction

1 From the introduction to Charles Michael Boland's *They All Discovered America* (New York: Doubleday and Co., 1961).

2 Frederick Pohl, *The Lost Discovery* (New York: WW Norton and Co., 1952); *The Sinclair Expedition to Nova Scotia in 1398* (Pictou, NS: Pictou Advocate Press, 1950); *Atlantic Crossings before Columbus* (New York: WW Norton and Co., 1961); and *Prince Henry Sinclair* (Halifax, NS: Nimbus Publishing, 1967); Michael Bradley, *Holy Grail Across the Atlantic* (Ontario: Hounslow Press, 1988) and *Grail Knights of North America* (Toronto: Hounslow Press, 1998); Andrew Sinclair, *The Sword and the Grail* (London: Century, 1993); Niven Sinclair, *Beyond Any Shadow of Doubt* (London: Private publication, 1998); Mark Finnan, *The Sinclair Saga* (Halifax, NS: Formac Publishing Co. Ltd., 1999); Stephen Sora, *The Lost Treasure of the Knights Templar* (Rochester, VT: Destiny Books, 1999); W. H. Hobbs, "The Fourteenth Century Discovery of America by Antonio Zeno," *Scientific Monthly*, No. 72, 1951, 24–31.

Chapter 1

1 Tim Wallace-Murphy and Marilyn Hopkins, *Rosslyn: Guardian of the Secrets of the Holy Grail* (Shaftsbury, UK: Element Books, 1999), p. 198.

2 Hermann Pálsson and Paul Edwards, trans. *Orkneyinga Saga,* (London: Penguin Books, 1981), 4, p. 26.

3 *Orkneyinga Saga,* 4, p. 26.

4 *Orkneyinga Saga,* 4, p. 27.

5 *Orkneyinga Saga,* 5, p. 27.

6 *Orkneyinga Saga,* 5, p. 28.

7 *Orkneyinga Saga,* 6, p. 28.

8 Wallace-Murphy and Hopkins, *Rosslyn: Guardian of the Secrets of the Holy Grail*, p. 199.

9 *Orkneyinga Saga,* 6, pp. 28–29.

10 *Orkneyinga Saga,* 7, p. 29.

11 *Orkneyinga Saga,* 8, p. 32.

12 *Orkneyinga Saga,.* 4, p. 26.

13 See Robert Wace, *The History of the Norman People: Wace's Roman de Rou*, trans., Elizabeth Van Houts (N.p.: The Boydell Press, 2004); Marilyn

Hopkins, Graham Simmans, and Tim Wallace-Murphy, *Rex Deus* (Shaftsbury, UK: Element Books, 2000) p. 107.

14 Louis Anatole de St. Clair, *Histoire Genealogique de la Famille de Saint Clair det ses alliances* (Paris: Hardy & Bernard, 1905.), p. 7.

15 Wace, *History of the Norman People.*

16 St. Clair, *Histoire Genealogique de la Famille de Saint Clair*, p. 7.

17 St. Clair, *Histoire Genealogique de la Famille de Saint Clair*, p. 8.

18 St. Clair, *Histoire Genealogique de la Famille de Saint Clair*, p. 8.

19 St. Clair, *Histoire Genealogique de la Famille de Saint Clair*, p. 8.

20 St. Clair, *Histoire Genealogique de la Famille de Saint Clair*, p. 9.

21 Wallace-Murphy et. al., *Rex Deus*, p. 105.

22 Wallace-Murphy et. al., *Rex Deus*, pp. 107–8.

23 Wallace-Murphy and Hopkins, *Rosslyn: Guardian of the Secrets of the Holy Grail*, pp. 97–98.

24 Wallace-Murphy et al., *Rex Deus*, p. 38.

25 Wallace-Murphy et al., *Rex Deus*, p. 41.

26 Wallace-Murphy et al., *Rex Deus*, p. 210.

27 Tim Wallace-Murphy, *The Templar Legacy and the Masonic Inheritance within Rosslyn Chapel* (Roslin, UK: The Friends of Rosslyn, 1994), p. 12.

28 Wallace-Murphy et al., *Rex Deus*, p. 95.

29 St. Clair, *Histoire Genealogique de la Famille de Saint Clair*, p. 10.

30 St. Clair, *Histoire Genealogique de la Famille de Saint Clair*, pp. 11–12.

31 St. Clair, *Histoire Genealogique de la Famille de Saint Clair*, pp. 15–16.

32 Wallace-Murphy, *The Templar Legacy and the Masonic Inheritance within Rosslyn Chapel*, p. 25.

33 Andrew Sinclair, *The Sword and the Grail* (London: Century, 1993), pp. 30–37.

34 St. Clair, *Histoire Genealogique de la Famille de Saint Clair*, p. 16.

35 John Robinson, *Dungeon, Fire and Sword* (London: Brockhampton Press, 1999), p. 20.

36 Robinson, *Dungeon, Fire and Sword*, p. 28.

37 Wallace-Murphy and Hopkins, *Rosslyn: Guardian of the Secrets of the Holy Grail*, p. 94.

38 Wallace-Murphy and Hopkins, *Rosslyn: Guardian of the Secrets of the Holy Grail* , p. 94.

39 Wallace-Murphy et al., *Rex Deus*, p. 109.

40 Wallace-Murphy and Hopkins, *Rosslyn: Guardian of the Secrets of the Holy Grail*, p. 97.

41 Wallace-Murphy et al., *Rex Deus*, pp. 113–14.

42 Wallace-Murphy and Hopkins, *Rosslyn: Guardian of the Secrets of the Holy Grail*, p. 97.

43 Wallace-Murphy, *The Templar Legacy and the Masonic Inheritance within Rosslyn Chapel*, p. 17.

44 Trevor Ravenscroft and Tim Wallace-Murphy, *The Mark of the Beast* (London: Sphere Books, 1990), p. 52.

45 HRH, Prince Michael of Albany, *The Forgotten Monarchy of Scotland* (Shaftsbury, UK: Element Books, 1998), p. 61.

46 Wallace-Murphy et al., *Rex Deus*, p. 168.

47 Alleged by Baigent, Leigh and Lincoln in *The Holy Blood and the Holy Grail*, (London: Book Club Associates, 1982); also by Andrew Sinclair in *The Sword and the Grail*, however we cannot locate any credible evidence whatsoever in support of this allegation.

48 Wallace-Murphy and Hopkins, *Rosslyn: Guardian of the Secrets of the Holy Grail*, p. 97; also, Robinson, *Dungeon, Fire and Sword*, p. 37.

49 Wallace-Murphy and Hopkins, *Rosslyn: Guardian of the Secrets of the Holy Grail*, pp. 95–96.

50 Wallace-Murphy et al., *Rex Deus*, p. 118.

51 Wallace-Murphy et al., *Rex Deus*, p. 120.

52 Wallace-Murphy and Hopkins, *Rosslyn: Guardian of the Secrets of the Holy Grail*, p. 99.

53 Robinson, *Dungeon, Fire and Sword*, pp. 320–23.

54 Wallace-Murphy et al., *Rex Deus*, pp. 119–20.

55 Wallace-Murphy and Hopkins, *Rosslyn: Guardian of the Secrets of the Holy Grail*, pp. 99–100.

56 Sinclair, *The Sword and the Grail*, p. 36.

57 Wallace-Murphy et al., *Rex Deus*, p. 128.

58 Wallace-Murphy et al., *Rex Deus*, pp. 121–22.

59 Wallace-Murphy and Hopkins, *Rosslyn: Guardian of the Secrets of the Holy Grail*, p. 112.

60 Wallace-Murphy et al., *Rex Deus*, p. 135.

61 Robinson, *Dungeon, Fire and Sword*, pp. 432–34.

62 Wallace-Murphy, *The Templar Legacy and Masonic Inheritance within Rosslyn Chapel*, p. 21.

63 Wallace-Murphy et al., *Rex Deus*, p. 177.

64 Rev. Fr. Hay, *The Genealogie of the St. Clairs of Roslin* (Scotland: Maidement, 1835).

65 Wallace-Murphy and Hopkins, *Rosslyn: Guardian of the Secrets of the Holy Grail*, p. 121.

66 HRH Prince Michael of Albany, *The Forgotten Monarchy*, p. 150.

67 Wallace-Murphy et al., *Rex Deus*, p. 177.

Chapter 2

1 Andrew Sinclair, *The Sword and the Grail* (London: Century, 1993), pp. 43, 129.

2 Robert Fossier, ed., *The Cambridge Illustrated History of the Middle Ages* (Cambridge: Cambridge University Press, 1986), vol. 3, 1250–1520, p. 65.

3 John Julian Norwich, *A History of Venice* (London: Penguin, 1983), p. 200.

4 Norwich, *A History of Venice*, p. 4.

5 Norwich, *A History of Venice*, pp. 13–16.

6 Norwich, *A History of Venice*, pp. 623, 631.

7 Norwich, *A History of Venice*, p. 77.

8 Stephen Runciman, *A History of the Crusades* (London: Pelican, 1971), vol. I, p. 312.

9 Runciman, *A History of the Crusades*, vol. I, p. 312.

10 Norwich, *A History of Venice*, pp. 79–80.

11 Albert of Aix, VII 225, pp. 521–23: translatio Sancti Nicolas, pp. 276–78.

12 Runciman, *A History of the Crusades*, Vol. II, pp. 464–67.

13 Anthony Bridge, *The Crusades* (London: Granada Publishing, 1980), p. 205.

14 Norwich, *A History of Venice*, pp. 122–23.

15 Norwich, *A History of Venice*, p. 123.

16 Bridge, *The Crusades*, pp 215–217

17 Norwich, *A History of Venice*, p. 127.

18 Norwich, *A History of Venice*, p. 128.

19 Norwich, *A History of Venice*, p. 128.

20 Bridge, *The Crusades*, p. 231.

21 Norwich, *A History of Venice*, pp. 130–40.

22 John Robinson, *Dungeon, Fire and Sword* (London: Brockhampton Press, 1999), p. 322.

23 Robinson, *Dungeon, Fire and Sword*, p. 322.

24 Robinson, *Dungeon, Fire and Sword*, p. 323.

25 Norwich, *A History of Venice*, p. 203.

26 Norwich, *A History of Venice*, p. 207.

27 Norwich, *A History of Venice*, p. 197.

28 Norwich, *A Short History of Byzantium* (London: Penguin, 1998), p. 341.

29 Norwich, *A History of Venice*, p. 211.

30 Norwich, *A History of Venice*, p. 212.

31 Cited in Norwich's *A History of Venice*, p. 212.

32 Norwich, *A History of Venice*, p. 212.

33 Fossier, *The Cambridge Illustrated History of the Middle Ages*, vol. 3, 1250–1520, p. 53.

34 Norwich, *A History of Venice*, p. 215.

35 Norwich, *A History of Venice*, p. 216.

36 Norwich, *A History of Venice*, p. 219.

37 Norwich, *A History of Venice*, p. 233.

38 Norwich, *A History of Venice*, pp. 246–47

39 Norwich, *A History of Venice*, p. 247.

40 Norwich, *A History of Venice*, p. 248.

41 Norwich, *A History of Venice*, p. 249.

42 Norwich, *A History of Venice*, p. 250.

43 Norwich, *A History of Venice*, pp. 250–51.

44 Norwich, *A History of Venice*, p. 251.

45 Norwich, *A History of Venice*, pp. 252–53.

46 Norwich, *A History of Venice*, p. 253.

47 Norwich, *A History of Venice*, p. 254.

48 Norwich, *A History of Venice*, p. 255.

49 Johann Reinhold Forster, *History of the Voyages and Discoveries made in the North* (Dublin: 1786), pp. 178, ff.

Chapter 3

1 Louis Anatole de St. Clair, *Histoire Genealogique de la Famille de Saint Clair det ses alliances* (Paris: Hardy & Bernard, 1905), p. 15.

2 St. Clair, *Histoire Genealogique de la Famille de Saint Clair*, p. 16.

3   Tim Wallace-Murphy and Marilyn Hopkins, *Rosslyn: Guardian of the Secrets of the Holy Grail* (Shaftsbury UK: Element Books, 1999), p. 200.

4   Andrew Sinclair, *The Sword and the Grail* (London: Century, 1993), p. 33.

5   HRH Prince Michael of Albany, *The Forgotten Monarchy of Scotland* (Shaftsbury, UK: Element Books, 1998), pp. 65, 150.

6   See the cover illustration of *An Illustrated Guidebook to Rosslyn Chapel*.

7   St. Clair, *Histoire Genealogique de la Famille de Saint Clair*, p. 18.

8   St. Clair, *Histoire Genealogique de la Famille de Saint Clair*, p. 19.

9   Scottish Advocates Library, *Genealogical and Topical Mss.* 22. 2. 9; also Alexander Sinclair, *A Sketch of the History of Roslin and Its Possessors* (Edinburgh: Irwin, Maxwell, Dick, 1856).

10 Frederick Pohl, *Prince Henry Sinclair* (Halifax, NS: Nimbus Publishing, 1967), p. 10.

11 Rev. Fr. Hay, *Genealogie of the St Clairs of Rosslyn* (Scotland: Maidement, 1835).

12 Pohl, *Prince Henry Sinclair*, p. 22.

13 Hay, *Genealogie of the St Clairs of Rosslyn*.

14 Lord Henry Sincleer, *The Descent and Pedegree of the most noble and ancient house of the Lords of Sincleer* (n.p., 1590).

15 Andrew Sinclair, *The Sword and the Grail*, p. 120.

16 Hjalmar R. Holand, *America 1355–1364* (New York: Duell, Sloan & Pearce, Inc., 1946), pp. 8–11.

17 Holand, *America 1355–1364*, pp. 11–12.

18 *Gronlands, Historiske, Mindesmerker* (Copenhagen: 1838–1845), vol. II, pp. 459–64.

19 Frederick Pohl, *The Lost Discovery* (New York: Norton and Co., 1952), p. 196.

20 Holand, *Explorations in America before Columbus* (New York: Twayne Publishers, Inc., 1956) p. 154.

21 Translation of the original letter, published by the Smithsonian Institution, *Miscellaneous Collections*, vol. 116, no. 3, 20.

22 Holand, *Explorations in America before Columbus*, p. 157.

23 Holand, *Westward from Vinland* (New York: Duell, Sloan, & Pearce, 1940), p. 91.

24 *Gronlands, Historiske, Mindesmerker*, vol III, pp. 120–22; also Professor Storm, "Studier over Vinlandsreiserne," *Aaboger for Nordske Oldkyndighed og Historie* (Copenhagen, 1887) p. 73.

25 Holand, *Explorations in America before Columbus*, p. 160.

26 Holand, *Explorations in America before Columbus*, p. 278.

27 Rolf M. Nilsestuen, *The Kensington Runestone Vindicated* (Lanham, MD: University Press of America, 1994), pp. 7–10.

28 Holand, *Explorations in America before Columbus*, p. 166.

29 See Rolf M. Nilsestuen, *The Kensington Runestone Vindicated*, pp. 7–10.

30 Norumbega was mentioned and its position described or indicated by Hjalmar Holand, Pierre Crignon, Verrazano, and Jean Alphonse.

31 Holand, *Explorations in America before Columbus*, p. 256.

32 See chapters 9 and 10 of this work.

33 Holand, *Explorations in America before Columbus*, p. 278.

34 Holand, *Explorations in America before Columbus*, p. 279.

35 The Knutson Expedition is also described by Bishop Olaus Magnusson in *Historia de gentibus septrionalibus* (Rome, 1528).

36 Holand, *Explorations in America before Columbus*, p. 284.

37 Gunnar Thompson, *The Friar's Map* (Seattle: Laura Lee Production & Argonauts of the Misty Isles, 1996), pp. 92–93.

38 Holand, *Explorations in America before Columbus*, p. 286.

39 Thompson, *The Friar's Map*, p. 3.

40 Thompson, *The Friar's Map*, p. 107.

41 Inscription by Mercator in the margin of his map of 1569.

42 Holand, *Explorations in America before Columbus*, p. 286.

43 Hay, *The Genealogie of the St Clairs of Rosslyn* and Andrew Sinclair, *The Sword and the Grail*, p. 121.

44 Advocates Library Edinburgh, *Genealogical and Topical Mss*, 22. 2. 9.

45 Niven Sinclair, *Beyond Any Shadow of Doubt* (London: private publication, 1998), Sections 2 and 6.

46 Andrew Sinclair, *The Sword and the Grail*, p. 121.

47 Jacopo Zeno, Bishop of Padua, *Biography of Carlo Zeno* (Thought to be written in 1460).

48 Andrew Sinclair, *The Sword and the Grail*, p. 121.

49 Pohl, *Prince Henry Sinclair*, p. 36.

50 Hay, *Genealogie of the St Clairs of Rosslyn;* Pohl, *Prince Henry Sinclair*, p. 32.

51 Niven Sinclair, *Beyond Any Shadow of Doubt*, Section 10.

52 Pohl, *Prince Henry Sinclair*, p. 27.

53 Pohl, *Prince Henry Sinclair*, pp. 27–28.

54 J. Storer Clouston, *A History of Orkney* (Kirkwall, UK: W. R. Macintosh, 1932).

55 *The Chartulery of St Giles*, an. Dom. 1362; Henry Lord Sincleer, *The Descent and Pedegree of the most noble and ancient house of the Lords of Sincleer* (n.p., 1590).

56 See Appendix A for extended pedigree.

57 Pohl, *Prince Henry Sinclair*, p. 36; Clouston, *A History of Orkney*.

58 Clouston, *A History of Orkney*.

59 Pohl, *Prince Henry Sinclair*, p. 30.

60 Pohl, *Prince Henry Sinclair*, p. 193; Andrew Sinclair, *The Sword and the Grail*, pp. 43, 129.

61 No. 813. Aug 2nd 1379. Marstrand. P298. No. 820. Sept 1st 1379. St. Andrews. P300.

62 Clouston, *A History of Orkney*, pp. 234–37.

63 Eric Linklater, *Orkney and Shetland, an historical and geographical survey* (London: Robert Hayle, 1965), p. 73.

64 Hay, *Genealogie of the St. Clairs of Rosslyn*.

65 Pohl, *Prince Henry Sinclair*, p. 43.

66 Pohl, *Prince Henry Sinclair*, p. 48; Andrew Sinclair *The Sword and the Grail*, p. 124.

67 *Larousse Encyclopaedia of Ancient and Medieval History* (London: Paul Hamlyn Ltd., 1965) p. 386.

68 Cited on page 125 of Andrew Sinclair, *The Sword and the Grail*.

69 Thormedus Torfaeus, *Orcades seu rerum Orcadensium historiae* (Copen-

hagen: HC Paulli, 1715), p. 177 *Diplomatorum Norvegicum*, vol. 55, no. 460, p. 358. Note: These are government records of Norway, some of which are cited in Thomas Sinclair's *Caithness Events* (Wick, UK: W. Rae, 1899).

Chapter 4

1   Niven Sinclair, *Beyond Any Shadow of Doubt* (London: Private publication, 1998), Section 4.
2   Based on original work done by the genealogist Nicolas Cram Sinclair of Edinburgh using among other sources: Peterkins Craven, *Rentals: St Clair's Records of the Earldom of Orkney* and Roland William St. Clair, *The St. Clairs of the Isles* (Auckland, NZ: H. Brett, 1890).
3   Eric Linklater, *Orkney and Shetland, an historical and geographical survey* (London: Robert Hale, 1965), p. 73.
4   The installation document is recorded in Munch's *Norske Folke Historie*, 2nd series, vol II, p. 95 and in *Diplomaticum Norvegicum*, vol. II, pp. 353–55.
5   Andrew Sinclair, *The Sword and the Grail* (London: Century, 1993), p. 125.
6   Frederick Pohl, *Prince Henry Sinclair* (Halifax, NS: Nimbus Publishing, 1967), p. 57.
7   *Icelandic Annals 1382*.
8   Pohl, *Prince Henry Sinclair*, p. 57.
9   Pohl, *Prince Henry Sinclair*, p. 60.
10 Pohl, *Prince Henry Sinclair*, p. 63.
11 Johann Reinhold Forster, *History of the Voyages and Discoveries made in the North* (Dublin: 1786), pp. 178, ff.
12 Pohl, *Prince Henry Sinclair*, pp. 65–66, 77.
13 Pohl, *Prince Henry Sinclair*, p. 54.
14 Pohl, *Prince Henry Sinclair*, p. 67.
15 Pohl, *Prince Henry Sinclair*, p. 67.
16 Andrew Sinclair, *The Sword and the Grail*, p. 125.
17 Niven Sinclair, *Beyond Any Shadow of Doubt*, Section 10.
18 Niven Sinclair, *Beyond Any Shadow of Doubt*, Section 10.
19 Pohl, *Prince Henry Sinclair*, p. 68.
20 Niven Sinclair, *Beyond Any Shadow of Doubt*, Section 10.
21 *Dimplomaticum Norvegicum*, vol. II, no. 515, p. 396.
22 Extract from *Diplomatorum Norvegicum* cited in Thomas Sinclair's *Caithness Events* (Wick, UK: W. Rae, 1899).
23 Andrew Sinclair, *The Sword and the Grail*, p. 126.
24 Pohl, *Prince Henry Sinclair*, p. 74.
25 Pohl, *Prince Henry Sinclair*, p. 75.
26 Pohl, *Prince Henry Sinclair*, p. 76.
27 Pohl, *The Sinclair Expedition to Nova Scotia in 1398* (Pictou, NS: Pictou Advocate Press, 1950), p. 6.
28 Andrew Sinclair, *The Sword and the Grail*, p. 128.
29 Tim Wallace-Murphy, Marilyn Hopkins, and Graham Simmans, *Rex Deus* (Shaftsbury, UK: Element Books, 2000), chapter 12.

30 Tim Wallace-Murphy and Marilyn Hopkins, *Rosslyn: Guardian of the Secrets of the Holy Grail* (Shaftsbury, UK: Element Books, 1999), pp. 103–4.
31 Andrew Sinclair, *The Sword and the Grail*, p. 108.
32 Forster, *History of the Voyages and Discoveries made in the North.*
33 Forster, *History of the Voyages and Discoveries made in the North.*
34 Andrew Sinclair, *The Sword and the Grail*, pp. 127–28.
35 R. H. Major, trans, *The Voyages of the Venetian Brothers Nicolo and Antonio Zeno to the North Seas in the XIVth Century* (London: The Haklyut Society, 1883), p 4. This is henceforth referred to as the Zeno Narrative.
36 Pohl, *The Sinclair Expedition to Nova Scotia*, p. 9.
37 Major, Zeno Narrative, p. 6.
38 Major, Zeno Narrative, p. 6.
39 Pohl, *Prince Henry Sinclair*, p. 83.
40 Pohl, *Prince Henry Sinclair*, p. 84.
41 Major, Zeno Narrative, p. 10..
42 Pohl, *Prince Henry Sinclair*, p. 85.
43 The notebooks of Robert Riddel in the Advocates Library, Edinburgh, also mentioned in Clouston, *Records of the Earldom of Orkney.*
44 Pohl, *Prince Henry Sinclair*, p. 88.
45 Roland William St. Clair, *The St. Clairs of the Isles*, p. 98.
46 Pohl, *Prince Henry Sinclair*, p. 89.
47 The original document is kept at the National Records Office in London.

Chapter 5

1 Aristotle, or a pupil, sometimes called pseudo-Aristotle. Wrongly assumed to be Aristotle. Latin translation of *de Mundo*, (Venice: 1521), 3, 392b.
2 Peter Kalkavage, trans. *Plato's Timaeus* (Newburyport, MA: Focus Publishing, 2001).
3 Didorus Siculus, *Bibliotheca Historica*, C.H. Oldfather, trans. (London: Heinemann, 1935), 9:19, 20.
4 Cited in Aelian's *Varia Historica* (Cambridge, MA: Harvard University Press, 1997), 3:18.
5 Plutarch's mention of lands in the Atlantic is made in his "Life of Sestorius" in *Plutarch's Lives,* John and William Landhorne, trans. (London: William Tegg, 1865) pp. 399–400.
6 Strabo, *Geographica*, Horace Leonard Jones, trans., vols. 1 and 2 (London: Heinemann, 1917 and 1923).
7 Cited by Strabo in *Geographica.*
8 Jordanes, De summa temporum de origine actibus gentis Romanorum (circa 551 C.E.), 1:4, 7.
9 Frances Gibson, *The Seafarers: Pre-Columbian Voyages to America* (Philadelphia: Dorrance & Co, 1974), p. 33.
10 Ivan Van Sertima, *They Came before Columbus* (New York: Random, 1976), pp. 1–10.
11 Alexander von Wuthenau, *The Art of Terracotta Pottery in Pre-Columbian Central and South America* (New York: Crown Publishing, 1969).
12 Van Sertima, *They Came before Columbus*, pp. xiv, xv.

13 Gibson, *Seafarers*, p. 45.

14 Cited in Gunnar Thompson, *American Discovery* (Seattle: Misty Isles Press, 1992), p. 23.

15 Nigel Davies, *Voyagers to the New World* (New York: William Morrow and Co., 1979), p. 60.

16 Joseph Campbell, *The Mythic Image* (Princeton, NJ: Princeton University Press, 1974), p. 133.

17 S. O'Riordain, and G. Daniel, *Newgrange*, also cited by Frances Gibson, *Seafarers*, p. 7.

18 Davies, *Voyagers to the New World*, p. 73.

19 Thompson, *American Discovery*, p. 143.

20 Scripps Howard News Service, 27 March 1991.

21 Charles Michael Boland, *They All Discovered America* (New York: Doubleday and Co., 1961), p. 24.

22 Thompson, *American Discovery*, p. 85.

23 Paul Johnson, *A History of Christianity* (London: Peregrine Books, 1978), p. 403.

24 William McGlone et al., *Ancient American Inscriptions* (Rowley, MA: Early Sites Research Society, 1993), p. 139.

25 McGlone et al., *Ancient American Inscriptions*, p. 140.

26 McGlone et al., *Ancient American Inscriptions*, pp. 154–55.

27 Ephraim, Stern, "What Happened to Cult Figurines," *Biblical Archaeological Review*, XV (4) 22–29, 53–54.

28 McGlone, *Ancient American Inscriptions*, pp. 251–68.

29 Letter to Jim Whittal of the ESRSS.

30 McGlone, *Ancient American Inscriptions*, p. 268.

31 Davies, *Voyagers to the New World*, p. 142.

32 Andrew Collins, *Gateway to Atlantis* (London: Headline, 2000), p. 115.

33 Peter James and Nick Thorpe, *Ancient Inventions* (London: O'Mara Books, 1994), p. 350.

34 Svetlana Balabanova, Franz Parsche, and Wolfgang Pirsig, "First Identification of Drugs in Egyptian Mummies," *Naturwissenschaften*, 79, 1992, p. 358.

35 Balabanova, "First Identification of Drugs in Egyptian Mummies," p. 358; also "Research Verifies the Use of Hashish, Cocaine, and Nicotine in Prehistoric Culture," *Sociology of Drugs*, March 1993.

36 TV program in the Equinox series, "Mystery of the Cocaine Mummies," shown by Channel 4 in England in 1996, repeated in 2000.

37 Lionel Casson, *The Ancient Mariners: Seafarers and Sea Fighters of the Mediterranean in Ancient Times* (Princeton, NJ: Princeton University Press, c. 1991); Boland, *They All Discovered America*, p. 55.

38 Thompson, *American Discovery*, p. 175.

39 Thompson, *American Discovery*, p. 175.

40 Robert and Jennifer Marx, *In Quest of the Great White Gods; Contact between the Old and the New World from the Dawn of History* (New York: Crown Publishers, 1992).

41 Thompson, *American Discovery*, p. 175.

42 Boland, *They All Discovered America*, pp. 56–58.

43 Boland, *They All Discovered America*, p. 67.

44 Gibson, *Seafarers*, p. 19.
45 Thompson, *American Discovery*, p. 175; Gibson, *Seafarers*, p. 19.
46 Gunnar Thompson, *The Friar's Map of Ancient America—1360* A.D. (Seattle, WA: Laura Lee Production & Argonauts of the Misty Isles, 1996), p. 27.
47 Bernard Assiwini, Abnaki historiographer, 1973.
48 Gibson, *Seafarers*, pp. 19–22.
49 Boland, *They All Discovered America*, p. 130.
50 Claimed in liber quator of *De Originibus Americanus*, published in the Hague in 1652.
51 Richard Haklyut, *English Voyages*, 16 vols. (Edinburgh: E. & G. Goldsmid, 1885–90).
52 Richard Deacon, *Madoc and the Discovery of America* (New York: George Baziller, 1967), p. 54.
53 Thompson, *The Friar's Map*, pp. 31–32.
54 Thompson, *The Friar's Map*, pp. 31–32.

Chapter 6

1 Else Roesdahl, *The Vikings* (London: Penguin, 1991), pp. 4, 16, 277–79.
2 John Haywood, *The Penguin Historical Atlas of the Vikings* (London: Penguin, 1995), pp. 58–59.
3 Haywood, *The Penguin Historical Atlas of the Vikings*, pp. 106–7.
4 Roesdahl, *The Vikings*, pp.. 262, 265–76.
5 Roesdahl, *The Vikings*, pp. 52, 78.
6 Haywood, *The Penguin Historical Atlas of the Vikings*, pp. 40–42; Roesdahl, *The Vikings*, pp. 83–93.
7 Thorleif Sjovold, *The Viking Ships in Oslo* (Oslo: Universitets Oldsaksamling, 1985), p. 6.
8 Sjovold, *The Viking Ships in Oslo*, pp. 69–70.
9 Sjovold, *The Viking Ships in Oslo*, pp. 53–68.
10 Sjovold, *The Viking Ships in Oslo*, pp. 10–36.
11 Sjovold, *The Viking Ships in Oslo*, p. 6.
12 Sjovold, *The Viking Ships in Oslo*, p. 7.
13 Sjovold, *The Viking Ships in Oslo*, p. 58.
14 Sjovold, *The Viking Ships in Oslo*, p. 56.
15 Sjovold, *The Viking Ships in Oslo*, pp. 53–55.
16 Sjovold, *The Viking Ships in Oslo*, p. 56.
17 Nigel Davies, *Voyagers to the New World* (New York: William Morrow & Co., 1979), p. 219.
18 Davies, *Voyagers to the New World*, p. 223.
19 Helge Ingstad, *Westward to Vinland* (New York: St. Martins Press, 1969), p. 32.
20 Ingstad, *Westward to Vinland*, p. 29.
21 Haywood, *The Penguin Historical Atlas of the Vikings*, pp. 40–42; Roesdahl, *The Vikings*, pp. 9–12.
22 Roesdahl, *The Vikings*, p. 14.
23 Frederick Pohl, *Lost Discovery* (New York: Norton and Co., 1952), p. 261.

24 *The Iselandingabok*, also cited in Gunnar Thompson, *The Friar's Map of Ancient America—1360 A.D.* (Seattle, WA: Laura Lee Production & Argonauts of the Misty Isles, 1996), pp. 51–52.

25 Thompson, *The Friar's Map*, pp. 51–52.

26 Holand was born in Norway in 1872 and emigrated to America in 1884. A university graduate, he became interested in history and runeology and was the author of ten works, mainly centered on the Viking explorations of the New World. This stone, inscribed with runic characters was apparently discovered circa 1823, but was not translated until 1902. Its discovery and translation are mentioned in Holand, *Explorations in America before Columbus* (New York: Twayne Publishing Inc., 1956), p. 80.

27 Pohl, *The Lost Discovery*, p. 105.

28 Pohl, *The Lost Discovery*, p. 105.

29 Roesdahl, *The Vikings*, p. 271 and Ingstad, *Westward to Vinland*, p. 32.

30 Hjalmar R. Holand, *Westward from Vinland* (New York: Duell, Sloan & Pearce, Inc., 1940), p. 61.

31 Haywood, *The Penguin Historical Atlas of the Vikings*, pp. 40–42; Roesdahl, *The Vikings*, p. 90.

32 *The Landamnabok*, The Book of Settlements.

33 Pohl, *The Lost Discovery*, pp. 15–16.

34 Haywood, *The Penguin Historical Atlas of the Vikings*, p. 96.

35 A. E. Nordenskiold, *Om Broderna Zenos Resor och de Aldasta Karter Ofver Norden* (Stockholm: Central-Tryckeriet, 1883), p. 40; also mentioned in Kare Prytz, *Westward before Columbus,* Liv Myhre and Charles De Stephano, trans. (Oslo: Norsk Maritant Forlag A/S, 1991), p. 10.

36 Pohl, *The Lost Discovery*, pp. 18–19.

37 *The Flateyabok*, also described in Pohl, *The Lost Discovery*, p. 21.

38 Pohl, *The Lost Discovery*, p. 26.

39 Holand, *Explorations in America before Columbus*, pp. 27–31.

40 Hjalmar Holand, *America 1355–1364* (New York: Duell, Sloan & Pearce, Inc., 1946), pp. 8–9.

41 Pohl, *Lost Discovery*, pp. 39–40.

42 Pohl, *Lost Discovery*, p. 40.

43 Pohl, *Lost Discovery*, pp. 44–46, being Pohl's understanding of the appropriate passages in the *Flateyabok*.

44 *The Flateyabok*.

45 Pohl, *Lost Discovery*, pp. 47–49.

46 *The Flateyabok*, also mentioned by Holand, *Westward from Vinland*, p. 27.

47 *The Flateyabok*.

48 *The Flateyabok*.

49 Holand, *Westward from Vinland*, p. 29.

50 Prytz, *Westward before Columbus*, p. 20.

51 Holand, *Explorations in America before Columbus*, p. 54 and America 1355–1364, p. 222.

52 Holand, *Explorations in America before Columbus*, p. 222.

53 Ingstad, *Westward to Vinland*, p. 44; Holand, *Explorations in America before Columbus*, p. 56.

54 Ingstad, *Westward to Vinland*, p. 44.

55 *The Graenlandingasaga*, also cited by Ingstad, *Westward to Vinland*, p. 45 and by Holand, *Explorations in America before Columbus*, p. 55.

56 *The Hauksbok.*

57 Ingstad, *Westward to Vinland*, p. 46.

58 *The Flateyabok* and *The Hauksbok.*

59 *The Hauksbok.*

60 Holand, *America 1355–1364*, pp. 213–15.

61 Ingstad, *Westward to Vinland*, p. 92.

62 Ingstad, *Westward to Vinland*, p. 25.

63 Ingstad, *Westward to Vinland*, p. 95.

64 Magister Adam of Bremen, *Gesta Hammaburgensis*, ch. 4, p. 38.

65 W. R. Andersen, *Viking Exploration and the Columbus Fraud* (Chicago: Valhalla Press, 1981), p. 47.

66 Ingstad, *Westward to Vinland*, p. 94.

67 Holand, *Explorations in America before Columbus*, pp. 90–91

68 The earliest maps locate Norumbega in New England between Cape Cod and the Hudson River. Norumbega is first mentioned in literature in a work entitled *Recherches sur les Voyages et decouvertes des navigateurs Normands*, by Pierre Grignon, published in 1539.

69 *Saga Hakon Hakonarsonar* (Codex Frisianus). This is a medieval manuscript that I have not seen in published form.

Chapter 7

1 Niven Sinclair, *Beyond Any Shadow of Doubt* (London: Private publication, 1998), Section 10.

2 Frederick Pohl, *Prince Henry Sinclair* (Halifax, NS: Nimbus Publishing, 1967), p. 91.

3 R. H. Major, trans., Zeno Narrative (London: The Haklyut Society, 1873).

4 Reported by Ivar Bardson, steward of the Bishop of Greenland.

5 Pohl, *Prince Henry Sinclair*, p. 95.

6 W. H. Hobbs, "Zeno and the Cartography of Greenland" *Scientific Monthly*, vol. 72, (January 1951), pp. 15–19.

7 Report in the Vatican Archives made by collectors of Peters Pence.

8 Andrew Sinclair, *The Sword and the Grail* (London: Century, 1993), p. 130.

9 Major, Zeno Narrative, p. 16.

10 Andrew Sinclair, *The Sword and the Grail*, p. 130.

11 Andrew Sinclair, *The Sword and the Grail*, p. 131.

12 Major, Zeno Narrative, p. 20.

13 Pohl, *Prince Henry Sinclair*, p. 102.

14 Andrew Sinclair, *The Sword and the Grail*, pp. 132–33.

15 Niven Sinclair, *Beyond Any Shadow of Doubt*, Section 10.

16 Major, Zeno Narrative, p. 25.

17 Andrew Sinclair, *The Sword and the Grail*, p. 134.

18 Michael Bradley, *Holy Grail Across the Atlantic* (Ontario: Hounslow Press, 1988).

19 Andrew Sinclair, *The Sword and the Grail*, p. 110.

20 Stephen Sora, *The Lost Treasure of the Knights Templar* (Rochester VT: Destiny Books, 1999).

21 Bradley, *Holy Grail across the Atlantic.*

22 Johann Reinhold Forster, *History of the Voyages and Discoveries Made in the North* (Dublin: 1786), p. 179.

23 Pohl, *Prince Henry Sinclair*, p. 85.

24 Major, Zeno Narrative, p. 30.

25 Pohl, *Prince Henry Sinclair*, p. 113.

26 Major, Zeno Narrative, p. 31.

27 Frederick J. Pohl, *The Sinclair Expedition to Nova Scotia in 1398* (Pictou, NS: Pictou Advocate Press, 1950), pp. 25–29.

28 Pohl, *Prince Henry Sinclair*, p. 128.

29 Augustus de Morgan, *Book of Almanacs* (London: 1850).

30 Major, Zeno Narrative, p. 31.

31 Major, Zeno Narrative, pp. 31–32.

32 Pohl, *The Sinclair Expedition to Nova Scotia in 1398*, p. 25.

33 Major, Zeno Narrative, p. 31.

34 Hobbs, "The Fourteenth Century Discovery of America by Antonio Zeno," *Scientific Monthly*, No. 72, 1951, 24–31.

35 *New Glasgow Evening News*, 1 August 1950.

36 Pohl, *Prince Henry Sinclair*, p. 120.

37 George Patterson, *A History of the County of Pictou Nova Scotia* (Montreal: Dawson, 1877), pp. 407–9.

38 Henry S. Poole, "A Report on the Pictou Coalfields of Nova Scotia," *Geological Survey of Cananda Annual Report*, vol. 16, (1901), p. 30.

39 From conversations with the authors during a research trip to Nova Scotia and New England in October 1999.

40 Major, Zeno Narrative, p. 31.

41 Major, Zeno Narrative, p. 30.

42 Confirmed by on-site investigation by the authors in October 1999.

43 Pohl, *The Sinclair Expedition to Nova Scotia in 1398*, pp. 33–34.

Chapter 8

1 Stephen Davis, *Mi'qmaq* (Halifax, NS: Nimbus Publishing, 1997), p. 5; Daniel N. Paul, *We Were Not the Savages* (Halifax, NS: Nimbus Publishing, 1993), p. 5.

2 Paul, *We Were Not the Savages*, p. 8.

3 Paul, *We Were Not the Savages*, p. 5.

4 Paul, *We Were Not the Savages*, p. 5.

5 Paul, *We Were Not the Savages*, pp. 5, 7.

6 Davis, *Mi'qmaq*, p. 23.

7 Ruth H. Whitehead and Harold McGee, *The Micmac* (Halifax, NS: Nimbus Publishing, 1983), p. 1.

8 Paul *We Were Not the Savages*, p. 7.

9 Paul, *We Were Not the Savages*, p. 14.

10 Bernard Gilbert Hoffman, *The Historical Ethnography of the Micmac of the Sixteenth and Seventeenth Centuries* (Thesis, University of California, 1955).

11 Paul, *We Were Not the Savages*, p. 7.
12 Whitehead and McGee, *The Micmac*, p. 5.
13 Whitehead and McGee, *The Micmac*, pp. 5-6.
14 Whitehead and McGee, *The Micmac*, p. 6.
15 Fr. Pierre Baird, *Relation of New France and the Jesuit Father's Voyages to that Country*, published as part of *Jesuit Relations*.
16 Whitehead and McGee, *The Micmac*, pp. 6, 9–11; see also Hoffman, *The Historical Ethnography of the Micmac of the Sixteenth and Seventeenth Centuries*, p. 190.
17 Whitehead and McGee, *The Micmac*, pp. 7–8; also Paul, *We Were Not the Savages*, p. 2.
18 Tim Wallace-Murphy and Marilyn Hopkins, *Rosslyn: Guardian of the Secrets of the Holy Grail* (Shaftsbury, UK: Element Books, 1999), pp. 53–54.
19 Wallace-Murphy and Hopkins, *Rosslyn: Guardian of the Secrets of the Holy Grail*, p. 54.
20 Paul, *We Were Not the Savages*, p. 2; Whitehead and McGee, *The Micmac*, p. 8; Davis, *Mi'qmaq*, p. 32.
21 Whitehead and McGee, *The Micmac*, p. 8.
22 Paul, *We Were Not the Savages*, p. 42; see also *Chief Seattle's Challenge* by J. Rich (Fairfield, WA: Ye Galleon Press, 1970).
23 Paul, *We Were Not the Savages*, p. 9.
24 Wallace-Murphy and Hopkins, *Rosslyn: Guardian of the Secrets of the Holy Grail*, pp. 71–72.
25 Paul, *We Were Not the Savages*, p. 18.
26 Paul, *We Were Not the Savages*, p. 19.
27 Fr Christian LeClerq writing in the seventeenth century.
28 Paul, *We Were Not the Savages*, chapter 5.
29 Paul, *We Were Not the Savages*, p. 48.
30 Nigel Davies, *Voyagers to the New World* (New York: William Morrow, Inc., 1979), p. 72.
31 Davies, *Voyagers to the New World*, p. 249.
32 A similar account is given in the work by Kare Prytz, Myhre and Stephano trans., *Westward before Columbus* (Oslo: Norsk Maritint Forlag A/S, 1991), p. 162.
33 Davies, *Voyagers to the New World*, p. 11.
34 Illustrated in Niven Sinclair's *Beyond Any Shadow of Doubt*, Section 10.
35 Max Lescarbot cited in Hoffman, *The Historical Ethnography of the Micmac of the Sixteenth and Seventeenth Centuries*, p. 527.
36 As a result of the Treaty of Utrecht.
37 Maurice Cotterrell, *The Prophecies of Tutenkhamun* (London: Headline Book Publishing, 1999), p. 321.
38 Illustrated in Niven Sinclair's *Beyond Any Shadow of Doubt*, Section 10.
39 Mark Finnan, *The Sinclair Saga* (Halifax, NS: Formac Publishing Co. Ltd., 1999), pp. 84–85.
40 John Robinson, *Dungeon, Fire and Sword* (London: Brockhampton Press, 1999), p. 298 and Stephen Runciman, *A History of the Crusades* (London: Pelican, 1971), vol. III, p. 257.
41 Frederick J. Pohl, *Prince Henry Sinclair* (Halifax, NS: Nimbus Publishing, 1967), p. 133.

42 Charles Godfrey Leland and John Dyneley Prince, *Kuloscap the Master and Other Algonquin Poems* (New York: Funk and Wagnalls, 1902), p. 16.

43 Pohl, *Prince Henry Sinclair*, p. 133.

44 Pohl, *Prince Henry Sinclair*, p. 134–35.

45 Finnan, *The Sinclair Saga*, p. 80.

46 Finnan, *The Sinclair Saga*, pp. 81–82.

47 Pohl, *Prince Henry Sinclair*, p. 134.

48 Pohl, *Prince Henry Sinclair*, p. 138.

49 Silas Rand, *Legends of the Micmacs* (New York: Longmans and Green, 1894), p. 14.

50 Rand, *Legends of the Micmacs*, p. 14.

51 Leland and Prince, *Kuloscap the Master*, p. 123.

52 Rand, *Legends of the Micmacs*, p. 14.

53 Rand, *Legends of the Micmacs*, p. 14.

54 Charles Godfrey Leland, *The Mythology, Legends and Folk-Lore of the Algonkins* (London: the Royal Society of Literature Transactions, series 2, vol. 14, 1886), pp. 78–80.

55 Rand, *Legends of the Micmacs*, pp. 228-29.

56 Rand, *Legends of the Micmacs*, p. 24.

57 Rand, *Legends of the Micmacs*, p. 73.

58 R. H. Major, trans., The Zeno Narrative (London: The Haklyut Society, 1873), p. 33.

59 Major, The Zeno Narrative, p. 34.

60 Leland and Prince, *Kuloscap the Master*.

61 The photograph appears in Stephen Davis's *Mi'qmaq*, p. 57.

62 Leland and Prince, *Kuloscap the Master*, p. 63; Andrew Sinclair, *The Sword and the Grail* (London: Century, 1993), p. 135.

63 Disclosed by the present Grand Chief to D'Elayne and Richard Coleman of the Prince Henry Sinclair Society of North America.

64 Since the probability of more than one voyage was first mentioned in an address given to the July meeting of the Society De Sancto Claro in Chicago during the Exposition of 1893, this matter has been completely ignored by Pohl, Bradley, Andrew Sinclair, Niven Sinclair, Mark Finnan, and William F. Mann, who have all written works, several in Bradley's case, on the Henry St. Clair voyage. Regrettably, after the original work done by Frederick Pohl, the others simply repeated his ideas uncritically, with little or no research of their own on the voyage itself. The one exception was Andrew Sinclair, who proposed Louisburg as Henry's point of landfall—a hypothesis based on dubious evidence that we cannot accept.

65 The necessarily brief account given here should be fleshed out by reading the detailed, rational, and horrifying account given by Paul in *We Were Not the Savages*.

66 Paul, *We Were Not the Savages*, pp. 48, 61.

67 Paul, *We Were Not the Savages*, pp. 62, 63.

Chapter 9

1 R. H. Major, trans., Zeno Narrative (London: The Haklyut Society, 1873), p. 32.
2 Major, Zeno Narrative, p. 32.
3 Major, Zeno Narrative, p. 32.
4 Frederick Pohl, Prince Henry Sinclair (Halifax, NS: Nimbus Publishing, 1967), p. 114.
5 Pohl, Prince Henry Sinclair, p. 14.
6 Pohl, Prince Henry Sinclair, pp. 143, 145.
7 Pohl, Prince Henry Sinclair, pp. 151, 152.
8 Major, Zeno Narrative, p. 10.
9 The boatstone kept on display in the J. V. Fletcher Library, Westford, MA.
10 Information given to Niven Sinclair by Mi'qmaq representatives at the Sinclair Symposium held in Kirkwall, Orkney, in 1997.
11 From a newspaper article written by Frank Glynn.
12 Rev. Edwin R. Hodgeman, The History of the Town of Westford in the County of Middlesex, Massachusetts, 1659-1883 (Westford, MA: Westford Town History Association, 1883), p. 306.
13 James P. Whittal, Jr., ed. T. C. Lethbridge–Frank Glynn, Correspondence 1950–1966 (Rowley, MA: Early Sites Research Society), p. 1.
14 Whittal, T. C. Lethbridge–Frank Glynn, Correspondence, letter dated 8 June 1954, pp. 31–32.
15 Whittal, T. C. Lethbridge–Frank Glynn, Correspondence, letter dated 20 October 1954, pp. 36–37.
16 Whittal, T. C. Lethbridge–Frank Glynn, Correspondence, letter dated 20 October 1954, pp. 31–32.
17 Whittal, T. C. Lethbridge–Frank Glynn, Correspondence, letter dated 1 June 1956, pp. 44–45.
18 This similarity to traditional medieval memorial brasses was a point we raised in our presentation to the Historical Commissioners of the State of Massachusetts in October 1999.
19 Whittal, T. C. Lethbridge–Frank Glynn, Correspondence, . letter dated 8 June 1956, pp. 45–46.
20 Whittal, T. C. Lethbridge–Frank Glynn, Correspondence,. letter dated 10 March 1958, p. 51.
21 This point is repeated in a letter from the Unicorn Herald, Sir Iain Moncrieffe of that Ilk, dated March 1973.
22 Dealt with at length in the book by Sir Iain Moncrieffe of that Ilk, The Highland Clans (New York: Clarkson W. Potter, 1982), pp. 160–62, 168.
23 Moncrieffe of that Ilk, The Highland Clans, final paragraph.
24 The full report of James P. Whittal's investigation of the Westford Knight is available for examination in the Jim Whittal Archive lodged with the Niven Sinclair Study Center at Noss Head, Caithness.
25 The Hildreth and O'Mara report is in the Whittal Archive. This matter was also the subject of an article in the New Haven Register in 1965.
26 Hildreth and O'Mara report.
27 See the letter from the Unicorn Herald, Sir Iain Moncrieffe of that Ilk, March 1973.

28 See the letter from the Unicorn Herald, Sir Iain Moncrieffe of that Ilk, March 1973.

29 Mark Rugg Gunn, *History of the Clan Gunn.*

30 Whittal, *T. C. Lethbridge–Frank Glynn, Correspondence*, letter dated 7 August 1963, pp. 59–60.

31 Whittal, *T. C. Lethbridge–Frank Glynn, Correspondence*, letter dated 2 June 1966, p. 61.

32 Andrew Sinclair, *The Sword and the Grail* (London: Century, 1993), pp. 143–44.

33 Erected by the Clan Gunn Association.

34 From a letter by Joseph M. Sinnot, submitted to the Historical Commissioners of the State of Massachusetts in support of moves to ensure the official preservation of the Westford Knight.

Chapter 10

1 Article titled "Yankee Explores the Legend of the Old Newport Tower," by the architect Conant, published by *Yankee Magazine* in 1954, p. 25.

2 *Newport History*, vol. 68, pt. 2, 1997, p. 65.

3 Whittal, *The Newport Stone Tower*, chapter 2.

4 Philip Ainsworth Means, *Newport Tower* (New York: Henry Holt and Co., 1942), p. 9.

5 Means, *Newport Tower*, pp. 9–12.

6 Conant, *Yankee Explores the Legend of the Old Newport Tower*, p. 25.

7 Conant, *Yankee Explores the Legend of the Old Newport Tower*, p. 25.

8 Earl Siggurson, "The Newport Tower," an article published by the *American-Scandanavian Review* found in the James Whittal Archive, Newport Tower file, 1971–1980.

9 Notes on the Newport Tower by Magnus Hrolf in the James Whittal Archive, Newport Tower file, 1991–2000.

10 Frederick Pohl, *Atlantic Crossings before Columbus* (New York: Norton & Co., 1961), p. 190; Andrew Sinclair, *The Sword and the Grail* (London: Century, 1993), p. 141.

11 Notes on the Newport Tower by Magnus Hrolf in the James Whittal Archive, Newport Tower file, 1991–2000.

12 Arlington Mallery, article published in *The American Anthropologist*, 60, (1958), p. 149.

13 Frank Glynn writing in 1961, reference found in the James Whittal Archive, Newport Tower file for 1961–1970.

14 Mallery, *The American Anthropologist*, p. 150.

15 Mallery, *The American Anthropologist*, p. 150.

16 Hjalmar R. Holand, *America 1355–1364* (New York: Duell, Sloan & Pearce, Inc., 1946), p. 36.

17 Mallery, *The American Anthropologist*, p. 150; Holand, *Exploration in America before Columbus* (New York: Twayne Publishing, Inc., 1956), p. 212.

18 The original copy of the Plowden Petition in the National Records Office in London.

19 Frederick Pohl, *The Lost Discovery* (New York: Norton & Co., 1952), pp. 182-84.

20 Means, *Newport Tower*, p. 9.

21 George G. Channing, *Newport Rhode Island 1793–1811*, p. 270.

22 Benson J. Lossing, *Pictorial Field Book 1855* (New York: Harper and Bros., 1962), p. 65.

23 Niven Sinclair, *Beyond Any Shadow of Doubt* (Privately published, 1998), Section 10.

24 George Gibbs, *The Gibbs Family of Rhode Island and some Related Families* (New York, 1933).

25 Article in *Scribners* magazine 1879.

26 Conant, *Yankee Explores the Legend of the Old Newport Tower.*

27 Reference found in the James Whittal Archive, Newport Tower file, 1940–1960.

28 Reference found in the James Whittal Archive, Newport Tower file, 1940–1960.

29 Photocopied article written by Hjalmar R. Holand in an unnamed magazine dated April 1953, vol. 12, no. 2, p. 62, found in the James Whittal Archive, Newport Tower file, 1940-1960.

30 See file of comparative studies between the Newport Tower and Round Churches in Europe contained in the James Whittal Archive.

31 See file of comparative studies between the Newport Tower and Round Churches in Europe contained in the James Whittal Archive.

32 Tim Wallace-Murphy, Marilyn Hopkins, and Graham Simmans, *Rex Deus* (Shaftsbury, UK: Element Books, 2000), p. 121.

33 Sue Carlson, *New England Historical Restorations,* 1997, found in the James Whittal Archive, Newport Tower file, 1991–2000.

34 Carl Christian Rafn, *Memoire sur la decouvertes de l'Amerique au dixieme siecle* (Copenhagen: Societé Royale des Antiquaires du Nord, 1843).

35 Comments contained in document entitled "Newport Stone Tower: Comments by European Architects and Historians" in the James Whittal Archive.

36 "Newport Stone Tower: Comments by European Architects and Historians" in the James Whittal Archive.

37 "Newport Stone Tower: Comments by European Architects and Historians" in the James Whittal Archive.

38 "Newport Stone Tower: Comments by European Architects and Historians" in the James Whittal Archive.

39 *Annual Report of the Board of Regents of Smithsonian Institution, 1953,* p. 391.

40 Gunnar Thompson, *American Discovery* (Seattle: Misty Isles Press, 1992).

41 Frederick N. Brown, "Answers to Riddles Revealed in Maps," *The Voyage of the Wave Cleaver,* vol. 1, no. 3, pp. 63–64.

42 Paraphrase of comments by David Wagner, New England historian and architect writing in 1997, his work is included in the Newport Tower file, 1991–2000 in the James Whittal Archive.

43 Means, *Newport Tower,* pp. 19–21.

44 George Gibbs Channing, *Early Recollections of Newport from the year 1793–1811* (Newport, RI: A. J. Ward, C. E. Hammett, Jr., 1868), p. 270.

45 "The Old Mill at Newport a New Study of an Old Puzzle," on file in the folder Newport Tower 1850–1900, James Whittal Archive.

46 "The Old Mill at Newport: A New Study of an Old Puzzle," on file in the Newport Tower folder, 1850–1900, James Whittal Archive.

47 Lossing, *Pictorial Field Book*, pp. 65–66.

48 "The Old Mill at Newport: A New Study of an Old Puzzle," p. 633, on file in the Newport Tower folder, 1850–1900, James Whittal Archive.

49 Hjalmar R. Holand, *America 1355–1364* (New York: Duell, Sloan & Pearce, Inc., 1946), p. 63.

50 Lossing, *Pictorial Field Book 1855*, p. 66.

51 Means, *Newport Tower*, p. 51. Arnold's birth on 21 December 1615 is recorded on the Parish Register at Northover, Ilchester.

52 Means, *Newport Tower*, p. 51.

53 F. A. Arnold, *An Account of the English Houses of the Early Propriators of Providence*, Rhode Island Historical Society Collections, XIV, no 2, 25–49, no. 3, pp. 68–86, Providence 1921.

54 Letter from Lord Willougby de Brooke to Means dated 21 October 1937.

55 Means, *Newport Tower*, pp. 184–87, 281.

56 Lossing, *Pictorial Field Guide 1855*, p. 65.

57 Rafn, *Memoire sur la decouvertes de l'Amerique au dixieme siecle*.

58 Original comment by Frölen made in *Nordens Belastada Rundkyrkor*, 1911, vol. I, pp. 17–43.

59 Andrew Sinclair, *The Sword and the Grail*, p. 145.

60 Manuel Luciano da Silva, "Finding for the Portuguese," published in *Medical Opinion and Review* March 1967.

61 Silva, "Finding for the Portuguese," p. 48.

62 Silva, "Finding for the Portuguese," p. 48.

63 Silva, "Finding for the Portuguese," p. 48.

64 Silva, "Finding for the Portuguese," p. 48.

65 Silva, "Finding for the Portuguese," p. 48.

Chapter 11

1 Front page of the report by William S. Godfrey, Jr., *Digging a Tower and Laying a Ghost, The Archaeology and Controversial History of the Newport Tower*, Thesis in partial fulfillment of a Ph.D. at Harvard University, Cambridge MA, 1951.

2 Godfrey, *Digging a Tower and Laying a Ghost*, p. 5.

3 Godfrey, *Digging a Tower and Laying a Ghost*, p. 5.

4 Godfrey, *Digging a Tower and Laying a Ghost*, p. 6.

5 Godfrey, *Digging a Tower and Laying a Ghost*, p. 13.

6 Godfrey, *Digging a Tower and Laying a Ghost*, p. 14.

7 Godfrey, *Digging a Tower and Laying a Ghost*, pp. 17, 18.

8 Godfrey, *Digging a Tower and Laying a Ghost*, p. 20.

9 Godfrey, *Digging a Tower and Laying a Ghost*, p. 22.

10 Godfrey, *Digging a Tower and Laying a Ghost*, p. 24.

11 Godfrey, *Digging a Tower and Laying a Ghost*, p. 38.

12 Godfrey, *Digging a Tower and Laying a Ghost*, p. 37.

13 Godfrey, *Digging a Tower and Laying a Ghost*, p. 14.

14 Godfrey, *Digging a Tower and Laying a Ghost*, p. 35.

15 Whittal, *The Newport Stone Tower*, ESRS 1995–6.

16 *Ground Penetrating Radar Survey of the Newport Tower Site*, published ESRS, 1994, p. 5.

17 Godfrey, *Digging a Tower and Laying a Ghost*, p. 137.

18 Godfrey, *Digging a Tower and Laying a Ghost*, p. 162.

19 Godfrey, *Digging a Tower and Laying a Ghost*, p. 177.

20 Godfrey, *Digging a Tower and Laying a Ghost*, p. 186.

21 Arlington Mallery, "Brief Comments" *American Anthropologist*, 60, (1958) p. 147.

22 Arlington Mallery's original report on the foundations of the Newport Tower, 1956.

23 Mallery "Brief Comments," p. 148.

24 English translation of an article by Heinemeier and Junger published in *Archaeological Excavations* in Denmark, 1992.

25 Article by James L. Guthrie on file in the James Whittal Archive in the folder "Comments on the Radio Carbon Dating of the Newport Tower."

26 Letter to Jim Whittal from Data-Roche Watchman Inc., dated 21 June 1996, filed as 25 above.

27 Letter to Jim Whittal from Data-Roche Watchman Inc., dated 21 June 1996, filed as 25 above.

28 Letter by Andre de Bethune published in the *Newport Daily News*, 8 July 1997.

29 Letter by Andre de Bethune published in the *Newport Daily News*, 8 July 1997.

30 The research papers on investigations into the forms of measure that may have been used in the Newport Tower are on file in the Jim Whittal Archive.

31 Godfrey, *Digging a Tower and Laying a Ghost*, p. 30.

32 Carlson, *New England Historical Restorations, 1997*, Whittal Archive, Newport Tower file, 1991–2000.

33 Andrew Sinclair, *The Sword and the Grail* (London: Century, 1993), p. 145.

34 James Whittal's report on the Newport Tower, see Whittal Archives.

35 James Whittal's report on the Newport Tower, see Whittal Archives.

36 Siggurson, The Newport Tower, Whittal Archive, Newport Tower file, 1971–1980.

37 Notes on the Newport Tower by Magnus Hrolf in the James Whittal Archive, Newport Tower file, 1991–2000.

38 Mallery, "Brief Comments," p. 149.

39 Mallery, "Brief Comments," p. 149.

40 Original document kept in the National Records Office, London.

41 Frank Glynn writing in 1961, reference found in the James Whittal Archive, Newport Tower file for 1961–1970.

42 Niven Sinclair, *Beyond Any Shadow of Doubt* (London: private publication, 1998), Section 10.

43 George G. Channing, *Newport Rhode Island 1793–1811*, p. 270.

44 See file of comparative studies between the Newport Tower and Round Churches in the James Whittal Archive.

45 List of comments contained in document entitled "Newport Stone Tower: Comments by European Architects and Historians," in the James Whittal Archive.

46 List of comments contained in document entitled "Newport Stone Tower: Comments by European Architects and Historians," in the James Whittal Archive.

47 *The Annual Report of the Board of Regents of the Smithsonian Institution,* 1953, pp. 388–91.

48 George Gibbs Channing, *Early Recollections of Newport from the year 1793–1811* (Newport, RI: A. J. Ward, C. E. Hammett, Jr., 1868), p. 270.

49 Carlson, *New England Historical Restorations,* 1997, found in the James Whittal Archive, File name, Newport Tower 1991–2000.

50 Hjalmar Holand, *Explorations in America before Columbus* (New York: Twayne Publishers Inc., 1956), p. 240.

51 Essay by James Whittal, Jr., James Whittal Archive.

52 *Ground Penetrating Radar Survey, Newport Tower Site,* ESRS 1994, p. 7.

53 *Ground Penetrating Radar Survey, Newport Tower Site,* ESRS 1994, pp. 11–13.

54 *Ground Penetrating Radar Survey, Newport Tower Site,* ESRS 1994.

55 *Ground Penetrating Radar Survey, Newport Tower Site,* ESRS 1994, pp. 11–15.

Chapter 12

1 Translation: To Nicolo and Antonio Zeno who in the fourteenth century explored/navigated the Northern Seas. By Decree of the Commune, 1881.

2 Document in the National Library of Scotland listed in the archive of the Advocates Library, Ms. 32. 2. 41.

3 Frederick Pohl, *Prince Henry Sinclair* (Halifax, NS: Nimbus Publishing, 1967), p. 170.

4 Rev. Fr. Hay, *The Genealogie of the St. Clairs of Roslin* (Edinburgh: Maidement, 1835).

5 Cited by Eric Linklater, *Orkney and Shetland, an historical and geographical survey* (London: Robert Hale, 1965), p. 73.

6 Document is in the National Library of Scotland listed in the archive of the Advocates Library, Ms. 32. 2. 41.

7 Earl Henry's supposed burial at St. Matthews at Roslin is claimed by Pohl, *Prince Henry Sinclair,* p. 171.

8 Pohl, *Prince Henry Sinclair,* p. 171.

9 Hay, *The Genealogie of the St Clairs of Roslin.*

10 Alexander Sinclair, *A Sketch of the History of Roslin and Its Possessors* (Edinburgh: Irvine, Maxwell Dick, 1856).

11 J. Storer Clouston, *A History of Orkney* (Kirkwall, UK: W. R. Macintosh, 1932), p. 247.

12 Henry II was indeed designated as Henry de Sancto Claro, Orcadie et Dominie de Roslyn, in a charter in the Hay collection.

13 *Genealogie of the House of Drummond,* p. 91, where it is claimed that the original deed is kept in the Perth Charter Chest with a copy in the Advocates Library.

14 Niven Sinclair, *Beyond Any Shadow of Doubt* (London: Privately published, 1998), Section 5.

15 Information gleaned as a result of conversations between the authors and the Sinclair clan chief, Earl Malcolm St. Clair of Caithness.

16 Hjalmar R. Holand, *Explorations in America before Columbus* (New York: Twayne Publishers, Inc., 1956), p. 256.

17 Andrew Sinclair, *The Sword and the Grail* (London: Century, 1993), p. 150.

18 Pohl, *Prince Henry Sinclair*, p. 177.

19 Pohl, *Prince Henry Sinclair*, p. 178.

20 The original *Discenza Patrizie* in several volumes is kept in the Corer Museum in St Marks Square, Venice.

21 *Discenza Patrizie*, final volume, S–Z.

22 *Discenza Patrizie*, final volume, S–Z.

23 These globes are on public display at the Corer Museum in Venice.

24 R. H. Major, trans., *Zeno Narrative* (London: Haklyut Society, 1835), p. 35.

25 Published in Italian under the title *Dello scoprimento dell'Isole Frislandia, Eslanda, Engrovelanda, Estotilanda & Icaria, fatto sotto il polo artico da due Fratelli Zeni, M. Nicolo il K. e M. Antonio con un disegno particolare did'tutte le dette parte did tramontana da lor scoperte*.

26 Including, among others, the Claus Magnus Map of 1529 and the Claudius Clavus Map of 1556—according to the cartographical scholar Erik Wilhelm Dahlgren.

27 Pohl, *Prince Henry Sinclair*, p. 180.

28 Essay by Norman Biggart in the Jim Whittal archive, partially reprinted in Niven Sinclair's *Beyond Any Shadow of Doubt*, section 16.

29 Biggart, partially reprinted in Niven Sinclair, *Beyond Any Shadow of Doubt*, section 16.

30 This possibility has been confirmed to the authors by the present Nicolo Zeno of Venice, who admits that the family archive is extensive, uncatalogued, and chaotic.

31 John Julius Norwich, *A History of Venice* (London: Penguin, 1983), p. 280.

32 Norwich, *A History of Venice*, p. 280.

33 P. Daru, *Histoire de la République de Venise*, vol. 4, (Paris: 1821), p. 118.

34 Norwich, *A History of Venice*, p. 461.

35 The Treaty of Tordisillas in 1494.

Chapter 13

1 Norman Biggart, "The Zeno Narrative—Interpretive Thoughts," James Whittal Archive and reprinted in part by Niven Sinclair in *Beyond Any Shadow of Doubt* (London: Privately published, 1998), section 16.

2 Frederick Pohl, "Prince Zichmini of the Zeno Narrative," *The Annals of the Society for the History of Discoveries*, vol II, Amsterdam, Israel, 1970.

3 Johann Reinhold Forster, *History of the Voyages and Discoveries Made in the North* (Dublin: 1786), pp. 178, ff.

4 Forster, *History of the Voyages and Discoveries Made in the North*, pp. 178, ff.

5 Pohl, "Prince Zichmini of the Zeno Narrative"; also cited by the same author in *Prince Henry Sinclair* (Halifax, NS: Nimbus Publishing, 1967), pp. 86–87.

6 Dr. Crawford's review of Pohl's *Prince Henry Sinclair*. Dr. Crawford is also the author of *A Lesson in the Art of Political Survival*, a treatise on the Life of the third St. Clair Jarl of Orkney.

7 Biggart, "The Zeno Narrative—Interpretive Thoughts."

8 Richard Haklyut, *Divers Voyages touching on the discoverie of America* (London: George Bishop and Ralph Newburie, 1582).

9 Jack Beeching, ed., *Richard Haklyut: Voyages and Discoveries* (London: Penguin, 1972), p. 19.

10 Beeching, *Richard Haklyut: Voyages and Discoveries*, p. 28.

11 Biggart, "The Zeno Narrative—Interpretive Thoughts."

12 Andrew Sinclair, *The Sword and the Grail* (London: Century, 1998), p. 114.

13 Biggart, "The Zeno Narrative—Interpretive Thoughts."

14 Biggart, "The Zeno Narrative—Interpretive Thoughts."

15 R. H. Major, trans., Zeno Narrative (London: Haklyut Society, 1835).

16 Johann Reinhold Forster, cited in Niven Sinclair, *Beyond Any Shadow of Doubt.*

17 John Fiske, *The Discovery of America—with some account of the Ancient Americans and the Spanish Conquest*, two volumes (Boston: Houghton Mifflin, 1892).

18 E.G.R. Taylor, *A Fourteenth Century Riddle.*

19 W. H. Hobbs, "The Fourteenth Century Discovery of America by Antonio Zeno," *Scientific Monthly*, No. 72, (1951), 24–31.

20 Ruscelli's *Ptolemy* (Venice, 1561). This work consists largely of maps. Few full copies of the original are in existence, but many of the original maps can be found in museums throughout the world.

21 *Encyclopaedia Americana.*

22 Taylor, *A Fourteenth Century Riddle.*

23 Major, Zeno Narrative, introduction.

24 Gunnar Thompson, *The Friar's Map*, (Seattle: Laura Lee Production & Argonauts of the Misty Isles, 1996) p. 167.

25 Thompson, *The Friar's Map*, p. 167.

26 Thompson, *The Friar's Map*, p. 169.

27 Arlington Mallery, *The Rediscovery of Lost America* (New York: E. P. Dutton, 1979).

28 Mallery, *The Rediscovery of Lost America.*

29 Charles Hapgood, *Maps of the Ancient Sea Kings* (New York: Chilton Books, 1966).

30 *Pre-Columbian Charts and Maps of the New World*, p. 152. As cited in Hapgood's *Maps of Ancient Sea Kings.*

31 Hapgood, *Maps of the Ancient Sea Kings.*

32 Hapgood, *Maps of the Ancient Sea Kings.*

33 Hapgood, *Maps of the Ancient Sea Kings.*

34 First reported in an Associated Press news dispatch on 26 October 1951.

35 Cited by Niven Sinclair in *Beyond Any Shadow of Doubt.*

36 Hapgood, *Maps of the Ancient Sea Kings.*

37 Fiske, *The Discovery of America*, vol. 1, p. 236.

38 Thompson, *The Friar's Map* is a work describing the voyage of Nicolas Lynne.

39 Original copies of the Higden Maps are kept in the Huntingdon Library, San Marino, CA.

40 Also compiled by Higden.

41 Cited by Helge Ingstad in *Westward to Vinland* (New York: St. Martin's Press, 1969), p. 96.

Chapter 14

1 Andrew Sinclair, *The Sword and the Grail* (London: Century, 1993), p. 154, who cites 1406 as the date of death of Antonio Zeno; also Frederic Pohl, *Prince Henry St. Clair* (Halifax, NS: Nimbus Publishing, 1967), p. 172, who cites 1405.

2 Alexander Sinclair, *Sketch of the History of Roslin and its Possessors*; Rev. Fr. Hay, *The Genealogie of the St. Clairs of Roslin* (Edinburgh: Maidement, 1835); also Andrew Sinclair, *The Sword and the Grail*, pp. 149–50.

3 Pohl, *Prince Henry St. Clair*, p. 173.

4 Thormodus Torfaeus, *Orcades seu rerum Orcadiensum Historia* (Copenhagen: H. C. Paulli, 1715).

5 Niven Sinclair, *Beyond Any Shadow of Doubt*, (London: Privately published, 1998), section 4.

6 J. Storer Clouston, *A History of Orkney* (Kirkwall, UK: W. R. Macintosh, 1932), p. 242.

7 Torfaeus, *Orcades*.

8 Bishop Tulloch, *Genealogy and Deduction of the Earls of Orkney*.

9 Tim Wallace-Murphy, *An Illustrated Guidebook to Rosslyn Chapel* (Roslin, UK: Friends of Rosslyn, 1993), p. 3.

10 Wallace-Murphy, *An Illustrated Guidebook to Rosslyn Chapel*, p. 4.

11 Thomas McGibbon and David Ross, *Castelated and Domestic Architecture of Scotland*, 5 vols. (Edinburgh: David Douglas, 1887–1892).

12 Tim Wallace-Murphy and Marilyn Hopkins, *Rosslyn: Guardian of the Secrets of the Holy Grail* (Shaftsbury, UK: Element Books, 1999), p. 10.

13 Rudolf Steiner, *Die Templlegende und die Goldene Legende*, lecture no. 93.

14 Tim Wallace-Murphy, *The Templar Legacy and Masonic Inheritance within Rosslyn Chapel* (Roslin, UK: Friends of Rosslyn, 1996), pp. 29–30.

15 Wallace-Murphy, *The Templar Legacy and Masonic Inheritance within Rosslyn Chapel*, p. 12.

16 Wallace-Murphy, *An Illustrated Guidebook to Rosslyn Chapel*, p. 14.

17 Wallace-Murphy, *The Templar Legacy and Mason Inheritance within Rosslyn Chapel*, p. 27.

18 Gedricke, eighteenth century historian of Freemasonry.

19 T. Ravenscroft and Tim Wallace-Murphy, *The Mark of the Beast* (London: Sphere Books, 1990), p. 63.

20 Wallace-Murphy and Hopkins, *Rosslyn: Guardian of the Secrets of the Holy Grail*, p. 10.

21 Tim Wallace-Murphy, Marilyn Hopkins, and Graham Simmans, *Rex Deus* (Shaftsbury, UK: Element Books, 2000), p. 236.

22 The Pilgrimage of Initiation is described in *Rosslyn: Guardian of the Secrets of the Holy Grail*.

23 The legend of descent from the High Priest of the Temple in Jerusalem is the main theme of *Rex Deus*.

24 Wallace-Murphy et al., *Rex Deus*, chapters 9, 10, 11.

25 Wallace-Murphy et al., *Rex Deus*, chapter 15.

26 Wallace-Murphy, *An Illustrated Guidebook to Rosslyn Chapel*, p. 3.

27 Wallace-Murphy et al., *Rex Deus*, p. 217.

28 Chris Knight and Robert Lomas, *The Second Messiah* (London: Century, 1997), p. 32.

29 Knight and Lomas, *The Second Messiah*, p. 32.

30 Wallace-Murphy, *The Templar Legacy and Masonic Inheritance within Rosslyn Chapel*, p. 23.

31 The original document is kept by the Grand Lodge of Scotland with a copy in the National Library in Edinburgh.

32 The original document is kept by the Grand Lodge of Scotland with a copy in the National Library in Edinburgh.

33 Wallace-Murphy et al., *Rex Deus*, p. 243.

34 Wallace-Murphy et al., *Rex Deus*, p. 244.

35 Wallace-Murphy et al., *Rex Deus*, p. 245.

36 Michael Baigent and Richard Leigh, *The Temple and the Lodge* (London: Corgi, 1992), p. 259.

37 Baigent and Leigh, *The Temple and the Lodge*, p. 351.

38 Wallace-Murphy et al., *Rex Deus*, pp. 257–58.

39 Baigent and Leigh, *The Temple and the Lodge*, p. 262.

40 Wallace-Murphy et al., *Rex Deus*, p. 219.

41 Wallace-Murphy et al., *Rex Deus*, p. 240.

Chapter 15

1 Position Paper on the Native American project in *Theology in the Americas* (Detroit II) July/August, 1980, p. 3.

2 Frederick Turner, *Beyond Geography, the Western Spirit against the Wilderness* (Piscataway, NJ: Rutgers University Press, 1992).

3 Daniel N. Paul, *We Were Not the Savages* (Halifax, NS: Nimbus Publishing, 1993).

4 Chief Seattle, cited by John M. Rich in *Seattle's Unanswered Challenge* (Fairfield, WA: Ye Galleon Press, 1970).

5 Chief Seattle's Address to the U.S. President in 1854 as cited by John M. Rich in *Seattle's Unanswered Challenge*.

6 John H. Neihart, *Black Elk Speaks* (New York: Washington Square Press, 1959), pp. 70-71.

7 Neihart, *Black Elk Speaks*, pp. 70–71.

8 Paul, *We Were Not the Savages*.

9 Martin Luther King's campaign for racial equality in the United States and countless "green campaigns" that have arisen right across the developed world.

10 Marilyn Ferguson, *The Aquarian Conspiracy* (London: Palladian, 1982).

11 Martin Luther King, Jr., *Stride towards Freedom* (New York: Harper, 1958), p. 72.

12 William McLoughlin, *Revivals, Awakenings and Reform* (Chicago: University of Chicago Press, 1978).

13 Rich, *Seattle's Unanswered Challenge*.

Epilogue

1 Kath Gourlay, article in the 1988 issue of the *Islander*, an annual publication describing events in Orkney.

2 Gourlay, article in the *Scotsman*, Monday, 4 January 2000.

3 Gourlay, article in the *Sunday Times* (Scottish Edition) 2 January 2000.

4 Letter from the Municipality of Venice to Mrs. D'Elayne Coleman, founder and President of the Prince Henry Sinclair Society of North America.

5 Evidence of official support of the Italian Navy for *Progetto Zeno* lies in the use of the Morosini Naval College for the launch of the project and the provision of an official naval escort for Laura's departure from Venice on 6 January 2000.

6 Letter of confirmation issued by *Communita Montana dell'Elba e Capria*, dated 16 December 1999.

7 Invitation issued by *Commune did Venezia*, December 1999.

8 The discourse was a brief précis of his work *Beyond Any Shadow of Doubt*.

9 From a letter by Niven Sinclair to the Clan Sinclair discussion list.

10 Described in an email from Laura Zolo to Niven Sinclair.

11 Described in an email from Laura Zolo to Niven Sinclair.

12 Further email from Laura to Niven Sinclair, later used as the basis for a newspaper article by Laura.

13 Speech kindly recorded by Rob Cohn of Halifax.

14 From comments made by Niven Sinclair and distributed to the worldwide Sinclair Clan at Christmas 2000.

15 From a superbly illustrated article by Don Julian titled "Nation to Nation—Chief to Grand Chief: Sword of Peace Presented to Mi'Maq," *Mi'qmaq-Maliseet Nations News*, November 2000.

16 Julian, "Nation to Nation—Chief to Grand Chief: Sword of Peace Presented to Mi'Maq," *The Mi'qmaq-Maliseet Nations News*, November 2000.

17 From comments made by Niven Sinclair and distributed to the worldwide Sinclair Clan at Christmas 2000.

18 Jackie Young, "Museum Musings," *Westford Eagle*, November. 2000.

BIBLIOGRAPHY

Anderson, Rasmus B. *America Not Discovered by Columbus*. Chicago: S. C Griggs & Co, 1877.

Anderson, W. R. *Viking Explorers and the Columbus Fraud*. Chicago: Valhalla Press, 1981.

Annual Report of the Board of Regents of the Smithsonian Institution, 1953. Washington, DC: U.S. Government Printing Office, Washington, 1954.

Baigent, Michael and Richard Leigh. *The Temple and the Lodge*. London: Corgi, 1992.

Bartlett, Robert. *The Making of Europe*. London: Penguin Books, 1994.

Bauer, Fred C. *Norse Visits to America*, with additional comments by James P. Whittal, Jr. Rowley, MA: Early Sites Research Society, 1990.

Beavois, Eugene. *Les Voyages Transatlantiques des Zenos*. Louvain, Belgium: J. B. Istas, 1890.

Beeching, Jack, ed. *Richard Haklyut, Voyages and Discoveries*. London: Penguin, 1972.

Boland, Charles Michael. *They All Discovered America*. New York: Doubleday & Co., 1961.

Bolton, Charles K. *Terra Nova, The North East Coast of America before 1602*. Boston: F. W. Faxon & Co, 1935.

Bradley, Michael. *Grail Knights of North America*. Toronto: Hounslow Press, 1998.

———. *Holy Grail Across the Atlantic*. Ontario: Hounslow Press, 1988

Bridge, Anthony. *The Crusades*. London: Grenada Publishing, 1980.

Brigham, Herbert Olin. *The Old Stone Mill*. Newport, RI: Franklin Printing House, n.d.

Cahill, Ellis. *New England's Viking and Indian Wars*. Peabody, MA: Chandler-Smith Publishing Inc,. 1986.

Channing, George G. *Newport Rhode Island 1793–1811*. Cited by Philip Ainsworth Means in *Newport Tower*.

Chapman, Paul H. *The Man Who Led Columbus to America*. Atlanta, GA: Judson Press, 1973.

———. *The Norse Discovery of America*. Atlanta, GA: One Candle Press, 1981.

Clouston, J. Storer. *A History of Orkney*. Kirkwall, UK: W. R. Mackintosh, 1932.

———. *Records of the Earldom of Orkney 1299–1614*, Second Series. Edinburgh: Printed for the Scottish Historical Society, 1914.

Collins, Andrew. *Gateway to Atlantis*. London: Headline, 2000.

Conchina, Ennio. *Dell'arabico—A Venezia tra Rinascimento e Oriente*. Venezia: Marsilio, 1994.

Davies, Nigel. *Voyagers to the New World*. New York: William Morrow & Co. Inc., 1979.

Davis, Stephen A. *Mi'qmaq*. Halifax, NS: Nimbus Publishing, 1997.

De Costa, B. F. *The Pre-Columbian Discovery of America*, Translations from the Icelandic Sagas. Albany, NY: Joel Munsell's Sons, 1901.

De Saint Clair, Louis Anatole. *Histoire Généalogique de la Famille de St Clair det ses alliances*. Paris: Hardy & Bernard, 1905.

Diplomatorum Norvegicum, Vol. 55. Christiana: R. J. Malling, 1852.

Enterline, James Robert. *Viking America*. New York: Doubleday & Co. Inc., 1972.

Finnan, Mark. *The Sinclair Saga*. Halifax, NS: Formac Publishing Co. Ltd., 1999.

Fischer, Joseph (S. J.). *The Discoveries of the Norsemen in America*, translated from the German by Basil H. Soulsby. London: Henry Stephens Son & Stiles, 1903.

Fiske, John. *The Discovery of America—with some account of the Ancient Americans and the Spanish Conquest*, two volumes. Boston: Houghton Mifflin, 1892.

Foote, P. G., and D. M. Wilson. *The Viking Achievement*. London: Sidgwick & Jackson, 1974.

Forster, Johann Reinhold. *History of the Voyages and Discoveries Made in the North*. Dublin: 1786.

Fossier, Robert, ed. *The Cambridge Illustrated History of the Middle Ages*. Vol. 3, 1250–1520. Cambridge: Cambridge University Press, 1986.

Gaddis, Vincent H. *American Indian Myths and Mysteries*. London: Signet, 1977.

Gathorne-Hardy, G. M. *The Norse Discoverers of America—the Wineland Sagas*. Oxford, England: Oxford University Press, 1921.

Gessing, Gutorm. *The Viking Ship Finds*. Oslo, Norway: A. W. Broggers Boktrykkeri A/S, 1938.

Gibbs, George. *The Gibbs Family of Rhode Island and some Related Families*. New York, 1933.

Gibson, Frances. *The Seafarers: Pre-Columbian Voyages to America*. Philadelphia: Dorrance & Co, 1974.

Godfrey, William S, Jr. *Digging a Tower and Laying a Ghost*. Ph.D. thesis, Cambridge, MA. 1951.

Goodwin, William B. *The Ruins of Great Ireland in New England*. Boston: Meador, 1946.

Gronlands, Historiske, Mindesmerker. Vols. 2 & 3. Copenhagen, 1838–45.

Grovier, Gabriel. *Découverte de L'Amérique par les Normands au Xme Siècle*. Paris: Maisonneuve & Cie, 1874.

Gunn, Mark Rugg. *History of the Clan Gunn*. Available from the Clan Gunn Association.

Haklyut Richard. *Divers Voyages touching on the discoverie of America*. London: George Bishop and Ralph Newburie, 1582.

———. *English Voyages*. 16 vols. Edinburgh: E. & G. Goldsmid, 1885–90.

Hapgood, Charles H. *Maps of the Ancient Sea Kings*. Philadelphia and New York: Chilton Books, 1966.

Hardy, G. M. *The Norse Discoverers of America—The Wineland Sagas, translated and Discussed*. Oxford, England: The Clarendon Press, 1921.

Haugan, Einar. *Voyages To Vinland, the First American Saga newly translated and interpreted*. New York: Alfred A Knopf, 1942.

Hay, Rev. Fr. *The Genealogie of the St Clairs of Rosslyn*. Scotland: Maidement, 1835.

Haywood, John. *The Penguin Historical Atlas of the Vikings*. London: Penguin Books, 1995.

Historic Newport. Newport, RI: Newport Chamber of Commerce, 1933.

Hjelmeseth, Eilert. *The Secret of Vinland*, trans. by Edna Rude, 1980.

Hobbs, W. H. "The Fourteenth Century Discovery of America by Antonio Zeno." *Scientific Monthly*, Vol. 72, January 1951.

――――. "Zeno and the Cartography of Greenland," *Scientific Monthly*, Vol. 72, January 1951.

――――. "The Zeno Map Revisited," *Imago Mundi*, Vol. 6, 1949.

Hodgeman, Rev. Edwin R. *The History of the Town of Westford in the County of Middlesex, Massachusetts, 1659–1883*. Westford, MA: Westford Town Historical Association, 1883.

Hodgeson, F. C. *Early History of Venice*. London, 1901.

Hoffman, Bernard Gilbert. *The Historical Ethnography of the Micmac of the Sixteenth and Seventeenth Centuries*. Ph.D. thesis, University of California, 1955.

Holand, Hjalmar R. *America 1355–1364*. New York: Duell, Sloan & Pearce, Inc., 1946.

――――. *Explorations in America before Columbus*. New York: Twayne Publishers Inc., 1956.

――――. *A Pre-Columbian Crusade to America*. New York: Twayne Publishers Inc., 1962.

――――. *Westward from Vinland*. New York: Duell, Sloan & Pearce, Inc., 1940

Honore, Pierre. *In Quest of the White God*. London: Futura, 1975.

Hopkins, Marilyn, Graham Simmons, and Tim Wallace-Murphy. *Rex Deus*. Shaftsbury, UK: Element Books, 1999.

Horn, Georg. *De Originibus Americanus*. The Hague: Johannis Mulieri, 1669.

Horsford, Eben Norton. *The Discovery of the Ancient City of Norumbega*. Boston and New York: Houghton Mifflin & Co., 1890.

Ingstad, Helge. *Westward to Vinland*. New York: St. Martins Press, 1969.

Irwin, Constance. *Fair Gods and Stone Faces*. London: W. H. Allen, 1964.

Jacopo, Bishop of Padua. *Biography of Carlo Zeno*. Publisher unknown.

James, Peter and Nick Thorpe. *Ancient Inventions*. London: O'Mara Books, 1994.

Joe, Dame Rita. *Lnu and the Indians we're called*. Nova Scotia: Ragweed Publishers, 1991.

Kirk, Poul. *Hope and Onefootland—Exploring Vinland, 1981.* Limited private edition from the Author, Eblerosestien 9, 3460 Birkerod, Denmark, 1981.

Knoup, James. *The Genesis of Freemasonry.* Manchester, England: Manchester University Press, 1947.

Leland, Charles Godfrey. *The Algonquin Legends of New England.* Boston: Houghton, Mifflin, 1884.

———. *The Mythology, Legends and Folk-Lore of the Algonkins.* London: Royal Society of Literature Transactions, series 2, vol. 14, 1886.

Leland, Charles Godfrey and John Dyneley Prince. *Kuloscap the Master and Other Algonquin Poems.* New York: Funk & Wagnalls, 1902.

Lewis, Archibald R. *The Northern Seas, Shipping and Commerce in Northern Europe* A.D. *300–1100.* New York: Octagon Books 1978.

Linklater, Eric. *Orkney and Shetland, an historical and geographical survey.* London: Robert Hale, 1965.

Lossing, Benson J. *Pictorial Field Book 1855.* New York: Harper and Bros., 1862.

Lucas, Fred W. *Annals of the Brothers Nicolo and Antonio Zeno.* London: Henry Stephens Son & Stiles, 1898.

Magnusson, Bishop Olaus. *Historia de gentibus septrionalibus.* Rome, 1528.

Major, Richard Henry, trans. *The Voyages of the Venetian Brothers Nicolo and Antonio Zeno to the Northern Seas in the XIVth Century.* London: The Haklyut Society, 1883.

———. *Voyages of the Zeno Brothers.* London: The Haklyut Society, 1873.

Mallery, Arlington. *The Rediscovery of Lost America.* New York: E. P. Dutton, 1979.

Marx, Robert and Jennifer. *In Quest of the Great White Gods: Contact between the Old and the New World from the Dawn of History.* New York: Crown Publishers, 1992.

McGlone, William R. and Philip M. Leonard. *Ancient Celtic America.* Fresno, CA: Panorama West Books, 1986.

McGlone, William R., Philip M Leonard, James L. Guthrie, Rollin W. Gillespie, and James P Whittal., Jr. *Ancient American Inscriptions.* Rowley: MA: Early Sites Research Society, 1993.

Means, Philip Ainsworth. *Newport Tower.* New York: Henry Holt & Co., 1942.

Morse, Rev. Abner. *Further Traces of the Ancient Northmen in America.* Boston: Dutton, 1861.

Mundy, Martin J. *The Irish in America One Thousand Years Before Columbus.* Boston: Angel Guardian Press, 1906.

Munn, W. A. *Wineland Voyages.* St. John's, Newfoundland: The Labour Press, 1931.

Neihart, John G. *Black Elk Speaks.* New York: Washington Square Press, 1959.

Nilsestuen, Rolf M. *The Kensington Runestone Vindicated.* Lanham, MD: University Press of America, 1994.

Nordenskiold, A. E. *Om Broderna Zenos Resor och de Aldasta Kartor Ofver Norden.* Stockholm, Sweden: Central-Tryckeriet, 1883.

Norwich, John Julius. *A History of Venice.* London: Penguin, 1983.

———. *A Short History of Byzantium.* London: Penguin Books, 1998.

Palsson, Hermann and Paul Edwards, trans. *Orkneyinga Saga.* London: Penguin Books, 1981.

Paul, Daniel N. *We Were Not the Savages.* Halifax, NS: Nimbus Publishing, 1993.

Pigafetta, Antonio, trans. by John Pinkerton. *To America and Around the World—comprising the Journal of the First Voyage of Christopher Columbus*, Markham, Clements S (trans for the Haklyut Society for the 1893 edition) plus, *Voyage Around the World* by Fernandez Magellan. Boston: Brandon Publishing Company, 1990.

Pohl, Frederick J. *Atlantic Crossings before Columbus.* New York:, Norton & Co., 1961.

———. *The Lost Discovery.* New York: Norton & Co., 1952.

———. *Prince Henry Sinclair.* Halifax, NS: Nimbus Publishing, 1967.

———. *The Sinclair Expedition to Nova Scotia in 1398.* Pictou, NS: Pictou Advocate Press, 1950.

———. *The Vikings of Cape Cod.* Pictou, NS: Pictou Advocate Press, 1957.

Prytz, Kare. *Westward Before Columbus*, Liv Myhre and Charles De Stephano, trans. Oslo, Norway: Norsk Maritimt Forlag A/S, 1991.

Rafn, Carl Christian. *Memoire sur la découverts de l'Amérique au dixième siècle*. Copenhagen: Societé Royale des Antiquaires du Nord, 1843.

Ramusio, Giovanni Batista. *Secudo Volume Della Navigatio et Viaggi*. Venice, 1559.

Rand, Silas. *Legends of the Micmacs*. New York: Longmans & Green, 1894.

Ravenscroft, Trevor & Tim Wallace-Murphy. *The Mark of the Beast*. York Beach, ME: Samuel Weiser Inc, 1997.

Rich, John M. *Seattle's Unanswered Challenge*. Fairfield, WA: Ye Galleon Press, 1970.

Robinson, John J. *Born in Blood*. London: Arrow Book, 1993.

———. *Dungeon, Fire and Sword*. London: Brockhampton Press, 1999.

Roesdahl, Else. *The Vikings*. London: Penguin Books, 1991.

Runciman, Stephen. *A History of the Crusades*, 3 Vols. London: Pelican, 1971.

Saga Hakon Hakonarsonar (Codex Frisianus). Medieval document.

Sertima, Ivan Van. *They Came Before Columbus*. New York: Random House, 1976.

Sewall, Rufus King. *Ancient Voyages to the Western Continent*. New York: G. P Putnam's Sons, 1893.

Shelton, F. H. *More Light on the Old Mill at Newport*. Newport RI: Newport Historical Society, 1917.

Sinclair, Alexander. *A Sketch of the History of Roslin and its Possessors* Edinburgh: Irwin, Maxwell, Dick, 1856.

Sinclair, Andrew. *The Sword and the Grail*. London: Century, 1993.

Sinclair, Niven. *Beyond Any Shadow of Doubt*. London: Private publication, 1998.

Sinclair, Thomas. *Caithness Events*. Wick, UK: W. Rae, 1899.

Sincleer, Henry Lord. *The Descent and Pedigree of the most noble and ancient house of the Lords of Sincleer*. N. p., 1590.

Sjovold, Thorleif. *The Viking Ships in Oslo*. Oslo: Universitetets Oldsaksamling, 1985.

Skelton, R. A., Thomas E. Marston, and George D. Painter. *The Vinland Map and the Tartar Relation*. New Haven, CT: Yale University Press, 1995.

Smart, T. H. *Pre-Columbian Historical Treasures—The Flatey Book and recently Discovered Vatican Manuscripts Concerning America as Early as the Tenth Century.* London, Stockholm, Copenhagen and New York: Norroena Society, 1908.

Stephenson, David. *The First Freemasons.* Aberdeen UK: Aberdeen University Press, 1989.

Storm, Professor. "Studier over Vinlandsreiserne." *Aaboger for Nordske Oldkyndighed og Historie.* Copenhagen, 1887.

Taylor, E. G. P. *A Fourteenth Century Riddle.* No publishing data available.

Thompson, Gunnar. *American Discovery.* Seattle, WA: Misty Isles Press, 1992.

———. *The Friar's Map of Ancient America—1360 A.D.* Seattle, WA: Laura Lee Production & Argonauts of the Misty Isles, 1996.

Torfaeus, Thormodus. *Orcades seu rerum Orcadensium historiae.* Copenhagen: H. C. Paulli, 1715.

Tulloch, Bishop. *Genealogy and Deduction of the Earls of Orkney.* No publishing data available.

Turner, Frederick. *Beyond Geography, the Western Spirit against the Wilderness.* Piscataway, NJ: Rutgers University Press, 1992.

Viking Ship Finds. published by the curator of the Gokstad museum in 1938.

Wahlgren, Erik. *The Kensington Stone—a Mystery Solved.* N.p.: University of Wisconsin Press, 1958.

Wallace-Murphy, Tim. *An Illustrated Guidebook to Rosslyn Chapel* Roslin, UK: The Friends of Rosslyn, 1993.

———. *The Templar Legacy and the Masonic Inheritance within Rosslyn Chapel.* Roslin, UK: The Friends of Rosslyn, 1994.

Wallace-Murphy, Tim and Marilyn Hopkins. *Rosslyn: Guardian of the Secrets of the Holy Grail.* Shaftsbury, UK: Element Books, 1999.

Whitehead, Ruth Holmes. *Stories from the Six Worlds, MicMac Legends.* Halifax, NS: Nimbus Publishing, 1988.

Whitehead, Ruth Holmes and Harold McGee. *The Micmac.* Halifax, NS: Nimbus Publishing, 1983.

Whittal, James P., ed. *Ground Penetrating Radar Survey of the Newport Tower Site, Touro Park, Newport Rhode Island.* Rowley, MA: Early Sites Research Society, 1994.

————. *T. C. Lethbridge–Frank Glynn, Correspondence 1950–1966.* Rowley, MA: Early Sites Research Society, 1998.

Wright, Ronald. *Stolen Continents.* Toronto: Penguin Books, 1993.

Zurla, D Placido. *Dissertazione intorno ai viaggi e scoperte settrionali de Nicolo ed Antonio fratelli Zeni.* Venice, 1808.

ABOUT THE AUTHORS

TIM WALLACE-MURPHY studied medicine at University College Dublin before going on to qualify as a psychologist. He has served his local community as a governor of the local technical college and as a member of the Careers Advisory Service, the Totnes Town Council, and, for over sixteen years, the Torbay and District Community Health Council, a body responsible for monitoring the quality of health care throughout the district.

Tim is a lecturer and author with an international reputation, and his work has been translated into many European languages. He has lectured in the United States, the United Kingdom, France, and Italy and was the driving force behind the foundation of the European Templar Heritage Research Network, which links scholars from all over the continent. He also organized the seminar "Who Was Jesus?" held at Dartington Hall near Totnes in 2003, and he acts as a tour guide around many of the major sacred sites in France. He is the author of *The Mark of the Beast* with Trevor Ravenscroft, *An Illustrated Guidebook to Rosslyn Chapel, The Templar Heritage and Masonic Inheritance within Rosslyn Chapel, Rosslyn: Guardian of the Secrets of the Holy Grail* with Marilyn Hopkins, *Rex Deus: The True Mystery of Rennes-le-Chateau* with Marilyn Hopkins and Graham Simmans, and the forthcoming work, *Custodians of Truth* with Marilyn Hopkins, also to be published by Red Wheel/Weiser.

MARILYN HOPKINS has been studying ancient and medieval history and esoteric spirituality for nine years, although her interest spans the past twenty years. She has contributed to seminars, talks, and lectures on subjects that include the Knights Templar, Rennes-le-Chateau, the Rosslyn Chapel, Western esoteric spirituality, and early voyages to America. She co-authored *Rosslyn: Guardian of the Secrets of the Holy Grail* with Tim Wallace-Murphy and *Rex Deus: The True Mystery of Rennes-le-Chateau* with Tim Wallace-Murphy and Graham Simmans. She is a shamanic practitioner, a spiritual healer, a natural dowser, and a practitioner in Indian head massage.

TO OUR READERS